THE CRASH

The accident was so sudden, so unexpected, that none of them even realized it had happened until it was almost over. There was Edward Pleasure changing gear as the car picked up speed. How fast were they going? No more than twenty-five miles per hour. Sabina said something and he half turned around to answer her. The headlights were shooting out, two separate columns, distinct from each other.

And then there was a cracking sound. It seemed to come from a long way away, but that wasn't possible. It had to be something in the engine. The car shuddered and lurched crazily to one side. Sabina cried out. There was nothing anyone could do. It was as if a giant hand had seized the back of the car and swung it around like a toy. Alex felt the tires slide helplessly across the road. Edward wrenched the steering wheel the other way, but it was useless. They were spinning out of control with the night sky rushing toward them. And then came the moment when the tires left the icy surface altogether, and with a surge of terror Alex knew that they had come off the edge of the rock face, that they were in the air with the black, frozen waters of Loch Arkaig far below.

For half a second the car hung in the air.

Then it pitched forward and plunged down.

⇥⇤

CROCODILE TEARS

ANTHONY HOROWITZ

PUFFIN BOOKS
An Imprint of Penguin Group (USA)

PUFFIN BOOKS
An imprint of Penguin Young Readers Group
Published by the Penguin Group
Penguin Group (USA)
375 Hudson Street
New York, New York 10014, U.S.A.

USA / Canada / UK / Ireland / Australia / New Zealand / India / South Africa / China
Penguin Books Ltd, Registered Offices: 80 Strand, London WC2R 0RL, England

For more information about the Penguin Group visit www.penguin.com

First published in the United States of America by Philomel Books,
an imprint of Penguin Young Readers Group, 2009
Published by Puffin Books, an imprint of Penguin Young Readers Group, 2010

LIBRARY OF CONGRESS CATALOGING-IN-PUBLICATION DATA IS AVAILABLE

Puffin Books ISBN 978-0-14-241719-5

Printed in the United States of America

Design by Katrina Damkoehler

9 10

The publisher does not have any control over and does not assume any responsibility
for author or third-party websites or their content.

To R & NA. 009.

CONTENTS

crocodile tears: fake or hypocritical tears. From the belief that crocodiles will pretend to cry in order to attract their victims . . . and will then cry for real as they devour them.

FIRE STAR

RAVI CHANDRA WAS GOING to be a rich man.

It made his head spin to think about it. In the next few hours, he would earn more than he had managed in the last five years: a fantastic sum, paid in cash, right into his hands. It was the start of a new life. He would be able to buy his wife the clothes that she wanted, a car, a proper diamond ring to replace the band of cheap gold she had worn since they were married. He would take the boys, aged four and six, to Disneyland in California. And he would travel to London and see the Indian cricket team play at Lord's, something he had dreamed about all his life but had never thought possible.

Until now.

He sat hunched up beside the window of the bus that was taking him to work, as he had done every day for as long as he could remember. It was devilishly hot. The fans had broken down once again and of course the company was in no hurry to replace them. Worse still, this was the end of June, the time of the year known in southern India as *Agni Nakshatram*—or "Fire Star." The sun was unforgiving. It was almost impossible to breathe. The damp heat clung to you from morning until night and the whole city stank.

When he had money, he would move from this area. He would leave the cramped two-bedroom apartment in Mylapore, the busiest, most crowded part of the city, and go and live somewhere quieter and cooler with a little more space to stretch out. He would have a fridge full of beer and a big plasma TV. Really, it wasn't so much to ask.

The bus was slowing down. Ravi had done this journey so many times that he would have known where they were with his eyes closed. They had left the city behind them. In the distance there were hills—steep and covered, every inch of them, with thick, green vegetation. But the area he was in now was more like a wasteland, with just a few palm trees sprouting among the rubble and electricity pylons closing in on all sides. His place of work was just ahead. In a moment, they would stop at the first security gate.

Ravi was an engineer. His identity badge with his photograph and his full name—Ravindra Manpreet Chandra—described him as a Plant Operator. He worked at the Jowada nuclear power station just three miles north of Chennai, the fourth largest city in India, formerly known as Madras.

He glanced up and there was the power station in front of him, a series of huge multicolored blocks securely locked inside miles and miles of wire. It sometimes occurred to him that wire defined Jowada. There was razor wire and barbed wire, wire fences and telephone lines. And of course, the electricity that they manufactured was carried all over India by thousands more miles of wire. How strange to think that when someone turned on their TV in Pondicherry or their bedside light in Nellore, it had all begun here.

The bus stopped at the security point with its TV cameras and armed guards. Following the 9/11 attacks on New York and Washington, nuclear power plants all over the world had become recognized as potential terrorist targets. New barriers had been added. Security forces had been enlarged. For a long time it had all been an incredible nuisance, with people ready to jump on you if you so much as sneezed. But it had been many years since 9/11. People had become lazy. Take old Suresh, for example, the guard at this outer checkpoint. He recognized everyone on the bus. He saw them at the same time every day: in at half past seven, out at half past five. Occasionally, he'd bump into them while strolling past the shops on Rannganatha Street. He even knew their wives and girlfriends. It wouldn't have occurred to him to ask for ID or to check what they were carrying into Jowada. He waved the bus through.

Two minutes later, Ravi got out. He was a short, skinny man with bad skin and a mustache that sat uncomfortably on his upper lip. He was already wearing overalls and protective steel-capped shoes. He was carrying a heavy toolbox. Nobody asked him why he had taken it home with him when normally he would have left it in his locker; nobody had cared. It was quite possible that he'd had to fix something in the apartment where he lived. Maybe he'd been moonlighting, carrying a few jobs out for the neighbors for a few extra rupees.

The bus had come to a final halt beside a brick wall with a door that, like every door at Jowada, was made of solid steel, designed to hold back smoke, fire, or even a direct missile strike. Another guard and more television cameras watched as the passengers got out and went through. On the other side of the door, a blank, whitewashed corridor led to a locker room, which was one of the few places in the complex that wasn't air-conditioned. Ravi opened his locker (there was a pinup of the Bollywood star Shilpa Shetty stuck in the door) and took out a safety helmet, goggles, earplugs, and a fluorescent jacket. He also removed a bunch of keys. Nuclear power stations do not use swipe cards or electronic locks on the majority of their doors. This is another safety measure. Manual locks and keys will still operate in the event of a power failure.

Still clutching his toolbox, Ravi set off down another corridor. When he had first come here, he had been amazed how clean everything was—especially when he compared it to the street where he lived, which was full of rubbish and potholes filled with muddy water and droppings from the oxen that lumbered along, pulling wooden carts between the cars and the motorized rickshaws. He turned a corner and there was the next checkpoint, the final barrier he would have to pass through before he was actually in.

For the first time, he was nervous. He knew what he was carrying. He remembered what he was about to do. What would happen if he were stopped? He would go to prison, perhaps for the rest of his life. He had heard stories about Chennai Central Jail, about inmates buried in tiny cells far underground and food so disgusting that some preferred to starve to death. But it was too late to back out now. If he hesitated or did anything suspicious, that was one sure way to get stopped.

He came to a massive turnstile with bars as thick as baseball bats. It allowed only one person in at a time, and then you had to shuffle through as if you were being processed, as if you were some sort of factory machine. There was also an X-ray scanner, a metal detector, and yet more guards.

"Hey—Ravi!"

"Ramesh, my friend. You see the cricket last night?"

"I saw it. What a game!"

Soccer, cricket, tennis . . . whatever. Sports were their currency. Every day, the plant operators passed it between them, and Ravi had deliberately watched Wimbledon the night before so that he could join in the conversation. Even in the cool of the corridor, he was sweating. He could feel the perspiration beading on his forehead and he wiped it away with the back of his hand. Surely someone would stop him and ask him why he was still holding on to his toolbox. Everyone knew the correct procedure. It should be opened and searched, all the contents taken out.

But it didn't happen. A moment later, he was through. Nobody had so much as questioned him. It had gone just as he thought it would. Knew it would. Nobody had lifted off the top tray of the toolbox and discovered the twenty pounds of C4 plastic explosive concealed underneath.

Ravi walked away from the barrier and stopped in front of a row of shelves. He pulled out a small plastic device that looked like a pager. This was his EPD—or Electronic Personal Dosimeter. It would record his own radiation level and warn him if he came into contact with any radioactive material. It had already been set with his personal ID and security clearance. There were four levels of security at Jowada, each one allowing access to areas with different risks of contamination. Just for once, Ravi's EPD had been set to the highest level. Today he was going to enter the heart of the power station, the reactor chamber itself.

This was where the deadly flame of Jowada burned. Sixty thousand uranium fuel rods, each one 3.85 meters long, bound together inside the pressure vessel that was the reactor itself. Every minute of the day and night, twenty thousand tons of fresh water were sent rushing through pipes both to cool the beast and to tame it. The resulting steam—two tons of it every second—powered the turbines. The turbines produced electricity. That was how it worked. In many ways it was very simple.

A nuclear reactor is at once the safest and the most dangerous place on the planet. An accident might have such nightmarish consequences that there can be no accident. The reactor chamber at Jowada was made out of steel-reinforced concrete. The walls were five feet thick. The great dome, stretching out over the whole thing, was the height and breadth of a major cathedral. In the event of a malfunction, the reactor could be turned off in seconds. And whatever happened in this room would be contained. Nothing could be allowed to leak through to the outside world.

A thousand safeguards had been built into the construction and the running of Jowada. One man with a dream of watching cricket in London was about to blow them apart.

The approach had come six weeks before at the street corner closest to his apartment: two men, one a European, the other from Delhi. It turned out that the second man, the one from Delhi, was a friend of Ravi's cousin Jagdish, who worked in the kitchen of a five-star hotel. Once they had recognized each other, it seemed only natural to go for tea and samosas . . . particularly as the European was paying.

"How much do they pay you at Jowada?" The European knew the answer without having to ask. "Only fifteen thousand rupees a month, yes? A child couldn't live on that amount, and you have a wife and a family. These people! They cheat the honest worker. Maybe it's time they were taught a lesson. . . ."

Very quickly the conversation was steered the way the

two men wanted it to go, and that first time, they'd left him with a gift, a fake Rolex watch. And why not? Jagdish had done them favors in the past, giving them free food that he had stolen from the kitchen. Now it was their turn to look after Ravi. The next time they met, a week later, it was an iPhone—the real thing. But the gifts were only a glimpse of all the riches that could be his if he would just agree to undertake a piece of business on their behalf. It was dangerous. A few people might be hurt. "But for you, my friend, it will mean a new life. Everything you ever wanted can be yours. . . ."

Ravi Chandra entered the reactor chamber of the Jowada nuclear power station at exactly eight o'clock.

Four other engineers went in with him. They had to go in one at a time through an air lock—a white, circular corridor with an automatic sliding door at each end. In many ways it looked like something out of a spaceship, and its purpose was much the same. The exit wouldn't open until the entrance had closed. It was all part of the need for total containment. The five men were dressed identically, with safety helmets and goggles. All of them were carrying toolboxes. For the rest of the day they would carry out a series of tasks, some of them as ordinary as oiling a valve or changing a lightbulb. Even the most advanced technology needs occasional maintenance.

As they emerged from the air lock into the reactor chamber, they seemed almost to vanish, so tiny were they in these vast surroundings, dwarfed by the gantries and walkways—bright yellow—overhead, by electric hoists and cables, soaring banks of machinery, fuel rod transportation canisters, generators. Arc lamps shone down from the edges of the dome, and in the middle of it all, surrounded by ladders and platforms, what looked like an empty swimming pool plunged twelve yards down, with stainless steel plates on all four sides. This was the reactor. Underneath a 150-ton steel cap, millions of uranium atoms were splitting again and again, producing unimaginable heat.

Four metal towers stood guard in the chamber. If they were shaped a little like rockets, they were rockets that would never fly. Each one was locked in its own steel cage and connected to the rest of the machinery by a network of massive pipes. These were the reactor coolant pumps, keeping the water rushing around on its vital journey. Inside each metal casing, a 50-ton motor was spinning at the rate of 1,500 revs per minute.

The pumps were labeled north, south, east, and west. The south pump was going to be Ravi's primary target.

But first of all he crossed to the other side of the reactor chamber, to a door marked EMERGENCY EXIT ONLY. The two men had explained everything very carefully to him. There was no point attacking the reactor cap. Nothing could penetrate it. Nor was there any point in sabotaging the reactor chamber, not while it was locked down. Any blast, any radiation leak would be contained. To achieve their aims, an exit had to be found. The power of the nuclear reactor had to be set free.

And there it was on the blueprint they had shown him. The emergency air lock was the Achilles' heel in the fortification of Jowada. It should never have been built. There was no need for it and it had never been used. The idea of a passageway between the reactor chamber and the back of the turbine hall, where it opened onto a patch of wasteland close to the perimeter fence, was to reassure workers that there was a fast way out should one ever be needed. But what it also provided was a single pathway from the reactor to the outside world. It was, in one sense, the barrel of a gun. All it needed was to be unblocked.

Nobody noticed Ravi as he strolled over to the emergency door, and even if they had, they wouldn't have remarked on it. Everyone had their own worksheet. They would assume he was just following his. He opened the inner door—a solid metal plate—and let himself into the corridor. This was identical to the one he had used to enter, the same size and shape as a passageway in an underground train station—only without the advertisements. About halfway along, there was a control panel fixed high up in the wall. Standing on tiptoe, Ravi unscrewed it, using one of the few real tools he had brought with him. Inside, there was a complicated mass of circuitry, but he knew exactly what to do. He cut two wires, took one of them, and attached it to a third. It was quite easy, really. The exit door slid open in front of him, revealing a patch of blue sky on the other side of another wire fence. He felt the sluggish air roll in. Somewhere, perhaps in the control room, someone would notice what had happened. Even now a light might be blinking on one of the consoles. But it would take a while before anyone came to investigate and by then it would be too late.

Ravi went back into the reactor chamber and over to the nearest of the four reactor coolant pumps. This was the only way that wide-scale sabotage was possible. What he was aiming for was known in the nuclear industry as a LOCA—a Loss of Coolant Accident. It was a LOCA that had caused the catastrophe at Chernobyl in the former Soviet Union and had almost done the same at Three Mile Island in Pennsylvania. The pump was locked in its cage, but Ravi had the key. That was one of the reasons he had been chosen for this job. The right man in the right place.

He stopped in front of the cylindrical wall, which rose more than sixty feet into the air. He could hear the machinery inside. The noise was constant and deafening. His mouth was dry now, thinking about what he was about to do. Was he insane? Suppose they traced this back to him? But then his mind drifted to all that money, to his wife, to the life they could finally lead. His family was not in Chennai today. He had sent them to friends in Bangalore. They would be safe. He was doing this for them. He *had* to do this for them.

For a few brief seconds greed and fear hung in the

balance, and then the scale tipped. He knelt down and placed the toolbox against the metal casing, opened it and removed the top shelf. The inside was almost filled with the bulk of the plastic explosive, yet there was just enough room for a digital display showing ten minutes, a tangle of wires, and a switch.

Ten minutes. That would be more than enough time to leave the chamber before the bomb went off. If anyone questioned him, he would say he needed to use the toilet. He would exit the same way he had come in, and once he was on the other side of the air lock, he would be safe. After the blast, there would be panic, alarms, a well-rehearsed evacuation, radiation suits for everyone. He would simply join the crowds and make his way out. They would never be able to trace the bomb to him. There wouldn't be any evidence at all.

People might die. People he knew. Could he really do this?

The switch was right there in front of him. So small. All he had to do was flick it and the countdown would begin.

Ravi Chandra took a deep breath. He reached out with a single finger. He pressed the switch.

It was the last thing he did in his life. The men from the street corner had lied to him. There was no ten-minute delay. When he activated the bomb, it went off immediately, almost vaporizing him. Ravi was dead so quickly that he never even knew that he had been betrayed, that his wife was now a widow and that his children would never meet Mickey Mouse. Nor did he see the effect of what he had done.

Exactly as planned, the bomb tore a hole in the side of the coolant pump, smashing the rotors. There was a hideous metallic grinding as the entire thing tore itself apart. One of the other plant operators—the same man who had been chatting about cricket just a few minutes ago—was killed instantly, thrown off his feet and into the reactor pit. The other engineers in the chamber froze, their eyes filled with horror as they saw what was happening, then scattered, diving for cover. They were too late. There was another explosion and suddenly the air was filled with shrapnel, spinning fragments of metal and machinery that had been turned into vicious missiles. The two closest men were cut to pieces. The others turned to run for the air lock.

None of them made it. Alarms were already sounding, lights flashing, and as the machinery disintegrated, it seemed that everything in the chamber had been slowed down, turned into a black-and-red hell. A cable whipped down, trailing sparks. There were three more explosions, pipes wrenching themselves free, fireballs spinning outward, and then a roar as burning steam came rushing out like an express train, filling the chamber. The worst had happened. Jagged knives of broken metal had smashed open the pipes, and although the reactor was already closing down, there were still several tons of radioactive steam with nowhere to go. One man was caught in the full blast and disappeared with a single hideous scream.

The steam thundered out, filling the entire chamber. Normally, the walls and the dome would have contained it. But Ravi Chandra, in almost the last act of his life, had opened the emergency air lock. Like some alien stampede, the steam found it and rushed through, out into the open air. All over the Jowada power station, systems were being shut down, corridors emptied, safety measures put into place.

But it was already too late.

The people of Chennai saw a huge plume of white smoke rise up into the air. They heard the alarms. Already, workers at Jowada were calling their relatives in the city, warning them to get out. The panic began at once. More than a million men, women, and children dropped what they were doing and tried to find a way through traffic that had come to a complete standstill. Fights broke out. There were collisions and smashups at a dozen different junctions and traffic lights. But it had all happened too quickly, and not a single person would have actually made it out of the city before the radioactive cloud, blown by a southerly wind, fell onto them.

The story appeared that night on television news all around the world.

It was estimated that at least a hundred people died in the one hour following the explosion. Of course, there

had been casualties within the Jowada power station itself, but far more people were killed in the madness to get
out of Chennai. By the following morning, the newspaper
headlines were calling it "A NUCLEAR NIGHTMARE"—in cap-
ital letters, of course. The Indian authorities were adamant
that the steam cloud would have contained only low-level
radiation and that there was no need for panic, but there
were just as many experts who disagreed.

Twenty-four hours later, an appeal was made to help
the people of Chennai. Further casualties were being reported. Homes and shops had been looted. There were
still riots in the streets and the army had been called in to
restore order. The hospitals were full of desperate people.
One British charity—it called itself First Aid—came forward with a comprehensive plan to distribute food, blankets,
and, most important of all, potassium iodate tablets for
every one of the eight million people of Chennai to coun-
ter possible radiation sickness.

As always, the world's people were unfailing in their
generosity, and by the end of the week First Aid had
raised over two million dollars.

Of course, if the disaster had been any greater, they
would have raised much, much more.

REFLECTIONS IN A MIRROR

ALEX RIDER TOOK ONE last glance in the mirror, then stopped and looked a second time. It was strange, but he wondered if he recognized the boy who was looking back. There were the thin lips, the slightly chiseled nose and chin, the light brown hair hanging in two strands over the very dark brown eyes. He raised a hand and, obediently, his reflection did the same. But there was something different about this other Alex Rider. It wasn't quite him.

Of course, the clothes he was wearing didn't help. In a few minutes, he would be leaving for a New Year's Eve party being held at a castle on the banks of Loch Arkaig in the Highlands of Scotland—and the invitation had been clear. Dress: black tie. Reluctantly, Alex had gone out and rented the entire outfit . . . dinner jacket, black trousers, and a white shirt with a wing collar that was too tight and squeezed his neck. The one thing he had refused to do was put on the polished leather shoes that the shopkeeper had insisted would make the outfit complete. Black sneakers would have to do. What did it all make him look like? he wondered as he straightened the bow tie for the tenth time. A young James Bond. He hated the comparison, but he couldn't avoid it.

It wasn't just the clothes. As Alex continued his examination, he had to admit that so much had happened in the last year that he'd almost lost track of who—and what—he was. Standing in front of the mirror, it was as if he had just stepped down from the merry-go-round that his life had become. He might be still, but the world around him was spinning.

Just two months ago, he had been in Australia . . . not on vacation, not visiting relatives, but, incredibly, working for the Australian Secret Intelligence Service, disguised as an Afghan refugee. He had been sent to infiltrate the people-smuggling gang known as the snakehead, yet his mission had taken him much further than that, setting him against Major Winston Yu and the potential devastation of a huge bomb buried deep beneath a fault line in the earth's crust. It had also brought him face-to-face with his godfather, the man he had known only as Ash. Thinking about him now, Alex saw something spark in his eyes. Was it anger? Grief? Alex had never known his parents, and he'd thought Ash would somehow be able to explain where he'd come from, to make sense of his past. But his godfather had done nothing of the sort, and their meeting had led only to betrayal and death.

And that was really it, wasn't it? That was what the boy in the mirror was trying to tell him. He was still only fourteen years old, but the last year—a year whose end they were about to celebrate—had almost destroyed him. If he closed his eyes, he could still feel Major Yu's walking stick smashing into the side of his head, the crushing

weight of the water under the Bora Falls, the punishment
he had taken in the Thai boxing ring in Bangkok. And
those were just the most recent in a string of injuries.
How many times had he been punched, kicked, beaten,
knocked out? And shot. His wounds might have healed,
but he would still be reminded of them every time he un-
dressed for bed. The scar left by the .22 bullet fired into
his chest by a sniper on a rooftop on Liverpool Street
would always be with him. Along with the memory of
pain. They say that never leaves you either.

Had it changed him? Of course it had. Nobody could
come through what he had and stay the same. And
yet . . .

"Alex! Stop admiring yourself in the mirror and get
downstairs." It was Sabina. Alex turned and saw her
standing in the doorway, wearing a silver dress with lots
of glitter around the collar. Her dark hair—she had
grown it long—was tied back. Unusually for her, she was
wearing makeup: pale blue eye shadow and pink, glossy
lipstick. "Dad's waiting. We're about to leave."

"I'll just be one minute."

Alex twisted the bow tie again, wondering what he had
to do to stop the darn thing from going crooked. He
looked ridiculous. Nobody under the age of fifty should
have to dress like this. But at least he'd been able to resist
Sabina's suggestion that he should go to the party
dressed in a kilt. She'd been teasing him about it since
Christmas.

Despite everything, the last six weeks had been fantastic for Alex Rider. First of all, Sabina and her parents had unexpectedly arrived in England. Edward Pleasure was a journalist. He had almost been killed once, investigating the pop singer Damian Cray. Alex had blamed himself for that, and when, at the end of it all, Sabina had left for America, he had been certain he would never see her again. But now she was back in his life, and although she was a year older than him, the two had never been closer. It helped perhaps that she was one of the few people who knew about his involvement with MI6.

Better still, the Pleasures had invited Alex to join them for the New Year at the house they had rented in the West Highlands of Scotland. Hawk's Lodge was a Victorian pile that had been named after an obscure poet rather than the bird. It stood, three stories high, on the edge of woodland with Ben Nevis in the background. It was the sort of house that needed roaring log fires, hot chocolate, old-fashioned board games, and too much to eat. Liz Pleasure, Sabina's mother, had supplied all of this and more from the moment they had arrived. In the past few days, the four of them had gone hiking and fishing. They had visited ruined castles and isolated villages and strolled along the famous white sands of Morar. Sabina had hoped it might snow—there was good skiing over at Aviemore and she had brought her gear with her—but although it was freezing outside, so far the weather had only managed a few flurries. There was no television in the house, and Edward had banned Sabina from bringing her Nintendo DS, so they had spent the evenings playing Scrabble or Perudo, the Peruvian game of liar dice, which Alex nearly always won. If there was one thing he had learned in his life, it was certainly how to lie.

Meanwhile, Jack Starbright, Alex's housekeeper and in some ways still his closest friend, was in Washington, D.C. She had been invited to Scotland too, but had decided to go home for New Year with her parents. Following her out of the house, it had crossed Alex's mind that one day she would go back to America for good. All her friends and family were there. He wondered what would happen to him if she did. She had looked after him since his uncle had died, and as far as he knew, there was nobody to take her place.

As if reading his thoughts, she had given him a hug while the taxi driver loaded up her suitcases.

"Don't worry, Alex. I'll see you in ten days. Just try and have a good time in Scotland. See if you can get past New Year without getting into trouble. Don't forget, school starts on the sixth."

And that was another reason to be cheerful. Alex had managed to complete an entire half term at Brookland without getting kidnapped, shot at, or recruited by one of the world's security agencies. He had begun to feel like an ordinary schoolboy again, getting told off for talking in class, sweating over his homework, listening for the bell that meant the end of day.

He took one last look in the mirror. Jack was right. Forget all this spy stuff. He'd had enough of all that. He was leaving it behind.

He went down two flights of stairs to the hall with its wood panels and rather gloomy paintings of Scottish wildlife. Edward Pleasure was waiting with Sabina. It seemed to Alex that the journalist had grown quite a lot older since they had last met. There were definitely more lines in his face, he now wore glasses all the time, and he had lost a lot of weight. He also limped, supporting himself with a heavy walking stick, metal tipped and with a metal handle shaped like a duck's head. His wife had bought it for him in an antiques shop in London. She had joked that if any of the people he wrote about ever tried to attack him, at least he'd have something he could use to defend himself.

The journalist had put on his own black tie for the evening, but Alex saw at once from his expression that something was wrong.

"What is it?" Alex asked Sabina.

"Mum's not coming," Sabina replied. She was looking glum. All her enthusiasm for the party had drained away.

"She says she's not feeling up to it," Edward explained. "It's nothing serious. She's just got a bit of the flu . . ."

"Then I think we should all stay," Sabina said.

"That's nonsense, Sabina. The three of you go and enjoy yourselves." Liz Pleasure had appeared at one of the doorways. She was a pleasant, easygoing woman with long, straggly hair. She didn't care how she looked and she liked to run a house without rules. Right now she was wearing a baggy jersey and jeans, holding a box of tissues. "I don't much like parties anyway, and I'm certainly not going out in this weather."

"But you don't want to be here for New Year on your own."

"I'm going to have a hot bath with some of that expensive oil your dad bought me for Christmas. Then I'm going to bed. I'll be asleep long before midnight." She went over to Sabina and put her arm around her. "Honestly, Sab, it doesn't bother me. We can celebrate New Year tomorrow and you can tell me what I missed."

"I don't even want to go to this stupid party!"

"That's not true. You love parties. And you look terrific . . . both of you."

"But Mum . . ."

"You have to go. Your dad's got the tickets and they cost a fortune." She beamed at Alex. "You look after her, Alex. And remember: This is a party in a real Scottish castle. I'm sure you're going to have a fantastic time."

There was no point in any further argument, and twenty minutes later, Alex found himself being driven along the twisting roads that led north to Loch Arkaig. The weather had turned worse. The snow that Sabina had been hoping for was falling more heavily, swirling in front of the headlights as they cut through the night. Edward Pleasure was driving a Nissan X-Trail that he had rented at Inverness Airport. Alex was glad he had chosen a four-by-four. The snow was already settling. Any thicker and they would need the extra traction.

Sabina was stretched out in the back, untangling her iPod. Alex was in the front. It was the first time he had been alone with Edward Pleasure since the south of France, and he felt a little uncomfortable. The journalist must have known about his involvement with MI6. Sabina would have told him everything that had happened. But the two of them had never discussed it, as if it was somehow impolite.

"It's good to have you with us, Alex," Edward muttered. He was deliberately keeping his voice down so that Sabina, plugged into Coldplay, wouldn't hear. "I know Sab was really glad you could tag along."

"I've had a great time," Alex said. He thought for a moment, then added, "I'm not sure about tonight, though."

Edward smiled. "We don't have to stay too long if you don't want to. But what Liz said was right. Nobody celebrates New Year like the Scottish. And Kilmore Castle is quite a place. Dates back to the thirteenth century. It was torn down in the Jacobite rising and stayed more or less in ruins until it was bought by Desmond McCain."

"Isn't he the man you're writing about?"

"That's right. He's the main reason we're going. The Reverend Desmond McCain." Edward reached down and flicked a switch, blowing hot air over the window. The windshield wipers were doing their best, but snow was still sticking to the glass. It was warm and cozy inside the car, in marked contrast with the world outside. "He's an interesting man, Alex. Do you want to hear about him?"

"Absolutely."

"Well, you've probably read a bit about him in the papers. He was brought up in an orphanage in east London. No parents. No family. Nothing. He'd been abandoned in a shopping cart, wrapped in a plastic bag . . . McCain Frozen Fries. That's how he got his name. He was fostered by a couple in Hackney, and from that moment things started going better for him. He did well at school . . . particularly at sports. By the time he was eighteen, he had become a famous boxer. He won the WBO world middleweight title twice, and everyone thought he'd make it a hat trick before he got knocked out in the first round by Buddy Sangster in Madison Square Garden in 1983."

"What happened to Buddy Sangster?" Alex asked. He'd heard the name somewhere before.

"It's funny you should ask. He died a year later. He fell under a train in the New York subway. They showed his funeral on TV. One of his fans even sent a hundred black tulips to the funeral. I remember hearing that . . ." Edward shook his head. "Anyway, Desmond McCain wasn't boxing anymore. His jaw had been smashed up pretty badly. He went to some plastic surgeon in Las

Vegas, but it was a botch job and it never healed properly. To this day he eats only soft food. He can't chew. But it wasn't the end of his career. He went into business . . . property development, and he was very good at it. There were a dozen tenants in Rotherhithe, down on the River Thames, and somehow he persuaded them to sell cheaply to him, and then he knocked down their houses and put up a bunch of skyscrapers and made a fortune.

"That was about the time that he became interested in politics. He'd given thousands of dollars to the Conservative party, and suddenly he announced he wanted to be a member of Parliament. Of course, they welcomed him with open arms. He was rich, he was successful—and he was black. That was part of it too. And the next thing you know, he managed to get himself elected in a corner of London that hadn't voted Conservative since the nineteenth century, and even then it had only been by mistake. People liked him. It was the typical rags-to-riches story . . . you could say plastic bag to riches in his case. He got a big majority, and a year later he was a minister in the department of sport. There was even talk that he could become our first black prime minister."

"So what went wrong?"

Edward sighed. "Everything! It turned out that his business hadn't been going as well as people thought. One or two of his developments had fallen behind schedule, and he had huge financial problems. The bank was closing in and it looked as if he might go bankrupt . . .

and of course you're not allowed to be a member of Parliament if that happens. Too unsightly for their taste. God knows what he was thinking, but he decided to set fire to one of his properties and claim the insurance. That was his way out of the mess. Well, the property in question was a twenty-four-story office building overlooking St. Paul's, and one night it simply burned to the ground. The next day, McCain put in a claim for fifty million dollars. Problem solved."

They came to a sharp bend in the road and Edward Pleasure slowed down. By now the whole road was snow covered, with dark pine trees looming up on both sides.

"At least that's what he thought," he went on. "Unfortunately for him, the insurance company smelled a rat. They started asking questions. Like, for example, why had the alarms been switched off? Why had the security staff been given the night off? There was a lot of gossip in the press—and then, suddenly, a witness turned up. It turned out there'd been a homeless person sleeping in the underground garage. He'd actually been there when McCain drove in with six gallons of gasoline and a cigarette lighter. He'd been lucky to get away alive. Anyway, McCain was arrested. There was a fairly sensational trial. He was sent to prison for nine years."

Alex had listened to all this in silence. "You called him Reverend McCain," he said.

"Well, that's the strange thing. In a way, McCain's whole life had been bizarre—but while he was in jail, he converted to Christianity. He did a correspondence course and became a priest in some church no one's ever heard of. And when he got out—that was five years ago—he didn't go back into business or politics. He said he'd spent his whole life being selfish and that he wanted to put all that behind him. Instead, he set up a charity. First Aid. That's what it's called. It provides a rapid response to emergencies all over the world."

"How much farther?" Sabina's voice came from the backseat. She was still plugged into her earphones.

Edward Pleasure held up a hand and opened it twice, signaling ten minutes.

"You interviewed him," Alex said.

"Yes. I've done a big piece for *Vanity Fair*. They'll be publishing it next month."

"And?"

"You'll meet him tonight, Alex, and you can see for yourself. He's got an enormous amount of energy and he's channeled it into helping people less fortunate than himself. He's raised millions for famine relief in Africa, bush fires in Australia, floods in Malaysia . . . even that accident in southern India. Jowada . . ."

Alex nodded. He'd read about it when he'd been working as a ball boy at Wimbledon. It had made the front pages. "The nuclear reactor . . . ," he said.

Edward nodded. "For a time it looked as if the whole city of Chennai could have been affected. Fortunately, it wasn't as bad as that, but a lot of people were killed in the panic. First Aid was up and running the very next day, getting antiradiation stuff to the women and kids, helping with supplies . . . that sort of thing. Nobody was quite sure how they got off the mark so quickly, but that's how they work. Instant response. Their aim is to be the first charity in."

"And you really think this man, McCain, is genuine? That he's turned a new leaf?"

"You mean . . . do I think he's another Damian Cray?" Edward smiled briefly. It had been his article exposing Cray as a maniac that had almost got him killed. "Well, I did have my doubts when I first met him. I mean, even if he wasn't a crook, he was a politician, which didn't exactly recommend him. But you don't need to worry, Alex. I did plenty of research into his charity. I interviewed him and a lot of people who know him. I spoke to the police and I opened many old files. The truth is, other than his past, I couldn't find anything bad to write about him. He really does seem to be a rich man who made a bad mistake and who's trying to make up for it."

"How has he managed to buy a castle? If he went bankrupt . . ."

"That's a good question. After he went to prison, he lost all his money . . . everything. But he had powerful friends—both in business and in politics—and they did what they could to help him out. Thanks to them, he managed to hang on to Kilmore Castle. He also has a

London apartment, and he's the part owner of a safari camp somewhere in Kenya." A car suddenly appeared in the road beside them, overtaking. Edward slowed down to let it pass. He watched as it was swallowed up by the whirling snow. "I'll be interested to hear what you think of McCain," he muttered.

"Is that why you're going?"

"When I met him, I mentioned I was planning to be in Scotland for the New Year, and he invited me. He gave me the tickets, which is just as well, since they cost one thousand dollars each."

Alex let out a low whistle.

"Well, it's for charity. All the profits will go to First Aid. There'll be a lot of rich people there tonight. They'll raise a fortune."

There was another brief silence. The road had begun to climb steeply uphill, and Edward shifted down a gear.

"We never really talked about Damian Cray," Edward muttered.

Alex twisted in his seat. "There's nothing to say."

"My book about him sold a million copies. But I never mentioned you, or your part in what happened."

"I prefer it that way."

"You saved Sabina's life."

"She saved mine."

"Can I give you some advice, Alex?" Edward Pleasure had to keep his eyes on the road, yet just for a moment he turned them on Alex. "Stay away from all that. MI6, intelligence, all the rest of it. I've got a good idea what's been going on over the past year. Sabina's told me some of it, but I have contacts in the CIA and I hear things. I don't want to know what you've been through, but believe me, you're better off out of it."

"Don't worry." Alex remembered what he'd been thinking back at Hawk's Lodge. "I don't think MI6 are interested in me anymore. They didn't even send me a Christmas card. That part of my life is over. And I'm glad."

The road was even steeper now, and the trees had fallen away on one side to reveal an expanse of black water, Loch Arkaig, stretching out below. It was still snowing, but the flakes didn't seem to be making contact with the half-frozen surface, as if the two were somehow canceling each other out. The loch was said to have its own monster—a giant water horse—and looking down, Alex could well believe it. Loch Arkaig had been left behind by the glaciers. Twelve miles long and in places three hundred feet deep, who could say what secrets it had managed to keep to itself for the past five million years?

And there was Kilmore Castle looming up above him, almost invisible behind the sweeping snow. It had been built on a rocky outcrop, above the loch, completely dominating the surrounding landscape, a massive pile of gray stone with towers and battlements, narrow, slit-like windows, soaring archways, and solid, unwelcoming doors. There was nothing about the place that could have been built for comfort. It existed only to rule and to keep those inside it in power. It was hard to imagine how it had ever fallen or, for that matter, how it had been built. Even the Nissan X-Trail, with its 2.5-liter four-cylinder turbo diesel engine, seemed to be struggling as it negotiated the series of tight hairpin bends that were the only way up. Had soldiers once come here on horseback? What medieval weapons could possibly have penetrated these massive walls?

They were in a line of traffic now with other partygoers, just visible behind the frosted windows of their cars. The last bend brought them to a wide-open space that had been converted into a parking lot with attendants in Day-Glo jackets frantically signaling where to go. Two fiery torches had been placed on either side of the main entrance, the flames fighting the snow. Men and women in heavy coats, their faces lost behind scarves, were hurrying across the gravel and bundling themselves in. There was something almost nightmarish about the scene. It didn't look like a party. These people could have been refugees running for their lives from some freak act of nature. All the while dressed to kill.

Edward Pleasure parked the car and Sabina took off her iPod.

"We don't have to stay until midnight," Edward told her. "If you want to leave earlier, just let me know."

"I wish Mum had come," Sabina muttered.

"Me too. But let's try and enjoy ourselves."

They got out of the car, and after the warmth of the interior, Alex was immediately hit by the deep chill of the night, the snow dancing in his eyes, the wind rushing through his hair. He had no coat and ran forward, hugging himself, using his shoulders to battle through the elements. It was as if the very worst of the winter had somehow been concentrated on this rocky platform, high above the loch. The flames of the fiery torches writhed and twisted. Somebody shouted something, but the words were snatched away.

And then they had reached the archway and passed through into an inner courtyard, where at least the wind couldn't penetrate. Alex found himself in an irregularly shaped space with high walls, cannons, a lawn under two inches of snow, and a huge bonfire. About a dozen guests were crowding around, feeling the warmth, and laughing as they brushed snow off their sleeves. A second archway stood ahead of him, this one with carved eagles and an inscription in Gaelic, the letters glowing red and shimmering in the light of the fire.

cha dèanaʀ sgʀios aiʀ nàimhdean gus
am biʒheaʀ ꜰios aiʀ cò iad.

"What's that?" Sabina asked.

Edward shrugged, but next to him one of the other guests had overheard. "It's the motto of the Kilmore clan," he explained. "This was their ancestral home. They were here for three hundred years."

"Do you know what it means?"

"Yes. 'You cannot defeat your enemies until you know who they are.' " The guest pushed forward and disappeared into the castle.

Alex looked at the inscription for a moment. He wondered if in some way it wasn't speaking to him. Then he dismissed the thought. A New Year was about to begin and with it a new set of rules. There were no more enemies. That was what he had decided.

"Come on, Alex . . ."

Sabina grabbed his arm and together they went in.

3

CARDS BEFORE MIDNIGHT

ALEX HAD NEVER BEEN to a party like it.

The banqueting hall at Kilmore Castle was huge, but even so, it was jammed with people: five or six hundred of them had been invited and this wasn't an invitation anyone was going to turn down, even if it came with a thousand-dollar price tag. Within minutes, Alex had recognized half a dozen TV celebrities and soap stars, a clutch of politicians, two celebrity chefs, and a pop star. The men were in black tie or kilts. The women had fought to outdo each other with yards of silk and velvet, plunging necklines, and a dazzling assortment of diamonds and jewels.

A whole army of waiters in full Scottish dress were fighting their way through the crowd carrying trays of vintage champagne while a trio of bagpipe players performed on a gallery above. There were no electric lights. More than a hundred candles flickered in two massive chandeliers. Torches blazed from iron braziers mounted in the walls. The center of the room was dominated by a massive stone fireplace with flames leaping up the chimney and throwing red shadows across the flagstone floor.

The Kilmores hadn't lived at the castle for centuries,

but they were certainly there tonight. Life-size portraits hung on the walls . . . grim-looking men with swords and shields, proud-eyed women in tartan and bonnets. Suits of armor had been placed in many of the alcoves, and crossed swords stood guard over every archway and door. The animals they had killed—stags, foxes, wild boar— looked down on the scene with their disembodied heads and glass eyes. Coats of arms dotted the walls, the fire-place, even the windows.

Desmond McCain must have spent a fortune on the party, ensuring that at the very least his guests would get value for their money. A buffet table reached from one end of the hall to the other, piled high with great slabs of beef and salads, whole salmon, venison, and—on a giant silver platter—a roast suckling pig complete with angry eyes and an apple in its mouth. There were dozens of different wines and spirits, punch bowls, and as many as fifty brands of malt whisky in bottles of various shapes. One archway led to a dance floor, another to a fully equipped casino with roulette, blackjack, and poker. Somehow, McCain had managed to park a brand-new Mini Convertible in the hallway. It was the first prize in a raffle that also included a Kawasaki 260X Jet Ski and a two-week Caribbean cruise—all of them had been given free to First Aid by wealthy sponsors.

Outside, the snow was still falling. The wind was cutting through the night like a scalpel. But all that was forgotten as, inside, the guests enjoyed the warmth of each other's company and the spirit of the celebration as the minutes ticked down to the New Year.

And yet, despite all this, Alex and Sabina felt out of place. Not many other teenagers had been invited, and the ones they met all lived locally, seemed to be at least six feet tall, and clearly regarded them as outsiders. Alex and Sabina ate together, had a couple of sodas, and made their way to the dance floor—but even here they didn't feel comfortable, surrounded by adults twisting and swaying to music that hadn't been popular in decades.

"I've had enough of this," Sabina announced as the band lurched into an ABBA classic.

Alex knew what she meant. The center of the dance floor was dominated by three bald men in kilts, jabbing their fingers into the air to the tune of "Money, Money, Money." He glanced at his watch. It was only ten past eleven. "I don't think we can leave yet, Sabina," he said.

"Have you seen my dad?"

"He was talking to one of the politicians."

"Probably hoping to get a story. He never stops."

"Come on, Sabina. Cheer up. This place is meant to be hundreds of years old. Let's go and explore."

They pushed their way off the dance floor and headed down the nearest corridor. The stone walls twisted around, and the music and the noise of the party were cut off almost at once. Another corridor led off of it, this one decorated with tapestries and heavy gilt mirrors with glass blackened by age. At the end, they came to a staircase that led to one of the towers, and suddenly they found themselves outside, surrounded by a low brick wall, looking out into the white-spotted blackness that the night had become.

"That's better," Sabina said. "I was suffocating in there."

"Are you cold?" Alex could see the snow falling gently onto her bare neck and shoulders.

"I'll be all right for a minute."

"Here." He took off his jacket and handed it to her.

"Thanks." She slipped it on. There was a pause. "I wish I didn't have to go back to America," she said.

The words jolted Alex. He had forgotten momentarily that she would be returning in a few days' time. She'd enrolled at a school in San Francisco, where the family was living, and it would be a while before they saw each other again. He'd miss her. The thought saddened him. He'd seen so much of Sabina over the Christmas break that he'd gotten used to having her around. "Maybe I could come over for the Easter holidays," he said.

"Have you been to San Francisco?"

"Once. My uncle took me on a business trip. At least, that's what he told me. He was probably working with the CIA, spying on someone or something."

"Do you ever think about Damian Cray?"

"No." Alex shook his head. The question seemed to

have come out of nowhere. Alex glanced at Sabina and was surprised to see that she was looking at him with something close to anger in her eyes.

"I do. All the time. It was horrible. He was crazy. And the way he died! I'll remember that for the rest of my life."

Well, that made sense. Sabina had been there at the very end. In fact, she had been at least partly responsible for his sensational death.

"I thought you said you were going to stop all that," she went on. "Playing at being a spy . . ."

"It was never my choice," Alex replied. "And anyway, I've already told your dad. I've stopped. It's not going to happen again."

Sabina sighed. "San Francisco's great," she said. "Great shops. Great food. Great weather. But I miss England." She paused. "I miss you."

"I'll come visit. I promise."

"You'd better. . . ."

They had only been outside for a couple of minutes, but in this weather it was more than enough. Alex could see the flakes of snow in Sabina's hair. "Let's go downstairs," he suggested.

"Yeah. Let's find Dad and get out of here. I'll go back to the main hall. You look in the other rooms. I want to get back to Mum, and if you ask me, this party sucks. All these men in kilts and not one of them with decent legs . . ."

She handed him back his jacket and the two of them made their way back down the twisting staircase, then split up, searching for Edward Pleasure. Alex watched Sabina hurry down the corridor, then went the other way, past more unsmiling portraits of long-dead ancestors. He wondered why anyone would want to live in a place like this. Maybe Desmond McCain needed somewhere to hide from the world. When he wasn't trying to save it.

He heard the murmur of voices, the clink of a glass, and a woman laughing. He had come to a set of double doors, opening into what must be the castle's library, with shelves of leather-bound books that looked at least a hundred years old and which were surely never read. He saw at once that the library had been converted into a casino, with card tables, a spinning roulette wheel, and croupiers in white shirts, waistcoats, and bow ties. As he walked in, the roulette ball tumbled into its slot with a loud clunk, the audience laughed and applauded, and the croupier called out "Eighteen, red, even . . ." and began to sort out the bets. There were almost a hundred people playing the different games, most of them holding drinks and one or two of them puffing at cigars. This must be the only room in the castle where smoking was allowed; a cloud of smoke hung in the air.

Alex didn't even notice himself entering the room, so spellbound was he. He looked briefly at the cards sliding across the green baize, the fresh bets stacking up in front of the roulette wheel, the men and women, some standing, some sitting, leaning forward, their faces flushed with excitement. The main focus of attention seemed to be at the far end of the room. There was a game in progress with six players—but one of them had just lost. Alex saw him throw his cards down with disgust and get up, leaving an empty chair. At the same time the winning player laughed a deep, rich sound that warmed the room.

Desmond McCain. It had to be him. Alex would have known it even if he hadn't been the only black man in the room. McCain was lolling back in his chair in front of a great window that had the effect of framing him, putting him at the center of the picture. Almost despite himself, Alex moved forward to get a closer look. He had been thinking about McCain only a few minutes ago. It couldn't hurt to see what the laird of Kilmore Castle was really like.

McCain was gathering up his cards, which almost disappeared in his oversized hands. He was a huge man with an extraordinary presence that somehow drew Alex to him. He was completely bald, with a round, polished head that had surely never seen a single hair. His eyes were a strange shade of gray—they were dark yet alight with electricity—and his smile was quite simply dazzling. Like everyone else, he was dressed in black tie, but unlike so many of the others, he looked completely comfortable, as if he always dressed this way.

He picked up a glass of whisky, which he drank as if it were a cocktail, using a straw at the side of his mouth, and Alex remembered what Edward Pleasure had told him about the boxing injury. It was true. The man he was looking at had received a blow that had permanently dislocated his jaw. Worse than that, it had been put back together in such a way that it no longer fit properly. It was as if someone had taken a photograph of his head, cut it horizontally in half, and then reattached the two pieces a few millimeters apart. His eyes and nose were no longer exactly over his mouth.

And there was something else. McCain said something, turned his head, and laughed a second time. That was when Alex saw it. He was wearing a silver crucifix, not around his neck but on his ear. It was less than a centimeter high, pinned into the lobe. The jewelry was quite striking set against the intense, dark skin. This was a man who wore his faith openly, who dared you to argue against it.

Alex drew closer. The six of them had been playing a version of poker—Texas Hold 'Em—in which five cards turned faceup are used by everyone at the table. And the stakes couldn't have been higher. Alex saw this at once from the number of different-colored chips spilling over the table—each one marked $50, $100, even $500. Each chip had been bought at its face value. The casino was using real money. Alex could feel the tension in the air. A scattering of cards, a few minutes' playing time, and thousands of dollars could be changing hands. At the moment, McCain was clearly in the lead.

There was a whole mountain of chips stacked up in front of him, and only one of the players—a man with a shock of silver hair and a thick, fleshy face—came anywhere close.

McCain looked up and noticed Alex. At once the smile was there, drawing him in, making him feel that the two of them had known each other for years.

"Good evening," he boomed. "Welcome to the Kilmore Casino. You're frankly a little young to be gambling, I'd have said. What's your name?"

"Alex. Alex Rider."

"And I'm Desmond McCain. We're just about to play the last hand. Why don't you join us? It's all for a good cause, so I think we can turn a blind eye to the age limit." He gestured at the seat that had just been vacated. Alex could already hear that his broken jaw made it difficult for him to speak. Words beginning with *f* or *r* came out slightly blurred. "The cards have been quite interesting this evening. Let's see if they have anything more to say before midnight."

Alex knew he was making a mistake. He was meant to be looking for Edward Pleasure. He had agreed with Sabina. They were going to leave. But it was almost as if McCain had challenged him. If he walked away now, he would look like some little kid who was out of his depth.

McCain had won the last hand and was neatly stacking up all the chips, including those of the man who had just left. Alex took his chair and sat down.

"Good!" McCain beamed at him. "Do you know the rules of Texas Hold 'Em?"

Alex nodded.

"We're taking this very seriously. It costs five hundred dollars to join the table—that money goes straight to First Aid—and minimum bets are fifty dollars. Have you brought your pocket money with you?"

A couple of the other players laughed. Alex ignored them. "I didn't bring any money at all," he said.

"Then we'll waive the entrance fee and I'll stake you. This is the last hand of the evening, so one thousand dollars ought to be enough." He slid the chips over. "It makes it more fun with more people. And you never know. You could win enough to buy yourself a new PlayStation!"

With Alex making up the numbers, there would be six players at the table: three men, two women, and him. McCain was at one end with a dark-haired woman—Alex vaguely recognized her as a television reporter—at his side. Then came an elderly man who could have been a retired soldier, sitting rigidly with a straight back and a face fixed in concentration. The silver-haired man came next. He reminded Alex of an accountant or a banker. The circle was completed by a Scottish woman with ginger hair, sipping champagne even though it was clear she'd already had more than enough.

The croupier shuffled the deck and each player was dealt two cards, facedown. These were known as the "hole cards." Alex had learned the basics of the game, playing with Ian Rider and Jack Starbright at an age when other children were probably reading Dick and Jane. Texas Hold 'Em is largely a game of bluff. You try to make pairs, three of a kind, a full house, and so on. But everything depends on your hidden cards. They may be great. They may be terrible. The secret is to make sure no one guesses either way.

Alex watched as McCain raised the corners of his cards with a thumb and smiled, not even attempting to conceal his pleasure. Of course, it was possible that he was bluffing, but Alex got the sense that this wasn't a man who was too clever when it came to hiding his emotions. He must have something good under there . . . high cards or a pair. Alex examined his own cards. There was nothing to get excited about, but he kept his own face blank.

"Come on, then," McCain said.

The croupier was a pale, serious-looking man in his late twenties. He looked uncomfortable having a teenager in the game, but dealt three more cards—"the flop"— faceup on the table. All six players would use these cards to try to create the best hand possible. The first one out was the jack of diamonds, a face card. Then came the seven of hearts. The third card drew a slight murmur from the people gathered around. It was the ace of spades. This was going to be an expensive game.

The betting began.

Alex looked at all the money he had been given, thinking there must be better ways to spend a thousand dollars. McCain started the bidding with two hundred dollars, and the reporter folded at once.

"There's no point playing against you, Desmond," she said. She had a thick Scottish accent. "You always win."

"'We are all running in the race,'" McCain said. "'But only one receives the prize.'" He laughed briefly. "That's Corinthians, chapter nine, verse twenty-four." He turned to the soldier. "Are you in, Hamilton?"

Hamilton also folded. The accountant, Alex, and the ginger-haired woman all slid their $100 chips in front of them.

Two more cards. Two more bets. By the time the last card had been dealt, this was what Alex was looking at, spread out on the green baize surface:

J♦ 7♥ A♠ 9♥ J♥

There were just three players remaining. The other woman had folded, leaving Alex, the accountant, and McCain to fight it out. The fact that the ace of spades had now been joined by a pair of jacks sitting faceup on the table made this an even more extraordinary game. McCain had asked if the cards had anything to say, and it seemed that they were screaming. If this had been a real casino, the betting might have climbed to hundreds of thousands of dollars. Even so, it was going to get expensive. Alex had just $700 left, yet the accountant had almost as much as McCain. And, even with such high sums, it was obvious that there was more to this than money. McCain was still relaxed, still smiling—yet he really wanted to win the game. It was his party, his castle, his evening. It was a matter of personal pride.

And the other people in the room had sensed it too. Alex realized that the roulette wheel had stopped spinning. Everyone had gathered around the table to watch this strange contest—two men, a boy, and five white rectangles that, combined with the turned-down cards, could mean so much or so little.

"Interesting cards," McCain muttered. "If either of you have another ace, you'll have two pairs. You could win the entire pot . . ."

Why had he said that, Alex wondered. The odds of two pairs at poker are not huge. Why even mention it? Was he perhaps challenging them? Or could it be that he was trying to divert their attention? Suppose he had three of a kind . . .

"I'll tell you what," McCain went on with a fast check of his watch. "It's the last game of the evening, so why don't we have a bit of fun?"

McCain lifted his hands theatrically, touched the two thumb tips together, then laid his palms flat on the table. There was a stir from the audience as he used the wedge to slide all his chips forward, the piles collapsing on top of one another as at least fifteen thousand dollars' worth of chips were spread across the table. One or two people clapped. Everyone knew what was happening here. It was all or nothing. This was one of those games that any serious gambler would remember for the rest of his life.

"I'm going to make it easy for you," McCain said. He ran a hand across his jaw as if he were trying to smooth it back into place. "I know the two of you don't have enough money to match my bet, but I'm feeling charitable." He smiled at his own joke. "Put all your money in and we'll call it even."

The accountant drummed his fingers on the table. "Are you trying to pretend you've got the third jack, Desmond?" he asked. He had a clipped, nasal way of speaking. His eyes were small and almost colorless; Alex watched them dart from McCain to the cards on the table and somehow knew that he was about to make a mistake. "I think you're bluffing," he went on. "You're just trying to scare us away. Well, it's not going to work." He slid his own pile into the center, the plastic chips mingling with McCain's. He'd added about ten thousand dollars of his own.

Twenty-five thousand dollars! Any thought of charity had suddenly disappeared. It was a fantastic sum of money to be determined by the turn of two cards.

Alex glanced at his own pile of chips. It looked pathetic in comparison with the others, but he assumed McCain's invitation extended to him. "I'm in," he said.

"All right, Leo!" McCain nodded at the accountant. "Let's see what you've got."

The accountant flicked over his two cards. There was a mutter of approval from the spectators. He did indeed have another ace—the ace of diamonds—plus a two of spades. Adding them to the faceup cards gave him two pairs—aces and jacks—a very good hand. McCain really would need three of a kind to do better.

It should have been Alex's turn to show his cards next, yet McCain ignored him. "Too bad, Leo!" he crowed. "'God hath delivered you into my hand'—as it says in the first book of Samuel, chapter twenty-three." The silver crucifix glimmered briefly as he leaned forward and picked up his cards. He paused for a moment, then turned them over, one at a time. The first card was the jack of clubs. Three of a kind. It beat Leo easily. But then came the real triumph. He turned over the second card to reveal the other black jack—the jack of spades. The audience exploded. The odds of getting four of a kind in Texas Hold 'Em are 4,165 to 1. It was incredible luck. It was almost miraculous.

Now Alex understood why McCain had talked about two pairs. He had actually been underselling himself to draw the other players in. And the tactic, at least in part, had worked.

"I have the knaves and that makes it my evening," McCain roared. His eyes were bright with pleasure. He leaned forward and began to sweep all the chips toward him.

"What about my cards?" Alex said quietly.

"Your cards?" McCain blinked. He had forgotten Alex was even there. He glanced down at the table as if to reassure himself. Nothing could beat four jacks, not with only one ace showing on the table . . . could it? He relaxed. "Do forgive me, Alex," he said. "I should have let you show your cards first. But everyone here would love to see them. What have you got?"

Alex waited a moment. He was aware that everyone was watching him. But for some reason he wanted McCain to remember this. Maybe it was just that he didn't like being taken for granted.

He turned over the eight of hearts. And then the ten of hearts.

There was a long silence as the truth sank in. Then the audience gasped. The seven of hearts, the nine of hearts, and the jack of hearts were already on the table, faceup. Put them together with Alex's cards and he had a straight flush . . . seven, eight, nine, ten, and jack of hearts. And in the rules of poker, a straight flush beats four of a kind.

Alex had won.

McCain froze with his hands still cradling the chips, and in that moment Alex stared at all the chips spread out in front of him. They were all his! He had just won more money than he had owned in his whole life. But even so, he regretted what he had done. McCain was his host.

This was meant to be his big night. Yet he had just been shown up in front of a large crowd of his friends by an unknown fourteen-year-old. How would he take it? Alex glanced up. McCain was staring across the table with raw anger in his eyes.

"I'm sorry . . . ," Alex began.

McCain slammed his hands together as if to break the mood. At the same time, he leaned back and roared with laughter. "Well, there's a lesson in pride," he exclaimed loudly, for everyone to hear. "I jumped in too quickly. I was too sure of myself, and it seems I've been undone by a child I don't even remember inviting. Never mind! Alex, you've beaten me fair and square." He used his huge hands to push the chips away as if trying to distance himself from them. "You can cash in your chips with the croupier. I bet you must be the richest thirteen-year-old in Scotland right now."

"Actually, I'm fourteen," Alex said. "And I don't want the money. You can give it all to First Aid."

That drew a round of applause from the audience. McCain stood up. "That's very generous of you," he said. "Donating my own money to my own charity!" He was joking, but there was an edge to his voice. "I can promise you it will be well spent." He moved away from the table, a few people patting him on the back as he left.

Alex glanced down one last time at McCain's cards: the knaves, as he had called them. They were strangely ugly—almost like freaks, joined at the chest, with flowing hair and strange multicolored tunics.

Scowling knaves versus his own brave hearts. But of course, it didn't mean anything. They were only cards, and even as he watched, they were swept away and shuffled back into the deck.

OFF-ROAD VEHICLE

4

TWENTY-FIVE THOUSAND DOLLARS.

Even as he made his way back into the main body of the castle, Alex thought about what he had just done. It had been an awful lot of money to give away without thinking. He could have held back a little of it, bought something for Jack or Sabina.

He shook his head, annoyed with himself. Charity was what the evening was all about. The money wasn't his and never had been. He remembered the look of anger in Desmond McCain's eyes as Alex had revealed his straight flush. McCain might be a born-again Christian, but he hadn't liked being beaten and somehow Alex doubted that he was going to be invited back.

Sabina had disappeared, but Alex stumbled across Edward Pleasure in yet another of the castle's many passageways, leaning on his walking stick while he talked on his BlackBerry. There was a spiral staircase just behind him, leading up to the next floor.

He closed up the phone as Alex approached. "That was Liz," he said. "She's not feeling any better and I'm beginning to think we ought to head back after all . . ."

"That's fine with me," Alex said. "In fact, Sabina was looking for you. She wants to leave too."

It was half past eleven. In just thirty minutes there would be the countdown to midnight, balloons, more champagne, and a chorus of "Auld Lang Syne" before what had been described as the biggest fireworks display in Scotland. Guests were already streaming past, making their way into the main room. But Alex didn't mind missing it. There was something about Kilmore Castle that he found unsettling. Maybe it was the fact that it was so ancient and remote, perched high above the loch as if it didn't want to belong to the twenty-first century. He would be glad to see in the New Year somewhere else.

"Let's wait here for Sabina," Mr. Pleasure said. "She's bound to turn up sooner or later."

Neither of them spoke. Alex could hear music coming from the dance floor—now they'd shifted into Michael Jackson. A few more guests hurried past. One of them recognized him from the casino and smiled at him. Once again, the two of them were alone.

"So, are you looking forward to school?" Edward asked, as much to fill the silence as anything else.

"Yes. I am." If the question had taken Alex by surprise, so did the answer. He really was looking forward to the start of the spring term. He felt safe at school. He felt normal.

"What was that essay you were working on?"

Alex had brought homework with him to Scotland. After taking so much time off, he was trying as best he could to catch up. "I'm doing a project about GM crops," he said.

"GM?"

"You know . . . genetically modified. It's something we've been looking at in biology. How scientists can muck around with crops and make them do different things." Alex dredged his mind, trying to remember what he'd been learning the term before. "It's something Prince Charles is always going on about," he said. "He's afraid they'll accidentally destroy the world."

"The real problem with GM crops could be the corporations who end up controlling them," Edward said. "Have you heard of the terminator gene?"

Alex shook his head.

"It's something they've built into plants that effectively turns them off. It stops them from reproducing. So if you want more wheat or barley or whatever, you have to go back to the same company and pay them. You see what I mean? Whoever controls the genes could end up controlling the world's economy. It might be a good subject for me to write about myself. The real danger of genetically modified food . . ."

There was the sound of footsteps coming down the spiral staircase and suddenly Desmond McCain was there, pacing toward them. Sitting at the card table, Alex hadn't realized how big the man was. He was almost seven feet tall, built like an American football player, with oversized shoulders and arms. Given his life story, he must have been at least fifty years old, but he looked much younger. He obviously still kept himself in shape.

Edward Pleasure turned around and recognized him. "Reverend McCain!" he exclaimed.

"Mr. Pleasure . . ." McCain came to a halt. Alex saw a hard-to-read emotion pass over his face. His eyes, ever so briefly, clouded over as the zigzag that was his mouth stretched tight. Then, just as quickly, the expression of unease was gone. He smiled. "I'm very glad you could make it to my little affair," he said. He gestured at Alex. "Are the two of you together by any chance?"

"Yes. Have you met?"

"Alex and I were playing cards just a few minutes ago." McCain's smile remained, but it seemed a little strained and artificial. "If I'd known he was your guest, perhaps I wouldn't have been so rash with my betting. He actually cleaned me out." They were now all standing on the same level, but McCain still loomed over them. "How is the article?" he asked.

"It's finished."

"I hope it won't contain any unpleasant surprises."

"You won't have long to wait. It should be out next month."

"Have you delivered it?"

"Not yet."

"I'm looking forward to reading it." McCain examined the journalist as if it was his mind that he was trying to read. For a moment neither of them spoke. Then McCain blinked as if he had suddenly lost interest. "But now you must forgive me," he said. "I have a speech to make.

Thank you so much for coming to Kilmore Castle. It was very good to see you again. And a pleasure to meet you, Alex."

He swept past them in the direction of the banqueting hall. Edward Pleasure was looking puzzled. "What was all that about?" he asked.

Alex shrugged. "I don't know." He hesitated. "I thought he looked upset about something. . . ."

"I thought so too."

"Maybe he's worried about what you're going to write."

"He shouldn't be. I've already told you. I had nothing bad to say. Actually, I think he's quite a remarkable man. Take tonight for example. All these people have come here because of him. And it's all for charity. He never rests."

He stopped as Sabina appeared, hurrying down the corridor toward them. "Dad!" she said. "I've been look-ing for you everywhere."

Edward Pleasure put an arm around her. "We're leav-ing," he said. "Mum's still awake. We can toast the New Year when we get in."

They had no choice but to leave through the banquet-ing hall. By now all the guests had assembled and were standing together, champagne glasses in hand, facing the gallery where the bagpipe players had been performing and where McCain was about to make his speech. At least nobody would notice the three of them as they left early. Alex and Sabina followed Edward Pleasure and they made their way down the side of the buffet table—which had been partly cleared—on their way out.

There was a sudden fanfare, a single trumpeter standing at the back of the hall, his instrument glowing golden in the candlelight. The notes echoed across the chamber and the guests stopped talking and looked up expectantly. McCain appeared on the gallery. Two of the Highland pipers walked behind him, flanking him, a guard of honor. Alex couldn't help wondering if they were about to burst into tune. But they stood back as McCain reached the front and looked down on the crowd.

"I want to thank you all for coming," he began, his voice booming out. "I'll be brief. It will turn midnight in exactly twenty minutes, and that's when the party really begins. For those of you who stay the course, we'll be serving haggis, neeps, and tatties, then a traditional Scottish breakfast to see you off. And the champagne will be flowing all night."

A few people cheered. The invitation had made it clear that everyone was welcome until sunrise.

"We're here to enjoy ourselves," he went on. "But at the same time, we can't forget the many terrible things that are happening around the world and the many millions of people who need our help. I want you to know that tickets sold for tonight's party, along with raffle tickets, our silent auction, and private donations, have raised a fantastic $875,000 for First Aid."

There was another burst of applause. Hearing it, Alex felt ashamed of himself. Whatever mistakes he had made in the past, McCain had more than redeemed himself. The whole evening was about helping other people, and in his own small way Alex had inadvertently spoiled it.

McCain held up a hand. "I have no idea how that money will be spent, but thank God it's there." He stressed the word *God* as if the two of them were personal friends. "This year, we had those terrible floods in Malaysia, the volcano eruption in Guatemala, and most recently, the incident at the Jowada power station in India, which could have been much, much worse. We were there first. Your money went straight to the people who needed it. Charity is the bond of perfectness, as it says in the book of Colossians. And the next time disaster strikes, wherever in the world it happens, we will be ready."

Edward Pleasure had retrieved his coat and slipped it on. One of the waiters had opened the door to reveal a maelstrom of snow against an unforgiving night. It was time to go. Alex took one last look back, and it seemed to him that at that moment, standing on his own in the middle of the gallery, Desmond McCain stared straight at him, locking him into a final eye contact that ignored the six hundred people between them.

"Alex?" Sabina called out to him.

And then they were gone, out of the warmth of the

castle, hurrying toward the car that Edward Pleasure was already unlocking, using the remote control on his key ring. The back lights blinked a welcome orange in the darkness. It had been snowing all evening. There was a carpet a couple of inches thick on the ground and on top of all the cars. If it continued much longer, Sabina might get her skiing break after all.

They threw themselves into the Nissan X-Trail, slamming the doors behind them and shaking loose some of the snow that had piled onto the car's roof. Once again, Alex was glad that they had an off-road vehicle. They would need it tonight.

"What a night!" Edward Pleasure muttered, echoing Alex's thoughts. He turned the key in the ignition and the engine began to throb reassuringly. He found the heating and turned it up as far as it would go. Alex was next to him. Sabina was once again in the back. "I'm afraid we're actually going to have New Year on the road," he said. "It'll take us at least an hour to get home."

"I don't mind." Sabina was already untangling the wires of her iPod. "That place gave me the creeps."

"I thought you liked parties."

"Yes, Dad. But not when I'm the youngest person there by about two hundred years."

They set off, the tires crunching on the newly laid snow. The weather had briefly cleared—which was just as well. Edward Pleasure would need all the visibility he could get to negotiate his way down the series of hairpin bends that led to the main road beside the loch. Alex took one last look at the great bulk of Kilmore Castle. He could see the firelight glowing behind the windows of the banqueting hall and could imagine McCain's speech ending, the balloons cascading, the kissing and the singing and then more drinking and dancing into the morning. He was glad they'd left early. He'd had a great time in Scotland, but, like Sabina, he'd felt slightly uncomfortable at the party. He loosened his bow tie, then pulled it off. He'd have preferred to have spent the evening at home.

The accident was so sudden, so unexpected, that none of them even realized it had happened until it was almost over. For Alex, it was as if the journey down the hillside had been broken into a series of still pictures. There was Edward Pleasure changing gear as the car picked up speed. How fast were they going? No more than twenty-five miles per hour. Sabina said something and he half turned around to answer her. The headlights were shooting out, two separate columns, distinct from each other.

And then there was a cracking sound. It seemed to come from a long way away, but that wasn't possible. It had to be something in the engine. The car shuddered and lurched crazily to one side. Sabina cried out. There was nothing anyone could do. It was as if a giant hand had seized the back of the car and swung it around like a toy. Alex felt the tires slide helplessly across the road. Edward wrenched the steering wheel the other way, but it was useless. They were spinning out of control with the night sky rushing toward them. And then came the moment when the tires left the icy surface altogether, and with a surge of terror Alex knew that they had come off the edge of the rock face, that they were in the air with the black, frozen waters of Loch Arkaig far below.

For half a second the car hung in the air.

Then it pitched forward and plunged down.

DEATH AND CHAMPAGNE

IT WAS LIKE DRIVING deliberately into a black wall. They couldn't stop. There was nothing they could do. The last thing Alex saw was Edward Pleasure clutching the steering wheel as if he had been electrified, his arms rigid, his eyes staring. Outside, the world had turned upside down. The headlights were bouncing off the surface of the loch, which hurtled toward them, filling the front window.

They hit the water. The actual impact was brutal, whipping them forward and backward at the same time. Alex realized that there must have been a thin coating of ice stretching across the lake—he heard it and felt it splinter. It was like smashing through a mirror into another dimension. The car didn't float, even for a second. Carried on by its own velocity, it plunged into the darkness, huge tentacles of water reaching out and drawing it in. The real world of Scotland and castles and New Year was wiped out as if it had never existed, to be replaced by . . . nothing. All the lights in the car had gone out. It was as if steel shutters had fallen on the other side of the windows. Alex would never have believed that darkness could be so total.

Something was pressing against him, smothering him. For a moment he panicked, punching out with his fists, trying to get whatever it was off him. He couldn't breathe. What was this huge thing pushing him back into his seat? Where had it come from? He forced himself to think straight, to fight against the sense of blind terror.

The air bag. That was all. It must have been activated at the moment of impact.

Air. He was going to need it. They were still sinking beneath the surface, getting deeper and deeper. He couldn't see anything, but he could feel the pressure in his ears. There was no letup. It was getting worse and worse. How deep was the loch? Some of these Scottish lakes continued down for hundreds of feet. They would keep going until they reached the bottom, and that was where they would die. What had seconds before been a $35,000 luxury car had become a steel coffin.

There was a soft thud and a shudder as the tires came into contact with mud. Alex was aware of a ton of blackness weighing down on him. They weren't moving anymore. That was something to be grateful for. But how far down had they gone? More to the point, how long did they have? The car wouldn't be able to keep the water out for more than a few minutes. It was even now splashing down onto his feet, presumably coming through the air vents on either side of the satellite navigation system. The water was freezing cold, numbing the flesh at first touch. Already it was over his ankles. It was as if his legs were being taken away from him, one inch at a time.

"Dad?" It was Sabina's voice, coming from the back-seat. She sounded a mile away.

"Are you okay, Sabina?" Alex asked.

"Yes. I think so. What about Dad?"

Edward Pleasure hadn't spoken since they had left the road. Alex reached out over the air bag and felt the worst. The journalist was resting against the steering wheel . . . unconscious, injured, perhaps even dead. It was impossible to say. Alex couldn't see anything. He drew his hand back and held it in front of his own face, so close that it was brushing against his nose. He couldn't see it. It was impossible to breathe normally. His heart was racing, trapped inside him, just as he was trapped in this car. He couldn't deny it. He was terrified.

He swallowed hard and somehow managed to speak. "Your dad's unconscious," he said.

"What happened?" He could hear the tears in Sabina's voice. Like him, she was struggling for control.

"I don't know."

"What do we do?"

It should have been silent here at the bottom of Loch Arkaig, yet Alex was aware of noise all around him. The engine was ticking and clanking as the engine cooled. There were strange, ghostlike echoes coming from the lake itself. The Nissan was groaning as it fought against the pressure outside. And—most terrible of all—a steady stream of water continued to splash into the cabin.

Alex felt the water rise over his knees, a blanket of ice. He was sure that it had only been at ankle level a few seconds ago, but time didn't exist down here. Seconds were hours and a whole life could be over in a minute.

There was the sound of fumbling in the back, then Sabina spoke again. "Alex . . . the door's locked."

"Don't even try to open it!"

Different thoughts were spinning uselessly through his mind. The Nissan might have a self-locking system. If the doors had locked themselves electronically, it would be impossible to get out. But there was no point in getting out anyway. Inside or outside they would die.

"What are we going to do?"

Alex was still blind. He reached up, hitting his hand on the ceiling. Where was the light switch over the mirror? He found it and turned it on. Nothing. Of course, the car's electrical circuits would have flooded. But then he remembered. Edward Pleasure had consulted a map just after they'd left Hawk's Lodge . . . and he'd used a flashlight. Where had he put it?

He pushed the air bag out of the way and reached for the glove compartment. Somehow he managed to get it open, and more water poured out. God! They couldn't have more than a few minutes left. The water had already risen over the edge of his seat, rushing between his legs. It was unbelievably cold. The whole lower part of his body no longer belonged to him.

But he had found what he was looking for. A heavy rubber cylinder. He flicked it on and to his utter relief it worked. The beam leapt out of his hand.

Alex had experienced more than enough in the past year, but he would never forget what he saw right then. It was the perfect nightmare.

The car was already half filled with water, which looked as black and as thick as oil. More of it was pouring out of the ventilation ducts, coming in two steady streams. Outside the windows there was nothing. The glass didn't even look like glass. They could have been buried alive rather than deep under the surface of Loch Arkaig . . . it would have made no difference. The two air bags took up most of the space in the front of the car. Edward Pleasure was slumped against his, a great gash on the side of his head. Alex undid his seat belt and twisted around. Sabina was looking more frightened than he had ever seen her. She had drawn up her legs as if she were cowering away from the water, but it had reached her anyway. It completely covered the backseat. The bottom of her silver dress was soaked. She was shivering with cold and fear.

They were in a tomb. And they were alone. Nobody would have seen them leave the road. Nobody would ever find them. It would simply seem that they had vanished into thin air.

"Alex . . ." Sabina was staring at the flashlight as if it could somehow save her life. "What happened?"

"I don't know. The car lost control."

"Is Dad . . . ?"

"He's okay. He's still breathing." The light flickered and for a brief second the darkness rushed in. It couldn't go out now! Alex tightened his grip as if he could somehow will the batteries to keep working. "We're going to have to open the window, Sabina."

"Why?"

"It's the reason the doors won't open. We have to make the pressure inside the car the same as the pressure outside."

"But then we'll drown."

"No." Alex shook his head. "We didn't sink that far. I don't think we can be more than sixty feet down."

"Sixty feet is a long way, Alex."

Alex drew a breath. He knew that there couldn't be too many more breaths in this cramped compartment available to him. The water was rising all the time, the air space beneath the ceiling becoming narrower and narrower. But once the water reached the level of the air vents, it would stop. They would be sitting in a bubble of air that would quickly diminish as they breathed out carbon dioxide. Sabina had been wrong. They wouldn't drown. They would suffocate.

"We have to get out of the car and swim for the surface," he said. "It's the only way."

"What about Dad?"

"Don't worry. I'll look after him."

"But how do we open the window?"

All the windows in the Nissan were electrically operated, and even if the battery still had power, it wouldn't
have been enough to move them. The pressure outside
was too great. A manual handle would have been equally
useless. They had to break the glass. Alex thought about
leaning back and kicking out, using the heel of his shoe.
But he knew it wouldn't work. He couldn't get the right
angle, and anyway, the glass was reinforced. He'd never
have the strength.

He needed a hammer or an ax. Something metallic. A
fire extinguisher? There wasn't one. Golf clubs? Edward
Pleasure had brought golf clubs with him, but they weren't
in the car. He'd left them back at Hawk's Lodge.

Then Alex remembered.

"Sabina, where's your dad's walking stick?"

"It's here."

"Pass it to me." He couldn't keep the panic out of his
voice. He could feel the seconds ticking away.

Sabina passed it across and Alex quickly examined it
in the tentative light. The handle was metal and shaped
like a duck's head. He could use it like a hammer . . .
except it was too long. He didn't have enough room to
swing it. It had to be shorter. How?

"Take this." He handed the flashlight to Sabina.
"Shine it on me."

"What are you doing?"

He didn't answer her. He took the walking stick and

fed it through the steering wheel, slanting diagonally across the dashboard so that the tip was in the far corner. The bulk of the walking stick was now in front of him. Using all his strength and his own body weight, he wrenched forward, pushing the stick in front of him. There was a creak of straining wood, but the stick held.

The water was rising over his chest. He could feel its grip, as cold as death. He tried again and this time he was successful. The walking stick snapped in half.

There was no time to lose. He let the bottom half drop and took the splintered end in his hand. He now had something like a hammer, about a foot long.

"I'm going to break the window," he shouted. "Take a deep breath. As soon as the water's over your head, you'll be able to open the door."

Sabina nodded. She was either too cold or too frightened to speak.

Alex clutched the walking stick. Then, at the last minute, he remembered something he had learned from his days scuba diving with his uncle. "Don't hold your breath!" he exclaimed. It was one of the most common reasons for diving accidents. If he and Sabina held their breath as they rose through the different pressure levels, they would end up puncturing their lungs. "Swim as fast as you can," he said. "But remember to hum as you go."

"What do you want me to hum, Alex? 'Auld Lang Syne'?"

Alex almost smiled. Only Sabina could still make jokes

at a time like this. Perhaps that was why the two of them were so close. "Hum anything, Sabina," he said. "As long as you're humming, your lungs will be open."

He unfastened Edward's seat belt and checked that the driver's door was unlocked. The car was filling more slowly now, but there couldn't be much more oxygen left. He tightened his grip on the broken walking stick, then swung it with all his strength, aiming for his own passenger window, as high up as possible. The duck's-beak handle slammed into the glass.

Sabina had aimed the flashlight toward him, and he saw a series of spidery cracks in the glass. Water oozed in, but the window held. Was it his imagination or was it already getting more difficult to breathe? He had seconds left. He swung the makeshift hammer again, then once more.

On the third strike, the window shattered, and Alex was almost torn out of his seat by the torrent of water that came rushing in, filling up the available space. The flashlight went out and the blackness returned so suddenly that he wondered if the force of the water might have knocked him out. But he was still conscious. Still thinking. Had Sabina managed to open her door? He couldn't worry about her. There was nothing more he could do. He had to get himself out. And Edward Pleasure too.

Fumbling, blind, he searched for the door handle. He had underestimated just how cold the rush of water would be. There were iron bands around his chest, crushing him, trying to empty his lungs. He squeezed the handle and felt the door open. At once he lurched sideways, fighting his way out of the car.

But he didn't dare go too far. Everything was black. If he lost contact with the car, he would never find it again, and Edward Pleasure would drown. With the icy water swirling around his face, he hooked a hand underneath the door frame and felt his way over the roof and down the other side. Where was the door handle? He was already beginning to strain for air. He should have opened it from the inside. That might have saved a few precious seconds.

His hand smashed into the side mirror, but it didn't matter because he couldn't feel anything. Somehow he managed to curl his fingers around the handle and pull. The door opened. Alex's own natural buoyancy was dragging him up, but he kicked out, forcing himself to stay down. He reached inside and put his arms around Edward Pleasure, yet he couldn't get him out. He seemed to be stuck, jammed against the steering wheel.

With his own air running out and the surface at least sixty feet away, Alex thought the unthinkable. It was like some devil voice whispering in his ear. _Leave him. Look after yourself. If you stay down here any longer, both of you will die._

It was the air bag pinning him in place. That was the problem. Alex still had the walking stick. At the last moment, almost instinctually, he had slipped it through his belt, taking it with him. Now he drew it out and, holding it this time by the handle, jabbed the splintered end into the nylon skin. He felt it puncture and there was a rush of bubbles against his fist. He was briefly tempted to breathe them in—but somehow he remembered that there would be nitrogen rather than oxygen inside the bag and it wouldn't do him any good. The bag crumpled. Alex pulled again. Edward Pleasure came free.

They were out of the car—but which way was up? Alex couldn't even see the bubbles escaping from his lips. Nor could he feel them. The intensity of the cold had punched right through him and his entire body was numb. He was still gripping Edward Pleasure and he kicked out with his legs, hoping that gravity, buoyancy, whatever would take him in the right direction.

The journalist was dragging him down. He was a dead weight in Alex's arms, and once again that voice was in his ear. *Let him go. Forget him. Save yourself.* But he just gripped all the tighter, kicked and kicked again.

Alex was following his own advice and humming—not a tune, more a soft moan of despair. Suppose he was wrong? The Nissan could have plunged a hundred feet or even more. He looked up but saw no light, no sign of the surface.

He kicked.

It didn't feel as if he was making any progress. And what about Edward? How could Alex be sure he was still alive?

His chest was beginning to ache. His lungs were screaming for air and Alex knew that he wouldn't be able to resist them much longer. It couldn't have taken him more than a minute to clamber across the car. Another minute to get Edward out. Perhaps another minute since then. Surely he could hold his breath longer than that!

But not in this cold. The icy chill of Loch Arkaig had weakened him. It was all over. His humming faltered and stopped. There was no more air to come out. With a sob of pure despair Alex opened his mouth . . .

. . . And breathed air. He didn't even know how or when he had reached the surface. He hadn't felt his shoulders break through. Somehow he was just there. As his vision cleared, he saw the blurred outline of the moon, lost behind clouds, and a scatter of still-falling snow. He had to struggle to keep Edward Pleasure's head above water, and he wondered, with a sense of dread, if the rescue had all been in vain. He wasn't sure that Sabina's father was still breathing. He looked horribly like a corpse.

And where was Sabina? Alex tried to call her name, but he was too frozen . . . his chest, his vocal cords. He jerked around in the water. There was Kilmore Castle, high above him. The shore was about sixty feet away. He was alone. She hadn't made it.

"Aaah . . ."

No. He was wrong. There was a splashing sound, the black surface of the lake parted, and suddenly Sabina was next to him with light rippling around her. Her face was white. Her long hair had come loose and was hanging into the water. She had tried to call his name, but it was too much for her. The two of them stared at each other, saying more with their eyes than they could ever have managed with words. Then Sabina reached out and took hold of her father, sharing the weight. The two of them began an awkward, stumbling swim to dry land.

And even as they went, Alex knew that their ordeal wasn't over yet. They hadn't drowned, but they could still die of cold. Their body temperatures must be dangerously low. Once they were on the shore, they would have to find help—and quickly, before their entire systems shut down. But how could they do it? Kilmore Castle was too high up, too far away. None of the guests would be leaving yet. And Edward Pleasure needed immediate help . . . unless it was already too late.

There was a loud bang and for a horrible moment Alex thought that someone was shooting at them, but a second later the sky exploded with a blaze of white and silver, and he realized McCain had just launched his first fireworks. So this was the New Year . . . and what a way to begin it, with this hideous midnight swim. All around him, the water shimmered with a brilliant array of colors as the display continued overhead. He could imagine the guests, sipping their champagne, wrapped up in their coats and scarves, as they watched from the battlements with the usual ooohs and aaahs as each five-hundred-dollar missile was outdone by the next. What would they think if they could see what was happening below? Death and champagne. It seemed incredible that the two could be so close, existing side by side.

It took them five minutes to reach the water's edge, and climbing onto the beach was a horrible, brutal experience. The beach was covered in shingle, slate gray and jagged. No feeling had yet returned to Alex's arms and legs, but if it had, he would have known only pain. He was filthy, covered in some oily film. Water was still streaming down his face. It was in his eyes and mouth. He must look barely human.

But his only thoughts were for Edward Pleasure. Helped by Sabina, he turned the journalist onto his back, then knelt beside him. The weeks he had spent in the Brecon Beacons being trained by the Special Operations Division of MI6 hadn't included lifesaving. Fortunately, he'd learned that at school. There was a hiss and a scream, and for a second the sky blazed red, illuminating Edward's face. His eyes were still closed. Alex checked that his mouth wasn't blocked. He found his heart, placed both fists on top of it, and pushed hard.

He did it again, then continuously. Sabina was shaking violently. She might have been sobbing, but she made no sound. She had no strength left. She could only watch in growing despair as Alex kept up the massage. Edward Pleasure lay flat out, still. But suddenly, on the tenth or eleventh attempt, he suddenly coughed and water gushed out of his mouth. Sabina grabbed hold of his arm. He opened his eyes. Alex let out a deep breath. He'd been about to try mouth-to-mouth resuscitation, and despite everything, a little part of him was relieved that it wasn't going to be needed.

Silver sparks crackled and exploded, hundreds of them, spread out across the darkness, then rained slowly down onto the loch.

We've got to get help. Alex tried to speak, but he was so cold, he couldn't make himself understood and the words came out as no more than single letters. "W-w-w . . . v-v-v . . . g-g-g . . ." His whole body was out of control. His teeth were chattering. The muscles in his neck and shoulders seemed to be locked rigid. He could see the snow settling on Sabina's and her father's hair. He had never been so cold. He hadn't thought it was possible for the human body to continue functioning at this temperature. A few more minutes out here and the three of them would freeze solid.

But the greatest miracle of the night was still to come. Alex heard the sound of footsteps on the shingle and turned around. There was a man hurrying toward them, carrying a blanket. He had appeared as if by magic. In fact, it seemed so unlikely that he was there at all that Alex wondered if he was hallucinating. It was impossible to make out the man's features in the shifting colors of the night, but vaguely Alex registered the fact that he wasn't dressed in black tie. He wasn't a guest from the party.

The man reached them. "I saw what happened!" he

exclaimed. "I thought you must be dead. Are you all right? Can you move?"

"Our car . . ." Alex pointed out at the loch. For a moment, the water blazed emerald green. A great circle of fire hung in the sky, then blinked out.

"I know. I saw. We have to get you, quickly, into the warm." The man draped the blanket over Sabina, and as he leaned forward another firework exploded, the glare revealing the side of his face. Alex saw that he was either Indian or Pakistani, a young man, in his very early twenties. As Sabina clutched the blanket and drew it around her shoulders, the man peeled off his coat and gave it to Alex. "Put this on," he instructed. "Do you think you can walk? My van is just up on the road. It's only five minutes from here. Once you're inside, you'll be okay."

Edward Pleasure was recovering his strength. He dragged himself up onto one elbow and broke into another fit of coughing. "What happened?" he asked. His voice was little more than a whisper.

"Not now, sir. Not now. We have to go."

The fireworks display had come to an end. In the far distance, Alex heard clapping and the blare of plastic noisemakers and paper horns. Slowly, the three of them staggered to their feet. Sabina and Alex had to support Edward Pleasure, and all three of them needed the help of the man who had come out of nowhere. Somehow he managed to guide them across the beach with the snow whirling around them as if unwilling to let them go.

A track led down from the main road and, on it, a white van sat with its headlights on and taillights blinking. The sight of it lent them new strength. They came off the shingle and threw themselves into the back.

"Don't worry!" Without his jacket, the man was shivering himself. He paused beside the doors. "I'll take you to a hospital. You'll be all right." He closed the doors, locking them in.

They were lying on the bare metal, a puddle of water surrounding them. Sabina was almost hidden in her blanket. Edward Pleasure was barely conscious. Alex heard the driver get into the front, and a few seconds later, they moved off. At the same time, he realized that his senses were returning. The man had turned the heat up to full and Alex could actually feel the warm breeze against his skin.

It took them an hour to reach an Inverness hospital, and Liz Pleasure arrived two hours after that. By then, all three of them had been treated for hypothermia and shock and were tucked up in bed with hot water bottles and soup, being looked after by nurses who had agreed to work through New Year's Eve and who, Alex decided, really were true angels. The man who had rescued them had left without even giving his name. He had told them he was a supplier—on his way to Kilmore Castle. But what had he been supplying so late into the night? Alex didn't think it right to ask him, but even now it struck him that something didn't quite add up. After all, the back of the van had been empty.

They were released the next morning, Edward Pleasure blaming himself for the car accident, all of them too
shaken to discuss it. Between them, they had decided to
cut the vacation short. The Highlands and lochs of Scotland held no attraction after what had happened. They
needed the reassurance of the city.

Waiting for the plane that would take them back to
London, Alex did wonder if he should tell them what he
knew, what he had seen one second before the car swerved
and left the road. But in the end he decided against it. He
still wasn't one hundred percent sure. He wanted to believe that he was wrong.

Just before the car had lost control, he had heard a
distant cracking sound. And at the same moment, out of
the corner of his eye, he thought he'd seen a tiny flash
of light in the darkness, behind them and high up above.
He hadn't imagined it. It had been there. And he understood exactly what it meant.

A marksman positioned in the battlements of Kilmore
Castle.

Edward Pleasure hadn't skidded on the ice. One of his
tires had been blown out and it had been done quite deliberately by someone who wanted to force them off the
road. Anyone else would have thought they were imagin-
ing it, but Alex knew better. He had been a target too
many times before. Someone had just tried to kill them.

But who?

Desmond McCain? Because he had lost at cards?

No—that was insane. There had to be someone else. An old enemy perhaps. Alex had plenty enough of them. Or maybe it had nothing to do with him. Edward Pleasure could have been the target. Journalists, too, had plenty of people who wanted to settle scores.

He said nothing. The last time he had been with the family, in the south of France, they had been attacked. How could he possibly tell them that it had happened a second time? Sabina would never want to see him again. It was much better to persuade himself that he was wrong, that he was tired, that he had an overactive imagination. Anyway, in a few minutes they would be in the air, flying south, leaving it all behind them.

And yet, secretly, he knew that he was lying to himself. As his flight was called and he picked up his carry-on luggage, Alex gritted his teeth. Trouble never seemed to leave him alone. Well, let it follow him to London. He'd just have to be ready for it when it showed up again.

NINE FRAMES PER SECOND

ALEX WAS GLAD TO BE HOME.

First of all, Jack was there, waiting for him, surrounded by presents she'd brought back from America. Alex sometimes wondered what people would make of the two of them, living together the way they did. With her baggy clothes, her wild red hair, and her constant smile, Jack was more like a big sister than a housekeeper. And although she was actually his legal guardian, she never nagged or lectured him. They were really just friends and Alex knew that he couldn't have gotten through the last twelve months without her. She knew what he was doing. She had tried to talk him out of it. But she had never stood in his way.

She'd bought him new jeans, two shirts, a Barack Obama baseball cap, and a pair of fake police sunglasses. And over their first dinner together, he had told her what had happened at Loch Arkaig . . . but with no mention of any sniper.

"I just don't believe it, Alex!" Jack exclaimed. "You go off for a nice New Year's Eve party and you end up sixty feet under a frozen loch. Only you could manage that."

"It wasn't my fault," Alex protested. "I wasn't driving."

"You know what I mean. How's Edward? How's Sabina?"

"They're okay. They were shaken up. We all were."

"I'm not surprised. Do you know how it happened?"

Alex hesitated. The one thing he wasn't going to do was lie to Jack. "Nobody's quite sure. They haven't gotten the car out yet. It's possible they never will. But Edward thinks one of the tires blew out. He felt something just before he lost control."

"And what about the man who helped you?"

"He didn't hang around. He didn't even wait to be thanked."

Alex wouldn't have mentioned the accident at all, but he knew it would come out the following weekend when he and Jack went to Heathrow Airport to say good-bye to Sabina and her parents, who were finally returning home.

It was an uneasy last meeting, the five of them standing together, hemmed in by the crowds and suitcases and bright lights of Terminal Three.

"We'll see you again in the spring," Edward Pleasure said, reaching out and shaking Alex's hand. "We've got a spare room and we can head up the coast. I'm sure you'd enjoy trekking in Yosemite, or we could stay on Big Sur."

Sabina's mother gave him a hug. "I know what you did," she said quietly. "Sabina told me. Edward would still be in that car if it hadn't been for you." Alex said nothing. For some reason, it always embarrassed him, being thanked. "I hope you'll come and see us. And you too, Jack. Maybe you should come over together."

And then it was Sabina's turn. She and Alex moved a little to one side.

"Bye, Alex."

"Bye, Sabina."

"I thought you were brilliant in the car. When I started to swim up to the surface, I was certain I was going to die. But I knew my dad would be all right because you'd promised you'd look after him."

"It seems that every time your family meets me, something bad happens," Alex said. It was true. In Cornwall, the south of France, and now in Scotland . . . sudden violence had never been far away.

"Will you come to San Francisco?"

"There'd probably be an earthquake or something."

"I don't mind. I still want to see you."

Sabina glanced at her parents. They were standing with their backs to her, talking to Jack. She quickly leaned forward and kissed Alex on the cheek. Then, suddenly, the three of them were picking up their carry-on luggage and making their way through to the security checks and passport control. Sabina looked back one last time and waved. Then they were gone.

The next day, Alex went back to school and the Christmas holidays were forgotten in a whirl of seating assignments, schedules, textbooks, new teachers, and old friends. Brookland was a sprawling, mixed comprehensive school half a mile north of Chelsea. It had been built only about ten years ago and it prided itself on its modern architecture, with double-height windows and bright primary colors. At the same time, though, it still had an old-fashioned, friendly feel. Everyone wore uniforms . . . sober shades of blue and gray. The school even had a Latin motto: *Pergo et Perago,* which sounded like the story of two Italian cannibals but which actually meant "I try and I achieve."

"No running in the corridor, Alex." Miss Bedfordshire, the school secretary, greeted Alex with one of her favorite phrases, even though Alex had only been walking quickly. She had stepped out of one of the classrooms, blocking his path.

"Hi, Miss Bedfordshire."

"It's good to see you. Did you have a good Christmas?"

"Yes, thanks."

"And do you plan to stay with us for the whole term? It would certainly make a nice change."

Alex had missed almost half the school year, and Miss Bedfordshire had always had her doubts about the series of strange illnesses that had been listed on his doctor's notes. "I hope so," he said.

"Maybe you should eat more fruit. You know . . . an apple a day."

"I'll give it a try."

Alex hurried on his way, aware that the secretary was watching him as he went. Sometimes he wondered how much she really knew.

And then there were twenty minutes of catching up with the usual crowd. Tom Harris was late as usual and looked incredibly scruffy in a new uniform, which was one size too big for him. His parents had recently gotten separated, and he had spent the Christmas holidays with his older brother in Naples. Alex had gotten to know them both when he'd come up against Scorpia for the first time—and Tom was the only boy in the school who was aware of his involvement with MI6. There were a couple of girls with him now, and together they all piled into the sports hall for Year Group Assembly.

This began, as usual, with a hymn, which the principal, Mr. Bray, insisted on—even though every other school in the area had dropped it. There were three hundred of them packed into the hall, and they were horribly out of tune. The last chords faded away and everyone sat down to listen to an uplifting speech, which, as usual, went on too long. This term, it was all about respect. "Respect for others; respect for yourself; above all, respect for the community." Alex noticed that Tom was listening intently, with one hand resting against the side of his head. Only he could see the white wires of an iPod trailing back down the other boy's sleeve and could hear the faint *tish-ta-ta-tish* coming from his ear.

Then it was on to school business. Mr. Bray introduced a new class tutor and mentioned a couple of
teachers who were leaving. "One last thing," he announced. "I'm very happy to tell you that the science
wing is finally opening again after the mysterious fire
that did so much damage back in May." Alex shifted
uncomfortably. He had been at the very center of the
fire and knew exactly what had caused it. He was glad
that Tom wasn't listening. Watching Alex squirm, and
knowing as much about him as he did, his friend might
have been able to put two and two together. "I hope
you'll enjoy the new facilities. I wish you all a hardwork-
ing and successful term."

The assembly finished and the lessons began. For Alex
that meant history followed by math and then social stud-
ies, a cheerful assortment for the first morning of the first
day of classes. After lunch, the first lesson of the afternoon was biology with John Gilbert, a young teacher who
had only arrived the summer before. He was curly haired
with glasses and specialized in brightly colored ties. He
hadn't been teaching long enough to lose his enthusiasm,
and it had been he who had given the class the project on
genetic engineering that Alex had described in Scotland.

"I hope you've all begun to think about this very serious subject," he began. "I'm going to want to see your
written work completed by midterm. And I've got some
good news." He picked up a letter and showed it to the
class. "At the end of last term, I wrote to the Greenfields

Bio Center in Wiltshire. I'm sure you know who they are . . . they're always in the news. Greenfields is a private organization, one of the world leaders in plant science and microbiology. They've been doing more than anyone else to develop new techniques in genetic engineering, and they've got a huge facility on the edge of Salisbury Plain. I asked if we could visit, look at their work, and maybe talk to some of their professors—and rather to my surprise, they've agreed. To be honest with you, I didn't think they'd allow school visits because so much of their work is secretive. But we'll be heading down there in a couple of weeks. I'll need to get permission from your parents, and I'll hand out forms at the end of the period. Don't forget to get them signed!"

He put the letter down and went over to the blackboard.

"Now, I want to find out how you're coming along with your projects. But first of all, I asked you to come up with some of the good things and the bad things about GM crops. Can anyone give me an example of how this science has helped society?"

GM crops.

Alex couldn't help himself. He remembered the moment he had told Edward Pleasure about his work just as Desmond McCain had come down the stairs, and suddenly he was back at Kilmore Castle, half an hour before New Year's. McCain had appeared alarmed about something. But what could it have been, and could it really have led to the gunshot and the near death in Loch Arkaig?

There had been no gunshot. Alex tried to force the idea out of his head. The car had blown a tire, that was all. And yet, he still remembered McCain, the gleaming, bald head, the silver cross, the strange line where the two halves of his head failed to meet.

No. This was crazy. McCain ran a charity. He had made a mistake in his life, but he had paid for it. He wasn't a killer.

"Rider?"

Alex heard his name, realized it had been called out twice, and forced himself to focus back on the class. Just as he had feared, Mr. Gilbert had asked him something and he hadn't even heard the question. He'd been miles away.

"I'm sorry, sir?" he said.

Mr. Gilbert sighed. "You don't turn up to school very often, Rider. But it would be nice if you actually listened when you did. Hale?"

James Hale was another of Alex's friends, a neat-looking boy with brown hair and blue eyes, sitting at the next desk. He glanced apologetically at Alex and then answered. "GM science can make crops grow extra vitamins," he said. "And there was a special sort of rice that was changed so that it could grow underwater for a few days without dying."

"Very good. It was called golden rice, and obviously it

was very useful in countries with too much rainfall. Anyone else?"

Alex made sure he concentrated until the end of the lesson. The first day of the term was far too early to get into trouble. Somehow he made it to 3:45 without further incident, and then he was part of the crowd, pouring out of the school gates with his backpack over his shoulder. For once, he hadn't brought his bike with him. Alex owned a Condor Junior Roadracer that had been built for him as a twelfth birthday present. But he'd noticed recently that it wasn't giving him a comfortable ride. The truth was that he was growing out of it, and the seat wouldn't adjust any more. He would be sorry to see it go. It belonged to his old life, before his uncle had died, and there was precious little of that left.

Perhaps it was thinking of his uncle that drove Alex to take a shortcut across Brompton Cemetery. This was where Ian Rider had been buried after the so-called car accident, the one that began with gunshots being fired into his uncle's car. It was at the funeral that Alex had first begun to learn the truth about his uncle, that he had never actually worked in a bank. He had instead lived and died as a spy. Alex often walked past the gravestone, but today, acting on impulse, he left the main path and went over to it. He looked at the name, carved in a square slab of gray marble, with the dates below it and a single line: A GOOD MAN TAKEN BEFORE HIS TIME. Well, that was one way to put it. Somebody had left flowers, quite recently.

Roses. The petals were dead and withered, but there was still a little color in the leaves. Who had been here? Jack? And if it was her, why hadn't she mentioned it to him?

Alex bent down and swept the plants to one side. He thought about the man who had looked after him all his life but who had been gone now for almost a year. He could still picture Ian Rider—halfway up a mountain, on a diving boat in full scuba gear, or racing on Jet Skis over the South China Sea. He had taken Alex all over the world, always challenging him, pushing him to the limit. Adventure vacations, he had called them. And how could Alex have known that all that time he was being trained, prepared to follow in his uncle's footsteps?

Footsteps that had brought him here.

"Alex Rider?"

They must have crept up behind him while he was crouching beside the grave, and even without looking up, Alex knew that somehow he was in trouble. There was something about the voice—soft and threatening, with a slight foreign inflection.

Slowly, Alex turned and looked up. Sure enough, there were three men standing at the foot of the grave, all of them Chinese, dressed in jeans and loose-fitting jackets. They were completely relaxed, as if they had strolled into the cemetery and come upon him by chance. But Alex knew that wasn't the case. They might have followed him from school. They might have known that he sometimes took this shortcut and waited for him. But there was nothing chance about this meeting. They were here for one single purpose.

"I'm sorry," Alex said. "My name is James Hale. You've got the wrong person."

Even as he spoke, he was glancing left and right. There was nobody else around. No passing vicar, no other kids from Brookland on their way home. Apart from his backpack, Alex had nothing with him. He knew he wasn't going to find any weapons in a cemetery, but there was always a chance that a gravedigger had been careless enough to leave behind a spade.

He was out of luck. There was an open grave, waiting for its occupant, about a dozen headstones away. But there was no sign of any tools. What else? A small stone angel stood above him, a monument to "a great dad, a much-missed granddad and a wonderful husband." Why did no one ever have anything bad to say about people who had died?

The nearest man smiled unpleasantly, revealing nicotine-stained teeth. "You are Alex Rider," he insisted. "This is the grave of your uncle."

"You're wrong. He used to live next door . . ."

Just for a moment, the three men hesitated, wondering if, after all, they had made a mistake. But then the leader made up his mind. "You will come with us," he said.

"Why? Where do you want to take me?"

"No more questions. Just come!"

Alex remained where he was, crouching beside the gravestone. He wondered what would happen next. He quickly found out. The man who had spoken made a signal, and suddenly all three of them were armed. The knives had appeared in their hands like some unpleasant magic trick. Alex examined the silver blades, one in front of him, one on either side. They were notched, designed to leave the most vicious wounds. Somehow the men had gotten into position, surrounding Alex, without seeming to move. They were standing in combat stance, the weight spread evenly over their feet, each knife exactly the same distance from the ground. These were professional killers. They had done this many times before.

"What do you want?" Alex demanded, trying to keep his voice neutral. "I don't have any money."

"We don't want money." One of the other men spat into the grass. He had furious eyes, lips twisted into a permanent sneer.

"Major Winston Yu sent us to see you," the leader said.

Winston Yu! So that was what this was about. Somehow the head of the snakehead that Alex had helped break up in Thailand had reached out from whatever hell he had been sent to. He had left instructions for revenge.

"Major Yu is dead," Alex said.

"You killed him."

"No. The last time I saw him, he was running away. If

he's dead, that's the best thing that ever happened to him. But it had nothing to do with me."

"You're lying."

"What difference does it make? He's finished. The whole thing's over. Coming after me isn't going to bring him back."

"You must pay for what you did."

They were about to make their move. Alex could almost see the knives jabbing forward, striking at his stomach and chest. They would leave him in the cemetery, bleeding to death, and the next funeral that took place here would be his. But he wasn't going to let that happen. He acted first. He was still holding the dead roses that he had been clearing from his uncle's grave. He could feel the sharp thorns digging into the palm of his hand.

Swinging his arm up, Alex threw them, scattering them across the first man's face. For just a second, the man was blinded, in pain, the thorns cutting into him. A single dead rose clutched at the skin under one of his eyes. Alex sprang up, then followed through with a powerful back kick, the ball of his foot ramming into the man's stomach. The man's eyes widened in shock and he crumpled, gasping for breath. That left just two.

They were already lunging toward him. Alex had to get out of their range, and there was only one way. He threw himself sideways, one hand down, cartwheeling over Ian Rider's gravestone. He needed a weapon and he snatched up the only one he could see—the stone angel from the grave next to his uncle's. He hoped the much-missed granddad wouldn't mind. The angel was heavy. Alex swung it around and hurled it at one of the men. It hit him in the face, breaking his nose. Blood poured over the man's lips and he reeled away, howling.

The last of the three men swore in Chinese and launched himself toward Alex, the knife swinging in great arcs, cutting at the air. Alex fled. With his attacker getting closer all the time, he ran over six of the graves, then leapt over the open trench. But the moment he landed, he stopped and turned around. The man had also jumped. He had been taken completely by surprise. He had expected Alex to keep running. Instead, he was in midair while Alex had both feet firmly planted on the ground. There was nothing he could do as Alex lashed out with a front jab—the *kizami-zuki* he had been taught in karate—leaning with all his weight forward for maximum reach.

Alex's fist caught the man in the throat. The man's eyes went white and he plunged down like a stone, disappearing into the grave. He hit the mud at the bottom and lay still.

The first man was now on his knees, wheezing, barely able to breathe. The second was still bleeding. Alex alone was unhurt. So what should he do now? Call the police on his mobile? No. The last thing he needed right now was a load of tricky questions.

He went back to Ian Rider's grave, snatched up his backpack, and walked away. But even as he went, there were questions of his own nagging at his mind. If Major Yu had given orders for him to be killed, why hadn't they just gone ahead and done it? They could have tiptoed up behind him and stabbed him. Why had they felt the need to announce themselves? And for that matter, why had none of them been carrying a gun? Wouldn't that have made the whole thing easier?

As Alex left the cemetery, he didn't see the fourth man, fifty yards away, hiding behind one of the Victorian mausoleums. This was an Englishman or an American, with fair hair hanging down to his neck, smiling to himself as he watched Alex through the 135mm telephoto lens that was attached to the Nikon D3 digital camera he was holding. He had taken more than a hundred shots of the encounter, clicking away at a rate of nine frames per second, but he took a few more, just for good measure. _Click._ Alex dusting himself down. _Click._ Alex turning away. _Click._ Alex heading for the main gate.

He had it all recorded. It was perfect. The man had been chewing gum, but now he took it out of his mouth, rolled it into a ball, and pressed it against one of the gravestones. _Click._ One final shot of Alex leaving the cemetery and the whole thing was in the bag.

7

BAD NEWS

ALEX WAS HAVING DINNER with Jack when the doorbell rang.

"Are you expecting anyone?" she asked.

"No."

The doorbell sounded again, longer and more insistent. This time Jack put down her knife and fork and frowned. "I'll get it," she said. "But why do they have to come at this time of night?"

It was half past seven in the evening. Alex had come home, changed, done his homework, and had a shower. He was sitting at the kitchen table of the Chelsea home that had once belonged to Ian Rider but which he and Jack now shared. He was wearing jeans and an old sweatshirt. His hair was still damp and his feet were bare. Jack liked to call herself a ten-minute cook because that was the maximum amount of time she spent preparing a meal. Tonight she had served a homemade fish pie, although Alex suspected she had cheated on the time.

He was feeling guilty. He hadn't told her yet about the fight at the cemetery, partly because he was waiting for the right moment, partly because he knew what she would say. There was no way that he could keep something like that from her, but he wasn't keen on ruining the evening.

He heard voices out in the hall—a man speaking, polite but insistent. Jack arguing. There was a pause, then Jack returned on her own. Alex could see at once that she was concerned.

"There's someone here who wants to see you," she said.

"Who is it?"

"He says his name is Harry Bulman."

Alex shook his head. "I've never heard of him."

"Then let me introduce myself . . ."

A man had appeared at the kitchen door behind Jack, strolling into the room, looking around him at the same time. He was in his thirties, with long, blond hair falling in a tangle, broad shoulders, and a thick neck. He was handsome—but not quite as handsome as he thought. There was an arrogance about him that presented itself in every move he made, even the way he had followed Jack in. He was dressed nicely in gray slacks, a black blazer, and a white shirt open at the collar. He had a gold chain around his neck and a gold signet ring with the letters _HB_ on his third finger. To Alex, it was as if he had stepped out of an advertisement for clothes . . . or perhaps for toothpaste. This was a man who enjoyed being himself and wanted to sell himself to the world.

Jack spun around. "I don't remember inviting you in."

"Please. Don't ask me to wait outside. If you want the truth, I've been waiting for this moment for quite a long time." He looked past Jack. "It's a great pleasure to meet you, Alex."

Alex slid his food aside. "Who are you?" he demanded.

"Do you mind if I sit down?"

"You don't need to sit down," Jack growled. "You're not staying long."

"You might change your mind when you hear what I've got to say." The man sat down anyway. He was at the head of the table, opposite Alex. "My name is Harry Bulman," he said. "I'm sorry I've come by so late, but I know you're at school, Alex—at Brookland—and I wanted to catch you while you were both in."

"What do you want?" Alex asked.

"Well, right now, I could murder a beer if there's one going." Nobody moved. "Okay. I'll get to the point. I've come here to speak to you, Alex. As a matter of fact, although you won't believe it, I want to help you. I hope the two of us are going to be seeing quite a bit of each other. I think we're going to become friends."

"I don't need any help," Alex said.

Bulman smiled. His teeth were as white as his shirt. "You haven't heard what I've got to say."

"Then why don't you get on with it?" Jack cut in. "Because we were having supper and we didn't want to be disturbed."

"Smells good." Bulman drew a business card out of his wallet and slid it across the table. Jack came over and

sat next to Alex. They both read it. There was the name—
Harry Bulman—and beneath it his job description: Free-
lance Journalist. There was also an address in north
London and a telephone number.

"You work for the press," Jack said.

"The *Mirror,* the *Express,* the *Star* . . ." Bulman nodded. "If you ask around, you'll find I'm fairly well
known."

"What are you doing here?" Alex asked. "You said
you could help me. I don't need a journalist."

"As a matter of fact, you do." Bulman took out a
packet of chewing gum. "Do you mind?" he asked. "I've
given up smoking and I find this helps." He unwrapped
a piece and curled it into his mouth. He looked around
again. "This is a nice place you've got here."

"Please get on with it, Mr. Bulman."

Alex could hear that Jack was running out of patience.
But the journalist had already outmaneuvered them twice.
He had simply walked in here, and for the moment nei-
ther of them was asking him to leave.

"All right. Let's cut to the chase." Bulman rested his
elbows on the table and leaned forward. "You might not
know this, but many journalists have a specialist area. It
might be food, sports, politics . . . whatever. My specialty
is intelligence. I spent six years in the army—I was in the
commandos—and I hung on to my old contacts when I
left. I always figured they might come in handy. I was
actually thinking about writing a book, but that didn't

work out, so I started touting myself around Fleet Street. MI5, MI6, CIA . . . any bits of gossip I managed to pick up, I'd string together as a story. It wasn't going to make me rich. But I did okay."

Alex and Jack were listening to this in silence. Neither of them liked the way it was going.

"And then, a couple of months ago, I started to hear these strange rumors. They began with an event that took place at the Science Museum last April, when Herod Sayle was about to launch his Stormbreaker computer system. What happened to the Stormbreakers, by the way? There was going to be one in every school in the country, but suddenly they were recalled and that was that. They were never seen again."

He waited for a response, but Alex simply met his questioning gaze with silence.

"Anyway, back to the Science Museum. It seems that someone, an agent of MI6 Special Operations, para-chuted through the roof and took a shot at Sayle. No name. No pack drill. Nothing unusual about that. But then I was talking to a mate in a pub, and he told me that the bloke at the end of the parachute wasn't a man at all. It was a boy. He swore to me that Special Operations had gone out and recruited a fourteen-year-old and that this was their latest secret weapon.

"Of course, I didn't believe it at first. But I decided to have a nose around, so I started asking questions. And do you know what? It all turned out to be true. MI6 had taken some poor bloody kid, trained him up with the SAS in the Lake District, and sent him out on active service no less than three times. It took me a while longer to find out the name of this boy wonder. In the SAS, he was known as 'Cub.' But I persisted . . . I'm not so bad at this job . . . and in the end I got what I wanted. Alex Rider. That's you."

"I don't know what you're talking about," Alex said.

"You're making a mistake, Mr. Bulman," Jack added. "Your story is ridiculous. Alex is still at school."

"Alex _is_ still at Brookland," Bulman agreed. "But according to the school secretary, a very nice lady named Miss Bedfordshire, he's been away an awful lot recently. Don't blame her, by the way. She didn't know I was a journalist. I pretended I was calling from the local council. But let me see . . ."

Bulman took out a notebook.

"You were away for the first time last April. You were also away at the end of last year. That would have been at exactly the same time that a teenage boy dropped in on an oil rig in the Timor Sea, fighting alongside the Australian SAS. And who was that kid at Heathrow Airport when Damian Cray had a nasty accident in a jumbo jet? Now there's a funny thing, isn't it? An international pop singer one minute—a multimillionaire—and the next minute the papers are announcing that he's had a heart attack. Well, I suppose I'd have a heart attack too if someone pushed me into the turbine of a plane." Bulman snapped the notebook shut. "Nobody's been allowed to write anything about any of this. National security and all the rest of it. But I've spoken to people who were at the Science Museum, at Heathrow, and in Australia." He fixed his eyes on Alex. "And they've all described you to a T."

There was a long silence. Jack's fish pie had gone cold. Alex was stunned. He had always supposed MI6 would protect him from publicity. He had never expected a journalist to turn up at his own home.

Jack was the first to speak. "You've got it all wrong," she said. "Alex took a bit of time off last term because he was sick. You can't possibly think—"

"Please don't treat me like an idiot, Miss Starbright," Bulman cut in, and suddenly there was steel in his voice. "I've done my homework. I know everything. So why don't you stop wasting my time and face up to the facts?" He reached into his jacket pocket and took out a bunch of photographs. Alex winced. He guessed what was coming even before the journalist spread them on the table. And he was right. The pictures had been taken just a few hours before in Brompton Cemetery. They showed Alex in action against the three men who had attacked him, kicking out in one frame, spinning over the gravestone in another.

"When were these taken?" Jack asked. She was obviously shaken.

"This afternoon," Alex replied. "They followed me

from school and came up to me in the cemetery." He looked accusingly at Bulman. "You set it all up."

The journalist nodded. "Believe me, Alex. They weren't going to hurt you. But I had to be one hundred percent certain. I wanted to see you in action for myself. And I have to say, you more than lived up to your reputation. In fact, I'm going to have to pay my people double what I promised them. You put two of them into the hospital! Oh . . . and there's something else you should know about."

Bulman produced a miniature tape recorder and pressed a button. At once, Alex heard his own voice, a little tinny and distant, but definitely him.

"Major Yu is dead."

"You killed him."

"No. The last time I saw him, he was running away. . . ."

"All three of them were wired up for sound." Bulman flicked the tape off. "You knew all about the snakehead, so don't play innocent with me. By the way, I never found out how Major Yu died. I'd be interested to know how it happened."

Alex glanced at Jack. They both knew there was no point denying it anymore. "What exactly do you want?" he demanded.

"Well, we could start with that beer I was talking about."

Jack stiffened. Then she stood up, went to the fridge,

and took out a can of beer. She gave it to the journalist without a glass, but he didn't seem to mind. He cracked it open and drank.

"Thank you, Jack," he said, all pretense of formality gone. "Look . . . I can tell you're both a bit thrown by this, and I can understand that, but you've got to remember what I said when I first came in. I'm on your side. In fact, I want to help you."

"Help me . . . how?"

"By telling your story." Bulman held a hand up before Alex could interrupt. "Wait a minute. Just hear me out." He had obviously rehearsed what he was about to say. "First of all, I think what's happened to you is an outrage. It's more than that. It's a national scandal. In case you hadn't noticed, the law says that you can't join the army until you're sixteen . . . and only after you've taken your school exams. So the idea that MI6 can just stroll along and use a kid like you quite frankly beggars belief. Did you volunteer?"

Alex said nothing.

"It doesn't matter. We can get to all that later. But the point is this: When this gets out, heads are going to roll. The way I see it, you're the victim in all this, Alex. Don't get me wrong. You're also a hero. If even half what I've heard about you is true, then what you've done is absolutely amazing. But it should never have been allowed to happen, and I think people are going to be horrified when the story breaks."

"The story will never break," Jack muttered. "MI6 won't let you write it."

"I'm sure they'll try to stop me. But this is the twenty-first century, Jack, and it's not so easy anymore. You think the Americans wanted anyone to know about the torture practices carried out in the Abu Ghraib prison in Iraq? Or what about all the British members of Parliament who were trying to hide their crooked expenses? There are no secrets these days. If they stop me from going to the newspapers, I can put it on the Internet, and once the story's broken, the press will come running. You'll see. And if we keep it exclusive—if we go to the _Sunday Times_ or the _Telegraph_—we'll clean up.

"But it's not just about the newspapers. The way I see it, there's a book in this. It shouldn't take more than three months to write, and it'll sell all over the world. Tony Blair was offered six million for his memoirs, which nobody even wants to read. I reckon we could make ten times that amount. Then there'll be syndication in the world press, exclusive interviews—Oprah Winfrey will pay a million alone—and almost certainly a bidding war for the rights to make a major Hollywood film. You're going to be the most famous person in the world, Alex. Everyone is going to want a piece of you."

"And who gets the money?" Jack asked. She already knew the answer.

"We'll come to an agreement, Jack. Whatever you may think of me, I'm not greedy, and there's going to be more than enough to go around. Fifty-fifty! Alex will tell me the full story and I'll write it down. I've got all the contacts . . . publishers, lawyers, that sort of thing. In a way, I'll be Alex's manager, and I promise you I'll look after him. Like I said, I'm a fan. And after what he's been through, he deserves to rake it in. From what I hear, MI6 hasn't even paid him a regular salary. Now that's what I call exploitation."

"Suppose I'm not interested," Alex said. "Suppose I don't want the story to be told."

Bulman drank more of his beer. The chewing gum was still in his mouth. "It's too late for that now, Alex," he explained. "It's going to happen anyway. The story's out there and someone's going to write it, even if I don't. If you sit back and refuse to cooperate, it'll only make it worse. You'll have to live with what people say about you and you won't get a chance to set down your own side of what happened.

"But in a way, if you don't mind my saying so, you're lucky that you've got me in the driver's seat. You think anyone else would offer you equal partnership? In fact, most other journalists would have just gone ahead and broken the news without even coming here. I can imagine you're probably a bit confused right now, and I'm sorry I pulled that stunt on you in the cemetery. But believe me, once you get to know me better, we're going to be friends. I'm a professional. I know what I'm doing."

Bulman finished his beer and crumpled the can. Alex

didn't know what to say. Too many thoughts were going through his head.

Fortunately, Jack was never at a loss for words. "Thank you for being so frank with us," she said. "But if you don't mind, we'd like a little time to think about what you've said."

"Of course. I can understand that. You have my number. I can give you one week." Bulman stood up. "I reckon it'll be quite fun, Alex. I'll come here every evening and we'll talk for a couple of hours. Then I'll write it up the next day while you're at school. You can read it over for accuracy on weekends." He gestured at the photographs. "You can hang on to those. I've got copies."

He went over to the door, then turned around one last time.

"You're a real hero, Alex," he said. "I hope I made that clear from the start. There aren't many boys your age who actually believe in their country. You're a patriot and I respect that. I'm really privileged to have met you." He waved a hand. "Don't get up. I'll show myself out." And then he was gone.

Neither Jack nor Alex said anything until they heard the front door close. Then Jack went out to make sure the journalist had really left. Alex stayed where he was. He was in shock. He was trying to think of what it would all mean. He would become world famous. There was no doubt of that. His photograph would be in all the newspapers and magazines, and he would never be able to walk down the street again, not without being pointed out as some sort of curiosity . . . a freak. He would have to leave Brookland, of course. He might even have to leave the UK. He could say good-bye to his home, to his friends, to any chance of a normal life.

He felt a black anger welling up inside him. How could he have allowed this to happen?

Jack came back into the room. "He's gone," she said. She sat down at the table. The photographs were still spread out in front of her. "Why didn't you tell me about the cemetery?" she asked.

There was no accusation in her voice, but Alex knew she was upset. "I wanted to," he said. "But it happened so soon after Scotland that I thought you'd be worried."

"I'd be more worried if I thought you weren't telling me when you were in trouble."

"I'm sorry, Jack."

"It doesn't matter." Jack gathered the photographs into a pile and placed them facedown. "He wasn't quite as clever as he thought," she said. "He didn't know everything about you. He'd only found out about three of your missions. And he said you trained in the Lake District. He got that wrong too."

"He knew enough," Alex said.

"So what are we going to do?"

"We can't let him write this story." Alex felt a hollow in his chest. "He doesn't care about me. He just wants to use me. He's going to ruin everything."

Jack reached out and took his hand. "Don't worry, Alex. We'll stop him."

"How?" Alex thought for a moment, then answered his own question. "We're going to have to go and see Mr. Blunt."

It was the only answer. They both knew it. There were no other options.

"I don't like you going back there." Jack was only saying what Alex was thinking. "Every time you set foot in that door, something bad comes out of it. I was beginning to think they'd forgotten all about you. This will just remind them . . ."

"I know. But who else is going to stop him, Jack? We need their help."

"They've never helped you before, Alex."

"This time it would be in their interest. They're not going to want Harry Bulman writing about them." Alex pushed his plate away. He had barely eaten, but he no longer had any appetite. "I'll go after school tomorrow."

"I'll come with you."

"Thanks."

He was going back. The decision had been made. But as Alex got up and helped clear the table, he wondered if in truth he had ever really left.

THE LION'S DEN

THE EVENING SEEMED TO have drawn in early on Liverpool Street. It was only half past four as Jack and Alex came out of the station, but already the streetlamps were on and the first commuters were on their way home, snatching their free newspapers without even breaking pace. There must have been a slight mist in the air, because it seemed to Alex that the offices were glowing unnaturally, the light behind the windows not quite making it to the world outside.

Punched in the chest.

Unable to breathe.

The pavement, cold and hard, rushing toward him.

This was where Alex had been shot, and he would never be able to return without experiencing it again. The flower seller that he saw now, standing across the road, the old woman coming out of the shop . . . had they been there that day? It had been five o'clock, almost the same time as now, but during the summer. There was the roof where the sniper must have lain concealed, waiting for Alex to come out. He had sworn that he would never come back here, yet here he was. It was like one of those dreams where you keep on running but always end up in the same place. Trapped.

"Are you okay?" Jack asked. She could see what was going on in his head.

Alex pulled himself together. "It feels strange, being back."

"Are you sure you want to go through with this?"

"Yes. Let's get it over with."

They stopped in front of a tall, classical building that would have been just as much at home in New York but for the Union Jack that hung limply from a pole jutting out of the sixteenth floor. A set of rotating doors invited them in, and set in the wall to one side a brass plaque read, ROYAL & GENERAL BANK PLC. LONDON.

Strangely, the bank was fully operational, with loan desks, cash machines, tellers, and clients, and Alex wondered how many people must have accounts here without knowing what the real purpose of the building was. The entire place belonged to the Special Operations Division of MI6. The bank was nothing more than a cover. And for that matter, how many men and women would come out of those doors, never to return? Alex's uncle had been one of them, dying for queen and country or whatever else motivated them. What difference did it make once you were dead?

"Alex?" Jack was watching him anxiously, and he realized that, despite what he had just said, he hadn't moved. "The lion's den," she muttered.

"That's what it feels like."

"Come on . . ."

They went in.

The doors spun them from the cold reality of the city to the warmth and deception of a world where nothing was ever what it seemed. They were in a reception area with a row of elevators, a marble floor, half a dozen clocks—each one showing the time in a different country—and the inevitable potted plants. But there would be hidden cameras too. Their images would already be on the way to a central computer equipped with face-recognition software. And the two receptionists, both female and pretty, would know exactly who they were before they said a word.

One of them looked up as they approached. "Can I help you?"

"We have an appointment with Mrs. Jones."

"Of course. Please take a seat."

It was all so normal. Alex and Jack took their place on a leather sofa with a scattering of financial magazines on the table in front of them. Alex had come straight from school, so he was still in his uniform. He wondered what he must look like to passersby. A rich kid, perhaps, opening his first account.

A few minutes later, one of the elevators opened and a dark-haired woman in a black suit stepped out. As usual, she wore very little jewelry, just a simple silver chain around her neck. This was Mrs. Jones, the deputy head of Special Operations and the second most important person in the building. Despite the impact that she'd

had on his life, Alex knew very little about her. She lived
in an apartment in Clerkenwell, near the old meat market.
She might have been married once. She had two children, but something had happened to them and they
were no longer around. And that was it. If she'd ever had
a private life, she'd left it behind her when she became a
spy—and the spy was all that was left.

"Good afternoon, Alex." She didn't exactly seem
pleased to see him. Her face was completely neutral.
"How are you?"

"I'm fine, thank you, Mrs. Jones."

"We're ready to see you." She turned to Jack. "I'll
bring Alex back down in about half an hour."

Jack stood up. "I'm coming too."

"I'm afraid not. Mr. Blunt prefers to see Alex on
his own."

"Then we're leaving."

Mrs. Jones shrugged. "That's your choice. But you
said on the telephone that you needed our help."

"It's all right, Jack." Alex could see the way this was
going, and he had quickly made his decision. It was always possible that Alan Blunt would agree to help him—
but it would only be on his own terms. Any argument and
Alex would be thrown out in the street. It had happened
before. "I don't mind seeing them on their own if that's
what they want."

"Are you sure?"

"Yes."

Jack nodded. "All right. I'll wait for you here." She glanced at the magazines. "I can catch up with the latest banking news."

Alex and Mrs. Jones walked over to the elevator, and she pressed the button for the sixteenth floor. Only she knew that the button had read her fingerprint and that if she hadn't been authorized to travel up, two armed guards would have been waiting when she arrived. She was also aware of the thermal intensifier concealed behind the mirror, as well as the early warning chemical detector that had been added recently. Even the floor was examining the soles of Alex's shoes. The dust and residue under his feet might, in certain circumstances, provide valuable information about where he had been.

Mrs. Jones seemed more relaxed now that the two of them were on their own. "So, how is school going?" she asked.

"Okay," Alex said. Mrs. Jones sounded friendly enough, but he had learned to treat even the most casual question with suspicion.

"And how was Scotland?"

How had she known he had gone to Scotland for the New Year? Did she know what had happened there? Alex decided to put her to the test. "I had a great time," he said. "I really liked Loch Arkaig. In fact, I made quite an in-depth visit."

Mrs. Jones didn't even blink. "I haven't been there myself."

They arrived at the sixteenth floor and left the elevator, walking down a heavily carpeted corridor with doors that had numbers but no names. They stopped outside 1605. Mrs. Jones knocked, and without waiting for an answer, they went in.

Alan Blunt was sitting behind his desk as if he had been there forever, as if he never left. He was the same gray man in the same gray suit with the same files open in front of him. Sometimes Alex tried to imagine the head of Special Operations with a wife and children, going to a film or playing sports. But he couldn't do it. Like Mrs. Jones, Blunt had no life outside these four walls. Was that what he had dreamed about when he was young, being locked into a job that would never let him go? Had he actually ever been young?

"Sit down, Alex." Blunt waved Alex to a chair without looking up from his paperwork. He wrote something down and underlined it. Alex wondered what he had just done. He could have been ordering extra office stationery. He could have just sentenced someone to death. The trouble with Blunt was that either way he would have shown the same lack of emotion.

He glanced briefly at Alex. "You're getting taller." He sounded disapproving—but that made sense. The younger and more innocent Alex looked, the more useful he was to MI6.

There was a long silence. Alex took the seat he had been offered. Mrs. Jones sat down beside the desk. Blunt made a few last notes, the nib of his pen scratching against the page. At last he finished what he was doing. "I understand you have a problem," he said.

Jack hadn't said very much on the telephone. She'd had enough dealings with MI6 to know that nobody says anything important on an unsecured line. So Alex quickly explained what had happened: the fight in the cemetery, Harry Bulman's visit, the newspaper story he was intending to write.

He finished talking. Blunt reached out and wiped a speck of dust off the surface of the desk.

"That's very interesting, Alex," he said. "But I'm not sure there's very much we can do."

"What?" Alex was astonished. "Why not?"

"Well, as you've often reminded us, you don't actually work for us. You're not part of MI6."

"That's never stopped you from using me."

"Perhaps not. But it's not our business to interfere with the freedom of the press. If this man, Bulman, has found out about your activities over the past year, there's not a great deal we can do. Are you asking us to arrange an accident?"

"No!" Alex was horrified. He wondered if Blunt was even being serious.

"Then what exactly do you have in mind?"

Alex drew a breath. Maybe Blunt was trying to confuse him deliberately. He wasn't sure how to respond.

"Do you really want him to go ahead and write this story?" he asked.

"I don't see that it matters one way or another. We can always deny it."

"What about me?"

"You can deny it too."

He could. But it would make no difference. Once Bulman's report came out, his life would still be in pieces. In fact, if MI6 denied the story, it would only make it worse. Alex would be left out in the cold. Once again, he felt a rising sense of anger. It was Blunt who had put him in this situation in the first place. Was he really going to sit back and wash his hands of the whole affair?

But then Mrs. Jones came to his rescue. "Maybe we could have a word with this journalist," she suggested. "It might be possible to make him see things from our point of view."

"Talking to him would only compromise us," Blunt insisted.

"I absolutely agree. But in view of what Alex has done for us in the past . . ." She hesitated. "And what he might do for us in the future . . ."

Blunt looked up, his eyes, behind the square gunmetal spectacles, locking into Alex's for the first time. "Would you ever consider coming back?" he asked.

It was as if the thought had only just occurred to him, but suddenly Alex understood. Everything in this room had been rehearsed. Mrs. Jones had known he had been to Scotland. They knew exactly what was going on at Brookland. They probably even got copies of his homework. And of course, they had steered this conversation exactly where they wanted. These two never left anything to chance.

"There's something you want," Alex said. His voice was heavy.

"Not at all." Blunt drummed his fingers. Then he seemed to remember something. He opened a drawer in his desk and took out a file that he laid in front of him. "Well, since you mention it, there is one thing. But it's a very simple matter, Alex. Hardly even worthy of your talents."

Alex leaned forward. The file that Blunt had selected was stamped with the usual red letters—TOP SECRET. But there was another word written underneath it in black ink. Alex read it upside down. GREENFIELDS. It meant something. Where had he heard it before? Then he remembered and he reeled back. He almost wanted to laugh. How did they do it?

Greenfields was the name of the research center that he was about to visit with the rest of his class. His biology teacher, Mr. Gilbert, had been talking about it only the day before.

"What do you know about genetic engineering?" Blunt demanded.

"I've been doing a project on it," Alex said. "But you already know that, don't you?"

"It's an interesting subject," Blunt continued in a tone of voice that suggested it was anything but. "Genetic science can do incredible things. Grow tomatoes in the desert or oranges the size of melons. There's no question that companies like Greenfields could change the way we live. Of course . . ." He drew his fingers beneath his chin. "There are also certain dangers."

"Whoever controls the food chain controls the world." Alex remembered what Edward Pleasure had said when they were in Scotland.

"Exactly. Anything that puts too much power into the hands of one individual is of interest to us. And there is one individual working at Greenfields who is causing us particular concern."

"His name is Leonard Straik," Mrs. Jones said.

"Straik is the director and the chief science officer. Aged fifty-eight. Unmarried. He was a brilliant student, studying biology at Cambridge back in the seventies. He invented something called the Biolistic Particle Delivery System—also known as the gene gun. It uses helium pressure to fire new DNA into existing plant organisms . . . something like that, anyway. The long and the short of it is that thanks to Straik, it's become much easier to mass-produce GM seeds.

"For twenty years, Straik ran his own company—

Leonard Straik Diagnostics . . . or LSD, as it was called. It all went well for a time, but like many scientists, he was less brilliant when it came to business and the whole thing collapsed. Straik lost all his money and went freelance. Six years ago he was hired as the director of Greenfields, and he has been there ever since."

"Why are you interested in him?"

"Because of something that happened a few months ago." Blunt opened the file. "Last November, the police got a call from a whistle-blower inside the company, a bio-technician by the name of Philip Masters. He said he knew something about Straik and wanted to talk. Given the security implications, the police passed the information to us and we arranged a meeting—but one day before it could take place, there was an accident and Masters was killed. Apparently he came into contact with some sort of toxic material and it poisoned his entire nervous system. By the time he turned up in the local morgue, he was unrecognizable."

"An accident . . ."

"Exactly. It seemed a bit of a coincidence, don't you think?"

"We don't like coincidences," Mrs. Jones said.

"Since then, we've been taking a close look at Greenfields," Blunt went on. "It's a major operation. As well as research and development, it's also one of the largest suppliers of genetically modified seeds in the world, using the gene gun that Straik pioneered. There are whole

countries—in Africa and South America, for instance—
that are dependent on them. We cannot risk having a
loose cannon at the center of an operation like that. Masters knew something about Straik. We need to know what
it was."

Alex nodded. He was beginning to see where this was
going.

"We've managed to put a tap on Straik's telephone
and we intercept all the calls he makes on his mobile. But
we need more than that."

"We want to get into his computers," Mrs. Jones
said.

Blunt nodded. "There may be nothing in all this. After
all, people die all the time. Accidents happen and there
are plenty of toxic plants on the site. I understand Straik
keeps a whole greenhouse full of them. He's been doing
research into natural cures . . . antivenoms. But we have
to get someone into Greenfields—and it can't be a security guard or a maintenance engineer. That's exactly
what he'd be expecting. We have to take a different
approach."

Alex had heard it all before. People with something to
hide would always suspect an adult, particularly if they
knew they were under surveillance. But nobody would
think twice about a schoolboy on a class visit. Alex remembered what Mr. Gilbert had said. _"I didn't think
they'd allow school visits because so much of their work is
secretive."_ But somehow they had been persuaded to

make an exception for Brookland. Had MI6 been working quietly behind the scenes?

"It would be easy for you to slip away from the group
during your visit," Mrs. Jones continued. "And it would
only take you thirty seconds to download everything from
Straik's computer."

"Won't it have a password?" Alex asked. "And how
would I even get into his office?"

"We can have a word with Smithers about all that,"
Blunt replied. "But it's up to you, Alex. It seems fairly
straightforward to me. We can't even be sure that Straik
is up to no good. It may all be a fuss about nothing. However, it seems that we can do each other a favor. You
agree to help us and we'll have a word with this man—
Harry Bulman—and see if we can persuade him to leave
you alone."

Blunt smiled, but Alex wasn't fooled. He knew exactly
what was going on. If he refused to help, his life would be
torn apart. Blunt was pretending to offer him a choice,
knowing exactly what Alex would do. The decision had
already been made.

He should have expected it. He had agreed to walk
into the lion's den—so he could hardly complain when he
got scratched.

"It's a pleasure to see you as always, Alex," Smithers said.
"I fancy you've grown a bit. Unless, of course, Mr. Blunt

has supplied you with a pair of my new sneakers. I'm rather pleased with them, I must say."

"Do they fire missiles?" Alex asked.

"Oh, no. Nothing like that. They're for use by agents who need to change their appearance rapidly in the field. There's a hydraulic system built into the heel, and they can add three inches to your height."

"Do you have a name for them?"

Smithers folded his arms across his ample stomach. "Pumps!"

The two of them were sitting in Smithers's office on the eleventh floor. The room looked ordinary enough, but Alex knew that everything in sight actually disguised something else—from the X-ray angle floor lamp to the incinerator "out" tray. Even the filing cabinet concealed an elevator to the ground floor. Smithers was exactly as Alex remembered him. He was dressed in an old-fashioned three-piece suit that must have been specially tailored to fit his bulk, with a striped tie that was surely the old-school variety. As usual, there was a broad smile across his face and above his various chins. Smithers was the one agent in MI6 that Alex was always pleased to see. He was also the only person Alex trusted.

"So I understand you're going to look into Greenfields for us," Smithers continued. "Very good of you, Alex. I'm always amazed how helpful you are."

"Well, Mr. Blunt is very persuasive."

"That's certainly true. At least it shouldn't be too dangerous this time . . . although do look out. That chap Masters was a bit of a mess. He'd definitely trodden on something that he shouldn't—so just make sure you look where you're going." Smithers coughed, realizing that he'd said too much, and continued hastily. "I'm sure no one will even notice you."

"How do I get into Straik's office?" Alex asked.

"I've got a few things for you right here." Smithers opened a drawer in his desk and took out an old-fashioned pencil case. It was made of tin, slightly battered, decorated with a picture of the Simpsons . . . the sort of thing he might have been given for Christmas three or four years ago. "It's very unlikely that you'll be searched," Smithers explained. "But we know Greenfields has a very efficient security system, so better safe than sorry."

He pushed the case forward. "The tin is rather clever," he explained. "I actually developed it for international air travel. It has a lead lining so it won't show any of the hidden circuitry if it passes through an X-ray machine. But at the same time, there are silhouettes of pens and rulers fused inside the lid, and if the tin is scanned, they'll show up as ghost images. You could carry anything you wanted inside and nobody would notice."

He opened the tin. Alex was surprised that it actually did contain pens and rulers—along with other pieces of school equipment. "Since this is a school trip, I've concealed all the gadgets inside things you might reasonably be expected to have with you," Smithers said. He picked out a rather large eraser with a pudgy finger and thumb. "The memory stick that you'll need for Straik's computer is inside this. Just tear open the eraser and plug it in. You won't need passwords or anything like that. It's completely automatic. In thirty seconds, everything that's inside the computer will be on the drive's memory."

He took out a library card. It was already stamped with Alex's name and had a magnetic strip on the back. "Straik's office will almost certainly be locked. This will get you in. It looks like a library card, but actually it's an all-purpose swipe card." He lifted the tin and for the first time Alex noticed a narrow slot near the bottom. "You take the library card and you swipe any door that you want to open. Then you feed it into the tin. There's a miniaturized flux reversal system hidden in the bottom. It will work out the code you need and reprogram the card. These are now standard equipment for all MI6 agents, although this is the first time I've hidden one in the bottom of a Simpsons pencil case!"

"How do I find Straik's office?" Alex asked.

"I'm working on that, Alex. Greenfields is a big place, and I doubt there'll be signs. But I've got a rather neat idea and I'll send it to you later."

Alex picked up a pencil sharpener. "What does this do?"

"It sharpens pencils." Smithers reached out for it. "But it also converts into a knife. It's tiny, of course, but the blade is diamond edged and will cut through almost anything. No need to worry about closed-circuit TV cameras. . . ." He took what looked like a small pocket calculator out of the tin. "Just press the plus button three times and it will send out a square wave frequency signal, which should jam any transmissions within fifty yards. On the subject of jam, it's almost time for tea. Would you like some?"

"No, thanks." Alex took the calculator. "Does it do anything else?"

"As a matter of fact, it's also an extremely sophisticated communications device. Press 911 and you can talk directly to us. It'll work anywhere in the world."

"911," Alex muttered. "In case of emergencies . . ."

Smithers smiled. "And finally, I know you like your explosions, Alex, so you'll enjoy this." He took the last two items out of the tin.

"They look like pens," Alex said.

"Yes, they do. They're gel-ink pens . . . but the gel in this instance is short for gelignite." Smithers held them in front of him. "There are two colors here. The red one is much more powerful than the black one. Remember that. It's the difference between blowing a door off its hinges and blowing the lock off a door. They both have time fuses concealed in the cap. Twist once for fifteen seconds, then pull the plunger upward to activate. You have a delay of up to two minutes. They're also magnetic. And, of course, they write."

He put everything back into the tin and closed the lid.

"There you are, old chap. Everything you need . . . nice and neat. I'm sure this mission is going to be a piece of cake—which reminds me once again that it really is time for tea. Are you sure you won't join me?"

"No, thanks, Mr. Smithers." Alex took the pencil case and got to his feet. "I'll see you."

"I'm sure you will, Alex. I don't know what it is about you, but you just don't seem able to stay away. Take care—and do come and see me again soon."

Back on the sixteenth floor, Alan Blunt was still behind his desk, listening as Mrs. Jones read from a report. It had been printed and handed to her only minutes before. There were just two pages: a black-and-white photograph followed by about fifty lines of text.

"Harry Bulman," she was saying. "Educated at Eton. Expelled when he was sixteen. Drugs. He went into the army, and it's true what he told Alex. He actually made it into the commandos, but they threw him out. Dishonorable discharge for cowardice. His unit came under attack in Afghanistan and he was found buried in a sand dune. He was hiding. After that, he managed to get odd jobs in journalism. Writing about defense issues some of the time, but mainly it was just smut. Three-in-a-bed headlines and that sort of thing. Married and divorced. No children. Lives in north London. Thirty-seven years old."

There was a brief silence as Blunt took this in. Nothing showed behind his eyes, but Mrs. Jones knew that he would be considering every possibility and that within seconds he would have come up with a plan of attack. This was his great strength. It was the reason why he had headed up Special Operations for so long.

"Invisible Man," he said. He had made his decision. "We'll give it to Crawley. He hasn't been out in the field for a while. He'll enjoy it."

"Right." There was a shredder beside the desk. Mrs. Jones fed her copy of the report into it and the blades began to rotate. Harry Bulman was looking out from the photograph. There was a half smile on his face, as if he was pleased with himself. Slowly, he disappeared into the machine, sliced into ribbons, dropping into the bin below.

INVISIBLE MAN

THERE WERE AT LEAST TEN THOUSAND GUESTS in the auditorium and they were all applauding. Harry Bulman made his way through the crowd, occasionally pausing to shake hands and to receive congratulations from people he didn't even know. Ahead of him, the stage beckoned. A dozen golden statuettes stood in a line and one of them had his name on it: Journalist of the Year. It was glimmering in the spotlight, twice the size of any of the others, and as he walked toward it, it seemed to grow even bigger. At the same time, a bell began to ring and . . .

He woke up. It was eight o'clock in the morning and his alarm had just gone off.

It had been a dream, of course, but a very pleasant one—and Bulman had no doubt that very soon it would become a reality.

He was going to be famous. Newspaper editors who were usually too busy to give him the time of day would be lining up to employ him. There would be television talk shows, celebrity parties, lots of awards. It occurred to him that maybe he had been a little too generous offering Alex fifty percent of his earnings. After all, he was the one doing all the work. It was *his* story. Maybe forty or even thirty percent would have been closer to the mark.

In fact, at the end of the day, the journalist didn't need to pay him anything at all. It wasn't as if Alex could do anything about it.

It was incredible, really, that the two of them had finally met. Bulman remembered the first time he had heard the story of a teenage spy. It had been in a pub, the Crown on Fleet Street, a late-night drinking session with an old friend in the police who had been at the Science Museum when the parachutist came through the roof. He hadn't believed it then, but something had told him to stick with it, and very soon he had found himself on what had become nothing less than a quest. He had spent months doggedly following leads that had gone nowhere, meeting contacts who had clammed up at the last moment, calling in favors, and, when necessary, making threats. Piece by piece he had put the story together. And in the end it had led him to Alex.

Bulman slept in a circular bed with black silk sheets on the top floor of a modern block of apartments in Chalk Farm. His bedroom had views of the railway lines leading into Euston Station. The place had been built only twenty years ago but already there were cracks appearing, maybe because of the vibrations from the trains. One was passing now. When he had first moved in here, the grinding wheels used to wake him up, but he had soon grown used to it. Now he quite liked it. He wouldn't have been able to afford the place if it had been anywhere quieter.

It was the start of a new week. Seven days since he

had been in Alex's Chelsea flat. In the end, he had de-cided to give the boy time to work things out and to recognize he had no alternative but to work with him. He and that housekeeper of his would have talked things over and probably blamed each other for what had happened. Now that he thought about it, maybe that was another interesting angle. The girl—Jack—was quite pretty. What was she doing, living with a fourteen-year-old boy? The _National Enquirer_ would like that! Well, this afternoon Bulman would go back. He would be there waiting with a glass of white wine and a digital recorder when Alex finished school.

He threw back the covers and went into the kitchen, where the plates from dinner last night—and the night before—were still stacked up in the sink. Bulman enjoyed good food, but he couldn't be bothered to cook for him-self and the packaging from frozen meals was spilling out of the garbage. He found a clean mug and made himself a coffee, glancing at the newspaper articles that were pinned to a corkboard above the sink. "Secrets of Army's Basra Breakfast." "Intelligence Chief Appears on Face-book." "SAS Commander Misses Flight." He wasn't proud of his work. Nobody took much notice of what he wrote, and the stories were always nearer the back of the paper than the front. What did it matter, anyway? They were read and then forgotten . . . if they were read at all.

That would all change soon.

Bulman opened the fridge. He took out the milk and

sniffed it. It was sour. He poured it into the sink and drank his coffee black. What was he going to do until four o'clock? It was a beautiful day, a cold January sun glinting off the railway tracks. He watched a second train rumble past on its way into town, packed with commuters on their way to their boring jobs. He could almost imagine them, squashed into the newspapers they were trying to read. A month from now, those newspapers would belong to him.

A late breakfast. Shopping. A couple of beers at the Groucho Club in Soho. He mapped out his day as he got dressed in his usual open-neck shirt, blazer, and slacks. He never wore jeans. He liked to look stylish. He fastened the shirt with brightly polished silver cuff links, each one decorated with a miniature engraving of the Fairbairn-Sykes dagger, used by the commandos since the Second World War. Finally, he scooped up the briefcase that he always carried with him, grabbed his wallet from the bedside table, finished his coffee, and went out.

There was a newsstand opposite the apartment with a display showing the morning headlines. "Journalist Killed." He couldn't help smiling as he read the words. He wondered if it was somebody he knew, probably taking a bullet in Afghanistan or somewhere else in the Middle East. He had often tried to get himself sent abroad (". . . our man, Harry Bulman, entrenched with the allied forces in Iraq . . ."), but none of the editors

had been interested. Well, serves the guy right, whoever
he was. Probably some stupid amateur who didn't know
when to duck.

He was about to cross the road and buy the paper
when he remembered that he had used the last of his
change down at the pub the night before. He'd been
drinking with a couple of freelance journalists and
somehow they'd all ended up around the slot machine,
shoveling coins in. At one stage he'd won more than
twenty-five dollars, but of course he'd put it all back in
again and lost it. That was his problem. He never knew
when to stop. He took out his wallet and opened it. All
he had was a couple of credit cards. He had no money
at all.

The nearest cash machine was at the traffic lights on
the other side of Camden Market. Bulman thought about
walking, but as luck would have it, a bus appeared at that
exact moment, rumbling toward him down the hill. At
least he had his pass . . . it was valid for any subway or
bus in London. He hurried over to the bus stop, arriving
just as the driver pulled in and the doors hissed open. A
couple of people got on ahead of him, but then it was his
turn. He pressed his card against the scanner. The machine made a discouraging sound.

"I'm sorry, mate," the driver said. "You've got nothing
left on your card."

"That's not possible," Bulman replied. "I took the subway last night and I had about thirty dollars left on it."

"Well, it's showing zero now." The driver pointed at the screen.

"Your machine must be broken."

"It worked for everyone else."

Bulman held his card against the screen for a second time—but with the same result. He glanced around. The bus was crowded with people waiting to move off. They were all watching him impatiently. "All right." He scowled. "I'll give you the cash."

But even as he reached into his pocket, he remembered that he didn't have any cash. The driver was glaring at him now. Bulman gave up. The bank was only a quick walk away. The sun was shining. "Forget it," he muttered. "I'll walk."

He stepped back onto the sidewalk. The doors closed and the bus moved off. Bulman was still holding his travel pass. He glared at it. When he had a spare minute, he would send a letter to Transport for London to complain. Maybe he would even write a newspaper article about his experience. Idiots. Why couldn't they get the technology to work?

It took him ten minutes to walk down to the bank, by which time it was almost nine o'clock. All around him, the shops were opening. People were hurrying out of the coffee shops, clutching their oversized cups, then disappearing into their offices . . . another busy London day. Propping his briefcase under his arm, Bulman selected a debit card and fed it into the machine. He needed money for breakfast, to pick up a few groceries—and later on, he might treat himself to a taxi over to Chelsea. He punched in his PIN, touched the box for $50, and waited.

The screen went black. Then a message came up.

CARD REJECTED. PLEASE CALL PROVIDER
FOR FURTHER SERVICE.

Bulman stared at the screen, then punched the Cancel button to get his card back. Nothing happened. Not only was the machine refusing to give him any money, it had decided to keep his card! There was nothing wrong with the account, he was sure of it. The last time he'd looked, he'd had over four hundred dollars in it. Someone must have vandalized the ATM, some lout who'd had too much to drink.

He'd have to find another cash machine and use his credit card for a cash advance. He walked only a block before finding one. Very cautiously, he typed in his PIN, taking care not to make any mistakes.

The same thing happened. A blank screen. A stark white message. His card was swallowed up.

He swore. A couple of people had lined up to use the same machine and they were looking at him with a sort of pity, as if they imagined that he was broke, that there was nothing in his account. What was he to do now? He was angry, humiliated, and hungry—he needed breakfast. He had no money and no way to travel.

Unless, of course, he used his car. Bulman had a sec-
ondhand Volkswagen parked around the corner from his
apartment. He didn't often use it during the day—there
was far too much traffic in London for his taste—but he
sometimes drove it at night, and he kept a spare twenty-
dollar bill in the glove compartment for emergencies.
That wouldn't buy him much, but it was better than nothing and he could use it for breakfast while he waited for
the bank to open. He'd feel better with a bit of food inside
him. Then he'd go in to the bank and shout at the silly fat
girl behind the teller's desk. (In his experience, bank tellers were always silly and fat.) And once it was sorted, he
would get on with his day.

He found the side street and strolled down to the spot
where he'd parked.

The car wasn't there.

Bulman stood on the sidewalk, blinking. He had the
beginnings of a headache. He had definitely parked in
this spot. He might have had a few too many drinks that
evening—and, yes, he was probably well over the limit—
but he was certain this was where he had left it. Now
there was a blue Volvo in his space. He looked up and
down the road. There was no sign of his Volkswagen. He
forced himself to think. Dinner, pub, slot machine, one
last drink, then home around midnight. The car had to be
here.

And yet it wasn't.

It had been stolen! Cars were always being taken in

this part of town! A lot of the residents had those clumsy-looking locks that fit over the steering wheel . . . but he had never bought one.

He shook his head. What a day this was turning into! He'd be in a bad mood when he caught up with Alex Rider later this afternoon. It would be their first session together—but even so, he was going to give the boy a hard time.

First things first. Bulman took out his mobile phone to call the police. He wondered what number to use. This wasn't really an emergency, but he decided to call 911 anyway. He thumbed the buttons and held the phone to his ear.

Nothing.

It wasn't ringing. There wasn't even a dial tone. Bulman brought the phone down—it was a brand-new BlackBerry—and examined it.

NO SIGNAL.

This was ridiculous. He was in the middle of the city. There was always a signal here. He walked a few paces up the sidewalk, held the phone up, tried it at a different angle. The message remained the same. He squeezed the phone so tightly that he was almost crushing it.

He forced himself to calm down. There was an old-fashioned telephone booth at the end of the road. He wouldn't need coins to make a 911 call. He would contact the police from there.

He retraced his steps and entered the phone booth. It was plastered with advertisements for models and smelled of cigarette smoke and urine. At least the phone itself seemed to be working. He balanced his briefcase against the glass and made the call.

"Which service do you require?" the operator asked him.

"My car has been stolen," Bulman said. He was almost relieved to hear another human voice. "I need to speak to the police."

There was a pause and he was put through.

"I'd like to report a stolen car," he said. "I parked it on Chilton Street last night and now it's gone."

"Can I have the license plate number?" It was a woman's voice. She didn't sound very concerned. She also spoke with a foreign accent, making him wonder if he'd been rerouted to a call center abroad.

Forcing himself not to lose his temper, he gave the license number. "KL06NZG."

"KL06NZG?"

"Yes."

"Is that a green Mercedes SLR Coupe?"

"No!" Bulman shut his eyes. His headache was getting worse. "It's a silver Volkswagen Golf."

"Can you give me the license number again?"

Bulman repeated it, pausing between each digit. Whoever was at the other end of the line obviously didn't have much skill with computers.

"I'm sorry, sir." The woman was adamant. "That number is registered to a Mercedes. Can I take your name?"

"It's Bulman. Harold Edward Bulman."

"And your address?"

He told her.

"Could you hold a moment?" There was another silence, longer this time. Bulman was about to hang up when the woman came back on the line. "Mr. Bulman, how long have you had this car?"

"I bought it two years ago."

"I'm afraid we have no record of that name or that address on our files."

This was the end. Bulman lost his temper. "Are you telling me that I don't know where I live and that I've forgotten the make and the color of my own car? I'm telling you, my car has been stolen. I left it here last night, and now it's gone."

"I'm sorry, sir. The license number you've given us doesn't match up with the information I have here."

"Well, your information is wrong." Bulman slammed the phone down. His head was throbbing.

He needed money. He felt naked without cash and he wanted to eat. He looked at his watch. At least that was still working. Half past nine. The banks would have opened by now. Bulman had plenty of ID on him, and he'd feel better once he had a full wallet. He could deal with the car later.

He turned and walked back the way he had come. Ten minutes later, he found himself in the local branch of his bank, talking to one of the managers who had a desk in the main hall. The manager was a young man, Asian, dressed in a suit, with a neat beard. He was clearly alarmed as this new customer came striding up to him, and Bulman realized that, what with all the tramping back and forth, trying to deal with all the events that seemed to have ganged up on him in the past hour, he must look half crazed. He no longer cared.

"I need to withdraw some money," he said. "And your machine doesn't seem to be working."

The manager frowned. "We haven't had any complaints."

"It doesn't matter. I don't need to use the machine. I want to withdraw some money from you."

"Do you have a card, sir?" Bulman handed over his last remaining credit card and watched as the manager brought up his details on the computer. He gazed at the screen, perplexed. "I'm very sorry, sir . . ."

"Are you saying I don't have an account with you?" Bulman's voice was quavering.

"No, sir. You used to have an account. But you closed it down a year ago. You can see for yourself." He swiveled the computer around and there it was, a row of zeroes at the bottom of his account. Every last penny had been removed exactly twelve months before.

"I never closed my account," Bulman said.

"Would you like me to talk to the head office? . . ."

Yet Bulman was already gone, spinning out of the

chair and making his way through the main door, out into the fresh air. What the hell was going on? His travel pass, then the bank cards, his mobile phone, his car, now his accounts . . . it was as if his identity was being taken from him one piece at a time. He leaned against the corner of the building, steadying himself, and as he stood there, a commuter hurried past, throwing a copy of his newspaper into a bin right in front of him, almost as if he wanted Bulman to see what was on the front page.

It was a photograph of himself.

Bulman gazed at it in horror, remembering the headline that he had seen as he came out of his apartment. "Journalist Killed." He was looking at the same headline now. He felt the sidewalk lurching underneath him as he stepped forward and plucked the newspaper out. The story was very short.

Harold Bulman, a freelance journalist who specialized in stories relating to the army and intelligence services, was yesterday morning found dead in his north London apartment. Mr. Bulman, 37, had been stabbed. Police today appealed for any witnesses who might have seen or heard anything between ten o'clock and midnight to come forward. Detective Chief Superintendent Stephen Leather, who is heading the investigation, said: "Mr. Bulman may well have made himself enemies in his line of work, and

at this stage we are not ruling anything out." Harold
Bulman was unmarried and had no close family or
friends.

_____

It was him. They were saying he was dead! How could
they have made a mistake like that? Was this the reason
why his phone wasn't working, why there was no money
in his account? Suddenly it all made sense. Somehow
he'd been confused with somebody else. And as a result,
a whole series of switches had been pulled as, automatically, his life was turned off.

He had to get to a telephone. He had to talk to his
editors, to the people who employed him. He had no
money. But there was a telephone in his apartment. That
was the answer. Bulman didn't want to be on the street
anymore, anyway. He had become a non-person, an invisible man. For some reason, he felt exposed. How could
he be sure that there wasn't someone out there who really
did want to stab him? He had to get back inside.

He was sweating by the time he got back to his apartment, and his hand shook as he tried to force the key into
the lock. It didn't seem to want to go in. In the end, after
three attempts, he realized that the key didn't fit. And that
was impossible too. Wasn't it? He had used it only last
night! But someone in the last twelve hours had gone out
and changed the lock.

"Let me in!" he shouted. There was nobody to listen
to him. He was shouting at the glass door and the brick-

work. "Let me in!" He kicked the door, using the sole of his foot. But the glass was reinforced, shatterproof, and the door was held in place by powerful magnetic plates. He kicked out a third time. He was screaming now. Anyone passing would think he was insane.

"Are you all right, sir? Can I help you?"

He hadn't heard the police car draw in behind him, but when he turned around, there were two policemen standing on the sidewalk. Bulman was glad to see them. After all, he'd been trying to call them just a few minutes ago.

"I'm locked out," he said.

"Do you live here, sir?"

"Well, obviously I live here. If I didn't live here, I wouldn't be trying to get in." Bulman realized he was being rude. He tried to force a smile to his face. "I have a home on the top floor," he explained. "This has never happened before . . ."

"Can I try for you?"

Bulman noticed that the policeman had dropped the "sir." He handed the keys over and watched as the policeman tried them in the lock—also without success. The policeman examined the keys, then the lock. He straightened up. "You're not going to open this door with these keys," he said. "The lock is Banham. These keys are Yale."

"But that's not possible . . ."

"What's your name?" the second policeman asked.

"It's Harry Bulman. I'm a journalist."

"And you say you live here?"

"I don't just say I live here. I do live here. But I'm locked out."

"Just one moment, sir."

The first policeman was talking on his radio. Bulman passed his briefcase from one hand to the other. It was suddenly feeling very heavy. Considering it was only January, the weather was far too hot. The second policeman was looking at him suspiciously. He was only about nineteen years old, with light brown hair and stick-out ears. He still had a schoolboy face.

"Are you sure this is where you live?" the first policeman asked. He had finished his radio conversation.

"Yes. Apartment thirty-seven. On the top floor."

"There was a Harold Bulman, a journalist, registered to this address, but he was killed two nights ago."

"No. That was in the newspapers. I just read it. But it's a mistake. I'm Harry Bulman."

"Would you have any identification on you?"

"Of course I have." Bulman took out his wallet. But two of his credit cards had been taken by the cash machines, and he had left the third in the bank. His driver's license was in the apartment. His fingers were shaking as he fumbled through his wallet. "I can give you ID once I get into my home," he said.

The two policemen looked at each other. The younger

one seemed to notice Bulman's briefcase for the first time. "What are you carrying?" he asked.

The question took Bulman by surprise. "Why do you want to know?" he snapped.

Before he could stop him, the first policeman had picked up the briefcase. "Do you mind if we look inside?"

"Yes. As a matter of fact, I do."

It was already too late. The policeman opened the briefcase and was looking at the contents, his face full of horror. With a sense that his whole life was draining away from him, Bulman leaned forward. He knew what was inside: a notepad, a couple of magazines, pens and pencils.

He was wrong. The policeman was holding the case open, and Bulman could clearly see a kitchen knife, about fifteen inches long, the blade covered in dried blood.

"Wait . . . ," he began.

The two policemen acted incredibly quickly. Without even knowing quite what had happened, Bulman found himself facedown on the sidewalk with his arms gripped behind his back. He felt the metal edges of the handcuffs bite into his flesh as they clicked shut. The first policeman was back on his radio, talking rapidly. Seconds later, there was a screech of tires and another police car drew up. More uniformed officers surrounded him.

"You have the right to remain silent . . ."

Bulman realized that he was being told his rights, but the words didn't quite register. They were booming in his ears. He felt himself being picked up and propelled toward the car. A hand was placed on his head to stop him from banging against the door frame. And then he was inside, being driven away at speed. They had even turned the sirens on.

An hour later, Bulman found himself alone in a bare brick interrogation room with a window set so high up, it showed only a small square of sky. They had taken his fingerprints and a swab from the inside of his mouth, which he knew would be used to check his DNA. There were two new officers sitting opposite him. They were older and more experienced than the men who had made the arrest, heavyset and serious. They had introduced themselves as Bennett and Ainsworth. Ainsworth seemed to be the senior of the two, bald, with small, hard eyes and a mouth that could have been drawn with a single pencil line. Bennett was slightly younger and looked as if he had recently been in a fistfight. He was holding a file.

Bulman had been given a little time to collect his thoughts. He had worked out what he was going to say. "Listen to me," he began. "This is all a stupid mistake. The way you've treated me is outrageous. I am a well-known journalist, and I'm warning you—"

"It's good to see you, Jeremy," Bennett interrupted.

"That's not my name."

"Jeremy Harwood. Did you really think we wouldn't

find you?" Ainsworth laid the file on the table and opened it. Bulman saw a black-and-white police photograph. Once again he recognized himself. But it had this other name underneath it.

He drew a breath. "My name is not Jeremy Harwood. My name is Harold Bulman."

"Harold Bulman is dead."

"No."

"We've already analyzed the blood we found on the knife in your briefcase. It's Bulman's. You killed him."

"No. You're making a mistake. This is all wrong." Bulman fought for control. How could this nightmare be happening?

Ainsworth flicked a page in a file. There were fingerprints—ten of them in a row—and what looked like a chemical formula. "We've checked your DNA and your fingerprints, Jeremy. They all match up. There's no need to pretend anymore."

"You escaped from Broadmoor two months ago," Bennett said.

Broadmoor? Bulman blinked heavily. That was where they sent the most dangerous prisoners in the country, the ones who were considered criminally insane.

"Why did you kill Harold Bulman?" Bennett asked.

"I . . . I . . ." Bulman tried to find the answer, but the words wouldn't come. Something had happened to his thinking process. He was aware that there were tears trickling down his cheeks.

"Don't worry, Jeremy," Ainsworth said. He sounded almost kind. "We're going to take you back. You'll be safe, locked up in your cell. You won't hurt anyone ever again."

"You'll be taken back to Broadmoor this afternoon," Bennett added.

"No . . ." The room was spinning in ever-increasing circles. Bulman gripped the table, trying to slow it down. "You can't—"

"We can. The arrangements have already been made."

The door suddenly opened and a third man came in. From the very start he didn't look anything like a policeman. He was more like a retired colonel, about fifty, with thinning hair and a face that was hurrying toward old age. He was wearing a suit that didn't match his brown suede shoes. "Thank you," he said. "I'll take over now."

He didn't exactly radiate authority, but there was something in his voice, an edge of steel, that cut straight to the point. The two detectives stood up immediately and left. The man took their place at the table, opposite Bulman. His eyes were empty and cold.

"My name is Crawley," he said. Bulman was still crying. There were tears dripping out of his nose. Crawley reached into his pocket and took out a tissue. "Use this," he suggested.

Bulman wiped his nose and ran a sleeve across his eyes.

"I work for the intelligence services," Crawley explained. "A branch of MI6."

And suddenly Bulman understood. It was like being slapped across the face. MI6! Who else could have twisted his life out of shape with such ease? If he hadn't been so terrified, he would have been furious with himself. He should have expected something like this. "Alex Rider . . . ," he rasped.

"I'm not saying I've ever heard of Alex Rider," Crawley responded. His voice was utterly flat. "But I am going to tell you this. I could snap my fingers now and a van would take you to a mental hospital and lock you up, and that is where you would spend the rest of your life. Harry Bulman would be dead and you'd be the lunatic who killed him."

"But . . . but . . ." Bulman couldn't talk. He could barely breathe.

"For that matter, I could eliminate you now myself," Crawley continued. "I actually know thirty-seven different ways to kill you in a manner that will look completely natural. Some of them are quick. Some of them hurt." He paused. "But those are not my instructions. I've been told to give you another chance."

"You bastard." Bulman was crying again.

"You can go home now. You can forget all about this. But if you ever go anywhere near Alex Rider again, if you approach any newspaper editor, if you so much as mention his name, we will hear about it, and next time we won't be so generous. We will wipe you off the face of the earth. Do you understand me?"

Bulman said nothing. Crawley stood up.

"From now on, we'll be watching you, Mr. Bulman," he said. "Every minute of every day. Please believe me. This was just a lesson. Next time it'll be for real."

He left the room.

Bulman stayed where he was. *Alex Rider.* The two words thundered through his head. *Alex Rider.* He knew that he would never write his story. His hopes of a major scoop had been destroyed, along with all his riches. He dragged himself to his feet. He was still trembling. *Alex Rider.* How he wished he had never heard the name.

GREENFIELDS

THE BUS HEADED WEST DOWN THE HIGHWAY, turning off at Junction 15, near Swindon. It passed through the attractive town of Marlborough, then on toward the vast area of empty grassland that was Salisbury Plain.

There was nowhere quite like it in the whole of England. Three hundred square miles in area, it had been inhabited long before the Romans had arrived. Stonehenge stood on its southern edge. Traces of hill forts dating back to the Iron Age were still dotted around. The plain was used by the army, frequently shut down for night exercises using tons of live ammunition. And one small part of it had been leased out to Greenfields for a research center that the authorities had decided was best kept hidden, in the middle of nowhere.

Alex Rider was sitting in the back of the bus next to Tom Harris and James Hale. There were forty students from Brookland on the trip, along with two teachers—Mr. Gilbert and a prim, slightly nervous woman named Miss Barry, who taught music but who had been included to help with discipline. They had been driving for over two hours now and the initial excitement had long since faded away, replaced by the dull sense of endlessness that comes with any highway journey.

Alex took out the postcard that had arrived the day before. It showed a picture of the Eiffel Tower in Paris. On the back, someone had written a date—2/25—and a message: *Paris is beautiful and fortunately we didn't manage to get lost. I hope you have a great time.* The signature was unreadable, but Alex recognized Smithers's writing. He had been expecting the card, and Smithers had told him how to use it. He slipped it away and turned to Tom.

"Can you do me a favor?" he said casually.

"Sure. What sort of favor?"

"While we're on this trip, I might have to disappear for a bit. So if there's any roll call, could you answer when you hear my name?"

Tom frowned. He spoke quietly so his voice wouldn't carry above the sound of the engine. "The last time you asked me to cover for you, we were in Venice," he said. "You're not doing that stuff again, are you?"

Alex nodded gloomily. He wasn't going to lie to his best friend.

"But I thought you'd finished with all that."

"Yeah. Me too. But it didn't quite work out that way." Alex sighed. "It's not anything dangerous, Tom. And it shouldn't take very long. I just don't want anyone to notice I'm missing."

"Okay. Don't get yourself killed."

They had been following a series of minor roads through swathes of green countryside that stretched to every horizon. This wasn't the England of pretty fields and hedgerows. There was something ancient and untamed about Salisbury Plain. It seemed to be completely deserted, with nothing—no buildings, no fences, no power lines, no people—for as far as the eye could see. There were a few clumps of trees huddled together on the hillsides, boulders and bits of debris thrown carelessly around. The wind was rippling through the grass, making strange patterns, like silent music chasing ahead of them as they rumbled slowly toward the top of a hill.

"Here it is," James said.

He was right. The Greenfields research facility had suddenly appeared in front of them, concealed in a miniature valley. It was somehow shocking after so much emptiness, like a glass-and-steel city, or perhaps a prison, or even a colony on another planet. It certainly looked completely alien here, in the middle of Wiltshire. The complex was shaped like a diamond, completely surrounded by a fence with links so tightly meshed that it was almost like a metal wall, glinting in the sun. A single sliding gate, heavily guarded, stood at the end of the tarmac road. At least the guards didn't seem to be armed—but they looked threatening enough, even without weapons.

"What is this place?" James muttered, staring out the window. "It seems like a lot of fuss for a bunch of vegetables."

There were about twenty buildings on the other side

of the fence. Many of them were indeed greenhouses, but they were enormous, taller and more solid than anything that might be found in any garden. The rest were either offices, warehouses, or factories, most of them low-rise but some of them five or six stories high, with radio antennas, satellite dishes, and tall silver chimneys built onto the roofs. To one side, Alex saw what might have been a welcome center, sleek and white. A second building right next to the gate was square and solid with a sign marked SECURITY. But his eye was drawn to the construction at the very center of the complex. It was a huge dome, like something out of a science-fiction film, filled with vegetation. He could make out the leaves of palm trees licking at the glass, twenty or thirty yards high. Vines and knotted foliage hung down on all sides. It was connected to other buildings by four glass corridors, radiating out like points on a compass. The Biosphere, Alex thought. He didn't know where he had gotten the name from, but it seemed right.

Greenfields looked brand-new. There was a network of black tarmac roads separated by perfect rectangles of freshly mown grass. Or perhaps the grass had been genetically programmed to grow to exactly the right height. Silent electric vehicles were ferrying men and women from place to place. Some of them—presumably the scientists—were wearing white coats. Others were in suits. The guards wore green camouflage jackets, as if to remind themselves that the environment was what this was supposed to be all about. And everywhere, on dozens of poles and on the sides of every building, sophisticated cameras and light sensors gazed down from every angle so that if a single wasp or bee had flown in, someone somewhere would have known.

There was a loud whine inside the bus as Mr. Gilbert turned on the intercom system. "Please don't be alarmed by all the security," he said. His voice, amplified and re-layed through the speakers, didn't sound very confident. "A lot of the work that they do here at Greenfields is sen-sitive. They have to protect themselves from competitors and from journalists and that sort of thing—and some of the plants they grow here have to be contained. I'm afraid we are all going to have to be searched as we go in—but it shouldn't take long. Please remember to leave all cam-eras and mobile phones inside the bus. They'll be perfectly safe here, and they won't be allowed inside."

There were general groans and protests, but as they drew closer to the gate, everyone began to open their backpacks, doing as they were told. They'd been on school trips before, but they weren't used to blank-faced guards and body searches. "I hope you know what you're doing," Tom muttered, glancing at Alex. Alex didn't reply. _"It's a very simple matter. Hardly worthy of your talents."_ He remembered Blunt describing the job. Why should he have been surprised by another lie?

The bus slowed down and stopped. They had reached the gate, which slid open slowly to allow them into a holding area. Someone rapped on the door and the driver opened it to allow a thin, unsmiling woman to step inside. Mr. Gilbert stood up and held out a hand, but she ignored him.

"Good afternoon," she said. Her voice was clipped and somehow artificial. She sounded like a speak-your-weight machine. "May I welcome you to Greenfields Bio Center. I am the supervisor here at Greenfields." She paused, running her eyes over the passengers as if committing the faces to memory. "My name is Dr. Myra Beckett, and I will be looking after you during your visit."

It was hard to say how old Beckett might be. She was a severe, very masculine woman in a white coat that hung loose from her shoulders and somehow defined her. There was so little emotion in her face that it was hard to imagine her doing anything that didn't involve books, Bunsen burners, and bottles of chemicals. Her dark hair was cut short, with bangs that cut diagonally across her forehead, the last strands touching her left eye. She wore circular, gold-framed spectacles that looked cheap and didn't flatter her. It was obvious that she didn't care about her appearance. She had no makeup and no jewelry. She made no effort to be polite.

"We have not had a visit from a school before," she continued. "We will be showing you our laboratories, some of our cultivation centers, and finally, there will be a lecture on GM technology by one of our experts. Any photography or recording is forbidden. When you leave this bus, every one of you will be searched. This was agreed with your school when you were invited. All mobile telephones are to be left behind. You will follow me now, please."

"What a charming woman," Tom muttered.

"Yeah. I'm really glad we came," James agreed.

The supervisor had climbed off. The two teachers and the rest of the Brookland crowd followed her into the square building that had been designed exactly like a security area in an airport. There were uniformed men standing behind silver tables, X-rays for hand luggage, and metal detectors that everyone would have to pass through. Alex was one of the first to be searched. He watched as his backpack, with the pencil case inside, disappeared into one of the machines. At the same time, he was briskly patted down by a tight-lipped guard. The postcard that Smithers had sent him was in his inside pocket, and the guard pulled it out, glanced at the picture of the Eiffel Tower, then handed it back to him. His backpack appeared on the other side of the machine, but before he could reach it, another security man picked it up.

"Is this yours?"

"Yes." Alex nodded. All around him, his friends were being processed.

It was as if the guard sensed that something was wrong. He examined Alex, then opened the backpack and looked inside.

"It's just my schoolwork," Alex said.

The guard ignored him. He rifled through the books, then took out the pencil case and opened that too. For a moment Alex was certain that every alarm in the place was about to go off. The guard took out the rubber eraser and turned it over between his fingers. But then, as if he had suddenly lost interest, he shoved everything back into the bag and handed it over.

"Next!"

Alex joined the others at the far end of the security hall. He noticed that Mr. Gilbert was looking fairly disgruntled, and he understood why. They were only on a school outing. They were being treated as though they might all be terrorists.

Beckett didn't seem to care. "We will now proceed into the complex," she announced. "Please stay together. Before we log in, does anyone need to use the toilet?" There was silence. "Good. Then come this way. . . ." She led them to a final barrier, and Alex noticed they were counted electronically as they passed through.

But at last they were inside Greenfields. Beckett gathered them in a group, standing in the open air with the great dome behind them. Now that he was closer to the glass, Alex could see that there was an entire ecosystem contained on the other side. Exotic-looking trees sprouted in all directions like green fireworks photographed just as they went off. There were strange plants and bushes fighting for space, some of them carrying ugly, brilliant-colored berries or fruit. It had to be hot inside. A thick layer of steam hung in the air and Alex noticed beads of moisture trickling down the panes. To his surprise, there was a movement and a man appeared briefly, covered from head to toe in a white protective suit. He was inside the dome, carrying a piece of measuring equipment. He stood briefly by the window. Then he was gone.

"You are going to be with us for two hours," Beckett began. She didn't sound pleased. Indeed, she was making it clear that this entire visit was an irritation. "We will start by looking at some of the laboratories where you will see some of our techniques, including genetic trans-formation, cloning, and the particle delivery system—we call it the gene gun—that fires new DNA into plants. The gene gun was developed by our director, Leonard Straik. You will visit some of the greenhouses and storage facili-ties where we cultivate and store fruits and vegetables, some of which have never before existed on this planet. After that, you will be taken to our lecture theater." She pointed at the white building that Alex had noticed from the brow of the hill. "There will be a discussion about the need for GM technology and the ways that it can help the future of the planet. And finally"—she smiled so briefly that it seemed to be no more than a nervous twitch—"you are invited to our canteen for a cup of our own Greenfields Bio Center Blend coffee, which has been genetically modified to deliver a more satisfying flavor.

"Please do not at any time separate from the group. This is the very first occasion that we have opened our doors for a school visit, and some of the guards are a little nervous. I would be very sorry if any of you delightful young people were asked to leave. Also, do not touch anything. You will be standing close to many chemicals and plant specimens. Any of them could be dangerous. Are there any questions?"

"What's in there?" someone asked.

Beckett turned around and looked at the central greenhouse. For a moment her eyes seemed to flash behind the circular lenses. "We call that the Poison Dome," she explained. "For many years, Greenfields has been researching natural poisons . . . which is to say toxins such as ricin and botulin, which occur in nature and have the ability to kill human beings. Inside the Poison Dome, we grow some of the deadliest plants on the planet, including water hemlock, deadly nightshade, elephant's ear, death cap mushrooms, and castor beans. The manzanilla tree has attractive fruit that you may choose to swallow. If you do so, it will kill you instantly. There is also a white resin dripping out of it that will blister your skin or blind you. The leaves of the ongaonga from New Zealand only need to touch you to produce hideous burns. It might interest you to know that a common nettle that you may find growing in your garden—*Urtica dioica*—injects you with five neurotransmitters when it stings you. The nettles in-side the Poison Dome have been genetically modified so that they will sting you with five hundred neurotransmit-ters. I would like to imagine the pain of such a death, but in truth, I do not have enough imagination."

She took out a tissue and touched it briefly against her lips.

"We are particularly interested in the way poisons in-teract," she continued. "So you will also find animal life in there, including specimens of the blue dart frog, which releases lethal toxins from its skin, the banana spider, the taipan snake, and the marbled cone snail. A single drop of its slime can kill an elephant." She paused and looked around the group. "If any of you would like to visit the Poison Dome, please let me know. Your visit will probably last about fifteen seconds before you die horribly."

Nobody spoke. Miss Barry, the music teacher, had gone very pale.

"Very well. Let us head over to the first laboratory. I will ask your teacher to take a roll call when we enter and again when we leave."

Tom Harris glanced at Alex, looking more doubtful by the minute. Alex shrugged. He was remembering what Blunt had told him about Philip Masters, how the whistle-blower had died. His body had been unrecognizable when it was found, and now Alex had a good idea what might have happened to him. Well, here was certainly one area of the Bio Center he'd be careful to avoid.

They went into one of the taller buildings with a steel chimney rising above them and smoke trickling into the sky. Beckett let them in using an electronic swipe card that she carried around her neck, and they passed into a clean, uncluttered passageway, where Mr. Gilbert took their names. As they set off once again, Alex made sure he was lingering near the back. They passed a restroom. Quickly he nudged Tom, who nodded back, and without hesitating Alex suddenly ducked sideways, throwing his weight against the door and plunging inside.

Suddenly he was alone, standing in a white-tiled room with two sinks and two mirrors in front of him. He waited until he could no longer hear the voices or the footsteps of his friends. Nobody had seen him leave. It was time to get started.

He took out the postcard with the view of Paris and went over to the sink. He ran a paper towel under the tap, then wiped it over the picture. The Eiffel Tower and its surroundings dissolved and disappeared. Underneath, there was an intricately drawn map of the Greenfields Bio Center, showing all the buildings and passageways, with two tiny lights already blinking. One was red. One was green. They told him where he was and where he had to get to.

He listened for a moment, and when he was sure that there was no one nearby, he slipped out into the corridor again, holding the postcard in front of him. According to the flashing display, the chief science officer—Leonard

Straik—could be found in the building next door to this one, but the two of them were connected by a walkway, so Alex wouldn't have to go back outside. All in all, he didn't think he was in too much danger . . . at least not yet. He was wearing a school uniform, part of an invited group. If anyone did run into him, it would be easy enough to claim that he had simply lagged behind and become lost. And anyway, what was there to worry about? The research center might look sinister and it might have poison at its heart, but nobody had suggested it was breaking any laws. He was here simply because one man, Straik, might be a security risk. His job was an easy one. And half an hour from now, it would all be over.

Even so, his nerves were jangling as he made his way forward, the flashing light in the display signaling his progress. He had been heading in the same direction as the school party until he came to an open area where three corridors met with a concrete staircase heading up to the next floor. That was where the light seemed to be directing him. He went up the first few steps, then flattened himself against a wall as he heard footsteps approaching. A man and a woman appeared, both of them wearing white coats, walking down one of the passageways below him. They were deep in conversation and didn't notice him. Alex waited until they were gone, then continued up.

The inside of the building was like a school or university. The walls were mainly whitewashed and bare, with signs pointing toward different blocks. There were no decorations, just fire extinguishers and display boards full of safety notices. The second floor was identical to the ground one, with doorways and interlinking corridors. Without Smithers's postcard, Alex wouldn't have had any idea where to go, but now he allowed it to lead him until he arrived at the glass bridge that led to the next building. It was more dangerous here. The bridge was about thirty feet long, exposed on both sides. From where he was standing, Alex could see electric vehicles passing each other on the road underneath. A couple of guards walked slowly past, and Alex saw that these two were armed. He recognized the familiar shape of 19mm Micro Uzi submachine guns, hanging lazily against their chests, and wondered if the weapons had been kept hidden deliberately when the school party arrived.

To make matters worse, there were also several cameras pointing his way. Alex could wait until there was no one around, but he would still be spotted if he tried to cross the bridge. He opened his bag, took out the pencil case, and found the pocket calculator. Jamming the cameras might well advertise that something was wrong, but he had no choice. He pressed the plus button three times, checked that the road was clear, then crossed the bridge.

He knew he was operating against the clock now. With the cameras down, security inside the complex would be heightened and it would be less easy to explain what he was doing if he was caught. He ran to the next corner, then jerked back as a door opened and a guard appeared, running down a corridor in front of him. It was obvious that Alex had passed from an academic or administrative block into an area reserved for senior management and executives. The floor was suddenly carpeted. There were paintings—highly detailed watercolors of different plants—on the walls. The lighting was softer and the doors were made of expensive wood. According to the navigation system concealed inside the postcard, Straik's office was nearby, and Alex also knew its number: 225. That was the date that Smithers had written above the message.

He found it at the end of the corridor around the next corner. As he approached, he heard a door open somewhere downstairs and someone calling out. There were more footsteps . . . someone hurrying. A telephone was ringing insistently. Nobody was answering it. They were only tiny details, yet Alex had the sense that something had changed inside Greenfields. The cameras were out of action, and that had made them nervous.

Was there anyone in Straik's office? There was only one way to find out. Alex took a deep breath and knocked. This was the moment of truth. If someone called out for him to come in, the whole thing would have been a waste of time.

There was silence.

Alex sighed. So far, so good. He took out the pencil

case and removed the library card. He had noticed a card reader built into the wall beside every door that he had passed, and Straik's was no different. Alex swiped his card through the reader, then fed it into the slot at the bottom of his pencil case. He felt the whole thing vibrate in his hand as the machinery that Smithers had built into the secret compartment did its work. A few seconds later, the library card slid out again. Alex swiped it a second time. The card had been reprogrammed. There was a click and Straik's door swung open.

Alex hurried in, closing the door behind him. He found himself in a large, comfortable office with views over the perfect lawn outside the security block. That was where they had gathered when they had first arrived, and for a fleeting moment Alex wondered if he had been missed yet. Had Tom been able to cover for him during the second roll call? He began to realize just how risky his plan had been—but it was too late now. He looked around him. Straik had four or five potted plants, which seemed to have been genetically modified to look artificial. There were half a dozen bookshelves, an antique mirror, and a glass-fronted cabinet with a scattering of scientific awards. A framed picture had recently been delivered but not yet hung. It was still in Bubble Wrap, leaning against the wall. Two designer armchairs sat side by side, opposite an antique desk. Straik's computer was on the desk.

Alex made straight for it. He just wanted to get this

over with and then join his friends. Once he was back with the school group, he would be safe. Even if the security people realized there was an intruder at large, they would never suspect him. He had to admit that Alan Blunt was right. Sometimes it did help to be fourteen.

Straik had a leather chair, a massive, swiveling thing that reminded Alex of the dentist. He sat down and took out the eraser that had come with the pencil case. Some of the gadgets that Smithers had supplied him with over the past year had been ingenious, but this one was very simple. He simply ripped the eraser in half, then pulled it apart to reveal the memory stick inside.

Straik's computer was already turned on, but Alex had no doubt that any important files would be encrypted and protected by a whole series of passwords. Fortunately, that wasn't his problem. Alex found the USB port. There was already a memory stick there and he took it out, laying it on the desk. Then he plugged in his own.

Immediately, the screen blazed into life with four columns of figures flickering and spinning crazily as the worm—or whatever was built into the memory stick— burrowed into the heart of the computer, sucking out its information. How long had Smithers said this would take? Alex thought he heard voices outside in the corridor, and he felt the cold touch of the air-conditioning against the sweat on his neck and brow. Half a minute. That was all. But the seconds seemed to stretch themselves in front of him as more and more files—thousands of them—appeared and disappeared, each one duplicated and stolen away.

57.2 GB downloaded of 85.3.

Alex forced his eyes away from the screen and looked at the desk, wondering what other secrets the director of Greenfields might have left scattered around. But there was nothing out of the ordinary: a diary with a few scribbled entries, some letters waiting to be signed. He glanced at them, but they were brief and uninteresting.

66.5 GB downloaded of 85.3.

He slid open one of the drawers. It held stationery—envelopes and headed notepaper, business cards, and a telephone directory. Two notebooks, both of them empty. He turned back to the screen. Only twenty gigabytes to go, but infuriatingly, the compuer seemed to have slowed down as whatever worms were hidden on the memory stick burrowed their way through the various firewalls. Even so, he wouldn't have time to go through the files. Most of them would make no sense to him anyway, and it would be impossible to tell which were important and which were simply routine.

71.1 GB downloaded of 85.3.

Alex knew that he was running out of time, that someone could arrive at any moment. Part of him was listening for footsteps in the corridor.

79.5 GB downloaded of 85.3.

The memory stick had almost done its work. But now

someone really was approaching! Alex could hear two men talking, getting closer all the time.

On the screen, the horizontal bar came to the end of its journey.

Download complete.

The memory stick had finished its work. The computer screen went blank. There was a faint bleep as the lock was activated. Alex snatched the memory stick and dived forward, making for the one hiding place he had seen inside the office. Already he was wondering what he would do if Straik decided to spend the whole day in his office. How would he get back to the school group? He would be trapped.

Alex had just managed to conceal himself when the door opened.

Two men came in.

From where Alex was crouching, he could see Leonard Straik as he approached the desk. The Greenfields director was reflected in the mirror, and with a sense of total shock, Alex realized that he recognized him. Silver hair rising up as if it had just been blown dry. Heavy lips and jowels. Small, watery eyes. The two of them had met recently. But where . . . ?

Then he remembered. Scotland. New Year's Eve. The man he had thought of as an accountant, playing cards with Desmond McCain. What had McCain called him? Leo. Of course! That was it. Leo was Leonard . . . Leonard Straik.

"Do you want something to drink? Tea? Coffee? We actually develop it ourselves, you know. But it still tastes disgusting."

"No. Not for me, thank you."

The other man came in, closing the door behind him. And that was an even bigger shock for Alex.

The second man was Desmond McCain.

CONDITION RED

"SO, IS IT READY FOR SHIPMENT?"

Alex remembered McCain's voice so well: not loud but deep and powerful, brimming with self-confidence. And yet he had difficulty pronouncing his words. His smashed jaw wasn't quite able to form them perfectly. He had taken one of the designer chairs and was sitting with his back to Alex, the silver crucifix in his ear just visible above his right shoulder. Meanwhile, Straik had taken his place on the other side of the desk. The two men had no idea that anyone else was in the room.

It was fortunate that Straik liked big paintings. Whatever it was that he had bought for his office had provided Alex with his hiding place. He was squashed up behind it, in the awkward, triangular space between the picture and the wall. There certainly wouldn't have been room for a full-grown adult here, and even he was cramped, the muscles in his thighs and shoulders already urging him to straighten up. He could make out a little of Straik and McCain reflected in the antique mirror, but he didn't dare lean too far forward. If he could see them, they would be able to see him.

"Of course it's ready," Straik replied. He sounded irritated. "I gave you my word, didn't I?"

"So where is it now?"

"The bulk of it is at Gatwick Airport. It's being carried out in a commercial Boeing 757. Completely routine. But I thought it might amuse you to have a look at it, so I've kept a sample for you here." Straik slid open one of the drawers of his desk and took something out. Alex craned forward, but he couldn't see what it was. "It took a little while longer than expected. We had problems with mass production."

"How much were you able to produce?" McCain asked.

"A thousand gallons. It should be more than enough. The main thing is to make sure that the temperature is kept constant when it's in the air. You have to remember, this stuff is alive. But that said, it's also fairly durable."

"How quickly will it work?"

"Almost immediately. You need to apply it in the morning. The process will begin at once, and within thirty-six hours it'll be unstoppable. There won't be anything to see, of course—not to begin with—but in about three weeks you'll have the attention of the entire world." Straik paused. "What about the shooting? All done?"

"I'm sending Myra to Elm's Cross tomorrow. We're closing it down."

"Getting rid of the evidence."

"Exactly."

"Well, in that case . . ."

Straik stopped. And in the silence, somehow Alex

knew that something had gone wrong. Crouching behind
the picture, he froze, afraid that the sound of his breathing or his heart beating would give him away.

"Someone has been in my office," Straik said.

"What?" The word came out like a whiplash.

"My desk . . ." Straik picked something up, and even
without seeing it, Alex knew what it was. The memory
stick that had been in the computer when he arrived. He
had taken it out to insert his own—but he hadn't had
time to replace it. "This was in my USB port when I came
down to meet you," Straik said. "I loaded it myself.
Someone's taken it out."

"Are you sure?"

"Of course I'm sure."

"Your secretary could have been in."

"She's not here."

Alex realized he couldn't hold his position much longer. He was desperate to straighten up, to allow his
muscles to stretch. At least there was one good thing.
The hiding place was so small that neither of the two
men would suspect for a minute that anyone else was
still in the room. But he had to know what was going on,
even at the risk of giving himself away. Very slowly, he
leaned forward a few inches to have a glimpse in the
mirror. McCain was holding the memory stick. Straik
was hunched over his computer, tapping furiously at the
keyboard, his little eyes focused on the screen. Two pin-
pricks of red had appeared in his cheeks.

"This computer has been compromised," he announced.

"Compromised?"

"Someone has attempted to download documents and files from the main drive. For all I know, they may have succeeded." Straik snatched up a telephone and dialed a number. There was a brief pause. Then he was answered. "This is Leonard Straik," he said. "I want an immediate status report." Another pause. Alex wondered what was being said at the other end of the line. It wasn't hard to guess. Then Straik spoke again. "I want you to put out a condition double red alert," he snapped. "All personnel to assemble immediately. This is not an exercise. We have a major security breach."

He hung up. "We have an intruder," he said to McCain. "Ten minutes ago, our entire surveillance system went down. Someone must be jamming the signal. This is what they were after." He nodded at the computer. "They must have left seconds before we arrived."

"What's a double red alert?"

"Any unauthorized person found wandering inside the Bio Center will be killed . . . no questions asked."

"Don't you have a bunch of schoolchildren here?"

"I haven't forgotten that, Desmond. I'm not an idiot—whatever you may think. My staff have special instructions." He turned off the computer. "I'm going to the control center. Are you coming?"

"Absolutely." It struck Alex that McCain sounded

more amused than alarmed. But that seemed to be his character. Whatever he might be up to, he didn't believe that anyone could get in his way.

The two of them stood up. Alex heard the swish of cloth as Straik came out from behind his desk. They went over to the door. It opened, then closed. Alex was on his own.

Gratefully, he uncurled himself from behind the picture. For a moment he stood where he was, trying to collect his thoughts. He was probably safe while he was in Straik's office, at least for the time being. Security would be searching for him—but this was the one place they wouldn't look. Even so, he couldn't stay here forever. With an intruder on the loose, the school visit might be cut short and the bus sent back to London. Alex had to be on it. He couldn't be left behind.

It was worse than that. Alex realized that his only chance of survival was to get back to Mr. Gilbert and the others. There had been nothing accidental about the death of the whistle-blower, and no matter what Blunt might have said, there really was something seriously unpleasant going on at Greenfields. Why else would the director be so keen to see that any intruder was killed? Alex had to get back to his class. No guard was going to fire at him when there were witnesses. Once he was back with the others, he would be safe . . . just one bored student among many.

He headed for the door, about to leave, when he noticed a glass vial resting on Straik's desk. It was a test tube, sealed at the top, with a muddy gray liquid inside. This must be the "sample" that he had heard the two men talking about. Alex had no idea what it contained, but another thousand gallons of it were on their way somewhere abroad. He still had the memory stick in his pocket, but on an impulse he went over and took the test tube too. Smithers would analyze it. And that would be the end of it. The liquid would surely reveal whatever was being planned.

He opened the door carefully, checked there was no one in sight, then stepped outside. He had decided to head back the way he had come. He had no idea where his friends were and he was furious that he had no way of communicating with them. Normally, he would have called Tom or James . . . but all their mobile phones had been left on the bus. What had the woman, Dr. Beckett, told them? The laboratories first. Then the greenhouses and storage centers. Finally, the lecture theater. Surely they couldn't be too hard to find.

Alex closed the door behind him and sprinted back around the corner, his feet making no sound on the carpet. The glass bridge was ahead of him, but even as he approached it, he heard men running toward him and spun back, ducking into a storage cupboard a second before they appeared. There were three guards and they were all armed. Alex watched them run across the bridge and disappear down another passage. Above his head, he noticed a light flashing red. He gritted his teeth. This had turned into a cat-and-mouse game with only one mouse and an awful lot of cats.

The bridge was clear and he crossed it into what he had thought of as the administrative block. He went back down the stairs but immediately realized that he had forgotten which way he had originally come from—left or right. The trouble was that every direction looked the same. He tossed a mental coin and set off, knowing almost at once that he was lost. He still had the postcard with its guidance system in his back pocket but it couldn't really help him now. All that mattered was to keep moving and not to be seen.

"Stop!"

The guard had stepped out of nowhere, blocking his way. He had a machine gun dangling around his neck and he was already fumbling with it, bringing it up and around. Alex turned and ran. He had taken no more than ten steps when a neon light fitting exploded with a shower of sparks and broken glass. At the same time, the walls and ceiling showered plaster on him. Alex hadn't heard much more than a whisper, but the guard was clearly firing in his direction, the bullets streaming over his head. The gun must have some sort of silencer attached to it . . . and of course, that made sense. These were the "special instructions" that Straik had issued. They couldn't risk the sound of gunfire, not when they had forty schoolkids on the site.

Alex hurtled down another corridor, past a series of open doors. He passed a laboratory, surprisingly cluttered and old-fashioned, with plant specimens on the work desks and bottles of different chemicals on the shelves. A woman in a white coat, holding a petri dish in the palm of her hand, looked up and momentarily caught his eye. Behind her, a man was taking a tray of flowers out of what looked like an industrial fridge. Alex wondered if his class had been here, perhaps a few minutes before. He was tempted to stop and ask. He could still pretend to be lost. He decided against it.

Double red alert. He had so far been spotted by one guard, and the fact that he was a boy in a school uniform hadn't made any difference at all. These people wanted him dead.

He heard shouting behind him. There was another light flashing in the corner of his eye. Alex hadn't even slowed down. He saw a glass door ahead of him and sprinted toward it, palms outstretched, praying that it wasn't locked. He pushed. It opened. He almost fell through as another blast of bullets fanned silently through the air, punching dotted lines across the wall beside him. But now he was outside and running. He saw the sleek white exterior of the lecture theater on the other side of the lawn, but he couldn't reach it. More guards in electric vehicles were racing toward him, moving fast. Alex felt a surge of despair. How could he have allowed Alan Blunt and MI6 to talk him into this? He'd promised Jack he wouldn't get into trouble again. He'd promised Sabina. More than that, he'd promised himself.

Anger spurred him on. He reached one of the greenhouses and plunged in through two sets of doors. It had been cold outside, but here the climate was subtropical. Hundreds of plants were arranged on shelves, some just a few inches tall, some bending against the roof high above. The greenhouses were actually more like glass factories, divided into dozens of different rooms, each one joined to the other by a maze of interlinking corridors. Huge silver pipes and watering systems snaked across the ceiling. There were banks of machinery controlling the lights, the temperature, and the humidity in all the different areas, ensuring perfect conditions for all this artificial life. Alex had to be safe here. The guards might have followed him in, but there were plenty of hiding places. Provided he kept moving, there was no way they would be able to find him.

The next attack took him completely by surprise. A cascade of bullets that seemed never-ending. They came from all sides, determined to kill the intruder even if it meant destroying the entire complex. Alex didn't hear a single shot, but inside the greenhouse the noise of bullets smashing glass was deafening. Windows shattered all around him. Alex threw himself to the ground as shards of glass, thousands and thousands of them, showered in all directions. Inches above his head, the plants were shredded, the very air turning green as it was filled with tiny cuttings of stalk and leaf. Terracotta pots exploded, earth showering out. Brightly colored flowers tore themselves apart. And still the bullets kept coming, hammering into the machinery, ricocheting off the metal pipes. Alex could just make out the dark shapes of the guards surrounding the building, destroying it. He wondered if they had all gone mad. Or was it that the work at Greenfields was finished and nothing mattered anymore, so long as nobody was able to escape with its secrets?

He scurried forward on his hands and knees, trying to lose himself farther inside the complex. He came to a brick wall with another bank of machinery and crawled behind it, putting a solid barrier between himself and the gunfire. Nobody could see him here. He patted his fingers against his forehead. When he examined them, they were stained with blood. None of the bullets had hit him. It must have been the falling glass. He brushed it out of his hair and off his shoulders. What must he look like? What would Mr. Gilbert say if he ever turned up?

He had to find the school tour! Surely they must have heard all the racket, even if the guards were using silencers. Another corridor led into the distance, this one with mirrored tiles instead of glass. He set off, still keeping low. Suddenly he was surrounded by brickwork. He had entered some sort of equipment room with spades and wheelbarrows. He could have been in an ordinary garden center rather than a top-secret research institute. There were even bags of fertilizer . . . as if he needed reminding of the sort of trouble he was in.

Somehow he had to find a way back outside. Then he would cut back to the lecture theater and hope to join the rest of Brookland there. At least he seemed to have lost the guards with their machine guns. Perhaps they were scouring through the wreckage, looking for a body. Alex checked the test tube that he had stolen from Straik's office. He had been carrying it in his top jacket pocket, and fortunately it was still in one piece. He slipped it back in and set off again, heading for a set of solid-looking doors and a sign: STRICTLY NO ADMITTANCE. AUTHORIZED PERSONNEL ONLY. The doors were locked and hermetically sealed, but there was another reader set in the frame. Alex still had the library card. He had reprogrammed it to open Straik's door, and presumably Straik had access to every zone in the Bio Center. So . . .

He tried it. It worked. The doors opened. Alex went in, smiling as they clicked shut behind him. It might well be that the guards were unable to follow him in here. How many of them, after all, would have been authorized?

He only realized where he was when it was too late. The shape of the building, the intense heat, the moisture running down the glass panes . . . all these should have warned him. But the door had already locked itself, and looking back, he saw that there was no reader on this side, no way back out. He stood where he was, feeling the heavy air on his cheeks and forehead. His clothes were already sticking to him. Something was buzzing loudly over his head. Alex closed his eyes and swore.

He had walked into the Poison Dome.

12

HELL ON EARTH

ALEX LOOKED AROUND HIM. He had once visited the greenhouses at Kew Gardens in London—and in some ways this was similar. The building itself was very elegant, the great dome supported by a delicate framework of metal supports. The whole area was about the size of a circular soccer field, if such a thing could exist. But unlike Kew Gardens, there was nothing beautiful or inviting about the plants that grew here. Alex examined the tangle of green in front of him, the trunks and branches crisscrossing each other, struggling for space. They all looked evil, the leaves either razor sharp or covered in millions of hairs. He remembered what Beckett had said. These were mutant organisms. Touching just one of them would bring pain and death. Fruits in the shape of half-sized apples hung over his head, and rich, fat berries clung to the bushes. But they were all hideous colors, somehow unnatural, warning him to stay away. He could hear droning. There were insects in here and they were big ones, from the sound of them. Bees, perhaps something worse.

Alex's skin was already crawling, but he forced himself not to move. The information that the Beckett woman had given him when he arrived might even now save his life. He mustn't brush against any of the plants here. They had been altered so that they were a hundred times more deadly than nature intended. And there weren't just plants. She had talked about the interaction of poisons. And so there were spiders and snails and . . . of course, the bees. Why had Straik created this place? Hell on earth. What was he trying to prove?

Alex couldn't go back. He remembered the shape of the dome, with the corridors branching out like points of the compass. He had come in as if from the south. Now he had to reach the other side and one of the other three exits. Two in and two out . . . that must be how it worked. From what he could remember, the lecture theater must be directly in front of him. So all he had to do was walk straight. And at least there was a path, a boardwalk made of wooden planks, stretched out ahead. And nobody would be looking for him in here. Nobody would be stupid enough to follow him in. He might be stung, bitten, poisoned, or scared to death, but at least he wouldn't be shot.

So . . .

There was no other way.

Alex moved forward, very slowly. Touching nothing. Not making a sound. If he was going to get out of here alive, he would have to take it literally one step at a time. Beckett had mentioned snakes . . . the taipan. Alex knew it to be the most venomous land snake in the world, fifty times more toxic than the cobra. But it was also nervous. Like most animals, it wouldn't attack a human unless it was threatened. So provided he didn't brush against anything, touch anything, step on anything, or alarm anything, he might come out of this all right.

One step at a time.

He followed the wooden boardwalk. The plants were horribly close to him. The nearest of them was an over-sized thistle that seemed to be straining to break free and attack him, like an angry dog. Then came a squat, ugly tree corkscrewing out of the earth with green scalpel blades instead of leaves. The smell of sulfur rose in his nostrils. The path was crossing a volcanic pool. A creeper hung in front of him. He resisted the urge to brush it aside and bent low, contorting himself to avoid coming into contact with it. If he made one miscalculation, even so much as an inch, he might dislodge something, and he knew that a single touch could finish him. Everything here was his enemy. Something buzzed close to his head and he jerked around, unable to control himself. His sleeve brushed against a jagged-edged nettle, but fortu-nately, the material protected him from the bristling hairs—or neurotransmitters, as Beckett had called them. Alex shrunk into his jacket, pulling it around him. Every fiber of his being was concentrated on the way ahead.

Something slithered onto his foot.

Alex stopped. He even stopped breathing. It was as if someone had drawn a noose tight around his throat. Try-ing not to panic, he looked down. He could already tell from the weight that this wasn't a snake. It was too small, too light. And it hadn't slithered, it had crawled. For a moment he couldn't see it and thought that perhaps, after all, he had imagined it.

He hadn't. It was almost worse than a snake. A glistening centipede, at least eight inches long, had settled on the top of his sneaker. The creature could have been drawn by a demonic child: red head, black body, bright yellow legs that seemed to be writhing with anticipation. Alex knew what it was. He had seen something exactly the same once on television. The giant redheaded centipede. Also known as the giant desert centipede. How had the narrator described it? Unusually aggressive and extremely fast . . .

And this one had decided to stretch itself out on his foot. What if it decided to explore a little farther, over his ankle and up his pant leg, for example? Alex stood as still as a statue. Without making any sound, he was screaming at the insect. *Go away! Go and explore a sulfur pit. Make friends with a marbled cone snail. But leave me alone!* Alex could see its antennae twitching as it made up its mind. He looked fearfully at his bare flesh just inches above his sock. He couldn't bear it any more. He suddenly lashed out, using every muscle in his leg as he kicked at the air. He thought the centipede would still cling on. It might get tangled in his laces. He was certain he was going to feel its bite. But when he looked down again, it was no longer there. He had managed to shake it free.

He needed a weapon . . . anything to protect himself from whatever might come next. Why couldn't Smithers have built a flamethrower into his Simpsons pencil case? Alex reached into his backpack once again. He had the two gel pens, but the last thing he wanted to do in here was set off an explosion . . . it would just advertise his presence to every living thing. That just left the pencil sharpener with the diamond-edged blade. He took it out and unfolded it three times, the plastic swiveling on concealed hinges. He was left with something that looked like a tiny ax or meat cleaver, barely three centimeters long. It might be useful for cutting through wire or even glass, but it wasn't much good for anything else. Even so, Alex felt a little more confident having it in his hand.

Where was the other door? The guards must still be looking for him, and he knew he had to get a move on, to find his way out of here as quickly as possible. But even so, he didn't dare hurry. He took another step and his foot came down on a little cluster of mushrooms, crushing them. Pale yellow liquid, like pus, oozed out from beneath his sole. A moth fluttered briefly in front of him. It was hard to believe that he was in an artificially created environment, a greenhouse—and not lost in the jungle. The pathway took him past a pool of boiling mud, bubbles rising slowly and heavily to the surface. A tall, twisted tree with lianas trailing from its branches grew beside it. Alex looked up, then ducked back as a globule of milky white syrup splashed down, oozing out of the bark. It missed his face by millimeters and he knew that if it had hit his eyes, he might well have been blinded.

The path curved around and Alex found himself in a slight clearing with a tiny river in front of him and a Japanese-style bridge. The pretty humpbacked structure looked ridiculous in this artificial jungle. Who could possibly want to come for a walk here among so much death? He could no longer see the glass windows that made up the outer walls of the Poison Dome and guessed that he must be at its very heart. Well, at least if he was halfway in, that meant he was also halfway out. Something buzzed past his head and he just caught sight of a giant wasp, legs trailing, barely able to stay in the air as it struggled against its own weight. What horrors were going to come next? He had to get out of here.

He crossed the bridge, still moving slowly. Silvery water flowed beneath, and as Alex passed across, it suddenly erupted in a frenzy. Some sort of fish life had detected his presence. Piranha . . . or something worse. Alex was beginning to wonder if the dome had really been built as a scientific experiment or if it wasn't just some huge toy, the fantasy of a sick mind. Straik might pretend to be studying poisons. In fact, he seemed more interested in sudden death.

He stepped off the other side of the bridge. That was when the man appeared.

It was a guard—or a gardener—dressed in a white protective suit that began at his ankles and continued all the way to his neck. His feet were weighed down by heavy-duty boots and he was wearing gloves that doubled the size of his hands. His head was completely enclosed in the sort of helmet that a beekeeper might wear, except that instead of a net, his face was covered by a plastic sheet. Alex was aware of two hostile eyes glaring at him, a small nose, and a mouth curled in a sneering smile. The rest of the man's features were hidden. He was holding a machete. He was pointing it directly at Alex.

Alex stopped with the bridge behind him. "Hi," he said. "Are you the park attendant? Because if so, maybe you could show me the way out."

The man tightened his grip on the weapon. Alex knew what was about to happen and he was ready for it. As the machete swung through the air, the blade aiming for his neck, he dropped down, then threw himself forward, ducking underneath the man's arm. For just a second, Alex was behind him and he slashed upward with his own, miniature blade. The man didn't even feel it. He spun around and brought both his hands plunging down, using the handle of the machete as a club. It smashed into Alex's shoulder and the pain ricocheted along his bones and muscles, all the way to his wrist. His hand fell open and the little knife dropped away.

The man came at him again, this time swinging the blade to force Alex away from him. Alex took one step back, then another. At the last second, he remembered the water behind him. The man was about to feed him to the fish. Alex stopped with his heels on the very edge of the bank. The machete sliced the air in front of him and at once he lashed out, his fist plunging into the man's abdomen. The protective suit absorbed much of the damage. Alex felt the hardened material take the skin off his knuckles. But the man had been winded and fell back. Alex lashed out with his foot, catching the man on his arm. The machete spun away and landed, point down, in a flower bed.

The man charged straight at him, almost knocking Alex off his feet. Alex was terrified he was going to step on a nettle or fall backward into one of the flower beds. The flowers growing near the river were like porcupines, with huge spikes and bulging, overripe berries that could have been disease-ridden eyes. For a moment Alex lost his balance and he lifted an arm to steady himself. He touched a spider's web hanging from a branch. He hadn't even seen it, but he felt it at once. A single strand of the web had wrapped itself across the flesh on the back of his hand. It burned into him like acid. Alex cried out.

The man reached for the machete, took hold of it, and suddenly he was coming again at Alex, chopping the air with a series of vicious blows. Alex looked left, right, then behind him. He had almost backed into another tree. The bark looked innocent enough, but he didn't dare touch it. It might contain ricin or botulin or any other toxin that Beckett had forgotten to mention. How far away was it?

Alex judged the distance carefully, then stood his ground. The man stumbled toward him. The heavy protective suit he was wearing was slowing him down. The blade slashed toward Alex's neck. At the very last second, Alex ducked and, just as he had hoped, he heard the clunk as it bit into the tree. The man pulled at it, but it was stuck fast. And that was when Alex twisted around and slammed his foot into the man's chest, putting all his strength behind it.

The man, thrown backward, slipped and fell on his back, landing in one of the beds of porcupine flowers. Even now, his suit should have protected him. But he had no way of realizing what Alex had done. Before he had lost it, he had used the little pencil-sharpener knife to make a slit that ran all the way from the man's waist to the back of his neck. There was a gap now that had allowed the spikes to go all the way through. The man screamed. Behind the mask, his eyes bulged and his entire body began to jerk, his legs kicking helplessly. Alex watched in horror as gray foam began to pour out of his mouth. Then suddenly his arms shot out and he lay still.

Alex didn't stay a moment longer than he had to. The noise of the fight would have disturbed whatever else was living in this nightmare place. If there were any other men working inside the dome, they would be on their way to investigate. He'd had enough. Still forcing himself not to panic, he pressed forward. A few minutes later, he was finally rewarded—a door! This one opened from the inside. Alex felt a great wave of relief as he swiped the card and passed through. The door swung shut. He had left the Poison Dome behind.

He examined the back of his hand. The web had left a white line running from one side to the other and the whole thing was swollen and painful. Well, he just had to be grateful that he hadn't actually met the spider. He rubbed the wound, but that only made it feel worse. He would just have to ignore it until he could get medical help. Where was he? The dome had brought him into another greenhouse, this one filled with troughs of what looked like wheat. He wasn't safe yet, but at least he was away from the shooting. Maybe the guards thought he was already dead.

He found a door and made his way outside again. In the distance he could hear shouting and two electric vehicles shot past, carrying more guards toward the noise. The lecture theater—white and modern—was right in front of him. Alex didn't know if the cameras were still jammed, nor did he care anymore. He was tired. His hand was hurting. His shoulder—where he had been hit with the handle of the machete—was on fire. There was still broken glass in his hair and he knew there must be quite a few cuts on his forehead and face. The next time Mr. Gilbert offered him a school trip, he would say he was sick.

He staggered forward, heading for the lecture theater. Maybe the rest of the school would already be there. He would slip in without being noticed and join the rest of the group. He could already see himself dozing off during the rest of whatever talk was going on.

Then the doors opened. Two guards stepped out. They saw Alex at the same moment that he saw them.

It wasn't over yet.

Alex turned around and ran.

13

EXIT STRATEGY

T OM HARRIS WAS GETTING WORRIED.

Almost an hour had passed since Alex had slipped away, disappearing into a restroom like some superhero about to change into costume and save the world. Only it wasn't like that. Tom knew that Alex didn't really want to work for MI6. He had said as much when the two of them were out together in Italy. So why had Alex chosen to go back to it all—and what could be such a big deal about a research center that seemed to be spending most of its time designing the perfect tomato?

After Alex had gone, the rest of the school party had been taken to one of the laboratories, where an earnest young scientist with a neatly trimmed beard had shown them the chemical process that put new DNA into a single plant cell. Tom had barely listened. He didn't find it easy to concentrate at the best of times. Now, his parents had recently separated. His father was living on his own in a motel in south London. His mother had taken up smoking again. They were both overachievers with a pile of diplomas between them, but what good had it done them? If Tom had his way, he would drop school entirely.

As they had moved from one laboratory to the next,

Tom had passed a window and had found himself looking for Alex. There was nobody in sight. But during the next demonstration—something to do with plants freeze-dried in liquid nitrogen—he had noticed a red light begin to blink discreetly in the corner of the room. Beckett had clearly seen it too. Tom saw her face change, a look of concern creeping into her eyes. It was an alarm. He was sure of it.

And then, in the distance, he heard something. The sound of breaking glass—a lot of it. Everyone else was too busy listening, taking notes. But Tom knew what it meant. Alex was on the run. Part of him was tempted to sneak out and join him.

It was lucky he didn't. As soon as the demonstration ended, Beckett insisted on a roll call to check that everyone was there, and—as promised—Tom stood in for Alex, doing a reasonable imitation of his voice.

"Rider?"

"Here, sir."

Only James Hale, standing next to him, saw what was happening and glanced at him quizzically. Tom shrugged but gave nothing away.

And now they were in some workshop, two floors down, underground. Tom wondered if they had been brought here on purpose, to stop them from hearing or seeing anything that might be going on outside. Another scientist—this one young, female, and Chinese—had arrived to show them the famous gene gun, developed, they were told, by the director of Greenfields. It was a rather ordinary-looking piece of equipment that resembled a small metal safe with a glass door. Nonetheless, this was at the heart of GM technology, the woman said. She opened the door and placed a round petri dish inside.

"The gene gun is a very effective way to deliver new DNA into a plant," she explained. "This is done by a system known as Biolistic Particle Delivery . . ."

As she continued, Tom noticed a guard, dressed in khaki, steal into the room. He approached Beckett and whispered urgently into her ear. Tom wasn't surprised when, a moment later, she stepped forward, interrupting the talk.

"I am very sorry, boys and girls," she exclaimed. "I am afraid we are going to have to end your visit to Greenfields. An emergency situation has arisen and you must return to your school bus at once."

"Wait a minute . . . ," Mr. Gilbert began. His face was indignant. They had driven a long way to visit the center and they had only been here for an hour.

"There will be no argument," Beckett snapped. "We will take the back staircase. Your driver has been instructed to meet you around the side of the building."

James moved closer to Tom. "This is about Alex, isn't it," he muttered.

"Alex is standing right next to me," Tom replied.

"Yeah. Sure." James nodded slowly.

The class was already filing out and the two of them followed behind.

The guards had seen him. If they had been carrying Uzis, he would have been dead already. One of them was coming after him, catching up fast. The other had stopped to talk into his radio, alerting the others.

Alex was getting tired. He was in pain. As he ran back toward the center of the complex, he was aware of just two things. He had to drop out of sight. And—if it wasn't too late already—he had to find his way back to his friends. There was safety in numbers. So long as he was part of Brookland School, inside the group, there was nothing that Straik or anybody else could do.

But where were they? There was no bus, no sign of anyone, and definitely no way out of the Greenfields Bio Center. The fence was too high and he could see the gate, over on his right, firmly closed. The Poison Dome, which he'd managed to break out of just a few moments before, was now on his left. Well, one thing was certain. He wasn't going back in there.

Alex heard a whine and saw an electric car with three more guards speeding across the lawn toward him. The door of one of the brick buildings opened and more guards poured out. These ones were armed. For just a second, Alex was tempted to hand himself over. He could still pretend he had lagged behind his class and gotten lost. Would they really be so quick to kill him?

Then he remembered the test tube in his top pocket. Straik knew someone had hacked into his computer. And there was a dead man in the Poison Dome. Alex put the thought out of his mind. It was obvious what they could— and would—do if they got hold of him, and right now they were just seconds away. He had to move . . . fast.

Ahead of him, a wide tarmac driveway ran straight between what looked like two rows of factories. This was the only way with no guards . . . and it might lead him back to the block where the school visit had begun. A single white-coated technician stood in his way, but he was busy with other things, funneling a steaming liquid from a steel cylinder into a heavily insulated container. Liquid nitrogen. It had to be. Alex had seen the same stuff—though in smaller quantities—at Brookland. And what were its properties? In physics class . . . yes . . . there was something he had been told.

The electric car was getting nearer. The guards who were on foot had brought up their machine guns, preparing to fire. A single cascade of silent bullets and he would be torn to shreds. Alex was already sprinting down the drive- way. As the stunned technician stood frozen in surprise, Alex leapt forward and seized the steel cylinder. Then, in a single movement—he spun around and hurled it behind him. The container hit the tarmac and the liquid nitrogen splashed out, immediately forming itself into marbles that bounced along the hard surface. At the same time, it began to evaporate, and suddenly there was a wall of white mist between Alex and his pursuers as the liquid reacted to the higher temperature and turned back into gas. The car swerved as for just a moment Alex disappeared from view. The technician was shouting, but Alex ignored him.

He raced over to the nearest door, using the library card to swipe his way in. He hoped the guards would be unaware that he could open any lock and would keep running. His eyes were watering and he could taste nitrogen gas at the back of his throat. If he had thrown the liquid in a closed room, he would have killed himself, suffocating as the oxygen was swallowed up. Now he found himself in a bare industrial building with cinder-block walls and cement floors. A series of furnaces stood in front of him, none of them operating. A metal staircase twisted upward. Alex was disappointed. He had hoped the building might offer more. Somewhere to hide. Some way of escape. Something.

He took the stairs. He would go up to the roof. There was a communication system built into the pocket calculator that Smithers had given him. He would use it to call MI6. With luck, they would respond before it was too late.

The staircase rose six floors. At the top he came to an old-fashioned door with a push bar. Even as he reached it, he heard the main door of the building crash open beneath him and knew that the guards had worked out where he had gone. He had to fight back a growing sense of hopelessness. There really didn't seem to be any way out of this mess. So what now? A fire escape. He would make his way from the roof back down again and find somewhere else to hide.

Alex had crashed through the door, which then slammed shut behind him. He found himself on a wide, flat roof covered with asphalt. A long silver chimney rose about fifty feet into the air, presumably carrying smoke from the furnaces that Alex had seen below. There were two air-conditioning units and a water tank. But that was all. There was no fire escape in sight. The roof had a low brick wall running all the way around the edge. The nearest building looked to be at least ten yards away—too far to jump. Alex was six stories up with no way to climb down. He was trapped.

He could imagine the guards already climbing the staircase, making their way toward him. Somehow he had to keep them at bay. There were a few pieces of scaffolding left over from building work lying on the ground beside the water tank. He snatched two of them, ran back to the door, and wedged them against the handle, slanting them into the ground. That would at least buy him a bit of time.

But he was still a sitting target. In a way, he had played right into their hands. They could leave him here all night and then pick him off at their leisure. Where were his friends? Alex ran back to the edge of the building, skidding to a halt beside the parapet. And finally he saw them.

The school bus was parked at the far end of the main driveway. The field trip must have ended early, as students were already loading up. Even as he watched, he saw Tom Harris and James Hale climbing on board, deep in conversation. He heard a couple of girls laughing. It seemed incredible that they could be unaware of what had been going on at Greenfields while they were being shown around. And there were the two teachers—Mr. Gilbert and Miss Barry! Alex tried to get their attention, tried to call out to them, but they were too far away and his voice was hoarse from the nitrogen. He could only watch in despair as the door hissed shut, sealing his friends inside. He twisted around and looked the other way. The gate was already sliding open. Straik was determined to get rid of the school party as quickly as possible. The best Alex could hope for was one last roll call, perhaps delaying their departure by another few minutes. Then they would be gone. He would be stuck here, on his own.

He sized up the angles. The bus would pass directly underneath him. Could he jump down? No. He was far too high up. Even assuming he timed it properly and landed on the roof, he would break his arms, his legs, and quite possibly his neck. Could he wave at the driver, somehow attracting his attention? Impossible. He wouldn't be seen at this height and there was nothing he could throw down.

He heard the sound of fists pounding against metal. A

single door was all that was between him and the armed
guards, wedged shut by two pieces of scaffolding. Desperately, Alex made a circuit of the roof. There were no
fire escapes, no ladders, no ropes, nothing. The bus engine had started. It was about thirty yards away at the end
of the driveway. At the other end, the gate was open, with
Salisbury Plain in clear view.

A cascade of machine-gun fire sent Alex diving for
cover. The noise was deafening and very near. But they
weren't shooting at him. Not yet. One of the guards at the
top of the stairs had sprayed the door with bullets. Alex
actually saw the metal bulging and blistering as it was
hammered. It was on the verge of being blown off its
hinges.

The chimney . . .

Alex was already up and running as the idea took
shape in his mind. The chimney was modern and silver,
and as far as he could see, its outer casing was fairly thin.
He didn't have time to work out the measurements, but
surely if it was laid out horizontally, it might reach across
to the next rooftop. He could use it as a bridge. And he
had the means to bring it down.

Another burst of machine-gun fire. The door shivered
in its frame. Feverishly, Alex reached into his backpack
and took out the red gel-ink pen that Smithers had given
him. Red was more powerful. It would do more damage.
That was what Smithers had said. He glanced back at the
door. White smoke was trickling through the cracks

around the side. How much longer would it hold? Alex had the pen in his hand. He twisted the cap once then pulled the little plunger to activate it. He felt it click and slammed the pen against the chimney, diving for cover behind one of the air-conditioning units. The pen stayed in place, held magnetically.

The bus had yet to move. The guards were hammering at the door now, using the stocks of their machine guns to finish the job. There was a brief pause and then an explosion, louder than anything that had gone before. Hopefully the bus driver would hear it. He would have to stop and find out what was going on! Alex was crouching with his hands over his ears. He felt the blast sear across his forearms and the top of his head and looked up just in time to see the chimney topple like a felled tree, the metal close to the base grinding in protest as it was torn apart.

It crashed down, but even as it fell, Alex saw that his plan couldn't work. The chimney was too short to reach the building opposite. It had fallen sideways, smashing into the low wall. The wall acted as a fulcrum, tearing the metal skin a second time. The chimney ended up tilting down toward the main driveway. What had been its top end was now about thirty feet above the road.

The door, meanwhile, had finally collapsed, blown off its frame from one last blast of machine-gun fire. Half a dozen men rushed out onto the roof.

The bus was now moving, slowly picking up speed,

roaring toward the gate as if desperate to get out of here. In a few seconds, it would pass directly beneath Alex.

One of the guards saw him and shouted. Alex stood where he was. The guard took aim.

As the bus drew closer, Alex sprinted forward, as if determined to throw himself off the side of the building. The guard fired. Bullets skidded across the roof of the building, ripping up the asphalt.

The chimney had been sliced open by the edge of the wall. It had almost broken in half. If it had, it would have fallen down to the road, blocking the bus. But it was being held in place by a small section of the metal skin, resting on the wall and acting like a hinge. Alex dived headfirst into the opening. The chimney was just big enough for him with his backpack still strapped to his shoulders. It was like being inside a slide at a swimming pool. The round silver surface offered no resistance and Alex shot down.

In the end, it was all about timing. If he had hit the road, he would have died. If he had started too soon, he might have missed the bus and been run over by it. But Alex had timed it perfectly. He shot out of what had once been the top of the chimney at the exact moment that the bus passed beneath him. For a brief second, he saw the roof, a yellow blur rushing past. He had only about fifteen feet to fall, but he knew that the impact was going to be painful.

It was worse than he imagined. The breath was smashed out of him. His neck and his spine almost separated. He was sure he had broken several of his ribs. He rolled, spinning toward the edge. If he kept rolling and fell off, he would be left behind after all and it would all have been for nothing.

Alex stretched out his arms and legs, spread-eagling himself, doing everything he could to stay in contact with the roof. He wondered why the driver hadn't stopped, but perhaps he hadn't heard anything above the noise of the engine.

The bus reached the security gate and passed through without slowing down. Then it was outside the complex, accelerating across Salisbury Plain.

Alex stayed where he was, battered and exhausted. He allowed the cold air to wash over him. Every part of him was in pain. Something was trickling against his chest and for a horrible moment he thought he had been shot. But it wasn't blood. The test tube had smashed. Smithers would just have to use whatever liquid he could separate from the fiber of Alex's jacket. Surely there would be enough of it to analyze.

Meanwhile, he couldn't travel all the way back to London on the roof.

Just before they reached the main road, Alex crawled over to the edge and lowered the top half of his body so that he was hanging, upside down, outside the window where he had been sitting. He was lucky. Tom Harris saw him, his eyes widening in disbelief. Alex made a sign with one hand. Tom nodded.

About one minute later, the bus stopped and Tom got out. Alex watched him rush behind a tree and pretend to be sick. He used the opportunity to slide to the edge and lower himself down. He limped over and joined his friend.

"Alex!" Tom looked horrified. "What happened to you?"

"Things didn't quite go as planned."

"You look awful!"

"Really? I feel great. . . ."

Tom helped Alex back to the bus. The two of them had to pass Mr. Gilbert, who was sitting in the front seat. Their teacher was even more shocked than Tom had been. He had only seen one boy leave the bus. So how was it possible for two of them to be returning?

"Rider!" he gasped. "What are you doing out of the bus? What happened to you?"

Alex didn't know what to say. He could only imagine what he must look like.

Tom came to his rescue. "He fell out of the window, sir. It's lucky we stopped."

"I don't believe a word of it! The windows don't even open—"

"It was the back door."

"Well . . ." The biology teacher was out of his depth.

He just wanted to get back to London. "You'll see the principal first thing tomorrow morning," he snapped. "Now get back to your seat."

Alex leaned on Tom and hobbled to the back of the bus past forty staring faces. Everyone would be talking about this at school the next day—but this was Alex Rider. Somehow, any strange behavior was to be expected. As for Alex, he still had the flash drive with its precious download and the sample from the test tube as an added bonus. He had completed his part of the bargain and he had come out of it more or less in one piece. And as he hadn't heard a word from Harry Bulman, he assumed that MI6 had kept their promise too.

He sank back into his seat, reflecting that his part in all this was over. He might never find out what McCain and Straik had been planning—but what did it really matter? It was none of his business and he was just glad that he would never see either of them again.

Desmond McCain was back in Straik's office, and for once it was clear that he had lost his composure. He was sitting cross-legged, one hand clenching and unclenching on his knee, and the crack that divided the two halves of his head seemed to have somehow widened as the damaged muscles in his jaw attempted to chew over what had happened. Even the silver crucifix earring had lost its shine.

"This intruder must have been in here, in the room, when we were talking," he growled.

"I would think so." Behind his desk, Leonard Straik licked his lips. He was blinking repeatedly.

"But where?" McCain's great white eyes slid slowly around the office. "There! Behind the picture!"

"I hardly think that there's room."

"Where else?" McCain paused, deep in thought. "What did he hear?"

"I don't think he could have heard anything very much, Desmond." Straik faltered. "We were only in here a couple of minutes. It's just lucky I noticed the flash drive."

"So he now has the contents of your computer."

"All the files are encrypted. And even if he manages to break into them, they won't give much away."

"What about the test tube?"

"I don't think that matters either. Of course, it's bad news. He'll have the sample analyzed—but it won't tell him very much. I don't think anyone will be able to guess its significance."

"You don't think." McCain's fist came pounding down on the side of his chair. Straik heard a dull crack. The arm of the chair had been broken in two. "Five years' work and hundreds of thousands of dollars! We're just a few days away from Poison Dawn, and you don't *think* we've been compromised! Obviously, this intruder came in here on the back of your blasted school visit. Why did you allow it in the first place?"

"We had no choice. We only rent this facility . . . the

land and the buildings. We have to do what the government tells us, and they insisted we have a couple of schools in. They insisted we educate schools about GM technology."

"So then it was a government agent who broke in?"

"I don't know, Desmond." Straik took out a handkerchief and wiped his brow. "But I don't think it was a coincidence that the cameras malfunctioned when they did."

"Did any of the guards see the intruder?"

"Quite a few of them did. And they're insisting it was a boy . . . a teenager."

"That doesn't make any sense at all. If it was a child, then the whole thing could have been . . . I don't know . . . a prank!"

"He blew up a chimney on the recycling unit. And he killed a guard in the Poison Dome."

"A teenager? Then who was he? What was he doing here?"

There was a knock at the door and Dr. Beckett came in, her white coat flapping behind her, carrying a file. There was something military about the way she walked, like a soldier delivering news of a defeat. "I have the photographs," she announced.

"I thought you said the cameras weren't working," McCain said.

"They were jammed for about forty minutes." Straik took the file. "But they were working when the bus first arrived, and I thought it might be worth our while to examine who exactly came here today."

McCain went over to the desk. The file that Beckett had brought contained a dozen photographs taken by the camera closest to the main gate. They were grainy, in black and white, but Mr. Gilbert and Miss Barry were clear enough, stepping down from the bus with the rest of the school group following behind. Straik and Beckett were both leaning forward, examining the pictures, when McCain suddenly stabbed down with his finger.

"Him!"

"Who is it, Desmond?"

"Don't you recognize him, you idiot? I don't believe it! It's impossible. But there's no doubt about it. It's the boy from Scotland."

"What boy?" Then Straik realized. "The boy from the card game."

"Alex Rider." McCain uttered the name with undisguised hatred. "That was what he called himself."

"I heard that name on the roll call," Beckett muttered. "But he never left the group."

"Somebody must have answered for him," McCain said. His finger was still pressing down on Alex, as if he could squash him like a bug. "It's definitely the same boy, and this is the second time he's crossed my path."

"I thought we'd dealt with him, Desmond." Myra Beckett stared at the picture in dismay. "You said he was in the car with that journalist—"

"Evidently, we failed." McCain twisted away. "Which means that that irritating journalist is still alive as well. This boy is no mere teenager, though. Who is this Alex Rider? Why is he interested in us?"

"We can find out," Straik muttered.

McCain nodded. "We have contacts. We need to use them. It doesn't matter how much it costs. Someone must know something about this boy . . . he clearly wasn't working alone." McCain took one last look at the photograph. With an effort, he broke free. "We'll locate him and we'll bring him back here."

"And then?"

"And then we'll find out what he knows."

14

FEELING THE HEAT

HENRY BRAY HAD BEEN THE PRINCIPAL at Brookland for seven years and assistant principal at another school for five years before that. He didn't often find himself lost for words, but right now that was exactly how he felt. Once again, he examined the boy in front of him while he tried to work out how to proceed.

Alex Rider was different from all the other boys at Brookland. He knew that. The unfortunate death of his uncle in a car accident almost a year ago had clearly sent him off the rails. That was understandable. But Alex had barely been in school since then, missing week after week because of so many different illnesses that in the end (Mr. Bray hadn't told anyone he'd done this) he had actually written to the doctor, suspecting that something might be going on. He had received a short note back. Alex had viral problems. His health was very delicate. The doctor—his name was Blunt—wouldn't be at all surprised if Alex had to miss a lot more school in the future.

Alex didn't look ill now. He looked as if he had been in a fistfight. There were a number of small cuts on his forehead and the side of his cheek, and from the way he was standing, Bray guessed he had hurt his shoulder.

He was here because of a report sent in by his biology teacher, Mr. Gilbert. But Alex didn't give any sign of being ashamed or nervous about what might follow. He was just angry.

Mr. Bray sighed. "Alex. You made a very good start in year seven. All your reports said the same. And I am well aware of your personal circumstances. I imagine you were very close to your uncle."

"Yes, sir."

"It doesn't help that you've had a lot of time off school . . . all these illnesses. Obviously, I've made allowances for you. But this business yesterday . . . frankly, I'm appalled. As I understand it, the bus had an emergency door that you opened, and you managed to fall out. Is that correct?"

"Yes, sir."

"I'm amazed you could be so irresponsible. You could have seriously hurt yourself. And there were other young people on the bus too. Didn't you stop to think that you might cause an accident? I can't imagine why you would do such a thoughtless thing." Mr. Bray took off his glasses and laid them on his desk. It was something he always did when he was about to pronounce sentence. "I hate the idea of your missing any more lessons, but I'm afraid I am going to have to make an example of you. You are going to have one day's suspension from school. You are to go home straightaway, and I've written a note for you to take with you."

Half an hour later, Alex crossed the school yard with a sense of injustice burning in him. He had survived poisonous plants and insects, hand-to-hand combat, and machine-gun fire. He had downloaded the contents of Straik's computer and stolen a sample of whatever he was brewing at Greenfields. Jack would have already delivered them to the MI6 offices on Liverpool Street. And what was his reward? To be treated like a naughty schoolboy, sent home with a note.

The first lesson had already begun, and nobody noticed Alex as he made his way out of the gates and down the road toward the bus stop. As he walked, he found himself going over the events of the day before. The appearance of Desmond McCain had completely thrown him. What was the head of an international charity doing in a bio research center in Wiltshire? He was planning something with Leonard Straik. That much was clear. The two of them had talked about shipping a thousand gallons of the liquid—and they had said that it was alive. But what was it and what was it for? The more Alex thought about it, the less sense it made.

McCain had been to prison once in his life, and he had to be heading that way again. Alex was certain now—not that he had ever really doubted it—that his near death in Scotland, along with Sabina and her father, had been no accident. McCain had tried to kill them. He was prepared to do anything to protect himself. MI6 had wanted to investigate Leonard Straik because he might be a security risk. In fact, he was using Greenfields for something much bigger than anyone suspected.

And then Alex remembered something he had overheard while he was in the office. McCain was going to send the Becket woman somewhere the following day—today. A place called Elm's Cross. The name rang a faint bell. Alex continued walking until he arrived at an Internet cafe not far from Brompton Cemetery. The place served disgusting coffee, but it charged only two dollars for half an hour on one of its ancient computers. At least it had broadband.

Alex paid and chose a computer at the very back, away from the window. The owner glanced at him briefly, then returned to a crumpled copy of _The Sun_. Alex Googled _Elm's Cross_ and waited for the page to come up on the screen. The results were disappointing. There was a packaging company with that name in Warminster, a restaurant in Bradford, and a film studio in west London that had apparently closed down a year ago. None of them could possibly be connected. Except . . .

"What about the shooting?"

Straik to McCain. When Alex had heard them, he'd automatically assumed that they were talking about guns. But suppose they had actually meant shooting film? Alex looked for more information about the studio. It was on the other side of Hayes, not far from Heathrow Airport. According to an old news report, a raft of British comedies had been shot there after the war, but the increasing noise of aircraft along with the decline in British film production had combined to put it out of business. There was talk of the land being developed . . . affordable housing and more office space. The last film that had been shot there was an advertisement for the shopping chain Woolworth's. It seemed appropriate. A few weeks later, Woolworth's had gone bust too.

Alex had made his decision. Jack wouldn't be expecting him, and even if the school had managed to tell her what was happening, she wouldn't be too worried if he took his time turning up. He would have to be careful. He was still in school uniform and that would certainly attract attention, being out on the street in the middle of the day—but he doubted there would be many policemen around, where he was going.

He took the subway from Fulham Broadway and a taxi the rest of the way. Elm's Cross was in a strange derelict area that had somehow been forgotten by the housing estates, the industrial zones, and the soulless strip malls that surrounded it. As Alex paid the taxi driver, there was a sudden roar and he looked up to see the underbelly of a 747 as it lurched out of the sky toward the main runway of Heathrow. In the distance he could make out the M4 highway, raised up on concrete spurs, injecting London with a never-ending stream of cars and trucks.

The driver looked at him suspiciously. "Shouldn't you be in school?" he asked.

Alex tipped him generously. "I'm on a school project," he replied. "We're writing about air pollution."

The lie had come easily. Alex could actually taste the exhaust fumes in the air, and he couldn't imagine what it would be like to live with it, day in and day out. He wondered what he was doing. Less than twenty-four hours ago, he had been congratulating himself on a mission accomplished. MI6 had what they wanted. So why was he here, quite possibly putting his head back in the noose?

He was angry. That was part of the reason. But Alex knew it was more than that. Mr. Bray might have given him the excuse, but there was part of him that needed to investigate, to uncover the answers. That part had been deliberately cultivated by MI6 and his uncle—Ian Rider. Using him wasn't enough. First, they had turned him into someone who _wanted_ to be used.

Alex hoisted his backpack onto his shoulder and set off. He had given the taxi driver an address about a quarter of a mile from his true destination—just in case he had taken it upon himself to call the police and warn them about a boy cutting off from school. He passed through an empty area with what looked like a reservoir on one side and a wide expanse of dirty, litter-strewn grass on the other. A wire fence stretched out ahead of him. Now he had to be careful. Desmond McCain had said he was coming here today. If he happened to drive past, Alex would stick out like a sore thumb, and this time there were no witnesses.

ELM'S CROSS STUDIOS
PRIVATE
WARNING: 24-HOUR SURVEILLANCE

The sign hung on the fence outside the main gate, but Alex wasn't sure he believed it. How could there be round-the-clock surveillance when there were no cameras? There were no guards in sight either. The paint on the sign had faded, with rust speckling through. And the gate itself was open, inviting him in.

Alex could see a paved driveway leading down to a cluster of buildings, most of them low-rise with long, narrow windows running horizontally, just beneath the roof. They might once have been surrounded by manicured lawns, but the site had become overgrown with long grass and shrubs running rampant. In the middle of it all, there was a row of three hangars, big enough to house planes . . . although they long ago would have ceased to fly. The whole place looked sad and abandoned.

He walked in. If security men appeared, he would just have to bluff it out. With a bit of luck, nobody here would know what had happened the day before. And although the guards at Greenfields had been armed, it was very unlikely that they would be toting guns right next to a major international airport.

Nobody stopped him. There were definitely no cameras. Alex passed a couple of Dumpsters, filled to overflowing. A lot of the contents were household rubbish—old cartons and broken pieces of furniture. But there were also oddities: a plastic cactus, a swordfish, a scaled-down replica of the Statue of Liberty missing the hand holding the torch. He thought he saw a car parked on the other side of some shrubs and was about to duck out of sight when he realized it was a black saloon BMW, left over from the Second World War, burned out and resting on bricks instead of tires. He was surrounded by the remnants of old films that had been made, seen, and forgotten. Elm's Cross had once been a dream factory, but the machinery had long since shut down.

He came to the first of the hangars, with the words **STUDIO A** stenciled in yellow letters on the corrugated iron wall. The huge sliding doors were open, but there was nothing inside apart from a puddle of oily water and a pile of broken wood. Cables hung down from the ceiling. A pigeon cooed somewhere in the rafters, the sound amplified by the empty space. The second hangar was the same. Alex was beginning to think he was wasting his time. There was nobody here. And what would someone like Desmond McCain want with an abandoned film studio, anyway? He must have been referring to a different Elm's Cross after all. Alex looked at his watch. Quarter past eleven. Jack would be wondering where he was. He took out his mobile phone, thinking he would call her. There was no signal.

"It's ready, ma'am . . ."

"Then I'll leave you to it."

Alex heard the voices and crouched behind a low brick wall—in fact made of painted cardboard and wood, another old piece of film scenery. He had already recognized the voice of Dr. Myra Beckett, and a moment later, there she was, walking out of the third studio dressed in a raincoat, which she had wrapped tightly around her waist. There were two men with her. Alex looked around for anyone else, but it seemed they were alone.

Beckett nodded at the men. "I'll see you back at Greenfields," she said.

For the first time, Alex noticed a couple of cars parked in the narrow driveway between Studios B and C. Beckett got into one of them and drove off. The two men went back into the studio. What could they possibly be doing there? Alex knew that he'd already been in enough trouble. Jack would kill him if she found out he'd come here. But he couldn't just back out now. He had to know.

Beckett had left. Alex crept over to the studio entrance, fearful that the two men would reemerge at any moment. He peered inside. There was no sign of them, but it seemed that this studio was still in use. He could make out powerful lights on the other side of a huge screen stretched over a metal frame. The screen was a barrier between Alex and whatever was happening, but at least it was dark on this side. He could hear the two men muttering in the distance and knew that, for the moment, he was safe. He slipped inside.

"Some of this stuff must be worth a fortune."

"You heard what she said. Leave it!"

The two voices carried easily in the enclosed space. Alex made his way along the back of the screen, keeping close to the outer wall. McCain was closing this place down. That is what he had said in Straik's office. Perhaps Mr. Bray had done Alex a favor after all. If he hadn't been suspended, he might never have had the opportunity to find out what was going on.

Then the two men appeared, coming around the side of the screen. But for the darkness, they would have seen Alex at once. Alex slipped behind a pile of boxes, crouching low. The men walked straight past him, so close that he could have reached out and touched them. He watched them disappear the way he had come. Good. Now he was on his own.

The sound of the door slamming shut echoed all around him like a gunshot. Alex twisted around, but he knew already there was nothing he could do. He heard the rattle of a chain being drawn through the handles, followed by the snap of a padlock. The men had finished here. They had left the lights on. But they had locked and bolted the main door. He heard their footsteps as they walked away and, a moment later, the sound of a car engine starting up. He would just have to hope there was another way out.

Alex straightened up, then continued around the side of the screen. And suddenly he was no longer in London, no longer in a grubby industrial area near Heathrow Airport.

He was in Africa.

Alex had never actually been to Africa, yet the scene that surrounded him was unmistakable. He was in the middle of a cluster of mud huts, half a dozen of them, with no windows and roofs made out of straw. They had been constructed close to each other in a dusty enclosure, surrounded by a wooden picket fence. An assortment of clothes, old but brightly colored, hung on a washing line between two stunted acacia trees. To one side, there was a well with a few objects—pots, pans, some tin plates—scattered around it. A shield shaped like a leaf and two wooden spears had been propped up against one of the doorways as if guarding the way in.

It was only when he looked up that the illusion was broken. Electric arc lamps blazed down from a network of catwalks high above. Together, they were creating the heat and light of an African summer's day. The giant screen was actually a cyclorama made out of a bright green fabric. Alex understood enough about film technology to know that a computer could insert anything into the green background. A flick of a switch and the village could be in a jungle, a desert, or beneath a clear blue sky.

But what sort of film was being made? With a shudder, Alex realized that the village was populated—but not with anything that resembled life. There were three dead cows lying on their sides, their legs rigid, their stomachs bloated, their eyes glassy and empty. They had to be made out of plastic. There was no smell, no flies swarming over them as there would have been out in the wild. But that didn't take away any of the horror. From the look of them, if these animals had been real, they would have died in pain.

They weren't alone. As Alex moved farther into the set, almost drawn in against his will, he saw what had once been a large bird, perhaps an eagle, now a crumpled heap of bone and feathers lying in the dust. It was only when he reached the edge of the village that he came upon the first human being. A little black boy, maybe two or three years old, was lying curled up, one matchstick arm drawn across his eyes. Alex felt sick. He could tell that it was just a dummy, not a real child. But who would create something like this? And why?

He had seen enough. He could work out the reason for all of this later. Alex just wanted to be back out in the fresh air. He looked around him for a second door and saw one, set in one of the walls of the hangar. He tried it, but it was locked too. There were no windows. He looked up. He could see two barred skylights set in the roof, but there was no way he was going to be able to reach them, even if he climbed up to the lighting platforms. A rectangular air-conditioning shaft ran the full length of the hangar, suspended from the ceiling by a series of metal brackets. He might be able to reach the skylights if he climbed on top of it—but even then, how would he cut his way through the bars?

Perhaps he could blow them up. He still had the second gel-ink pen that Smithers had given him. He was already taking off his backpack when he remembered. He had left the pencil case with the pen and the pocket calculator beside his bed. He checked his mobile. There was no signal. So it looked as if he was just going to have to wait here until someone came back.

And then the whole world burst into flames.

Alex didn't know what was more shocking—the fact that it was so silent, or so unexpected. All around him the ground simply erupted, tongues of fire shooting upward as if powered by hidden pipes below. Alex could have been in the middle of a minefield. About half a dozen bombs, incendiaries perhaps, were being set off, one by one. Alex was thrown off his feet. He knew that if one of the devices went off directly underneath him, he would be killed. He threw his arm across his eyes, protecting them from the heat.

Now he understood what Beckett and the two men had been doing. Closing this place down meant destroying it. The three of them must have just finished laying the explosive charges when he had come across them. They had been set off either by timer switches or remote control. It made no difference either way to Alex. The flames were roaring all around him. It was as if he had been locked inside some huge oven. He had only minutes to break out of here. Very soon he would begin to suffocate. And if he passed out, that would be the end of him.

Everything in here would burn. There would be nothing left.

The green screen had caught alight. Alex saw it dissolve like a huge sheet of paper, turning black and then orange and red as the flames burst through. His eyes were streaming now. It was difficult to see, almost impossible to think. The doors were locked. The skylights were out of reach. The walls were metal. The mobile was dead. He had nothing with him. There was no way out.

The air-conditioning shaft . . .

It was a square tunnel hanging underneath the ceiling, plugged into the wall. It brought air into the building. So it had to lead outside. The silver shaft was big enough to crawl through, and Alex thought he could make out an access panel. He wiped a sleeve against his eyes. All the clothes on the washing line were ablaze. One of the huts had vanished, consumed by a whirlpool of fire. Suddenly, all the lights blinked out. The main electric cable must have melted. Now the hangar was an intense red, lit only by the inferno that was destroying it.

Coughing, forcing himself to suck in the hot air, Alex started forward. Without knowing quite why, he grabbed hold of the shield and carried it over to the ladder. It would make it more difficult to climb, yet somehow he had a feeling he would need it. He reached out and grabbed the first rung. It was already warm. In a minute's time, it would be too hot to hold.

Dragging the shield with him, he climbed up to the

walkway. The air-conditioning shaft was directly above him, running about thirty yards to the far wall. He was going to have to climb into it and then crawl the whole distance with the flames roaring underneath him. Alex stared at the distance across the studio with a sense of despair that made him weak. It was going to be like feeding himself into an oven. If he didn't move fast, he would roast before he reached the other end.

But would there even be a way out? There had to be. There was no other choice.

The access panel to the ventilation shaft was fastened with four nuts and bolts. Alex was lucky. They turned in his hand. But even that wasn't easy. The smoke was blinding him. There was a foul chemical smell—many of the props must have been made of synthetic materials—and even as he dragged at what little air remained, he felt sick. Finally the fourth bolt came free and the panel fell away, bouncing off the walkway and spinning down below. Alex watched it disappear into the fire. There was nothing but fire now. Beckett and her colleagues had done their work all too well.

He pulled himself into the open shaft, sliding the shield in front of him. Now he was glad that he had brought it. Even as he crouched in the square corridor, he could feel the metal underneath him heating up. The shield would at least protect his hands. Quickly, moving with difficulty in the confined space, he tore off his backpack and dropped it ahead of him. Then came his jacket. He folded it under his knees. It would have to provide a cushion against the heat. He was already sweating. He could see the air rippling in front of him. He fixed his eyes on the end of the tunnel. There was a square of daylight, another access panel. That was what he had to reach.

He set off.

He could no longer see the flames, but he could imagine them, stretching out, licking the metal surface directly beneath him. He was shuffling forward as quickly as he could, his hands resting on the shield, his knees on the jacket. But there wasn't enough room to move properly. For just one moment he lost his balance and his palm and five fingers landed on the metal. He winced. The surface was already too hot to touch. He wasn't going to make it. The end was too far away.

Push the shield. Draw in his knees. Push the shield. Draw in his knees.

His head was swimming. There was almost no air left in the tunnel. And the jacket was burning. Most of his weight was on his knees, and he could feel the heat coming through. There was a dull clang behind him and he glanced back to see that the access panel was filled with smoke and the metal was buckling. There was certainly no way back. It occurred to him that the entire shaft could come free, that the brackets holding it up could melt or break loose and that the whole thing could plunge down, smashing into the studio floor and the roaring fire below. But he couldn't let that possibly stop him.

His knees were hurting now and he'd had to move his hands to the very edge of the shield, gripping the sides. It was fortunate that the African shield seemed to be the real thing. If it had been made of plastic, it would already have melted. Alex could hear someone grunting and realized it was him. Every movement was an effort: fighting the heat, fighting to breathe, forcing himself not to give up. He was more than halfway across. He could see the exit—a metal grille—ahead of him. He wouldn't have time to turn any screws, even assuming there were any. What if the grille was welded into place? No. Don't even think it. Alex shuffled faster and faster. Draw in the knees. Push the shield.

The last ten yards were the worst. Alex's vision was blurred. He could feel tears streaming down his face. But then he was there. The grille was in front of him. He reached out and grabbed hold of it, curling his fingers over the metal slats. It wouldn't move. He shook it. Something whispered behind him and he turned around to see a ball of fire rolling in slow motion from the far end toward him. There was only one thing to do. He slid the shield behind him then somehow maneuvered himself so that he was lying on his back. His shoulders screamed at him. The metal was too hot. He could smell his own clothes beginning to burn. He lashed out with both feet, smashing them into the grille.

Nothing.

The fireball was getting closer, floating in space, already halfway down the shaft. He kicked a second time and the grille swung open. Still on his back, Alex drew himself forward, using the balls of his feet. He hooked his heels over the edge of the wall and somehow spilled out into the open.

He was falling. How high up was he? Had he done all this just to break his neck when he hit the concrete below? But he was lucky. The ground rose up at the back of the studio and he hit soft grass, the slope of the hill. He rolled over several times, then came to a halt. There were flames above him, shooting out of the little square that had just provided him with an exit. Although the metal walls were keeping most of it contained, smoke was seeping through the cracks, rising into the air. Alex heard the glass shatter as the skylights broke and thicker smoke began to billow out. Coughing, wiping his eyes, he got to his feet.

The first fire engines arrived ten minutes later, followed by the police. A pilot coming in to land at Heathrow had seen what was happening and radioed the authorities. By the time the firemen bundled out and began uncoiling their hoses, the whole of Studio C was a raging inferno. Not a single piece of evidence of the filming would remain inside.

The firemen did what they could, but in the end it was easier just to let the building burn. Meanwhile, the police checked the rest of the complex, making sure there was no one else around. None of them had noticed a single schoolboy limping along the main road, looking for a taxi to take him home.

"ALEX RIDER IS AN AGENT working for the Special Operations Division of MI6. I know that's hard to believe, but I promise you it's true. He lives in Chelsea, just off the King's Road, with a housekeeper who acts as his guardian. Her name is Jack Starbright. He has no relatives that I know of. His uncle, a man named Ian Rider, was also a spy, but he was killed. That was when the kid got recruited."

Harry Bulman unwrapped a stick of chewing gum, rolled it carefully between his finger and thumb, and slid it into his mouth. He was sitting in a makeshift office that stood on the edge of a building site in London, not far from King's Cross. There was a cheap desk, three plastic chairs, and a fridge with a kettle and coffee mugs. The walls were covered with architect's drawings. Outside, work had finished for the day and it looked as if everyone had gone home. There were two men with him. He recognized one of them. Desmond McCain had been in the papers often enough for his face to be familiar. He was dressed entirely in black, one leg crossed over the other, his hands resting in his lap. Bulman could see his own reflection in the brightly polished leather of McCain's shoe. The other man had been introduced as Leonard Straik. He was older than

McCain, with silver hair rising over his forehead. He looked nervous.

Bulman was also neatly dressed. He had put on a suit and tie for this meeting, and his briefcase, with all his notes, was at his feet. But something had gone out of him since he had turned up at Alex's house. His confidence and swagger had been replaced by a dull sense of resentment. He was a man who had been injured, and it showed. He talked slowly, measuring his words, and the hatred in his voice was unmistakable. Even the way he chewed the gum had a mechanical quality. He could have been chewing raw flesh.

After he had been released by the police, Bulman had gone home. He had opened a bottle of whisky and drunk half of it, staring at the wall. He had been terrified. In a matter of hours, his entire life had been stripped away from him and—this was the worst part—it could happen again at any time. The man called Crawley had made it absolutely clear. They could just snap their fingers and he would vanish off the face of the earth, spirited away to some mental hospital where he would be left to rot. They were probably watching him even as he sat there. He wondered if his apartment was bugged. Almost certainly. For the first time in his life, he sensed how powerless he would be if the system—society, the government, whatever—turned against him. They had given him a warning and it had struck him in the heart.

Harry Bulman was many things, but he wasn't stupid.

He knew that there was going to be no newspaper story about Alex Rider, no front-page headlines, no publishing deal. Even if he dared try again, there wasn't an editor in town who would go anywhere near him. The Internet? Despite what he had told Alex, he knew there was no point in posting the story in cyberspace. It would do nothing for him, other than getting him killed.

But what rankled him most wasn't Crawley. It wasn't MI6. It was that he had been defeated by a fourteen-year-old boy. Mr. Alex Bloody Rider. The kid was probably laughing at him.

When the phone had rung a few weeks later and Bulman had heard the voice of one of his contacts, the ex-soldier who had helped him put the story together in the first place, the reporter was tempted to hang up. Fortunately, the man didn't mention Alex Rider. He simply said that something interesting had turned up and he wondered if Bulman would like to meet at the usual place.

The usual place was the Crown pub on Fleet Street. Bulman used his old army training to make sure he wasn't being followed, but he still insisted on walking to a second pub on the other side of town before he said a word. And even then, he chose a back room with the music turned up loud and nobody else in sight.

And that was when he heard that someone else was now asking questions about Alex Rider, and that they were prepared to pay good money for information. It was all being done very discreetly. The friend didn't even know who wanted to know—but the money involved had a lot of zeroes and there was a telephone number he could pass on if Bulman was interested.

Bulman took twenty-four hours to come to a decision. Every instinct told him that Alex Rider had an enemy and that they weren't doing this to buy him a surprise present for his birthday. There was a risk putting himself forward. He could be walking into a trap. But even as he mulled it over, two thoughts stayed in his mind. The first was the money, which he needed. The second was the possibility that he could do Alex serious harm.

In the end he made the call.

He had been passed from one anonymous voice to another. There had been three different people asking him questions before he had finally been told to come here, and he was fairly sure that his own background, everything about him, would have been checked. But the way that it was all being handled reassured him. Whoever these people were, they were afraid of being found out, just like him. And the more careful they were, the safer he would be.

Finally, the date for this meeting had been set. According to the signs on the street, this was the site of a new hostel for the homeless being built by the international charity First Aid. Even so, Bulman was astonished to find himself face-to-face with the Reverend Desmond McCain. Of course he remembered the story of the Parliament member who had gone bad, the building that had burned down and the false insurance claim. He'd heard that McCain had reformed. For the past five years he had been devoting himself to charity projects. Well, obviously he wasn't quite as saintly as people thought. It had already occurred to Bulman that there might be another story in all this, but of course, he kept the thought to himself.

There had been no pleasantries and no introductions. No offers of tea or coffee. After Bulman had sat down, McCain had opened the meeting as if he really were a vicar addressing his congregation.

"I appreciate your coming here today, Mr. Bulman. It is most generous of you. I understand you have information about a boy named Alex Rider. Please would you be good enough to tell me everything you know."

And Bulman had done just that. Once he had started, he found it all pouring out of him, everything he had learned during his research. It had been difficult to stop.

"They recruited a child!" McCain had listened in silence, but now he turned to Straik. "'For they are a wicked generation, children who have no faith.' We should have been warned by the book of Deuteronomy, chapter thirty-two."

"He's been incredibly successful," Bulman said, although it annoyed him to have to admit it. "I have notes on his last three assignments, and there may have been others."

"You have his address?"

"I've actually been to his house. I know where he goes to school. I've written it all down for you. I can tell you everything you want to know." Bulman didn't want to push his luck, but he couldn't resist asking a few questions of his own. It was too good an opportunity to miss. He began innocently. "What is this place? You're building a hostel?"

"It's a dreadful thing, the number of young homeless people there are in London," he said—and to Bulman's surprise, he actually had to brush away a tear. "Out on the streets with no food or shelter! First Aid was given this land by one of the city's most prominent developers, and I'm happy to say that we have raised enough cash to build somewhere they can be looked after with food and warm clothes."

"You do a lot of charity."

"I have made it my life's work."

It was the moment to ask what Bulman really wanted to know. "So why are you interested in Alex, Mr. McCain?" he continued casually. "I have to tell you, whatever you do with that kid is fine with me. But I would be interested to know—"

"I'm sure you would, Mr. Bulman." The round white eyes settled on him, and for a moment he shuddered. "You are a journalist, I understand."

"That's right."

"I would hate to think that you might be tempted to write about this meeting today."

"That depends how much you're going to pay me."

"We've already agreed on the price," Straik muttered. "Twenty thousand dollars, in cash."

Bulman licked his lips. He could taste the mint from the chewing gum. "I agreed to that price before I realized that Mr. McCain was involved," he said. "But I thought, under the circumstances, that we might renegotiate."

"I agree with you," McCain said. "That's exactly what I've decided to do."

He took out a gun and shot the journalist three times; once in the head, once in the throat, and once in the chest. Bulman's last gesture was one of surprise. His eyes widened even as his hands flew up and his body jerked in the chair. Then he slumped back. Blood trickled down from the three bullet holes, spreading across his shirt.

"Was that completely wise?" Straik asked.

"It was unavoidable," McCain replied. He slipped the gun back into his pocket. "He wasn't going to keep quiet. He was greedy. A week from now or a year from now, he would have made himself a nuisance."

"I'm sure. But are we safe?"

"I would doubt very much that he told anyone he was coming here. There's nothing to connect him with you or me. He was a journalist. Now he's a dead journalist. Who really cares about the difference?"

"And what about Alex Rider?" Straik got up and went over to the window. He made a signal and a moment later there was the sound of an engine starting up. "We can't go ahead, Desmond. Poison Dawn is finished."

"No." McCain hadn't raised his voice, but the single word was dark and thunderous. The two of them had known each other for years, but at that moment Straik wondered if he fully understood what went on inside the other man's head. There was a sort of madness there. He wouldn't listen to any argument. "We have been planning this too long," McCain said. "We've spent too much time and too much money. Everything is in place."

"But if MI6 knows what we're doing . . ."

"They can't know. It's impossible."

"They sent the boy. First to Scotland and then to Greenfields."

"I'm not so sure." McCain glanced at Bulman as if he'd forgotten that he'd just shot him and was expecting him to make some comment. "When Alex Rider came to Kilmore Castle, he was a guest of another journalist, Edward Pleasure. There was a teenage girl too. When he came to Greenfields, he was with a school party. It was quite different. I don't quite know what's going on here, but it may not be quite as cut and dried as it seems."

"Even so . . ."

McCain held a hand up for silence. "We are not canceling Poison Dawn," he said. "And certainly not yet. It seems to me that we have to meet with this Alex Rider and have a little talk."

"You think he'll just walk in here?"

"I have something else in mind." McCain stood up. "We are about to make an unimaginable amount of money," he said. "Two hundred million dollars. Maybe more. But that means we have to take risks. More than that, we have to make sure that we move one step ahead of the opposition. And that's exactly what we're going to do."

He reached forward and grabbed Harry Bulman by the front of his shirt. The journalist had never been a small man, and now he had become, in every sense, a dead weight. Even so, McCain pulled him effortlessly to his feet and dragged him over to the door. Still holding him, he stepped outside. A mechanical digger had started up while he was talking with Straik and it was waiting for him on the other side of the door with its metal arm raised. There was a driver sitting behind the window, smoking. McCain threw down the body and the driver revved up the engine and trundled forward. There was a crunch of machinery as the arm was lowered and the dead man was picked up. Then the digger reversed, carrying Bulman toward the muddy excavation that would soon be his grave.

McCain watched him go. "Well, it looks as if Mr. Bulman finally got what every journalist wants," he said.

Straik glanced at him.

"A scoop."

McCain had made his decision. He set off, avoiding the puddles so that he wouldn't get his shoes dirty as he made his way toward his car.

"So what exactly do you think is going on?"

Even as Alan Blunt posed the question, a waiter approached his table with the main course: steak and kidney pie for him, a tuna salad for Mrs. Jones. The two of them preferred not to talk as the plates were positioned and the wine was poured. They were having lunch at Blunt's club, the Mandarin, in Whitehall. And although all the waiters had received security clearance, the two of them preferred not to talk while there was any chance of being overheard. A great many members of the Mandarin were either politicians or intelligence chiefs, and it was said to be the most unfriendly place in London. Nobody trusted anybody. Members very rarely spoke to each other at all.

That morning, Blunt and his deputy had been given a full briefing by the chief science officer at MI6, a fiercely intelligent woman called Redwing. She had analyzed the liquid that had seeped into Alex Rider's jacket after the test tube he had stolen had smashed. Her report—she was always thorough—had begun with wool, polyester, and apple juice. The first two, of course, were the materials of the jacket itself. The third had perhaps been a spill during school lunch.

But the rest of the ingredients had been more interesting. According to Redwing, the test tube had contained something that she called _bitrites infestans_. This was essentially a biological soup that seemed to have been developed from a variety of different mushrooms. It was too soon to say which mushrooms exactly had been used, but preliminary tests were surprising. The liquid was completely harmless. It even had a nutritional value. Although it would taste disgusting, it could be consumed by humans or animals with no side effects. Redwing had eaten once or twice at the Mandarin, so she had concluded by saying, "They could serve it at your club, Mr. Blunt, and you might not even send it back. Why they're making so much of it is a little puzzling. A thousand gallons? Is that what your agent said? Well, I can't tell you what they're going to do with it, but I can assure you that the worst it would give you is indigestion. . . ."

Alex had told Jack what had happened at Greenfields, and she had in turn informed MI6. The appearance of Desmond McCain, the chase through the complex, the Poison Dome, the escape from the roof . . . they knew all of this. But, like Alex, they still had no clear idea what exactly was going on.

The waiter retreated and Mrs. Jones tried to answer Blunt's question. "I'm not at all surprised that McCain is up to no good," she said. "He has a criminal record, after all."

"Didn't he convert to Christianity?"

"So he claims—and to be fair, his charity, First Aid, has done some very good work. But after what Alex has told us . . ."

"Of course." This time, Blunt was going to believe everything Alex had said. After all, as much as it embarrassed him to admit it, the boy had been right in the past and MI6 had been proved wrong. "Is there any link between McCain and this man Leonard Straik?" he asked.

"None that we've been able to find."

"What do we know about McCain's movements in the past five years?"

"I'm having a report prepared. It'll be on your desk this afternoon."

Blunt broke the crust on his pie and examined the contents. The food at the Mandarin Club was not good, but the members liked it that way. It reminded them of school. "I have to say, I'm quite worried about all this," he said. "I always had a feeling that the department would have to turn its attention to GM food one day. There are people out there doing things that half the world doesn't even understand."

"We are what we eat." Mrs. Jones had lost her appetite. She put down her knife and fork.

"That was why I was interested in Mr. Straik. And if he's working hand-in-hand with McCain, that's certainly alarming. We need to know what the two of them are up to."

"What about Alex?" Mrs. Jones asked.

"As usual, Alex has done an extremely good job. We really are going to have to make sure we recruit him full-time after he finishes college. He's already shown himself to be more resourceful than a great many of our adult agents." Blunt stuck his fork into the pie and pulled out a piece of rather fatty meat covered in thick brown gravy. "But as far as this business is concerned, he's no longer involved. Maybe you should drop him a note, Mrs. Jones. We've treated him badly in the past, but perhaps we could send him a brief thank-you? And maybe we should enclose a bag of candy."

Alan Blunt began to eat his lunch. He was still puzzled about the mushroom soup, but his department would work on it. That was the important thing. In the meantime, Alex Rider was already out of his mind.

16

SPECIAL DELIVERY

ALEX COULD TELL JACK was in a bad mood. She had
made the breakfast as she did every morning—boiled eggs
for him, fruit and muesli for her. There had been a freshly
ironed jacket waiting for him in his room. But she had
stamped around the kitchen in silence, and when she
had loaded the dishwasher, she had slid the plates in as if
she had a personal grudge against them.

He knew what had upset her. "Jack," he said. "I'm
sorry."

"Are you?" She lifted up the toaster and wiped away
imaginary crumbs.

"I am. Really."

Jack turned around and let out a sigh. She could never
stay angry for long and they both knew it. "I just don't
understand you sometimes," she said. "We both agreed
that Greenfields wasn't your business. You did what you
were told and you were lucky to get out alive. So what on
earth did you think you were up to?"

"I don't know." Alex thought for a moment. "I just felt
angry after being told off by Mr. Bray. And I thought, if
I could only find out what McCain was doing . . ."

"What exactly *is* he doing?" Jack sat down at the table.

"You say there was a film set, an African village. But why? What's the point?"

"I've been thinking about that. McCain runs a charity. First Aid. They have appeals all over the world. Maybe that's his plan. He wants to raise money for something that hasn't happened."

"A fake charity appeal."

"Exactly. He shows a film of some village that doesn't exist. People send in money. He gets to keep it."

Jack thought about it for a moment, and then shook her head. "It wouldn't work, Alex. These days, everything is on TV or in the newspapers. People would find out soon enough if it wasn't true."

"Can you think of anything else?"

"No. But I think we should go back to MI6 and leave it to them this time." She glanced meaningfully at him. "Okay?"

Alex smiled. "That's what I'd already decided," he said. "Do you mind going back?"

"Of course not," Jack replied. "I'm beginning to wonder where this is all going to end. You go to a party in Scotland and you end up at the bottom of a lake. A school field trip almost lands you in the hospital. And now this!" She took one of Alex's toast slices and bit it in half. "The trouble is, you've got too much of the spy in you. It's all your uncle's fault. And your father's. And your grandfather's. For all we know, he was probably a spy too."

Alex looked at his watch. It was a quarter past eight. "I ought to be on my way to school," he said.

"Yes." Jack nodded. "Let's not get into any more trouble with Mr. Bray."

Alex ran up to his room, collected his books, and put on the spare jacket. He was about to leave when he noticed the black gel-ink pen that Smithers had given him resting on his desk. On impulse, he slipped it inside his pocket. He knew that Tom Harris would get a kick out of seeing it.

He hurried back downstairs and out through the hall, calling out a last "Good-bye!" as he went.

"Don't forget your scarf!" Jack called back.

She was too late. It was cold outside but dry, and there was no wind. Alex hoisted his knapsack over his shoulder and made his way along the backstreets that would lead him to the King's Road.

This part of Chelsea was full of elegant townhouses standing side by side with expensive cars parked outside. In a few months, the trees would blossom and the wisteria would tumble down the brickwork. Ian Rider had liked being here because it was quiet and private and yet still in the middle of the city. He'd always had a hatred of the suburbs. "A nice place for children and vets." Alex could still hear his slightly cryptic remark.

There was a FedEx van at the end of the street, badly parked across the corner, and two men dressed in overalls examining a clipboard that they held between them. They were obviously lost, and as Alex approached, one of them came over to him.

"Excuse me, mate," he said. "We've got a delivery for Packard Street. You wouldn't know where it is, would you?"

Alex shook his head. "There's no Packard Street around here."

"Are you sure? That's what it says here." The man held out the clipboard, inviting Alex to take a look.

It was the empty van that alerted him.

The doors of the van were open, and if they were making a delivery to an address in Chelsea, why was there nothing inside?

Alex jerked back, but it was already too late. The two men had maneuvered Alex between them so that they were perfectly placed, one of them in front of him, one of them behind. He heard the clipboard hit the sidewalk. It was just a prop. They didn't need it anymore.

One of the men grabbed him by the throat. Alex twisted around, trying to break free. At the same time, he saw something that sent a chill up his spine. The second deliveryman had produced a hypodermic syringe. They weren't here to kill him. They were here to take him. The van was for him.

Alex put everything he had been taught into action. He knew that it would be almost impossible even for two grown men to drag him into the van . . . unless they made contact with the needle. That was what he had to avoid. So he didn't waste any energy trying to break free of the neck lock. It was too strong anyway. Instead, he used the man's own strength against him, levering himself back, raising both legs off the ground and lashing out. The man with the syringe had been looking for somewhere to plant it, and with a smile of satisfaction, Alex saw the soles of his shoes smash into it, breaking it against the man's chest. If they'd been planning to knock him out, they could forget it. Now it would be twice as hard to make him disappear.

So far, no more than about ten seconds had passed since the attack had begun, and Alex knew that time was on his side. The streets of Chelsea might be quiet, but it was eight thirty in the morning and people would be on their way to work. He couldn't call for help. He was still being strangled. But someone would see what was happening. They had to.

Sure enough, a figure turned the corner and Alex was overjoyed to see the blue-and-silver uniform of a policeman. Alex felt the man behind him loosen his grip as the policeman ran forward, and he gratefully sucked in air.

"What's going on here?" the policeman demanded.

"They . . . ," Alex began, and stopped as he felt something stab him in the back, just above his waist. A second needle! The man who had been holding him must have taken it out of his pocket. But surely . . .

The policeman wasn't doing anything, and even as the

strength drained out of him and his legs buckled, Alex understood. The policeman wasn't any more real than the deliverymen had been. They were all in it together. Alex had been tricked and there was nothing he could do as whatever drug had been pumped into him coursed through his system. He saw the street tilt and then turn sideways and knew that the only reason he wasn't lying flat on the sidewalk was because the deliverymen had caught him and were carrying him into the van.

He was angry with himself. Only a few minutes ago, Jack had been accusing him. He could have died at Elm's Cross and she would have never known what had happened to him. He had promised her it would never happen again. And yet it already had. In a few hours, the school would report him missing. She would think he had betrayed her again. If he died, he would never be able to tell her the truth.

This was all his fault. He shouldn't have gone to the film studio. He should never have gotten involved with Desmond McCain in the first place. He wished he could call Jack and tell her. But it was too late. Barely conscious, already unable to struggle, he was bundled into the back of the van. He didn't even hear the doors slam shut.

Alex opened his eyes.

Someone was doing something to his head. A lock of light brown hair twisted, falling in front of his eyes. At the same time he heard the snip of scissors. He was sitting in a chair in what looked like a hotel room. They hadn't tied him up, but they didn't need to. He was still drugged and couldn't move. He'd been taken out of his school uniform and dressed in an ill-fitting tracksuit. They were cutting his hair. The two deliverymen were standing over him. There was a window covered by a blind and, at the very corner of his vision, an unmade bed. No carpet. His feet seemed to be resting on some sort of metal shelf, but he didn't have the strength to look down.

The two men were talking, their voices like distant echoes that he couldn't make out. One of them noticed he was awake and grabbed his head, squeezing his cheeks between thumb and fingers. More of his hair tumbled down into his lap. He could feel the cold air touching his scalp.

"He's back," the man said.

"Good."

A woman appeared from nowhere—she must have been standing behind him—and Alex recognized Myra Beckett, the supervisor of Greenfields. Bizarrely, she was dressed as a nurse, complete with a starched white hat. The diagonal fringe of dark hair looked more severe than ever, as if it had been sliced with a single sword stroke. Her eyes, behind the round, gold glasses, were slightly crazy. Alex's mouth was dry and he was feeling sick, but he managed to swear at her, a single venomous word.

"We'll do it now," she said.

They took hold of his arm and rolled up his sleeve. Alex winced as they gave him another injection, a long needle sliding into the flesh just above his wrist. But this time they didn't remove it. Beckett taped it in place and Alex saw there was a tube connecting it to a plastic box about the size of a cigarette packet, which they taped to his arm.

"This IV will continue to give you a timed injection of the drugs we are using over the next few hours," Beckett explained. "You will not be able to move or to speak. There will be other side effects. Try to breathe normally."

Alex felt a wave of a nausea. He was completely help-less. And whatever these people were planning, it wasn't going to end in this room.

The men rolled back his sleeve, hiding the plastic box. Alex knew that it was pumping its venom, drip by drip, into his bloodstream. He tried to jerk his arm but he had no strength at all. He swore at Beckett a second time, but his voice was no longer working and all that came out was an inarticulate grunt.

Beckett leaned over him and pressed a pair of glasses onto his face. Alex tried to shake them off, but they were tight-fitting, hooked over his ears. "You can take him out now," she said.

He was in a wheelchair! Alex didn't realize it until one of the men spun him around and pushed him out the door. They turned into a long corridor. "Wait a minute,"

Beckett said. She stepped forward and crouched beside Alex so that her face was close to his. "What do you think?" she asked, with a thin smile.

There was a full-length mirror at the end of the corridor. Alex stared at himself in shock and disbelief. His hair had been cut so hideously that he looked two years older than his true age and completely pitiful. The tracksuit was the color of a nasty bruise. It was one size too big and it was covered in stains, as if he was unable to feed himself. His skin was pale and unhealthy. The glasses he had been given were deliberately ugly; black plastic with thick lenses. They hung slightly crooked on his face.

The drugs had attacked his muscles, paralyzing him and somehow changing the shape of his entire body. His jaw hung open and his eyes were glazed. Alex knew exactly what they had done. They had turned him into a foul parady of a disabled person. They had made him look brain-damaged . . . but worse than that, they had removed his dignity too. In a way, it was a brilliant disguise. People might glance at him in the street, but they would be too embarrassed to look twice. Beckett was taking their prejudices and using them to her own advantage.

Beckett must have given a signal. Alex was taken down the corridor and around to an elevator. After that, the extra drugs must have kicked in, because his world seemed to skip and jump.

He had the foggy sensation of being on the street and wheeled into the van.

He was in the van.

He was at Heathrow Airport! Hadn't he been here just a few weeks ago with Sabina and her parents? The terminal lights hurt his eyes and he saw people staring briefly at him, then turning away, ashamed of themselves. He tried to call out for help, but the low, pathetic mumbling that came out of his lips only added to the impression that he was handicapped. They had no idea what was going on. They wouldn't even begin to guess that he was being kidnapped, spirited away in front of their eyes.

Passport control. They had provided Alex with fake documents, of course, but it seemed to him that the official didn't look too closely. A boy in a wheelchair accompanied by a nurse. The two men had stayed behind.

"Jonathan loves flying on big airplanes. Don't you, Jonathan!" Beckett was talking to him, addressing him as if he were six years old.

I'm not . . . Alex wanted to tell the passport officer his real name. But nothing resembling a word came out.

And now he was in some sort of lounge.

Now being wheeled down a corridor.

On the plane. A seat had been taken out to make room for the wheelchair. Other passengers were passing him, carrying their luggage. He saw them glance in his direction. Each time the reaction was the same. Puzzlement, the realization that something was wrong, then pity, and finally a sense of embarrassment. The drug was making his knee twitch. His hand, resting on the knee, was doing the same.

"Try to get some sleep, Jonathan," Beckett said. "It's a long flight."

Where were they taking him? And why? Did they really think they could get away with this, whisking him out of the country with a fake ID? Jack would already know he was missing. The school would have called her and she would have alerted MI6. They would be looking for him. Every airport would be watched.

Except . . .

What day was this? He could have been kept drugged for a few hours or a week. Or a month. Alex had no control over his body, but they had left his mind intact . . . hadn't they?

He was alert enough to realize it wasn't completely hopeless. Everything led back to Desmond McCain. MI6 knew what had happened at Greenfields. Jack would tell them about Elm's Cross. They would track down McCain and that would lead them to him.

They were in the air. How was that possible? Alex couldn't remember taking off. How long had they been flying? He tried to work out where they might be going. It had been light when they were on the runway, and it was still light now. If they had been in the air for a while, that would suggest, at the very least, that they weren't heading east. The different time zones would have brought the night in faster. South, then, or west? He couldn't turn his head—the muscles in his neck refused to work—but as they had filed past, he had noticed that many of the other passengers were black, dressed in clothes that were too brightly colored for the UK. They could be going home.

Africa.

Food was served—but not to him. The stewardess smiled at him sadly, as if understanding that he couldn't feed himself. Beckett brought out some baby food and tried to force it into his mouth with a spoon. Using all his remaining strength, Alex kept his mouth shut. He wasn't going to be humiliated by her any more than he had been already.

Hours passed, yet Alex hardly was aware of it.

They were on the ground.

The doors were open.

And then Alex was being wheeled through an arrivals hall, and a poster on the wall answered the question he had been asking himself for the past how-many hours. A brightly dressed black woman with a huge smile, holding a basket of fruit. And a caption.

SMILE! YOU'RE IN KENYA.

Kenya! Vaguely, Alex remembered something that Edward Pleasure had told him. *"He's the part owner of a safari camp somewhere in Kenya."* The words might have been spoken a century ago and on a different planet. Had he really once been in Kilmore Castle, dancing with Sabina? What would she say if she could see him now?

The plastic box was still resting against his arm, and he actually felt the whole thing vibrate as the timing mechanism clicked in, sending another spurt of the liquid into his veins. He felt unconsciousness returning and didn't even try to fight it. He was on his own, thousands of miles from home. He had fallen into the hands of a ruthless enemy and nobody knew where he was. Ahead of him, a set of automatic doors swung open. Alex was wheeled into the dark.

17

A SHORT FLIGHT TO NOWHERE

MOVEMENT RETURNED, one twitch at a time.

Alex had no idea how long he had been here, but he guessed that it couldn't have been much more than twenty-four hours. He had watched the sun rise, not out of the window but through the cloth that made up the wall. He was lying on his back on a comfortable bed in what seemed to be a cross between a luxury hotel room and a large tent. The floor was made of polished wood. There was an expensive-looking wardrobe, a carved wooden table, and two chairs. A fan hung from the ceiling above his head, turning continuously. He was completely enclosed by a mosquito net that rippled in the breeze. But the walls were made of canvas. The windows consisted of two flaps, fastened from the outside.

Where exactly was he? From the sounds that surrounded him—the chatter of monkeys, the occasional bellow of an elephant, the constant whoops and screams of exotic birds—it seemed that he was in the bush, somewhere in the middle of Kenya.

That tied in with his memories of the journey here, even if they were still confused. There had been the poster he had seen. SMILE! YOU'RE IN KENYA. As if he had felt remotely like smiling! They had gone through passport control, and after that the drug must have kicked in again. They had driven across a city, but he had barely seen any of it. It had been late evening. Nairobi? And then there had been a second, smaller airport and another plane, this one a four-seater with propellers. They had bundled him in, leaving the wheelchair behind. And then . . .

He had woken up here, on his own. It was dark . . . evening or night. But they had left two little battery lights on—battery, not electric. At least he could see, even if he couldn't yet move. The plastic box had been removed from his arm and a dirty bandage stuck over the puncture where the needle had gone in. That had been the first thing he had noticed—and he'd been grateful for it. With the drug no longer pumping into his system, he had begun to recover. He could lift his hand. He could turn his head from side to side, taking in the sweep of the room. Eventually he had stood up and tottered on unsteady legs into the bathroom, behind the bed, separated by a screen. He had thrown up and that made him feel better. Then he had taken a cold shower, the water washing away some of the horror of the past day.

He had still been too weak to make his way outside. He had decided he would wait for the sun. Once again he had fallen asleep, but this time more normally.

And now it was morning. Alex rolled off the bed and stood up. He had slept in his shorts. The tracksuit that they had dressed him in was lying on the floor, a crumpled heap. He noticed that his school uniform had been brought over from England. It seemed somehow strange to see it, but of course he had been wearing it when he was kidnapped. He went over to it, feeling in the inside pocket of his jacket.

Yes. It was there. He had been carrying the black gel-ink pen that Smithers had given him and nobody had thought to remove it. It wasn't as powerful as the device that had brought down the factory chimney, but it might still be useful. At the very least, it gave Alex hope. McCain had made his first mistake.

He was now moving completely normally. They had used a powerful drug on him, but it had left his system completely. Just to be sure, he forced himself to do twenty push-ups, then had another shower. He got dressed in his own pants and shirt, leaving off the jacket. Although it was early morning, it was already warm. He could feel the sun beating through the walls of the tent and the fan was having to fight against the sluggish air. He slipped the gel-ink pen into his pants pocket. From now on, he would make sure it never left him.

The front of the tent was sealed up. There was a large flap with a zipper running around the side. Well, if this was his prison, it was a very flimsy one. Alex went over and unzipped it. At once he saw the green of the jungle, confirming what he had guessed. He was in the bush. But the way was blocked by a guard, a black man dressed in jeans and grimy shirt, a rifle strapped over his shoulder. Alex realized that he must have been there all night.

The guard turned around and scowled. "You stay inside." That seemed to be the limit of his English.

"What time do you serve breakfast?" Alex asked. He
had already decided. He wasn't going to let these people
think he was scared.

"Inside." The guard brought the rifle around.

Alex raised his hands and retreated. There was no
point starting a fight. Not yet.

Breakfast came half an hour later: tea, canned orange
juice, and two slices of toast, carried in by a second guard.
Alex wolfed it down. It had been a long time since he had
last eaten and his stomach couldn't have been more
empty. There was a bottle of water in the tent, and he
drank that too. He had no idea what was going to happen
to him. He would take any food or water he could get.

Why had they brought him here? Alex almost admired
McCain. The man must have nerves of steel, kidnapping
him in broad daylight, smuggling him out of England
through one of the world's busiest airports. But what was
the point? McCain must have identified him as the intruder at Greenfields. He would have remembered their
meeting at the castle in Scotland. Maybe he had decided
to take revenge. After all, he had already tried to kill Alex
once.

And yet, somehow, Alex didn't believe it. Whatever
McCain was planning, the stakes were too high. This
wasn't personal. This was business. McCain needed Alex
for a reason.

And now Alex was completely in his power. It was probably best not to think too much about what might lie ahead.

Instead, Alex thought about Jack. What would she be doing now? And what about MI6? Once they'd realized he was gone, they'd have spared no effort. Every intelligence agency in the world would be looking for him. Surely someone would remember a fourteen-year-old boy being taken through passport control, even if he was in a wheelchair. The trail would lead to Kenya and they must know that McCain had a base here.

Except that McCain would have covered his tracks. He knew exactly what he was doing. Alex was going to have to rely on his own resources to get himself out of this mess. He would just have to wait for an opportunity and take it when it came.

The tent flap suddenly opened and Myra Beckett stepped inside. She had changed once again, wearing a safari outfit—a loose shirt and long pants in different shades of brown. The clothes made her look more masculine than ever. She was carrying what looked like a leather cloth.

She wasn't alone. A guard had come with her, but not the one he had seen earlier. This one had on dirty jeans and a black sleeveless T-shirt. Alex noticed the knotted muscles of his arms and the machete hanging from his belt. He had narrow, mean eyes. He was looking at Alex as if the two of them had been lifelong enemies.

"I heard you were up," Beckett said. "How are you feeling?"

Alex wasn't sure what to say. Just seeing her made him feel sick again. "Never better," he muttered.

"The serum that we injected you with was my own invention, and I'm very pleased with the way it worked. It was derived from the water hemlock that we cultivate at Greenfields. The effect is not dissimilar to a snake bite, only far less permanent. Can I trust you to behave yourself? If not, we can always inject you with some more."

"What do you want with me?" Alex asked.

"You'll find out in good time. For the moment, let me introduce you to Njenga." She gestured at the guard. "He's a Kikuyu tribesman, as are all the guards here, and they will do anything we tell them. There are no other jobs, you see. You might like to know that the Kikuyus once fought against the British with a ferocity that made them a source of great terror. One of their tricks was to impale their victims with a spear up their backside, then leave them to die slowly on the side of a hill. I mention this only as a warning not to annoy them."

"Nice to meet you, Njenga," Alex said.

Njenga's scowl deepened.

"Where's McCain?" Alex demanded.

"The Reverend McCain won't be here until later today. It is very likely that your friends in MI6 are watching him, so he had to take a more roundabout route. But he's hoping to have dinner with you this evening. In the mean-time, I thought you might like to come with me."

"Where are we going?"

"Oh—nowhere in particular." Beckett smiled, her lips barely moving. "A short flight to nowhere." She lifted the piece of leather and Alex saw that it was a flying cap. "You don't mind another plane?"

"Do I have any choice?"

"Not really. This way . . ."

She led him out of the tent.

He was in a safari camp. The tent where he had spent the night was one of a dozen, each one surrounded by a wooden veranda and built into the embrace of a wide river that swept around them. Alex looked at the silver water rippling past, with a tangled wall of green rising in a steep bank on the other side. This really was a beautiful spot. He heard chattering above him and looked up to see a family of gray monkeys leaping from the branches of a juniper tree, using their hands and tails. Some of the mothers had tiny babies clinging to their chests.

"The monkeys are a nuisance," Beckett muttered. She snapped out an order in another language and one of the guards standing beside the path lifted his rifle and fired. A dead monkey plunged out of the tree and crashed to the ground. The others scattered. "The guards are equally accurate with guns and spears," she went on. "They keep the population down."

"What is this place?" Alex asked. He was careful not

to react to what he had just seen. He knew it had been done for his benefit.

"This is the Simba River Camp, a business that belongs to Mr. McCain. I take it you know which country you're in?"

"Kenya."

"That's right." Another hint of a smile. It was as if she had forgotten how to do the real thing. "We're on the edge of the Rift Valley. Simba River Camp was once a world-class safari lodge with visitors from America, Europe, and Japan. Brad Pitt once stayed here. Unfortunately, it became a victim of the global recession. The visitors stopped coming and the business went bust."

Looking around, Alex could see it for himself. His was the only tent that had been occupied. The others were empty and falling into disrepair. The path that they were following had been neglected, with weeds and wild grass breaking through. They passed a swimming pool, but it had no water and the cement was cracked. All around, the vegetation was tumbling over itself, out of control. If the camp was left to itself for much longer, it would be swallowed up, disappearing into the bush, and nobody would know that it had ever existed.

They came to a beaten-up Land Rover with dirty windows and wires tumbling out of the dashboard. Njenga climbed into the driving seat with Beckett next to him. Alex went in the back. He was moving completely normally now and he was glad of it. Even on this short journey, he might get a chance to break away.

"It's seventy miles to the next camp, and I doubt that you'd ever find it," Beckett said. She must have seen what he was thinking. "So please don't entertain any foolish ideas. The Kikuyus are also excellent trackers. They would be able to follow your trail in the darkness, even in the pouring rain. I'm afraid Njenga would enjoy hacking you to pieces. That's the sort of person he is. If I were you, I wouldn't give him the opportunity."

They rumbled along a dirt track for a couple of minutes, passing through a wire fence with a rusting gateway and leaving the camp behind them. Almost at once they came to an airstrip—a dusty orange runway that had somehow been cut through the long grass. A dilapidated wooden hut stood to one side, with a wind sock hanging limply from a pole. This must have been where Alex landed when he was brought to Simba River Camp, although he had no memory of it.

There was a plane parked on the grass next to a line of about thirty oil drums. Alex had never seen anything quite like it. It was like an oversized toy with two seats, one behind the other, three wheels, and a single propeller at the front. It had no cabin or cockpit. A slanting window would protect the pilot, but any passenger would be sitting outside, feeling the full force of the air currents. A single wing, on struts, stretched out from left to right, and Alex saw a series of rubber tubes running all the way to the tips. These were connected to two plastic drums lashed to the side of the plane just behind the passenger seat.

It was a crop duster, but a very old one. It should have been in a museum. Alex wondered if it could really fly.

"This is the Piper J-3 Cub," Beckett told him. She had taken off her glasses and was putting on the flying cap, fastening it under her chin. She was also wearing a leather jacket, which she had brought from the Land Rover. Alex noticed that she wasn't offering him anything to keep him warm. "Twenty-two feet long. Sixty-five horsepower engine. They used them for training during the war. Please, get in."

Njenga stood near the car. Alex was feeling increasingly uneasy, but he did as he was told. There was a metal lever between the seats connected to a control box, with two sets of wires running toward the wings. When he sat down, it was right in front of him. There was almost no room for his feet. Myra Beckett got into the front and made a few checks. She produced a pair of goggles and slipped them over her eyes. Then she flicked a switch and the propeller began to turn.

It took a full minute to blur and then come up to speed. Alex could feel the high-pitched buzz of the engine and knew that from this point on there would be no more conversation. That suited him. He had nothing to say to the woman.

Njenga moved forward and pulled the chocks from under the wheels. Alex clicked on his seat belt. The Piper rolled forward.

They taxied to the end of the runway, bumping up and down on the uneven surface. At least Beckett seemed to be an experienced pilot. She spun the plane around, then raced back again, the engine straining like an overworked lawnmower. Alex wondered if they had enough speed to get into the air, but after one last bump they were up, with the wind rushing past and the ground sweeping away below.

Alex looked back. He could see Njenga standing on his own beside the car and behind him, separated by a line of brush, Simba River Camp, with the water now a silver ribbon twisting around it. The far bank rose steeply, then sloped down again, opening onto a great savannah that fanned out to the horizon. He saw a herd of antelope, startled by the sound of the engine, racing across the plain as if it were a bed of hot coals, their feet barely touching the grass. In any other circumstances, it would have been a beautiful sight. The flat African landscape, with its burned-out yellows and browns, had a true majesty. The sun was shining. The sky was a brilliant blue. Just for a moment, he was able to forget the trouble he was in.

Beckett had taken the Piper to a height of perhaps one thousand feet, at the same time tilting away from the river, heading north. Alex could see the compass on the control panel in front of her. He studied the land-scape, holding up a hand to protect his eyes from the slice of the wind. They were flying over a sprawl of green, but there were hills ahead of them, gray and rocky, rising up to the east and west, then closing together to form an upside-down V. In the far distance, he made out what looked like a man-made wall, but it would have to be a very big one if he could see it from here. Over to one side, he noticed a track winding up into the hills, and an electricity pylon. Had Beckett been lying when she said there was no one around for seventy miles? There seemed to be signs of civilization much closer than that.

They flew over a wheat field. The entire valley between the hills had been planted with the crop, which looked almost ready to harvest. Alex could see thousands of golden blades bending in the breeze. He wondered how it could possibly grow out here in this heat, and a moment later he got his answer. The wall he had seen was a dam built into the neck of the valley. The plane flew over it and suddenly they were above water, a huge lake stretching out to the mountain range on the far shore. The water must somehow feed into the river. It would also be used to feed the crops.

Beckett pulled on the joystick and the Piper Cub performed a tight circle, the whole continent tipping on its side. Alex felt his ears pop and he was glad he was belted in. For a few seconds he had almost been upside down, and in a plane like this it would be easy enough to tumble out. They were flying back exactly the same way they had come. For a second time, they passed over the lip of the dam. The wheat field lay ahead of them, less than half a mile away.

For the first time, Beckett turned around and called out to him. Her eyes, behind the goggles, looked enormous. "When I tell you, I want you to pull the lever." Alex could barely hear what she was saying. She repeated herself, stressing each word. He nodded.

Pull the lever? What was this all about? Alex wondered if he might be about to eject himself, if this hadn't all been some cruel and horrible trick. But he had no choice but to play along, and anyway, if he refused, it would be easy enough for her to reach back and do it herself.

They swept in low over the wheat and Beckett signaled with one hand. Alex pulled the lever. At once, there was a gurgle. Alex felt the rubber pipes under his feet swell as liquid rushed through them, and seconds later a spray began to burst out from beneath the wings, spreading out in the air and falling evenly onto the crop. He wondered why he was even remotely surprised. The plane was a crop duster and that was what they were doing. Dusting the crops.

They flew over the field four times before the liquid ran out. Alex could only sit there, watching the artificial rain, completely mystified. At last, Beckett turned around again. "Now we can go back!" she shouted.

It took them just a few minutes to return to the runway.

Njenga was still waiting for them, leaning against the Land Rover in the heat of the sun. Alex saw his head turn slowly as they approached. He had been smoking a cigarette. He dropped it and ground it out under his foot.

They landed. The plane rattled back to the grass and came to a standstill. Myra Beckett flicked off the engine, then took off her goggles and helmet and climbed down. Alex followed her. He was glad to have his feet back on the ground. He stood there, waiting for her to explain herself.

"Did you enjoy that?" she asked.

"What was it all about?" Alex demanded. Suddenly he was angry. "Why don't you stop playing games with me? I don't know what you're doing, but you've got no reason to keep me here. I want to see McCain. And I want to go home."

"Desmond will be here this evening and he will explain everything to you, including the purpose of our little flight today. But I'm afraid I have to tell you there's no chance of your going home."

"Why not?"

"Because we're going to kill you, you silly boy. Surely you must have realized that. But first we're going to hurt you. You see, there are things we need to know. I'm afraid you do have a very unpleasant time ahead of you. If I were you, I'd get as much rest as you can."

She untangled her eyeglasses and put them back on. Then, with a brief laugh, she walked back to the waiting car.

18

WOLF MOON

ALEX HEARD DESMOND MCCAIN arrive later that afternoon. He came in a plane that was larger than the Piper, with a deeper, more solid-sounding engine. Alex didn't actually see it—he hadn't been allowed out of his tent since the flight with Myra Beckett—but he heard it land.

He had been on his own all afternoon. Only once, a Kikuyu guard had come in carrying a meager lunch on a tray: fruit, bread, and water. He refused to think about what the Beckett woman had told him. He had been threatened before and he knew that part of her plan was to weaken him psychologically, to sap his resolve.

Instead, he used the time to collect his thoughts. He presumed the crop duster had been carrying the liquid that had been developed at Greenfields. But what was the point of spraying a single field in Kenya, and why had Beckett made such a big deal of it? Alex tried to connect the dots. An international charity, a dead African village mocked up in a film studio, his own kidnapping, the wheat field. The more he thought about it, the more unsettled he became, and in the end he pushed it out of his mind and dozed off. He would let McCain explain himself when the time came.

But the sun had set and darkness fallen before Beckett returned to the tent.

"The Reverend McCain would like you to join him for dinner," she announced.

"That's very kind of him." Alex swung himself off the bed. "I hope it's better than the lunch."

Once again, they left the tent.

Simba River Camp looked better at night than it had in the day. There was a full moon and the pale light softened everything and made the river sparkle. There were a few lights burning in the camp, but they were hardly needed when the sky was so full of stars. The air smelled of perfume. Cicadas were already at work, grinding away in the shadows.

Alex followed the woman to what was clearly the center of the camp, a circular clearing with the river on one side and acacia trees on all the others, the wide branches stretching out as if to form a protective screen. Two wooden buildings stood opposite each other. One was a welcome center and administrative office. The other combined a bar, lounge, and restaurant. It had a thatched roof that was much too big for it, almost thrown over it like pastry on a pie. There were no windows or doors . . . in fact, no walls. Alex could imagine the guests meeting here for iced gin and tonics after their long day spotting wild game . . . except the tables were piled up in the corner and the bar was closed.

He noticed a satellite dish mounted on the roof of the

first building and realized there must be a radio somewhere inside. Might it be possible to send out a message? He doubted it. There were yet more guards patrolling the area—there must have been a dozen of them altogether—these ones armed with spears, which they carried as if they'd had them from the day they were born. Guns and spears. It seemed a strange combination in the twenty-first century, but Alex guessed that in the hands of the Kikuyu tribesmen, one would be just as dangerous as the other.

"Over here, Alex."

There was a raised platform close to the river with a bonfire burning low to one side. The embers were glowing bright red and the smell of charcoal crept into the air. A table and chairs had been laid out on the platform with two white china plates, two crystal wine glasses, but only one set of silver knives and forks.

"You're not joining us?" Alex asked.

Beckett added a couple of branches to the fire. "Mr. McCain has asked to eat with you alone."

"Well, you can do the washing up."

"Still making jokes? We'll see if you find this all so amusing tomorrow."

She spun around and left him. It occurred to Alex that she might be annoyed that she hadn't been invited. He still hadn't worked out what her part in all this might be. She was a scientist, after all. What had persuaded her to throw in her lot with Desmond McCain?

Alex sat down. A bottle of French wine, already opened, stood next to a jug of water. He helped himself to the water. His eye fell on one of the knives. It looked sharp, with a serrated edge. Would anyone notice if it was missing? He glanced around, then slid it off the table and into the waistband of his pants. He felt the blade against his skin, strangely comforting. He would use his bread knife when it was time to eat.

He glanced over at the river, wondering what animals might gather there in the night. There was no fence, no barrier between them and the camp. He had seen monkeys and antelope. Might there be lions too? Despite everything, he had to admit that this was a memorable place, with the river sweeping around, the fire blazing, the African bush with all its secrets. He looked up at the night sky, packed with so many stars that even in the vastness of the universe they seemed to be fighting for space. And there, right in the middle of them, huge and pale . . .

"They call it the Wolf Moon."

The voice came out of the shadows. Desmond McCain had appeared from nowhere, walking up to the table in no particular hurry. Alex wondered how long he had been standing there, watching him. McCain was dressed in a gray silk suit, black polished shoes, and a black T-shirt. He was carrying a laptop computer that seemed to weigh nothing in his hand. His face gave nothing away. He sat at the table and laid the computer down. Then he unfolded his napkin and looked at Alex as if noticing him for the first time.

"American Indians call it that," he went on. "But I have heard the name used here too. It is also known as the Hunger Moon, which is strangely appropriate. I have been waiting for it. The moon is important to my plans."

"There's a name for people with an interest in the moon," Alex said. "They're called lunatics."

McCain laughed briefly but without making any sound. "The late Harold Bulman told me a great deal about you," he said. "I was impressed by what I heard, but I have to say I am even more impressed now. Any other boy who had been through what you have been through would be a sniveling wreck. Far away from home. Transported in a manner that could not have been agreeable. And you're still brave enough to trade insults with me. At first I was disinclined to believe that the British intelligence services would have recruited a fourteen-year-old child. But I'm already beginning to see why they chose you."

"Bulman is dead?" Alex wasn't sure what else to say.

"Yes. He told me what I wanted to know and then I killed him. I enjoyed doing so. If you have learned anything about me, Alex, it won't surprise you that I have a strong dislike of journalists." McCain picked up the bottle. "Will you have some wine?"

"I'll stick to water."

"I'm glad to hear it. You're too young to drink." Mc-Cain poured himself a glass of the wine. Alex saw the swirl of red against the side of the glass. "Did you have a good day?" he asked. "Did Myra look after you?"

"She took me for a ride in the crop duster."

"Do you know that she taught herself to fly? She never had a single lesson. She merely had a complete understanding of the laws of physics and worked it all out. She is a remarkable woman. When this is over, she and I plan to get married."

"You must let me know what to buy you."

"I doubt that you'll be invited, Alex." McCain still hadn't drunk any of the wine. He was gazing into the glass as if he could see his future in it. "The meal will be brought over very shortly. Have you ever eaten ostrich?"

"They don't serve it in the school cafeteria . . . at least not that I'm aware of."

"The meat can be quite tough, and you will need a sharp knife to cut it. I notice that your knife is missing. Can I suggest you return it to the table?"

Alex hesitated. But there was no point denying it. He took out the knife and placed it in front of him.

"What were you going to do with it?" McCain asked.

"I just thought it might come in useful."

"Were you planning to attack me?"

"No. But that's a good idea."

"I don't think so." He raised a hand and almost at once something whipped past Alex's head and buried itself in a tree. It was a spear. Alex saw it quivering in the trunk. He hadn't even seen who'd thrown it. "You can see that it would be a great mistake to try anything unwise," McCain continued, as if nothing had happened. "I hope I have made myself clear."

"I think I get the point," Alex said.

"Excellent."

"Are you going to tell me why I'm here?"

"All in good time." McCain turned his head and for a moment the flames were reflected in his silver crucifix. It was as if there were a fire burning on the side of his face. "I am sure you will have worked out that I risked everything bringing you here. Your disappearance has already been reported on the English news and the police forces of the world are united in the search for you. But I am also playing for an enormous prize, Alex. It is a little bit like that poker game that first brought us together. All gamblers know that the greater the reward, the greater the risks."

"I suppose you want to take over the world," Alex said.

"Nothing as tiresome as that. World domination has never seemed particularly attractive to me." He glanced up. "But it seems that dinner is about to be served. We can talk further as we eat."

Two guards had appeared, carrying the dinner. They

laid the food down on the table and disappeared. Alex had been served a barbecued meat, sweet potatoes, and beans. McCain had a bowl of brown sludge.

"We have the same food," McCain explained. "Unfortunately, I am no longer able to chew." He took a small silver straw out of his top pocket. "My meal has been liquified."

"Your boxing injury," Alex said.

"It wasn't so much the injury as the operation that I underwent afterward. My manager decided to send me to a plastic surgeon in Las Vegas. I should have known it would be a botch job. His clinic was above a casino. I take it you are familiar with my past?"

"You were knocked out by someone called Buddy Sangster when you were eighteen."

"It happened at Madison Square Garden in New York, two minutes into the middleweight championship. Sangster destroyed not only my hopes of becoming world champion, but my career. Then the surgeon made it difficult for me to speak and impossible to eat. Since then, I have only taken liquids, and every time I sit down for a meal, I remember him. But I had my revenge."

Alex remembered what Edward Pleasure had told him. A year later, Buddy Sangster had fallen under a train. "You killed him," he said.

"Actually, I paid to have him killed. An international assassin known as the Gentleman did the job for me. He also took care of the plastic surgeon. It was very expensive and, in truth, I would have preferred to have done it myself. But it was too dangerous. As you will learn, Alex, I am a man who takes infinite care."

Alex wasn't hungry, but he forced himself to eat the food. He would need all his energy for what was to come. He tried a mouthful of the ostrich. It was surprisingly good, a bit like beef but with a gamier flavor. He would just have to do his best not to picture the animal while he ate. Meanwhile, McCain had leaned down and was busily sucking. His own brown porridge entered his mouth with a brief slurping sound.

"I am going to tell you a little about myself," McCain went on. "This is the third time you and I have encountered each other, Alex. We are enemies now and tomorrow, I'm afraid, we are going to have no time for idle chat. But I am a civilized man. You are a child. Tonight, under the Wolf Moon, we can behave as if we are friends. And I welcome the opportunity to tell my story. I've often been quite tempted to write a book."

"You could have the launch party back in jail."

"I would certainly be arrested if I were to make public what I'm about to tell you—but there is no chance of that happening."

McCain put down his straw and dabbed at his lips with his napkin. His mouth was slanting the wrong way, as if it had been further dislodged by the food.

"I began my life with nothing," he said. "You have to remember that. I had no parents, no family, no history, no friends, no anything. The people who fostered me in east London were kind enough in their own way. But did they care who or what I was? I was just one of many orphans that they took in. They were do-gooders. This was my first lesson in life. Do-gooders need victims. They need suffering. Otherwise they cannot do good.

"I grew up in poverty. I went to a tough school, and from the very first day, the other children were very cruel to me. I can assure you that it is not a good start in life to be named after a bag of frozen food. I was bullied unmercifully. My color, of course, was against me. If you had ever been a victim of racism, Alex, you would know that it goes to the very heart of who you are. It destroys you.

"I soon came to understand that only one thing would keep me safe and separate me from the herd. Only one thing would make a difference. Money! If I was rich, people wouldn't care where I came from. They wouldn't tease or torment me. They would respect me. That is the way modern life works, Alex. Look at self-satisfied pop singers or greasy, semi-literate athletes. People worship them. Why?"

"Because they're talented."

"Because they have money!" McCain almost shouted the words. His voice echoed across the clearing and a couple of the guards turned toward him, checking that everything was all right. "Money is the god of the twenty-first century," he continued, more quietly. "It divides us and defines us. But it is no longer enough to have enough.

You have to have more than enough. Look at the bankers with their salaries and their pensions and their bonuses and their extras. Why have one house when you can have ten? Why wait in line when you can have your own private jet? From the age of about thirteen, I realized that was what I wanted. And very soon, that is what I shall have."

He had forgotten his food. He still hadn't tasted the wine, but he held it in front of him, admiring the deep color, balancing the glass in the palm of his hand as if afraid of smashing it. Once again, Alex was aware of the power of the man. He could picture the huge muscles writhing underneath the silk suit.

"I had little education," McCain went on. "The other children in my class saw to that. I had no prospects. I was, however, strong and fast on my feet. I became a boxer, which has seen more than one working-class boy rise to riches and success. And for a time, it looked as if the same might happen to me. I was known as a rising star. I trained in a gym in Limehouse and I threw myself into it. Sometimes I would go there for ten hours a day. This was in many respects the happiest time of my life. I loved the feel of my fist smashing into an opponent's face. I loved the sight of blood. And the feeling of victory! Once I knocked a man out. I thought for a moment I had killed him. It was a truly delicious sensation.

"But, as I have explained to you, my dream came to an end. My manager dropped me. The press, which had once fawned over me, forgot me. I returned to London with no money and no job. I had to move back in with my foster parents, but they didn't really want me. I was no longer a cute little boy that they could feel good about helping. I was a man. There was no room for me in their life.

"My foster father managed to get me a job with a real estate developer, and that was how I found myself in the lucrative world of property. It was an area in which I had almost immediate success. At that time, it was easy to make a fast profit and I began to do well. People noticed me. You could not be a successful black person in Britain without standing out, and as I moved up the ladder, more and more businessmen wanted to be seen with me, to pretend that they were my friends. People liked inviting me to dinner parties. They thought of me as a bit of a character—particularly after my brief fame in the boxing ring.

"I made a large donation to the Conservative party, and as a result I was asked if I would like to become a prospective member of Parliament. I accepted and I was duly voted in, even though the seat had been Labour for as long as anyone could remember. Success followed success, Alex. I became a junior minister in the department of sport. I would often find myself on the terrace outside the House of Commons, sipping champagne with the prime minister. The entire cabinet came to my Christmas parties, which became famous for their fine vintage wine and chicken pies. I gave talks all over the country. And, thanks to my property empire, I was getting richer than ever. I still remember buying my first Rolls-Royce. At the time, I couldn't even drive—but what did I care? The next day I went out and hired a chauffeur. By the time I was thirty, I had a dozen people working for me."

He spread his hands. "And then it all went wrong again."

"You were sent to prison for fraud." Alex remembered what Sabina's father had said.

"Yes. Isn't it amazing how quickly people desert you? Without a moment's hesitation, my so-called friends turned their backs on me. I was thrown out of Parliament. All my wealth was taken from me. Journalists in the main newspapers jeered and mocked me in a way that was every bit as bad as the boys I had once known at school. In prison, I was beaten up so often that the hospital reserved a bed for me. Other men would have chosen to end it all, Alex—and there were times when even I considered dashing my head against a concrete wall. But I didn't—because already I was planning my comeback. I knew that I could use my disgrace as just one more step on the journey I had been born to make."

"You didn't convert to Christianity," Alex said. "You just pretended."

McCain laughed. "Of course! I read the Bible. I spent hours talking to the prison chaplain, a pompous fool who couldn't see farther than the end of his own dog collar. I took a course on the Internet and got myself ordained. The Reverend Desmond McCain! It was all lies . . . but it was necessary. Because I had worked out what I was going to do next. I was going to be rich again. Fifty times richer than I had ever been before."

Alex had left most of his food. One of the guards came over and took the plates away, removing McCain's unfinished food. Another brought over a basket of fruit. In the brief silence, Alex listened to the sounds of the night: the soft murmur of the river as it flowed past, the endless whisper of the undergrowth, the occasional cry of some animal far away. He was sitting in the open air, in Africa! And yet he couldn't enjoy his surroundings. He was sitting at a table with a madman. He knew it all too well. McCain might have suffered hardships in his life, but what had happened to him had nothing to do with his background or his color; they were convenient excuses now. He had been a psychopath from the start.

"Charity," McCain said. "A very wise man once defined charity in the following way. He said it was poor people in rich countries giving money to rich people in poor countries." He smiled at the thought. "Well, I have been thinking a lot about charity, Alex—and in particular how to use it for my own ends." For a moment he looked up at the night sky, his eyes fixed on the full moon. "And in less than twenty-four hours, my moment will come. The seeds have already been sown . . . and I mean that quite literally."

"I know what you're doing," Alex interrupted. "You're faking some sort of disaster. You're going to steal the money for yourself."

"Oh—no, no, no," McCain replied. He lowered his head and gazed at Alex. "The disaster is going to be quite real. It's going to happen here in Kenya and very soon. Thousands of people are going to die, I'm afraid. Men, women, and children. And let me tell you something rather disturbing. I really want you to know this.

"I can see the way you're looking at me, Alex. The contempt in your eyes. I'm used to it. I've had it all my life. But when the dying begins—and it will be very soon—just remember. It wasn't me who started it."

He paused. And somehow Alex knew what he was going to say next.

"It was you."

19

ALL FOR CHARITY

THE GUARDS HAD SERVED COFFEE and McCain had lit a cigarette. Watching the gray smoke trickle out of the corner of his mouth, Alex was reminded of a gangster in an old black-and-white film. As far as he was concerned, the habit couldn't kill McCain quickly enough.

McCain stirred his coffee with a second silver straw. The night had become very still, as if even the animals out in the bush had decided to listen in. The breeze had dropped and the air was heavy and warm.

"There are two ways to become rich," McCain began again. "You can persuade one person to give you a lot of money—but that means finding someone who is wealthy and stupid enough in the first place, and it may involve criminal violence. Or you can ask a great many people to give you a little money. This was the thought that obsessed me while I was in prison, and it was there that I came up with my idea. It was easy enough to fake my conversion to Christianity. Everyone likes a sinner who repents. And it certainly impressed the parole board. I was released a long time before I had completed my sentence and I immediately set up my charity, First Aid. The aim, as I described it, was to be the first organization to respond to disasters wherever they took place.

"I would imagine that you know very little about international charity, Alex. But when a catastrophe occurs—the Asian tsunami in 2004 is a good example—people all over the world rush to respond. Old-age pensioners dip into their savings. Ten dollars here, twenty dollars there. It soon adds up. At the same time, banks and businesses fight to outdo each other with very public displays of generosity. None of them really care about people dying in undeveloped countries. Some donate because they feel guilty about their own wealth. Others, as I say, do it for the publicity—"

"I don't agree with you," Alex cut in. He was thinking of Brookland School and the money they had collected for Comic Relief. There had been a whole week of activities and everyone had been proud of what they had achieved. "You see the world this way because you're greedy and mad. People give to charity because they want to help."

"Your opinions mean nothing to me," McCain snapped, and Alex was pleased to see that he was annoyed. The anger was pricking at his eyes. "And if you interrupt again, I'll have you tied down and beaten." He leaned forward and sucked at his coffee. "The motives are irrelevant anyway. What counts is the money. Six hundred million dollars was raised for the tsunami in the United Kingdom alone. It's very difficult to say what a charity like Oxfam raises over a period of twelve months, but I can tell you that last year they raised the same figure—six hundred million in Great Britain. That was just one office. Oxfam also has branches in a dozen other countries and subbranches in places like India and Mexico. You do the math!"

McCain fell silent. For a moment, his eyes were far away.

"Millions and millions of dollars and pounds and Euros," he murmured. "And because the cash comes so quickly and in such large amounts, it is almost impossible to follow. An ordinary business has accountants. But a charity operates in many countries, often in appalling conditions—which makes it much less easy to pin down."

"So basically you're just a common thief," Alex said. He knew he was treading close to the line, but he couldn't resist needling McCain. "You're planning to steal a lot of money."

McCain nodded. Surprisingly, he didn't seem to be offended. "I am a thief. But not a common one at all. I am the greatest thief who ever lived. And I do not need to take the money. People give it to me willingly."

"You said you were going to create a disaster."

"I'm glad you were listening. That is exactly what I am going to do . . . or perhaps I should say it is exactly what I have done. What *we* have done. The disaster is already happening, even as we sit here in this pleasant night air."

He stubbed out his cigarette and lit another.

"People need a reason to give money, and my genius,

if you will forgive the word, has simply been to work out that the reason can be created, artificially. I can give you an example. A serious accident took place last year at the Jowada nuclear power station in Chennai, southern India. You may remember reading about it in the newspapers. That was a fairly simple matter, a bomb carried into the plant by one of my operatives. I have to say that the results were disappointing. The full force of the blast and the resulting radioactivity were contained and did less damage than I had hoped. But even so, First Aid was the first on the scene and received more than two million dollars in donations. Some of it, of course, we had to give away. We had to buy large quantities of some sort of antiradiation drug, and we had to pay for advertising. Even so, we made a tax-free profit of about eight hundred thousand dollars. It was a useful dress rehearsal for the event I was planning here, in Kenya. It also helped us with our operating costs."

"And what are you planning here? What do you mean when you say I started it?"

"We'll come back to you in a minute, Alex. But what I am planning here is a good old-fashioned plague. Not just in Kenya, but in Uganda and Tanzania too. I am talking about a disaster on a scale never seen before. And the beauty of it is that I am completely in control. But I don't need to describe it to you. I can show you. I am, as you will see, one step ahead of the game."

McCain opened his laptop computer and spun it

around so that Alex could see the screen. "When the disaster begins, a few weeks from now, other charities will rush to the scene. In a sense, all charities are waiting for bad things to happen. It is the reason for their existence. We need to be faster than them. The first on the ground will scoop the lion's share of the money. So we have already prepared our appeal . . ."

He pressed the Enter button.

A film began to play on the computer. Slowly, the camera zoomed in on an African village. At first, everything seemed normal. But then Alex heard the buzz of flies and saw the first dead bodies. A couple of cows lay on their sides with bloated stomachs and rigid, distended legs. The camera passed an eagle which seemed to have crash-landed, slamming into the dust. And at the same time, he heard a voice speaking in a soft, urgent tone.

"Something terrible is happening in Kenya," the commentary began. "A dreadful plague has hit the land and nobody knows how it began. But people are dying. In the thousands. The oldest and the youngest have been the first to go . . ."

Now the camera had reached the first child, staring up with empty eyes.

"Animals are not immune. African wildlife is being decimated. This beautiful country is in the grip of a nightmare and we urgently need money, now, to save it before it's too late. First Aid is running emergency food supplies. First Aid is already on the ground with vital medicine and fresh water. First Aid is funding urgent scientific research to find the cause of this disaster and to bring it to an end. But we cannot do it without you. Please send as much as you can today.

"Call us or visit our website. Our lines are open twenty-four hours a day. Save Kenya. Save the people. How can we ignore their cry for help?"

The final image showed a giraffe stretched out in the grass with part of its rib cage jutting through its side. A telephone number and a web address were printed over them with the First Aid logo below.

"I am particularly pleased with the giraffe," McCain said. He tapped the keyboard and froze the picture. "Many people in the first world just look away when a child or an old woman dies in the street. But they'll weep over a dead animal. A great many giraffes and elephants will die in Kenya in the next few months. It should double the amount we receive."

Alex sat in silence. Everything that McCain was saying sickened him. But it was worse than that. He knew exactly what he was looking at. The African village on the screen. He had been there. He had stood in the same village when he had broken into the Elm's Cross film studio. The only thing that was different was the backdrop. The green cyclorama was gone, replaced by swirling clouds and forest.

"You've made it all up," he gasped. "It's all fake. You built the village. It's a set."

"We were merely preparing ourselves for the reality," McCain explained. "As soon as the first reports of the Kenyan plague hit the press, we will come forward with our television appeal. There will be advertisements in all the newspapers and on posters. This will happen not just in England but in America, Australia, another dozen countries. And then we will sit back and wait for the money to flood in."

"And you're going to keep it! You're not going to help anyone!"

McCain smiled and blew smoke. "There's nothing anyone can do," he said. "Once the plague begins, there will be no stopping it. I can tell you that with certainty because, of course, I created it."

"Greenfields . . ."

"Exactly. I wish my good friend Leonard Straik was here to explain the science of it, but I'm afraid he met with an accident and won't be joining us. You could say he choked on a snail. Except the snail in question was the marbled cone variety and deadly poisonous. I have a feeling that Leonard's heart had exploded before I forced it down his throat."

So McCain had murdered Straik. Presumably, he didn't want to share his profits with anyone. Alex filed the information away. He had to find a way to contact MI6.

"It works like this," McCain explained. He was enjoying himself and he didn't try to hide it. "You don't seem to have spent a lot of time at school, Alex, but can I assume you've heard of genes? Every single cell in your body has about thirty thousand of them—and they are basically tiny pieces of code that make you what you are. The color of your hair, your eyes, and so on. It's all down to the genes.

"Plants are made up of genes too. The genes tell the plant what to do . . . whether to taste nice or not, for example. Now, what Mr. Straik and his friends at Greenfields were doing was changing the nature of plants by effectively adding a single gene. Plants are more complicated than you might think. For example, the information required to make a single stalk of wheat would take up one hundred books with one thousand pages each. And here's the remarkable thing. If you added just one paragraph of new information—the equivalent of an extra gene—you would change the entire library. Your wheat might still look like wheat, but it would be very different. It might not be quite so tasty, for example, if eaten with milk and sugar for breakfast. It might, in fact, kill you.

"Do you see where I'm going with this? I'm talking about taking something very ordinary and agreeable and turning it into something lethal. And this actually happens in every kitchen in the world almost every day of the week! Only, in reverse. Let me try to explain it to you.

"I'm sure you enjoy potatoes. Young boys like you eat them all the time . . . as chips or as fries. It probably never occurs to you that you are actually eating a poisonous plant. Not many people realize that the potato is closely related to deadly nightshade. Its leaves and flowers are extremely toxic. They won't kill you, but they would make you very sick indeed. What you actually eat is the tuber, the bit that grows underground.

"The tubers, of course, are delicious—but they can also be made to harm you. If you leave them out in the sun, even for one day, they turn green and taste bitter. If you eat them after that, you will be sick. And why has this happened? There's a gene—a genetic switch—hidden inside the potato tuber. It's completely harmless and almost invisible—but the sunlight seeks it out and turns it on. And once that happens, the potato tuber behaves differently. It goes green. It becomes poisonous. You have to throw it away.

"For the last five years, Greenfields Bio Center has been supplying seed to grow wheat in several African countries. The wheat has been genetically modified to need less water and to produce extra vitamins. But what nobody knows is that Leonard Straik used his particle delivery system to add an extra gene to the package. Like the potato gene I just told you about, it's harmless. A loaf of Kenyan bread made out of home-grown Kenyan wheat will be fine. But once the genetic switch has been activated, although the wheat will look exactly the same, it will begin to change. It will quietly produce a toxin known as ricin. Ricin normally grows in castor beans and is one

of the most lethal substances known to man. A tiny cap-
sule of the stuff would kill an adult. And very soon it will
be growing all over Africa."

"That stuff I found in your office," Alex muttered. "In
the test tube . . ."

"You're very quick," McCain said. "The more I get to
know you, Alex, the more I like you. Yes. That is our activating agent. It is a sort of mushroom soup. And this is
very important. It's not a chemical, it's a living organism—
which is to say it can reproduce itself.

"Again, I can explain this to you by taking you back to
the kitchen. If you place an ordinary mushroom on a
piece of paper and leave it overnight, you'll notice a black-
ish sort of dust covering the surface the next day. What
you are looking at are spores. If they are released outside,
the spores will spread—a little bit like the common cold,
traveling from one field to another. It may interest you to
know that the Irish Potato Blight of 1845, which caused
the death by starvation of almost a million people, was
caused by a spore attacking the potato crop.

"I can see from your face that you're beginning to
understand the exact purpose of the flight that you took
this morning. You were kind enough to help Dr. Beckett
by pulling a lever inside the Piper Cub, and when you did
this, you sprayed a single field of genetically modified
wheat with the activating agent. Leonard Straik told me
that it would take exactly thirty-six hours for the reaction
to occur. So, at sunset tomorrow, the genetic switch will

be thrown and the wheat in the field will begin to produce ricin. But that will only be the start of it. Once the spores have done their work, they will move on. The wind will carry them to the next field and to the one after that. Nothing will be able to stop them. Nothing will stand in their way.

"The birds will be the first to die. A little peck of poisoned wheat and they'll look like the plastic eagle you saw in that film. Then it will be the turn of the people. It's hard to believe that a loaf of bread in the local baker's or wrapped in plastic on a supermarket shelf will contain enough poison to kill an entire family. But it will. It will have become a slice of death. Animals will die too. It will be as if God has passed judgment on the whole of Kenya.

"Except that it won't stop at the borders. Greenfields has sold millions of seeds to the African people . . . in Uganda, Tanzania, and all around. Soon the contamination will have spread across the whole continent."

"They'll realize," Alex said. "People will know that the wheat is poisoned and they'll stop eating it. They'll burn the fields."

"That's exactly right, Alex. It will all be over very quickly. It won't even make a great economic difference to Kenya. They only grow 135,000 tons of wheat a year, and a lot of their food is imported. But that's why First Aid has to act fast. It'll be in the initial panic, the first weeks, that we'll make our billions. First Aid will publicize the catastrophe to the world, and people will rush to give money without thinking. And what do you think they'll do when they discover that it's only the wheat that has mysteriously developed this sickness, that the plague can be contained? Do you think they'll ask for their donations back? I don't think so.

"And anyway, it will be too late. By then, I will have moved to Switzerland. I already have a new identity waiting for me. I will have plastic surgery . . . this time, I think, more successfully. I will reemerge as a slightly mysterious billionaire businessman, but I don't think people will ask too many questions about who I am or where I've come from. I already discovered this when I was partying in politics. When you are rich, people treat you with respect."

McCain fell silent. He had completed his explanation and sat back, almost exhausted, waiting for Alex to respond. There was a sudden hiss as one of the logs in the fire collapsed in on itself and a flurry of sparks leapt into the night air. The guards had disappeared from sight, but Alex knew they would be watching and would come in an instant if they were needed. He felt sick. It had been a final twist, a little act of extra cruelty to make him pull the lever that had released the spores. There had been no real reason for it. It was just how McCain and his fiancée got their kicks.

"So what happens next?" he asked. "What do you want with me?"

"Is that all you want to know? Haven't you got anything to say about my plan?"

"I think your plan is as sick as you are, Mr. McCain. I'm not interested in it. I'm not interested in you. I just want to know why I'm here."

Perhaps McCain had been expecting applause or at least some sort of reaction from Alex; he was clearly disappointed, and when he spoke, his voice was sullen. "Very well," he said. "I might as well tell you."

He had finished his second cigarette. He ground that out too.

"I have been thinking a great deal, Alex, about how you managed to cross my path on two occasions. The first time was at Kilmore Castle in Scotland. You were with the journalist Edward Pleasure. Why were you there?"

"I'm a friend of his daughter." Alex couldn't see any harm in admitting the truth. "He invited me."

McCain considered for a moment. "Pure coincidence, then. Unfortunately for you, I was concerned about Pleasure," he continued. "I had been warned that he might be dangerous and I wondered how much he knew about me. I only agreed to be interviewed by him because to have refused might have raised his suspicions. And then, when I heard the two of you talking about genetic engineering—"

"You thought he was talking about his article?" Alex almost wanted to laugh. "I was telling him about my homework! He'd asked me how I was doing at school!"

"I believe you, Alex. But at the time, I couldn't take any chances. If Pleasure had found out about my involvement with Greenfields, he would have put this entire operation in jeopardy."

"So you decided to kill him. You had one of your people shoot out his tire."

"Actually, Myra did it for me. She was there too that night. Of course, there was a certain risk attached. But as I have already told you, I am something of a gambler. Perhaps that's why I allowed myself to lose my temper when you managed to beat me at cards."

He lifted a hand and waved. It was a signal. Two guards, both carrying rifles, began to approach the table. Beckett was with them.

"The first time we met may have been a coincidence," McCain said. "The second time most definitely was not. You were sent to Greenfields by MI6. There is no point in attempting to deny it. You were carrying equipment that allowed you to jam the surveillance camera, and you also exploded a chimney on the recycling unit roof. It is therefore absolutely critical for me to discover how much the intelligence services know about me and in particular about this operation. In short, I need to know why you were at Greenfields. How much of my conversation with Leonard Straik did you overhear? What were you able to tell MI6?"

Alex was about to speak, but McCain held up a hand,

stopping him. Beckett and the two guards had reached the table. They were standing behind Alex, waiting to escort him back to his tent.

"I do not want to hear any more from you tonight," McCain said. "It is already clear to me that you are brave and intelligent. It is quite possible that you would be able to deceive me. So I want you to consider the questions I have asked you. I will ask them again in the morning.

"But the next time I put them to you, it will not be over a pleasant dinner." McCain leaned forward, and Alex saw the ferocity in his eyes. "'Behold, I have the keys of hell and death,' as it says in the book of Revelation. Tomorrow, I intend to torture you, Alex. I want you to sleep tonight in the knowledge that when the sun rises, I am going to inflict terror on you such as you have never known in your life. I am going to strip you of your courage and your bravado so that when you open your mouth and speak to me, you will tell me everything I want to know and won't even contemplate lying. Over this table, you have made some jokes at my expense, but you will not be making jokes when we meet again. You must be prepared to shed tears, Alex. Leave me now. And try to imagine, if you will, the horror that awaits you."

Alex felt the two men grab hold of his arms. He shrugged them off and stood up.

"You can do what you like to me, Mr. McCain," he said. "But your plan will never work. MI6 will find you and they'll kill you. I expect they're already on their way."

"You're right about one thing," McCain replied. "I can do anything I like to you. And very soon I will. Good night, Alex. I'll leave you to your dreams."

Alex was taken away. The last thing he saw was Myra Beckett standing behind McCain, massaging his shoulders. McCain himself was leaning forward with his elbows on the table, his hands in front of his face. He looked very much as if he was at prayer.

20

PURE TORTURE

THE SUN ROSE ALL TOO SOON.

Barely able to sleep, Alex watched the sides of his tent turn gray, silver, then finally a dirty yellow as the morning light intensified. He had lost his watch and he had no idea of the time, but being so close to the equator, he suspected the sun was up early here. When would they come for him? Exactly what sort of torture did McCain have in mind?

He lay back and closed his eyes, trying to fight off the demons of fear and despair. The fact was that he was completely in McCain's power. And McCain wasn't taking any chances; two Kikuyu guards had stood watch outside his tent all night. He had heard them murmuring in low voices and had seen the occasional flare of a match as they lit cigarettes. Once, he thought he had heard a plane flying low overhead, but apart from that there had been nothing except the usual eternal sounds of the bush. Alex had been left entirely on his own, unable to sleep. Right now, he was close to exhaustion. He could see no way out.

The sun was getting stronger by the minute. Alex thought of it beating down in the Simba Valley, just two miles to the north. The wheat would be growing taller, turning gold. And the deadly spores that he himself had released would be activating themselves. By the end of the day, they would have begun to spread, lifted by the breeze, carrying poison and death all over Africa. Alex's eyes flicked open and suddenly he was angry. Why was he wasting time and energy worrying about himself when, in a few hours, an entire continent might begin to die?

Without any warning, the flap of the tent opened and Myra Beckett stepped inside, dressed in white with a round straw hat—the sort of thing a schoolgirl might have worn a hundred years ago. She had clipped two dark lenses over her spectacles to protect herself from the sun's glare. They made her look less human and more robotic than ever.

She was obviously surprised to see Alex lying on the bed, seemingly relaxed. "How did you sleep?" she asked.

"I slept very well, thank you," Alex lied. "Have you brought my breakfast?"

The woman scowled. "I think you will find you _are_ the breakfast." She gestured at the exit. "Desmond is waiting. Let me show you the way . . ."

It was another beautiful day with just a few wisps of cloud in an otherwise perfect sky. There was a familiar chatter above Alex's head and he looked up to see that at least one monkey had dared to come back, looking down on him with shock-filled eyes as if it knew what was about to happen. Birds with long tails and brilliant plumage hopped along the pathways. There would have been a time when tourists would have woken up to this scenery and thought themselves in heaven. But one sight of the glowering guards reminded Alex. McCain had turned it into his own peculiar version of hell.

"It's not very far," Beckett said. "Please, follow me."

She led him out of the camp, away from the landing strip, and also away from the open area where he had eaten the night before. Alex was still wearing part of his school uniform—the shirt, pants, and shoes. Even with his sleeves rolled up, he was still too warm and sweaty, but they hadn't bothered to give him any fresh clothes. He had just one crumb of comfort. The gel-ink pen was in his pants pocket. Even now he might get a chance to use it. He had no other surprises left.

With two guards behind him and the woman a few steps ahead, he was taken down a path that followed the edge of the river. The camp disappeared behind them, and looking ahead in the far distance, Alex saw a family of elephants washing themselves in the sparkling water. It was an extraordinary sight, but Alex couldn't enjoy it. Not when it might be the last thing he ever saw.

Desmond McCain was waiting ahead of them, dressed comfortably in a well-tailored safari suit with a white silk neckerchief. It seemed they had arrived at their destination. Alex looked around him. He didn't like what he saw.

A steep slope ran down to a stretch of sandy shingle,

a narrow beach at the very edge of the water. There was a stepladder, about twenty feet high, standing on the beach, and above it a metal pipe that had been fastened to the branch of a tree. The pipe ended with two handles and reminded Alex of a periscope in a submarine. A wooden observation platform had been constructed at the top of the slope. This was where McCain was standing.

Alex had already worked out what might be going on here and was making calculations. If he walked down to the beach and climbed the ladder, he would be able to reach the handles. Then the ladder could be taken away and he would be left hanging from the pipe. He would be close enough to the platform to be able to talk to McCain and to hear what he had to say—but not close enough to reach him. Because the pipe was rigid, he wouldn't be able to swing back and forth. In other words, he would simply have to stay there until his arms grew tired and he dropped.

The question was—why? What was the point?

"This will not take very long, Alex," McCain said. He had watched Alex taking everything in. "I will talk to you a little bit, and then, I'm afraid, we will begin. As I have already told you, I need most urgently the answer to three questions. What was it that brought you to Greenfields? Why did MI6 send you? And how much do the intelligence services know about Poison Dawn?"

Alex had already decided what he was going to say. "You don't need to play your sadistic games, Mr. McCain," he said. "I'll tell you what you want to know anyway."

McCain held up a hand. "I don't think you were listening to me last night. Of course you will tell me what I want to hear. That is the point I'm trying to make. You will tell me anything to protect yourself. But I have to be one hundred percent certain that you are telling me the truth. There cannot be even the tiniest margin of doubt."

"And you think torturing me will achieve that?"

"Normally, no. There are many horrible things I could do to you, Alex. We have electricity here and wires attached to various parts of your body could produce excruciating pain. My Kikuyu friends could take you far beyond the limits of endurance using only their spears, perhaps heated first in the flames of a fire. We could cut pieces off of you. We could boil you alive. And do not think for a single minute that I would hesitate to do any of this because you are fourteen. MI6 clearly does not think of you as a child, so why should I?"

"Is part of the torture boring me to death?" Alex asked.

McCain nodded. "Bravely spoken, Alex. Let us see how brave you are ten minutes from now." He took out a handkerchief and wiped his brow. The sun was beating down on his bald head, and beads of sweat were standing out. "The pain that you are about to experience is going to be all the worse because you will inflict it on yourself. You will, as it were, cooperate with your torturers. And you will do so to escape the terror that lies below." He took out a gun, an old-fashioned Mauser with a shortened barrel and a white ivory plate over the grip. It looked like something out of a museum. "I would like you now to go down to the river," he explained. "If you refuse to do so, if you attempt to run away, I will shoot you through the knee."

Alex stood where he was. Beckett was smiling properly for the first time, and he realized that she knew what to expect, that she had seen this all before. The two tribesmen were covering him with their rifles. If McCain missed with his pistol, they would certainly gun him down before he'd taken a single step. He glanced at the beach and at the river. There was nobody else down there. He had a nasty feeling he wasn't going to be alone for long.

"I'm waiting, Alex," McCain said.

Without speaking, Alex made his way down the slope. Now McCain and the others were directly above him, looking down from the protected height of the observation platform. Alex was reminded of a Roman emperor and his entourage. They were in the royal box. He was the gladiator, about to entertain them.

"This is part of the River Simba," McCain explained. "It runs all the way up to the Simba Dam and Lake Simba beyond. It is the water from this river that will be feeding my wheat field, Alex. And as you are about to learn, it is infested with crocodiles."

"Here comes one now!" Beckett crowed.

Crocodiles.

Alex turned to see a dark shape on the opposite bank slither forward and launch itself into the water, followed quickly by a second. There was something strikingly evil about the way they moved. They twisted and sliced their way through the water like two knife wounds, and somehow they managed to swim—or slither—very quickly without seeming to be in a hurry. They would be across the river in less than a minute. They somehow knew he was here. But then, of course, they had been fed this way before. And Alex had a feeling they were hungry.

Alex looked up. Beckett was gazing at him with her mouth open, and he could see the saliva glistening on her lips and tongue. McCain was next to her, his gun held loosely, watching with interest. He glanced back. The crocodiles were halfway across the river. His first instinct was to run, but he knew he would be shot if he tried. Nor would he be allowed back on the platform. Everything had been carefully arranged. There was only one way of escape.

Sick with himself, knowing that he was doing exactly what McCain wanted, Alex climbed the stepladder. He was trying not to panic, but now his every instinct was driving him up, out of harm's way. As he drew nearer to the top, he felt the whole structure tremble underneath him and for one terrible moment he thought he was going to fall. Somehow, he managed to steady himself. He reached the top even as the first crocodile heaved itself out of the water and began to crawl toward him.

Alex turned back and looked at it. It was a mistake. In an instant he felt the terror that McCain had promised him, the deep-rooted fear of this ancient monster that had to be hot-wired into every human being. The crocodile that had just emerged was almost twice his own size, from the ugly snout to the writhing tip of its tail. Its great mouth was open, with two lines of ferocious white teeth waiting to snap shut on his arm or leg. That was how they operated, of course, clamping down on their victim and then dragging them back into the water. And only when the bones were loose and the flesh had begun to decompose would they begin their feast.

But worst of all were the eyes, midnight black, snake-like, and swollen on the side of its head, surely too small for its body and filled with hatred. They really were the eyes of death. Alex had heard it said that crocodiles wept as they attacked their prey, but there would be no pity in those eyes. They were part of a machine that existed only to kill.

The second crocodile was a little smaller and much quicker. Alex saw it overtake the other, scuttling over the shingle on its short, squat legs, all the way to the foot of the ladder.

He climbed the last few steps, using his hands to steady himself at the top. If he fell! . . . He could imagine it. Smashing into the shingle. Perhaps breaking an ankle or a leg. And then being torn apart between the two animals as they fought over him. There could be no more horrible death.

The crocodile threw itself at the ladder and the whole thing shuddered. How many people had McCain terrorized in this way? He looked up. He still wasn't level with the observation platform. He knew what he had to do. With dreadful care, he balanced himself on the highest step. The handles at the end of the pipe were directly above him. Swaying, using his arms to steady himself, he reached up and grabbed hold of them. His fingers closed around them even as the larger crocodile reared up, throwing its entire weight against the ladder. The whole thing came crashing down. Alex was left dangling in space.

And now he saw how McCain had arranged things.

He was facing McCain, the two of them level with each other, no more than a yard apart. The two crocodiles were directly underneath Alex, climbing on top of each other, snapping at the air. For the moment he was safe. But he was stretched out, hanging in space, clinging to the pipe by his fingers. His wrists and arms were already feeling the strain as they supported his entire body weight, and the burn of lactic acid was building up in his shoulders. It was just as McCain had said. He was actually inflicting the pain on himself, and it would get worse the longer he hung there. In the end, of course, he would have to let go. And that was the horror of it. Once he dropped, there would only be more pain and then death. How long did he have?

"The longest anyone has ever remained where you are is eighteen minutes," McCain said. He spoke slowly and evenly. He didn't have to raise his voice to make himself heard. "The man in question had lost his sanity before the end. He was giggling as he fell. But you, Alex, you have one hope, one chance of survival. My men can shoot at the crocodiles and scare them away. But first you have to answer my questions, and you have to make me believe you. If you can make that happen, then you will be safe."

Alex swore. It was difficult to speak. All his concentration was fixed on his hands, the increasing pain in his arms, the need not to let go.

"I dislike that sort of language, Alex," McCain said. "I am, after all, an ordained priest. Would you like me to go away for five minutes and come back when you're in a better frame of mind?"

One of the crocodiles leapt toward him. Instinctively, Alex pulled his legs up, curving them in toward his stomach. The movement put extra strain on his arms, but he actually heard the jaws of the animal snap together and he knew there were mere inches between it and his ankles.

"No," he shouted. His voice was strangled. He didn't sound like himself. But he had to get this over with. "Ask me what you want."

He had been hanging for less than a minute. It already felt longer. He would never manage another five, let along another seventeen. In his desperation, he found himself twisting around. His wrists crossed and he had to jerk his body to bring himself face-to-face with McCain.

"The first question, then." McCain paused. He was speaking deliberately slowly. He knew that every second only added to the torture. "Why were you at Greenfields?"

"It was a school trip."

"You're still lying to me, Alex. I'm going to leave you for a little while . . ." McCain turned his back on Alex and walked away. Below, on the beach, the crocodiles were writhing together in a frenzy of claws and scales and black eyes and teeth.

"It's the truth!" Alex shouted after him. His hands were sweating, making it even more difficult to keep his grip. "It was a biology project for my teacher Mr. Gilbert. But then MI6 asked me to help them. They weren't interested in you. It was Leonard Straik."

McCain turned back. "Go on."

"There was someone in Greenfields. An informer . . ." What was his name? Alex thought back desperately. "Philip Masters. He'd gone to the police and then he was killed. That was why they wanted to find out about Straik."

"You broke into his computer."

"They gave me a memory stick. That was all they asked me to do."

"What about Poison Dawn?"

"They never said anything about Poison Dawn. They never even mentioned it to me. I'm telling you, they only knew about you and Straik when I told them I'd seen you together."

"That was very unfortunate. What else did you tell them?"

"I told them I heard the two of you talking . . . but you didn't say anything that made any sense. I gave them the stuff I found in Straik's office." To Alex, it was as if his arms were being torn out of his shoulders. He could feel his body hanging in space. He didn't dare look at the crocodiles below. "But I never even spoke to them again. I don't know what they know. They don't know anything else. . . ."

McCain let him dangle in silence. Ten seconds dragged to twenty and then to half a minute. Alex felt every one of them. He could feel his bones wrenching in their sockets and knew that McCain was doing this on purpose. He was staring straight into Alex's eyes as if trying to read what was going on inside his mind. Alex tried to ease his grip, but his palms were so slippery that the smallest movement could make him fall. Beckett had moved closer to him. She was breathing heavily, watching Alex struggle with evident delight. He could see himself reflected in the dark circles of her glasses.

The silence stretched out. Alex could actually smell the crocodiles; a deep, sickly odor of stale fish and decaying meat that rose up and crept into his nostrils. He was finding it difficult to breathe. The pain was getting worse and worse. All the muscles in his upper body were burning.

"I believe you," McCain said at last. "You are telling the truth."

"Then get rid of them!" Alex jerked his head down at the two crocodiles. They were silent now, as if they knew it was only a matter of time before they were given what they wanted.

Another long pause. Alex's arms screamed.

"I'm afraid not," McCain said.

"What?" Alex shouted the word.

"You have annoyed me very much, Alex. I tried to kill you when you were in Scotland, and it would have been a lot better if I had. Your activity at Greenfields very nearly brought an end to an operation that has taken me five years and a great deal of money to develop. Thanks to you, my name is now known to MI6, and that will make my future life more difficult. And, added to that, you are a very rude and unpleasant boy, and all in all, I think you deserve to die." He turned to Myra Beckett. "I know you enjoy this, my love, so you can stay to the end. I'll be interested to know how many minutes he manages to hang on before he falls. I somehow doubt that he'll beat the record."

The woman took out her mobile phone. "I'll take photographs for you, Dezzy."

McCain took one last look at Alex. "I hope you die

painfully," he said. "Because although you have not lived long, I really think you deserve a painful death."

He signaled to the guards and the three of them walked away. But he had given his gun to Beckett. She was holding it in one hand, the mobile phone in the other. Behind him, Alex heard a splash. A third crocodile had launched itself into the river and was already wriggling its way across.

"Four minutes." The woman glanced at her watch. "I do not think you will make it to five."

And she was right. Everything was pain and with every second the pain was getting worse. Alex couldn't swing himself to safety. He couldn't climb. He couldn't move. He could only fall.

He closed his eyes and knew that very soon he would do just that.

21

RAW DEAL

SEVEN MINUTES. MAYBE EIGHT MINUTES. Alex wasn't even sure why he was hanging on anymore. The sooner he dropped, the sooner it would all be over. His whole body was racked by pain and his blood was pounding in his ears and behind his eyes. With every second that passed, the strength was draining out of his arms. He tried to accept what was about to happen: his fingers slipping out of the metal handles, the short fall down to the riverbank, the jarring impact, and then the final horror as the crocodiles attacked.

Myra Beckett leaned forward. "Do you have any last words?" she asked. "Any good-byes you want to make? I can record them for you." She held out her mobile phone.

"Go rot in hell." Alex's eyes felt as if they were swollen shut, but he forced them open, staring straight at her.

"You are the one on the way to hell, my dear," she said.

Her eyes widened. She took a step forward as if something had surprised her. Once again she opened her mouth and Alex thought she was about to speak, but instead, a stream of blood poured over her lower lip. A moment later, she pitched forward and fell and Alex glimpsed the hilt of a knife jutting out of the back of her neck. Desperately clinging onto the handles, he corkscrewed around and looked down. The woman had landed in the middle of the crocodiles. She was still alive. He heard her scream as she was torn apart, her arms and legs being pulled in three directions. He turned away. He couldn't watch any more.

He was going to join her. His own strength was gone. He felt his fingers opening. But then suddenly there was a man on the observation platform, leaning out, reaching toward him, and even as he wondered where the man had come from, he knew that he had seen him somewhere before.

"Alex!" the man called. "Take my hand."

"I can't reach . . ."

"One effort. You can make it."

The distance was too great. Alex would have to let go with one hand and throw himself sideways, reaching out with the other. If he miscalculated or if the man was tricking him, that would be it. The crocodiles would get a second feed.

"Now!" The man couldn't shout. They were too close to the lodge. His voice was an urgent whisper.

Alex did as he was told, stretching as far as he could, using every muscle to propel his body away from the handles. The man was leaning out. And somehow, just when Alex was certain he would fall, they managed to lock together, wrist in hand and hand over wrist.

"Okay. I've got you. I'll take your weight."

Alex let go of the handle. He felt the man pull him toward the platform. Even so, there was one dreadful moment when he was sure they had overbalanced and they would fall together. He came crashing down. But he was right on the edge of the platform. He clawed at the wooden planks and managed to find some purchase. His legs were dangling below him, but then he pulled himself forward and rolled over on his side. He was lying next to the man who had just rescued him. He was safe.

For a few seconds he lay in silence, recovering his breath and waiting for his jangling nerves to calm down. Then he looked up. "Who are you?" he asked.

"Not now." The man was Asian, young, with very dark skin and close-cropped hair, dressed in camouflage khakis with a harness for three knives slanting across his chest. One knife was missing.

Alex knew him at once. With a sense of astonishment he remembered where they had met before. It was the man from Loch Arkaig, the driver of the white van who had appeared from nowhere when he had crawled out of the freezing water. He had driven Alex, Sabina, and Edward Pleasure to the hospital. And now he was here! What sort of guardian angel was he, operating on two sides of the world?

"My name is Rahim," the man said. "But now we must leave. When they find the woman is missing, they will come looking for her. Here . . . give me your shirt."

Alex didn't know what the man was thinking, but this was no time for an argument. He stripped off his school shirt and handed it over. Rahim took out a second knife and cut the shirt to shreds, then tossed it down to the crocodiles. There were only two of them down there, fighting over what was left of the woman. The other had returned to the river, dragging part of her with it.

The pieces of Alex's shirt fluttered down onto the riverbank. "It may fool them," Rahim said. "It may not. Let's go."

"Go where?"

"I have a camp."

Alex followed Rahim off the observation platform and away from the river, heading into the bush. He was alarmed to see that Rahim was limping badly and that the back of his jacket was covered in sweat. The man had a fever. Alex had also seen it in his eyes. He was a soldier of some sort, extremely fit. But he was also hurt. It was only willpower that was keeping him going.

Even so, they kept up a fast pace for the next fifteen minutes, finally arriving at a clearing dominated by a huge *Kigelia africana,* or sausage tree, with its strange black pods hanging underneath the branches. This was where Rahim had set up a makeshift camp. Alex saw a back-pack, a few tins of food, and—at least this answered one of his questions—a parachute made of black silk, bunched up and tucked under a bush. A very sophisticated-looking gun was leaning against the trunk of the tree. It was a

Dragunov SVD99 gas-operated sniper rifle, built in Russia but used extensively by the Indian army.

Rahim went over to the backpack and took out a spare T-shirt. He threw it over to Alex. "Here. You can wear this." He opened a water bottle and drank, then offered it to Alex. Alex took a swig. The water was warm and tasted of chemicals.

"You were in Scotland," Alex said.

"Yes." Rahim had obviously been drained by what he had just been through. The sweat was pouring down his face and he was breathing heavily, fighting against the fever. Now Alex saw that one of his legs was bleeding. It was probably bandaged underneath his pants, but the blood was seeping through. He sat down and began to untie his shoelaces. He was wearing heavy combat boots.

"How safe are we here?" Alex asked.

"Not safe. The Kikuyu will be able to track us. Maybe McCain will think you are dead. But he is already nervous. He will not take any chances."

"You're hurt." Alex handed back the water bottle. "What can I do to help you?"

"I was unlucky." Rahim drank a second time. "I parachuted in last night." Alex remembered hearing a plane. It had passed over the safari lodge, flying close to the ground. "I landed badly in a thornbush and cut my leg open. The wound has become infected. But I have taken antibiotics and I will recover. There is nothing you can do."

"You've told me your name, but you haven't said why you're here." Rahim didn't reply, but Alex had already worked it out for himself. "You were at Kilmore Castle, so you must be interested in McCain."

Rahim nodded.

"Who are you working for?"

Rahim took a deep breath and shifted his position. The movement caused him pain. "I know who you are," he said. "You are Alex Rider. You are a part-time operative working with the Special Operations Division of MI6. They are looking for you. They have put out the call to every intelligence department, including mine."

"But you didn't come here looking for me."

"I did not expect to find you here, Alex." Rahim smiled, and at that moment Alex saw how very young he was, perhaps only twenty-three or -four. There might be less than ten years between them. "I was sent here for one reason only. It was the same reason that I was sent to Kilmore Castle, and this is now the second time you have got in my way. I am here to kill Desmond McCain."

"Why?" There were so many questions Alex wanted to ask, and he was aware of time ticking away. The tribesmen could come looking for them at any time. But at least the rifle might put the odds more on their side.

Rahim took a plastic bottle out of his pocket. "I will

tell you," he said. He tipped two pills into the palm of his hand and swallowed them dry. He grimaced. "I am a spy like you, Alex. I belong to a division of the Indian secret service called RAW. It stands for Research and Analysis Wing, and it deals in counterterrorism, foreign affairs, and covert action. My own department goes further than that. Our activities often come under a single word. Revenge."

"This is about the nuclear power station," Alex said. "The one that McCain tried to destroy."

Rahim nodded. "The Jowada facility in Chennai. We know that he bribed a man by the name of Ravi Chandra to carry a device into the building. It was a lamentable lapse in security, but the security at Jowada was in general a disgrace. Unfortunately, we were unable to question Chandra because he died in the initial explosion. McCain took a great deal of care. There were a number of connections between him and the man who paid Chandra, but we investigated, and in the end we found a link with First Aid. Suddenly everything made sense. Even so, we cannot prove the case against McCain, nor do we need to. Sometimes RAW deals with its enemies in a simpler and more direct way. I was sent to Scotland to kill him there, and I was checking out the castle when your car went off the road and into the lake. That was fortunate for you. And it is even more fortunate that I should be here a second time. That business with the crocodiles . . ."

Rahim gave Alex the ghost of a smile. "I have never seen anything like that."

"How were you going to kill him?" Alex asked.

"I was planning to shoot him, but as I discovered last night, that will not be as easy as I thought. He is well protected by his Kikuyus. However, I have come well prepared. I can also blow up his plane."

"You have plastic explosive?"

"Of course." Rahim gestured at his backpack. "McCain flies a four-seater 172 Skyhawk."

Alex nodded grimly. "I know. That's what brought me here."

"I will blow it up in midair. In a way, that is the better option. It is part of my brief that RAW should not be seen to have been involved. A bomb, I think, will be more anonymous than a bullet casing."

"I'm afraid you're going to have to think again, Rahim." Alex went over to the Indian agent and sat down next to him. His thoughts had already raced ahead. "I have to contact MI6," he said.

"You want to let them know you are safe."

"More than that. Do you have a radio?"

"I have a laptop equipped with a demodulator. It will produce a baseband output that can be picked up by satellite. Do you have an address?"

"No." It only occurred to Alex now. Even after all the missions he had undertaken for MI6, they had never given him an e-mail address or a telephone number. On the other hand, he'd been supplied with gadgets. What had happened to the pocket calculator with the built-in communications system? It was a shame it hadn't been in his pocket when he was snatched.

"It's not a problem," Rahim said. "We can contact the Intelligence Bureau in New Delhi. They will pass on any message to Liverpool Street. What is it you want to say?"

Quickly, Alex told Rahim everything that he had learned from Desmond McCain the night before . . . the genetically modified wheat crop, the spores, the plan to poison half the continent. "We have less time than you thought," he said. "And killing McCain right now isn't going to do anyone any good. We have to go up to the Simba Valley. It's only two miles from here."

Rahim shook his head. "I'm sorry, Alex. I don't have enough explosive to blow up an entire wheat field."

"That's not my idea." Alex was remembering what McCain had told him, and what he had seen for himself when he was flown in. "There's a place called the Simba Dam," he explained. "It's on the edge of a big lake. If we could blow it up, we could flood the valley. We could put the whole crop underwater before it has a chance to do any harm. But we have to do it today. Right now. McCain said that the spores would start working at sunset. It must be about midday now."

"Alex, I know this dam," Rahim said. "I studied the whole area before I parachuted. It is what is known as a double curvature arch dam . . . which is to say that it curves against the side of the valley and also against the valley floor, making it doubly strong. I have just one kilogram of plastic explosive. That would not be nearly enough even to make a crack in the wall."

"There must be some sort of pipe or valve—"

"There will be a whole series of pipes carrying the water down the hill. Simba Dam is used for irrigation purposes, but there are also two hydroelectric turbines." Alex was impressed. Rahim had clearly done his homework. "It might be possible to attack the bottom outlet valve or the scour valve that is next to it. Either of them would release enormous amounts of water." He shook his head. "But it cannot be done."

"Why not?"

"Because I cannot do it. My leg is infected. I was barely able to limp to the river. The Simba Dam is three miles from here."

"I could go on my own."

"That I will not allow."

Alex thought for a minute. "You parachuted in," he said. "How were you planning to leave?"

"McCain has a crop duster as well as the Skyhawk. I imagine he used it to spread this spore of his that you described? I can fly. I was intending to steal it."

"Then you could fly me to the dam?"

"There is nowhere to land. I might be able to slow the plane to as little as thirty-five miles per hour and fly low over the water to allow you to jump, but even so, the chances are high that you would be killed."

For a moment, Alex lost his temper. "We can't just sit back and do nothing!"

"No, Alex. We can contact the Intelligence Bureau as I have already suggested. They will, in turn, speak to the British authorities. Together they will know what to do." Rahim went on quickly, before Alex could interrupt him. "I have my instructions. I am here to kill McCain. I was acting improperly when I decided to rescue you, and I can assure you my superiors will not be amused when I make my report." He broke off. He was sweating again and his eyes were unfocused. Alex could almost see the disease attacking his system. "My laptop . . ." Rahim pointed at the backpack. He was too weak to go over himself.

Alex stood up. He went over to the backpack and opened. Everything was packed very neatly inside. There was a laptop computer, maps, a compass, ammunition for the Dragunov, medical supplies, spare clothes, and food. Much of the space was taken up by a silver box about the size of a car battery with two switches and a clock set behind glass. Alex knew at once what it was. Rahim must have been planning to conceal it in the Skyhawk's hold.

"Bring it to me," Rahim said.

Alex left the bomb and carried the computer over. Rahim opened it, booted it up, and then handed it across.

"It will be easier if you do it," he said. "But I suggest you don't take too long. We will have to move from this place before the Kikuyu come looking for us, and I need to break into the Cessna and prepare it for its last flight."

Alex crouched down. It felt weird to be tapping away at a keyboard, sitting in the dust in the middle of the African bush. He also wondered what the British or the Indian authorities would be able to do. Another six hours and it might be too late. He briefly outlined the location of the valley, the crop that McCain was growing there, his plan to bring famine and disease to Kenya. Finally, he added a PS.

Please let Jack Starbright know where I am
and tell her I'm all right.

If there was one good thing to come out of all this, at least Jack would know that he hadn't been hurt. He quickly read the page over and pressed Send.

He looked up. Rahim had slumped forward. Alex went over and examined him. The RAW agent wasn't exactly asleep. He was unconscious, breathing heavily. He had been knocked out—either by the fever or by the medicine he had been taking to fight it. Alex eased him gently to the ground, then looked back in the direction of the lodge. Everything was silent in the bush as even the animals slept in the midday sun. It was very hot, but at least Rahim was tucked away in the shade of the sausage tree.

What would MI6 do when they received the news?

Alex had visions of Alan Blunt and Mrs. Jones confer-
ring with the appropriate ministers at Downing Street. A
new government had recently been voted in. They probably wouldn't even know he existed, so they would have
to be persuaded he was reliable, that his information was
accurate. And then they would have to make a decision . . .
but what exactly were their options? They could send in
troops with flamethrowers, but that might take days. In
fact, Alex couldn't even be certain that the Indian secret
service would pass the message on in time. After all, they
had their own agenda. They simply wanted McCain
dead.

He didn't like it, but he knew what he had to do. He
took the map out of Rahim's backpack and studied it.
Simba River Camp was clearly marked—and there was
the track that he had seen from the air. It led all the way
to the dam, rising up the side of the valley. He could follow the river for the first mile and then cut across the
countryside using the compass. It wouldn't be too difficult to pick up the track. There was electricity up there.
He had seen one of the pylons. If he could find it again,
it would lead him to the dam.

Finally, Alex examined the bomb. It wasn't very complicated either. All he would have to do is set the timer,
which operated like an ordinary alarm clock, then activate it by throwing a single switch. What was it that

Rahim had told him? He had to locate one of the two main valves. That was where he would place the bomb.

Alex took out the medicine, then put on the backpack and tightened the straps. He felt bad just walking out on Rahim, particularly after the agent had just saved his life. But at least he could make sure that he wasn't found by the Kikuyu tribemen. He would follow the path back to the river where he had first been taken. He would do his best to cover his tracks, and then he would set off in another direction, making sure that he disturbed the vegetation as much as possible. If McCain did realize that Beckett was missing and sent his men after him, they would follow the new path. Rahim would be left alone and Alex had no doubt that, once he woke up, he would be able to look after himself.

The decision was made. Alex looked up at the sky. The sun was directly overhead, beating down on him. It was midday. Before long it would begin its journey down.

Alex took a swig out of the water bottle and set off. Two miles in this unfamiliar countryside would take him as many hours. He just hoped he wasn't already too late.

22

MARGIN OF ERROR

ONE O'CLOCK IN THE AFTERNOON, London time.

The navy blue Jaguar XJ6 drove around Trafalgar Square and then headed down Whitehall, in the direction of Big Ben and the Houses of Parliament. The weather forecasters had been predicting snow, but so far it had held back. Even so, it was a hard, cold day, with the wind skittering along the sidewalks. Inside the car, the heat had been turned up and the windows were tinted. Both of these helped keep the winter at bay.

The Jaguar passed the famous Banqueting House, where the first King Charles had lost his head, and turned onto Downing Street. The black steel gates opened automatically to admit it. It stopped outside Number Ten and two people, a man and a woman, got out. As always, there was a handful of news reporters in the street, making their broadcasts against the backdrop of the most famous door in the world, but none of them noticed the two new arrivals, and if they had, it would have been extremely unlikely that they would have recognized them. Alan Blunt and Mrs. Jones had never been photographed. Their names didn't appear on any government profiles.

Neither of them needed to knock. The door swung open as they approached and they passed into the brightly colored entrance hall with a surprisingly long corridor stretching out in front of them. They made no sound at all as they walked along the plush carpets, beneath the chandeliers, toward the far staircase. As usual, the walls were lined with paintings that had been borrowed from a central government reserve. They were by British artists, most of them modern and rather bland.

Blunt examined them as he continued forward, not because he was interested in art—he wasn't—but because they might give him some insight into the mind of the man who had chosen them. There was a new prime minister in Downing Street. He had been voted in just a month before, And what did the paintings say about him? He liked the countryside, fox hunting, and windmills. His favorite color was blue.

Of course, Blunt already knew everything about the new man—from the state of his marriage (happy) to the last payment he had made on his credit card (£97.60 for a meal at The Ivy). There wasn't a single prime minister in England who hadn't been thoroughly checked by MI6: their families, their friends and associates, what websites they liked to visit, where they took their vacations, how much money they spent every week. There was always a chance that the information might reveal a security risk or something that the prime minister didn't want anyone to know.

The two of them reached the staircase and began to climb up to the first floor, passing the painted portraits and photographs of past prime ministers, spaced out at regular intervals. There was a man in a suit waiting at the top, gesturing toward an office. The building was full of young men in suits, some of them working for Blunt, although they probably didn't know it. Blunt and Mrs. Jones went into the office and there was the prime minister, waiting with two advisers, sitting behind a desk.

"Mr. Blunt . . . please, take a seat."

The prime minister wasn't happy, and it showed. Like all politicians, he didn't entirely trust his spy masters and he certainly didn't want one sitting opposite him now. It wasn't fair. He hadn't been in power very long. It was certainly too soon for his first international crisis. There were two men sitting with him, one on each side. They were trying to look relaxed, as if they just happened to be passing and had decided to pop in for the meeting.

"I don't think you've met Simon Ellis," the prime minister said, nodding at the fair-haired, rather plump man on his left. "And this is Charles Blackmore." The other man was also young, though with prematurely gray hair. "I thought it might be helpful if they joined us."

Blunt hadn't met either of them, but of course he knew everything about them. They had both been at Winchester College with the prime minister. Ellis was now a junior civil servant in the Treasury. Blackmore had left a career in television to become director of strategy and communications. The two men loathed each other. The prime minister didn't know this. They were also loathed by almost everyone else.

"Well . . . ," the prime minister began. He licked his lips. "I've read your report on the situation in Kenya and it does seem to be very alarming. But the first question I really do have to ask you is—why did your agent feel it necessary to send his information via the Indian secret service?"

"I'm afraid I can't answer that," Blunt replied. "We only know what you know, Prime Minister. It's all in the file. Our agent was kidnapped and smuggled out of the country against his will. Somehow he must have managed to break free and fell in with an agent from RAW."

"Research and Analysis Wing," Blackmore muttered helpfully.

"We have no idea what RAW was doing in Kenya, and so far they've refused to tell us. I'm afraid foreign intelligence agencies are always overcautious when it comes to protecting their own. But if I may say so, Prime Minister, it's completely irrelevant. What matters is the report itself and the very serious threat it contains."

The prime minister picked up a sheet of paper that had been lying in front of him. "This was sent by e-mail," he said.

"Yes."

"And it suggests that this man, Desmond McCain, is engaged in a plot to poison the wheat crop in Kenya for his own financial gain."

Blunt blinked heavily. "I'm glad you had time to read it," he muttered.

The prime minister ignored the rudeness. He put the paper down. "What makes you believe this information is reliable?" he asked.

"We have absolutely no reason to doubt it."

"And yet I understand that this agent of yours, the one who sent the report—which, incidentally, has no fewer than three spelling mistakes—is only fourteen years old."

There was a long pause. The two advisers glanced at the prime minister, urging him on.

"Alex Rider. Is that his name?" the prime minister asked.

"He's never let us down in the past," Mrs. Jones cut in. She was carrying a slim leather case, which she opened. She took out a thin file marked TOP SECRET in red letters and handed it across. "These are the details of just four of the assignments he's undertaken on our behalf," she continued. "The most recent of them was in Australia."

"Shouldn't he be in school?"

"He called in sick."

"Let me have a look . . ." The prime minister opened the file and read it in silence. "You certainly seem to have a very high opinion of him," he remarked. "And let's say for the sake of argument that it's justified. Let's assume that everything that he has told you is true—"

"Then by four o'clock this evening, the wheat field will have been activated," Blunt said. In fact, Alex's e-mail had crossed two time zones. He had sent it at midday. It had arrived in New Delhi at half past two, Indian time. They had kept it for three hours before they had sent it to MI6 where it arrived at noon, UK time. Four o'clock in England would be seven o'clock in Kenya, and sunset. They had less than three hours in which to act. "The wheat will have been turned into a million doses of ricin," Blunt went on. "At the same time, the spores that McCain sprayed onto the field will take off and begin to spread across the rest of Kenya. It will settle on the next field and then the one after that. It's impossible to say how many millions of seeds Greenfields has supplied over the past five years. All we know for sure is that within three months, the entire country will be poisoned."

"We can let McCain know we're onto him," Ellis said. "There's not going to be any charity appeal. Once he knows that, there'll be no point in going ahead."

"I agree." Blackmore nodded his head, secretly annoyed that he hadn't spoken first.

"We don't have any way to contact McCain, short of parachuting into Simba River Camp," Blunt replied. "And anyway, we're too late. There's a biological clock that's already ticking. The damage has been done."

"So what do you suggest?"

"We need to speak to the Kenyan government and send in troops. The field has to be neutralized, probably with flamethrowers. And we also have to find Alex Rider. We've heard nothing more from him. I want to know he's safe."

Although she didn't show it, Mrs. Jones was surprised. It was the first time she had ever heard Blunt show any concern for Alex. Even when he had been shot, Blunt's main concern had been keeping the story out of the newspapers.

"I'm not sure that's possible, Mr. Blunt." The prime minister shifted uncomfortably in his seat. "It might be a bit awkward explaining to the Kenyan authorities that a British citizen has just launched a biochemical attack on their country . . . and let's not forget that Greenfields actually receives government funding! Of course, it wasn't my government that agreed to it, but even so, the political fallout could be appalling. Frankly, the less said the better. And I definitely think we ought to handle the situation ourselves."

"I have an SAS task force on standby," Blunt said.

"It would still take too long to fly them to Africa," Blackmore said. He glanced at the prime minister, waiting for permission to continue. The prime minister nodded. "But in my view, we can do better than that," he said. "We have an RAF Phantom squadron in Akrotiri, Cyprus. They're already fueling. They can be in the air in half an hour."

"And what do you intend to do with them?" Blunt asked.

"It's very simple, Mr. Blunt. We're going to bomb the entire wheat field. After all, thanks to your agent, we know exactly where it is."

"But won't the bombs do McCain's work for him? You'll actually blow the spores into the air. You'll spread them all over Africa."

"We don't believe so. The Phantoms will be carrying AGM-65 Maverick air-to-surface tactical missiles with infrared tracking. They'll be able to pinpoint the target exactly. Each plane has six missiles. Each missile contains eighty-six pounds of high explosive. The advice we've been given is that there's a 99.5 percent probability that every single one of the spores will be destroyed in the firestorm."

"That still leaves room for error," Blunt said.

"And what about Alex?" Mrs. Jones added. "For all we know, he could still be in the area. Are we going to launch a missile strike against him too?"

"I don't think we have any choice," Ellis said. He reached down and picked a speck of dust off his tie. "There's no reason to believe he's anywhere near the target area."

"And if he is?"

"I'm sure you'd agree that we can't allow one life to get in the way. Not when we're trying to save thousands."

There was a brief silence. The prime minister was looking more uncomfortable than ever. But then he spoke again. "I think we've come to a unanimous decision, Mr. Blunt."

"You certainly have," Blunt muttered.

"And before you leave, there is one thing I do have to ask you. Exactly how many agents do you have who are underage . . . which is to say, sixteen years old or younger?"

"We have only one," Blunt replied. "There is only one Alex Rider."

"I'm very glad to hear it." The prime minister looked apologetic. "To be honest, I was rather horrified to discover that the British secret service would even consider employing a minor. I can see from his file that he's been tremendously useful to you and he certainly deserves our gratitude. But putting children into danger, no matter how compelling the reason . . . well, I'm not sure the public would stand for it. In my view, recruiting him in the first place was a serious error of judgment."

"Well, if your Phantom jets manage to kill him, that won't be a problem anymore, will it," Blunt said. He was speaking evenly and without emotion, but it was the nearest Mrs. Jones had ever seen him come to losing his temper.

"I hope it won't come to that, Mr. Blunt. But whatever happens, I want to make it clear that my government will not tolerate this sort of thing again. This is Alex's last assignment, do you understand me? I want him back at school."

The meeting was over. Blunt and Mrs. Jones stood up and walked out of the room, back down the stairs, and out into the street where their car was waiting for them.

"The man is an idiot," Blunt snapped as they swept through the gates at the end of Downing Street. "He talks about a 0.5 percent margin of error. But I spoke to Redwing, and she thinks it's much higher. These missiles of his won't kill the disease. They'll spread it . . . farther and faster than anyone could imagine."

"What about Alex?" Mrs. Jones asked.

"I'll talk to RAW the moment we get back. But their man has gone silent. Nobody knows what's happening in Kenya." He glanced briefly out of the window as they turned into Whitehall. "It looks as if, once again, Alex Rider is on his own."

"Where did you find this?"

Desmond McCain was sitting behind the folding table that he used as a workplace in his own private cabin at Simba River Camp. The room was similar to the one in which Alex had been kept, except that there was no bed and the walls were decorated with photographs of the office buildings that McCain had once developed in the east end of London. Although the fan had been turned to full speed, the air was still hot and sluggish. There was sweat on his head and on his face. It was seeping through the shoulders of his jacket.

He was looking at a leather shoe, one he recognized. The last time he had seen it, it had been on Myra Beckett's foot. In fact, it still was. The foot, bitten off just above the ankle, was still inside.

"It was beside the river, sir."

Njenga was also in the room, standing with his legs apart and his hands behind his back. He had become the leader of the dozen men working for McCain. The rest of them spoke only Bantu, but he had been to school in Nairobi and spoke fluent English. McCain took one last look at all that remained of his fiancée. A single tear stole out of his eye and crept down his cheek. He wiped it away with the back of his hand.

Also on the table was a scrap of material, part of Alex's shirt. McCain examined it. "What about this?" he asked.

"It was in the same place."

"By the river."

"Yes, sir."

McCain held the shirt in his huge hands, tugging at it with his fingers. It had been more than two hours since he had noticed that Myra was missing and had sent out his men to find her. They had come back with this. What could possibly have happened? He had left her standing on the observation platform, waiting for the child to come to the end of his strength and to fall as, inevitably, he must. There was no way that Alex Rider would have been able to reach her. Nor could he have escaped. It had all been too carefully arranged. And yet there was something . . .

"There is no blood on this shirt," he said. "We've been tricked. Somehow, the child got away."

Njenga said nothing. The rule here was to speak only when it was essential.

"He can't have gone far, even with a two-hour start. He has nowhere to go. He won't have crossed the river, not knowing what's in it. So it should be a simple matter to track him down." McCain had come to a decision. "I want you to take the men—all of them—and set off after him. I'm not asking anything clever. I want you to bring him back to me alive if you possibly can. I would like to have the pleasure of finishing this once and for all. But if you think he's going to get away, then kill him and bring me back his head. Do you understand? This time, I want to be sure."

"Yes, sir." Njenga showed no concern about killing and decapitating a child. All that mattered to him was the money that would come to him at the end of the month.

"Go now. Don't come back until the job is done."

A few minutes later they all left, twelve men carrying a variety of weapons, including spears, knives, and machetes. Half of them had guns. Njenga himself carried a German-manufactured Sauer 202 bolt-action hunting rifle equipped with a Zeiss Conquest scope. He knew he could shoot the eye of an antelope out at two hundred yards. He had done so many times.

They found two tracks at the river. The first one went into the bush and came back again. The second, which was much clearer, headed off toward the north. This was the path they chose. Alex Rider had a two-hour start, but they were Kikuyu tribesmen. They were taller, faster, and stronger than him. They knew the land.

They set off at a fast run, dodging through the undergrowth, confident that they'd catch up with him in no time at all.

23

SIMBA DAM

THE BIRDS PERCHED HIGH UP in the camphor tree were definitely vultures. The shape was unmistakable—the long necks and the bald heads—and the way they sat, hunched up and still. There were about ten of them, ranged across the branches, black against the afternoon sky. But the question Alex had to ask himself was: Were they waiting for him?

He had no idea how long he had been running for, but he knew he couldn't go on much longer. He was dehydrated and close to exhaustion, his arms covered in scratches, his face burned by the African sun. The bits of his school uniform that he was still wearing couldn't have been less well suited to this sort of terrain. The black polyester pants trapped the heat, and his lace-up dress shoes had caused him to slip twice. Each time he had come crashing down to the ground, he had wearily reminded himself that there was a bomb strapped to his back. Not that he could have forgotten it. The weight of Rahim's backpack was dragging him down, the straps cutting into his shoulders. Well, if the bomb went off, the vultures would have their feast. It would just come in snack-sized pieces.

The journey should have been simple. After all, he had

seen where he had to go from the air. Unfortunately, the landscape looked very different at ground level when he was stuck in the middle of it. The sudden rising hills, the thick vegetation, the spiky shrubs that forced him to turn another way . . . all these had been flattened out when he was in the Piper Cub. The bush had swallowed him up. The dam, the pylons, the track had all disappeared.

He had to rely on the map and his own sense of direction. To start with, he had kept the river on his right—near enough to glimpse the water through the trees but not so close as to attract the attention of whatever might be lurking within it. That was his greatest fear. He was in the middle of a killing field—and he wasn't being escorted around like a tourist in a four-by-four. It had been midday when he set out and most of the animals would have been asleep, but the sun was already beginning to cool and very soon they would awaken and begin their ceaseless search for food. Was he prey? He could imagine his scent creeping out. All around him, invisible eyes could be watching his progress, already measuring the distance. He had seen elephants, monkeys, and, of course, crocodiles. What other horrors might be waiting for him around the next corner if he was unlucky? There could be lions or cheetahs. He had thought of taking the Dragunov sniper rifle or searching Rahim's pockets for other weapons, but in the end he had decided against it. Rahim might need them when he recovered consciousness. Now he wished he hadn't been so generous.

After about half a mile, he had turned away from the river, heading in what he hoped would be the direction of the dam—and it was then that his progress became harder. This time it was the map that was deceiving him. It hadn't showed that the ground sloped steeply uphill, although he should have worked it out for himself. Rahim had told him that the water held back by the Simba Dam flowed through two hydroelectric turbines. Since water only flows downhill, it was fairly obvious that he would have to climb.

It was hard work, weighed down in the hot sun. And the African landscape was huge. He knew he had only two miles to cover, but somehow the distances seemed to have been magnified so that even a shrub or a tree right in front of him always took too long to reach. Worse still, after leaving the river behind him, Alex had lost all sense of direction. The colors were too muted: the pale greens and browns, the faint streaks of yellow and orange. You could hide a herd of elephants here and not see them. There was nowhere for the eye to focus. There were no people, no houses, nothing that looked like a pathway or a road. This was the world as it must have been long ago, before man began to shape it to his needs. Alex felt like an intruder. And he was utterly lost.

But as long as he was climbing uphill, he had to be going the right way. He stopped and took out Rahim's water bottle. He had already drunk from it three times, and he had tried to ration himself, but even so, he was surprised to find it almost empty. He finished the last drops and slung the empty container into the bush. Let the Kikuyu tribesmen pick it up. Alex had no doubt that they were already closing in behind him.

The bush ahead suddenly parted. Alex froze. It was an animal of some sort, small and dark, hidden by the long grass. And it was headed toward him. For a moment he felt the same uncontrollable terror that McCain had inflicted on him at the crocodile pit. If this was a lion, then it was all over. But then he relaxed. The animal was a warthog. For a moment it stared at him with its small, brutish eyes. Its upturned nose sniffed the air, and Alex could imagine it asking itself the same question it must ask every day. *Food?* Then it made its decision. This creature was too big and probably wouldn't taste very nice. It turned around and fled the way it had come.

Alex looked back. What time was it? There was a mountain ridge over to the west, lost in the heat haze like a strip of gray silk. The sun was sinking slowly behind it and there was already a faint moon visible against the clear blue sky. A meeting place of night and day. Alex wiped a grimy hand over his face. A mosquito whined in his ear. He wondered if Rahim had woken up yet. What would the Indian agent do when he discovered he was alone?

A movement caught his eye. At first, Alex thought he had imagined it—but there it was again. An animal? No. About a dozen men were making their way toward him.

They were still at least half a mile away, far down at the bottom of the slope that Alex had been climbing. They were spread out in a line and Alex could just make out their black faces, the combat clothes they were wearing, and the weapons they carried or had strapped to their backs. He knew exactly who they were. He also knew that if he had seen them, they had seen him. If he stayed where he was, they would be with him in less than fifteen minutes.

Forcing himself on, he broke into a run. There was a thicket of trees to one side and he made for it, wondering if he might be able to lose himself among the trunks and branches. But it was a foolish hope. Alex knew that McCain's men must have been tracking him from the start and that a single broken blade of grass or a fallen leaf would have been like a flashing neon sign for them. Now it was just a question of speed. Could he reach the dam before they caught up with him? Could he detonate the bomb? Alex had no doubt that he was going to be captured and killed. But he would die more happily if he knew that he had beaten McCain.

The wood ended as suddenly as it had begun. On the other side was a field and the first man-made object that he had seen since he set out . . . the remains of a low wooden fence. He leapt over it and continued running, aware that he was surrounded by a very different sort of vegetation. It was wheat! Incredibly, he had actually found his way to McCain's wheat field. So the dam must be directly ahead of him. He still couldn't see it, but he knew it was there. If he just continued forward he would have to come upon it.

Suddenly, he was racing through the stalks. He could feel it scratching at his ankles and his hands. It surrounded him. And with a jolt of horror he wondered if it had switched yet, if the spores had done their work. If so, he was running through a vast field of poison. Each one of these bright yellow blades could be the death of him. The very air he breathed could be full of ricin. Grimly, Alex kept his lips tightly shut and his arms held high. It seemed incredible to him that McCain could have done this: taken something as natural, as universal as a wheat field and turned it into something deadly.

He glanced back. There was no sign of his followers. Seeing them had given him new speed and determination. Over to one side he saw the electricity pylon that he had spotted before, or one identical to it—not steel, but wood, and only four or five yards high. It was still a quarter of a mile away, but he made for it. The wires would lead to the turbines and the turbines had to be somewhere beneath the dam. He tried to remember on which side he had seen the track. That would be the fastest way forward. Was it possible that Njenga had come after him in the Land Rover? No. Alex would have heard the engine by now.

The wheat, waves and waves of it, crunched beneath his feet as he drove his way through it. He liked the sound that it made. He wanted to crush as much of it as he could, but the field seemed to go on forever, trapped between the two rock faces that rose up on each side.

Where was the dam? He should have been able to see it by now.

The wheat suddenly ended—so abruptly that it was as if Alex had fallen from one world to another. He was on the track! There it was, right underneath him. So how far did he have to go? How much farther *could* he go? He glanced back. There was still no sign of the Kikuyu tribesmen, but the wheat would cause them no problems. In fact, the trackers would have a field day. Alex would have left a highway for them to follow. He had to keep up his pace. They would surely have doubled theirs.

The track had once been covered with asphalt, but it was full of potholes now, with weeds and wild grass sprouting through. Alex guessed it would be used both by the farmers coming up to harvest the wheat and by technicians working on the hydroelectrics. He could make out tire tracks and hoofprints. It was an easier surface for running, but he was still going uphill and his mouth was dry. He resisted the temptation to look back. He had no time to waste. His muscles were taut and his whole body was tingling with the anticipation of a knife or a bullet in his back.

And then the track turned a corner and there, ahead of him, was the Simba Dam.

It was completely bizarre and out of place. That was

Alex's first thought. This huge gray wall had been constructed in the middle of all this unspoiled nature, and it
had no right to be there. It wasn't exactly ugly. Indeed,
the great curve, stretching from one side of the valley
to the other, had a certain gracefulness. Beaten by the
sun, the concrete had faded so that it blended in with
the rocks that surrounded it. But it was still a scar. In a
strange way, it reminded him of what had happened to
McCain's face. The dam cut the landscape in two, and
the two halves didn't quite meet.

Alex stumbled to a halt and stood there panting, his
entire body covered in sweat. He desperately needed a
drink. He wished now he had taken more care with his
water supply.

There was no sign of the lake from where he was
standing at the very foot of the dam, surrounded by dis-
carded pieces of cement and broken rocks that must have
been blasted during the construction. The surface of the
water had to be about ninety feet above him and, of
course, on the other side. He could see enormous slots in
the wall, oversized letter boxes with what looked like
metal gates cutting them in half. Presumably these could
be raised or lowered to allow the water to spill through.
Alex tried to imagine the amount of pressure that must be
pushing against the wall itself, the tons and tons of water
being held back. There was nobody here. Somewhere—
perhaps in Nairobi—someone would press a button and
a sluice would open. And then some of the water—just a

few million gallons—would rush down a series of hidden pipes to the turbines, where its energy would be siphoned off to provide electricity before it was finally released to feed the crops.

Suddenly the bomb he was carrying felt very small. As he followed the track to its end, the Simba Dam loomed over him, much bigger and more complicated than anything he had imagined. It curved in two directions, forming a letter C around him but also slanting out over his head, away from the water. What had Rahim called it? A double curvature arch dam. Now that he was here, it was easier to understand what that meant.

Two drainage slipways ran up on either side. These were basically curving roads running up the side of the hill, though so steeply that no car would be able to make the journey. Alex guessed that they had something to do with the water, which could be directed down them and into the valley if there happened to be heavy rainfall and the threat of a flood. Two concrete staircases had been built next to them, one for each slipway, with about a hundred steps leading up to the top. There was one other way up, a single ladder clinging to the face of the dam, leading to two inspection platforms, one above the other, and finally to the lip of the dam itself. The ladder was dangerous because it wasn't quite vertical. Following the curve of the wall, it slanted outward. It was also narrow, steep, and covered in rust.

Alex took this all in, then turned his attention to a

construction directly in front of him. It looked like something out of the Second World War . . . a solid concrete bunker with an entrance and three barred windows. A pair of fat steel pipes jutted out, pointing at him like the cannons of two tanks that might have been parked next to each other inside. Both of them were capped, making them look like oversized industrial oil cans. They were connected to the dam by hydraulic steel claws with a network of smaller pipes, wires, and taps around them. The concrete underneath them was stained. It had recently been wet.

Alex knew that he was looking at the two valves that Rahim had described. His targets. He took one quick look back over his shoulder, then hurried forward. He had perhaps five minutes to position the explosive before the Kikuyus arrived. Even as he ran, he wriggled out of the backpack and opened it. The concrete building had a sort of entrance, a narrow slit that led into an inner chamber with more pipes and machinery. While he was in here, Alex would be out of sight. Surely he couldn't have left a trail on the broken rock and other debris in front of the dam. With a bit of luck, the trackers wouldn't be able to find him . . . until it was too late.

He had the bomb in his hands. It couldn't have been more old-fashioned or easier to understand. That was what made terrorism all the more frightening—the fact that it relied on such simple devices. The glass window in front of the clock face opened and Alex was able to take the single hand and move it as many minutes as he wanted, up to sixty. He made a quick calculation. It would take him about two minutes to climb up to the top of the dam, using one of the staircases beside the slipways. Once he was there, he would be safe from the torrent of water. But what about the Kikuyus? Suddenly, Alex had an idea.

He turned the hand of the clock to the figure 5, then pressed the two switches. A green light came on and the clock began to tick. So it was done. Alex looked around him. It didn't matter which valve he chose. He just had to hope that the explosion—contained within the concrete walls—would be strong enough to rupture them both. He placed the bomb on top of one of the pipes, wedging it against the ceiling. Now to get away.

He slithered out of the opening and stopped in dismay. He saw three Kikuyu men just a short distance ahead of him. They had almost reached the end of the track and were gazing at the dam as if it had deliberately chosen to block their path. There was no more than fifty yards between them. They saw Alex at once. One of them called out. The other threw his spear. It fell short. None of them seemed to have guns.

Alex began to run. He headed for the nearest slipway, but he hadn't even begun to climb when another of McCain's men appeared at the top, pointed down, and shouted. Alex realized what had happened. The dozen tribesmen had arrived at the dam and, as he had hoped, they had lost his track. So they had separated. They were all around him now, coming at him from all sides.

And he had made a terrible miscalculation.

There were just four and a half minutes until the bomb would go off. He didn't have time to go back into the bunker and change the time of the detonation . . . he'd be trapping himself and it would only draw attention to what he had done. He had to move quickly—and preferably up. If he stayed here, he would be killed by the blast or drowned in the rush of water. The slipway on the right was covered. Alex looked the other way. Yet another tribesman had appeared and was scampering down. The three men who had first seen him were getting closer.

That just left the rusty, winding ladder, running up the side of the bunker onto the roof and then up toward the two platforms.

Alex grabbed hold of the first rung and began to climb.

The F-4 Phantom 11 fighter jets had taken off at exactly 3:45 P.M. local time, their Rolls-Royce Spey engines powering them down the runway and into the air, climbing at 40,000 feet per minute. There were three of them. They had leveled off at 80,000 feet, moving into a classic arrow formation, before turning south toward Africa. Each one carried eight missiles. Between them, they were confident that they had enough firepower to turn McCain's wheat field into a blazing hell in which nothing, not so much as a single microbe, would survive.

There was, of course, the faintest possibility that the initial force of the impact would propel some of the mushroom spores into the air, ahead of the flames. These spores would then travel very fast and very far and do their lethal work elsewhere. But as is so often the way with British politics, a decision had been made. If it was later shown to be wrong, all the evidence would be gently massaged to show that no other decision had been possible. Not that the public would ever hear about this. The orders that the three Phantom pilots had received were top secret. Their flight plan had not been recorded. As far as the world was concerned, they hadn't even taken off.

And when the three planes crossed the Kenyan border, heading west from the Indian Ocean, the urgent inquiries from air traffic control in Nairobi were ignored. Later, it would be explained that they had accidentally strayed off course during a training mission. Profuse apologies would be offered to the Kenyan government. But for now, they were observing strict radio silence.

The Phantoms were equipped with the Northrop target identification system, essentially a telescopic camera fitted to the left wing and connected to a radarscope inside the cockpit. As Alex began to climb the ladder at the Simba Dam, the planes began to drop altitude, flying toward the Rift Valley at just under 1,200 miles per hour.

Inside their cockpits, the pilots made their final preparations. There would be no need for a flyby. The target coordinates were locked in. Once they had visual contact, they would open fire.

Alex was halfway up the ladder, with the first maintenance platform stretching out above his head. It was hard work, climbing up. Because of the curve of the dam, he was leaning outward, and the force of gravity was against him; every time he pulled himself up another rung, he felt himself being dragged backward. The sun was now beating down on him, burning his shoulders and back. He forced himself to keep going. He was painfully aware of the bomb he had activated and that was ticking away even now. If only he had given himself more time! If it went off before he reached the top of the dam, there was a good chance the ladder would be blown off the wall— and him with it. He was already too high up. If he fell, he would die.

He grabbed hold of the next rung and looked back, only to see two of the tribesmen who had raised the alarm—at this height they were no more than toy figures—running down to the foot of the dam. The third was holding back. None of them seemed anxious to climb the ladder after him. Why?

He looked up and saw the reason. They had no need to follow him. Another Kikuyu man had reached the center of the dam and was already climbing down.

There was no way out. Alex consoled himself with the knowledge that nobody knew about the bomb apart from him and that in about two or three minutes it would explode, releasing millions of gallons of water that would flood the valley, drowning the wheat. It would be mission accomplished . . . except that he wouldn't be around to see it. Somewhere in his mind, he wondered if anyone would ever discover what had happened. Perhaps Rahim would make a report if he managed to get away. *He died fighting for what he believed in.* Alex could already see the words inscribed on the medal. Jack could wear it at his funeral.

But he wasn't ready to give up yet. He couldn't go back down. He saw that the third Kikuyu was aiming another spear at him. That was why he had positioned himself farther back. Well, he would be in for a surprise when the valve smashed. A spider down the bath drain! He was about to find out what it felt like. Alex seized hold of the next rung and pulled. Once again, the curving wall pushed him backward, as if it were desperate to make him let go.

The man above him was getting closer. It was Njenga, McCain's first in command. He had already reached the upper platform and was dragging the rifle off his shoulder, bringing it around to pick off Alex. But Njenga knew that he too had made mistakes. First, as he'd approached the dam, he had instructed his men to separate. He had been confused by all the different concrete ramps and stair-

ways, the various outbuildings with their tanks and pipe-
work. He had assumed Alex would try to hide and had
given the order to spread out and search for him.

And he had spotted Alex too late. From where he was
standing, the slant of the dam put him at a disadvantage.
So long as Alex remained underneath him, he was slightly
tucked away, out of sight, and Njenga couldn't get off a
clear shot. Why, then, was the boy still climbing? He had
just reached the lower platform and was continuing up
the next stretch of the ladder that would bring the two of
them face-to-face. There was no need for shooting just
yet. Njenga laid down the rifle, took out his machete, and
smiled to himself. How far did the boy think he would be
able to climb without hands?

He waited. Alex was getting closer.

Alex knew he couldn't risk going any farther. He could
see Njenga's machete blade dangling in the air directly
above him. If he climbed another few rungs, he would be
in range. He would have to wait for the explosion. Perhaps the shock of it might change things, rearrange them
in his favor. It was all he could hope for.

At the bottom of the dam, the Kikuyu tribesman threw
his spear. The black needle with its vicious silver point
flashed toward Alex. He saw it out of the corner of his
eye. The man who had thrown it must have been fantasti-
cally strong, as there were at least twenty yards between
them. But the spear was off target. It was going to hit the
wall just to his left.

At the very last second, Alex let go of the ladder with one hand, his whole body swinging around as if on a hinge. He stretched out with his free hand and caught the spear in midair, then, using all the strength in his shoulder, swung himself back again. At the same time, he lunged upward. He had grabbed hold of the spear at the very bottom end. The beaten metal tip sliced into Njenga's leg, just above the ankle. Njenga screamed and toppled sideways.

Then the bomb went off.

Alex felt the entire ladder jerk violently. He was almost thrown off—and would have been if he hadn't been expecting the shock wave and prepared for it by wrapping himself around the metalwork, clinging on with his arms and his legs. He felt himself being slammed away from the wall of the dam and cried out as a ball of flame rushed past his back and shoulders, shooting into the air. But he was still there. The ladder had held. He hadn't been thrown off.

Njenga was less fortunate. Shocked and in pain, with blood pouring out of the wound in his leg, he was caught off balance and plummeted down. He managed one twist in midair before dashing onto the rocks below.

And instantly he was gone. Alex must have positioned the bomb perfectly. It had completely smashed the bottom outlet valve and ruptured the other valve too. It was as if the two biggest taps in the world had been turned on simultaneously. The water didn't just rush out—it erupted with such force that it seemed to obliterate the entire landscape—the rocks, the vegetation, and, of course, the three Kikuyus who had been standing in its path. They were simply washed away, smashed out of existence by a thundering white locomotive that roared over them, taking them with it.

How many thousands of gallons of water were being released by the second? It was impossible to say. The water didn't even look like water. It was more like smoke or steam—only more solid. Alex saw a huge tree uprooted as if it were no more than a weed, a boulder pushed effortlessly aside. And then the flood reached up for him. He felt the spray whipping into the back of his legs, and looking down, he saw that almost all the ladder had been ripped away, that the twisted metal ended just a few rungs beneath his feet. If he stayed here for a minute more, he too would be sucked into the vortex and obliterated.

Once again he began to climb. The sound of the water was pounding in his ears, deafening him, and he remembered the huge lake that the Simba Dam had been containing and wondered how much longer the curving wall could hold it. The lake was a monster that had been given its first taste of freedom. This one torrent might not be enough. It would demand more.

Alex was soaked from the spray. He was blistered by the sun. He was close to exhaustion. Yet somehow he dragged himself up to the platform where Njenga had been standing and then onto the last ladder that led to the top. He didn't dare look back. He could still hear an incredible, explosive pounding, the sound of the third day when God created the oceans. Surely it must have been like this. And he knew that very soon, the river that he had created would reach the wheat field. Every last stalk would be drowned. Maybe the water would even reach the Simba River Camp and destroy that too. He liked the idea of McCain disappearing in a swirl of mud and stones and broken trees. It was nothing less than he deserved.

He reached the top of the ladder and rolled over a low wall with a road on the other side. Dripping wet, gasping for breath, he knelt for a moment, taking stock of his surroundings.

The track that he had followed from the wheat field rose up past one of the slipways and continued over the lip of the dam, where it became a bridge, a dead straight line that crossed from one side to the other. That was where he was now. He had climbed over one hundred feet. The ground, with the churning water, was a long, long way down. On the other side of the dam, in front of him, the lake stretched toward the horizon, completely calm and undisturbed by what was taking place below. Alex could see distant mountains, the clouds, and the emerald sky, all reflected in the mirror of the surface. He turned back. From here he could make out the sweep of the land, a great plain with the silhouettes of trees and, in the far distance, a herd of gazelles, lost in their surroundings.

And there was the wheat field with the first finger of water trickling through it, widening with every second that passed. In another minute it would begin to drown. In five, it would no longer exist. At least there was that.

But once again he was trapped. The remaining Kikuyu tribesmen were on top of the dam, in two groups, left and right. They had already seen him and were shouting among themselves, excitedly raising their rifles, taking aim. Alex was midway between them. Did they know what had happened while he was on the ladder? It made no difference. They would have fired at him already, except they had to be careful. If they missed, there was a chance they might hit each other.

They began to move forward. Alex could only stand and wait.

The road trembled. Alex felt it, like an earthquake beneath his feet. At first he thought it must be tiredness, that he had imagined it. But then it happened again and this time it was stronger. The entire wall of the dam was shifting. The Kikuyus had felt it too. They stopped dead in their tracks, looking at each other for explanation. The answer was obvious.

The dam was breaking apart. Perhaps the bomb had damaged some of the joints where the individual blocks of concrete had come together in the construction. Or there could always have been a hairline crack, a weakness just waiting for the moment to bring an end to the whole thing. Well, that moment had come. Alex was thrown sideways as the ground tilted. He saw more water gushing out of a newly formed crack. Part of the wall crumbled, huge pieces of masonry tumbling in slow motion, disappearing into the chaos below. He knew that there were just seconds left before the whole thing collapsed. Even if he tried to run, it would be too late.

The Kikuyus were retreating, panic etched into their faces. They had forgotten him. They had to get off the dam and back onto dry land. Two of them lurched into each other and then both of them were knocked sideways, thrown off their feet by the cement floor, which tilted up beneath them, their weapons clanging to the ground. They screamed as they fell over the edge.

Alex fought for balance. Something was coming toward him. What was it now? A plane—but a strange one, small, like a toy. Alex recognized the Piper Cub. It was flying over the lake, heading toward him, so low that the wheels were almost touching the water. Was it McCain? Had he come for revenge? But then he saw a rope trailing from the back and a dark figure hunched over the controls. Rahim! He must have recovered to find Alex missing and somehow guessed what he planned to do. Rahim had come for him. He had told Alex he could fly. He had also said that he could slow the plane down to thirty-five miles per hour. He was steering it straight into the headwind, using the air currents to slow himself down. If he went any slower, he would surely stall.

He knew what Rahim had in mind. But he couldn't do it. Alex would be torn in two.

Another explosion of concrete and water. Part of the dam tumbled like a house of cards, sinking into itself. The ground tilted crazily. Once again, Alex had to struggle to stay on his feet.

The plane was so close that Alex could see the concentration on Rahim's face as he fought to keep himself in the air. The end of the rope was skimming the surface of the lake, snaking a line through the water. The plane looked slow, but the rope was whipping toward him, almost a blur.

There was no other way.

Blindly, Alex reached up and felt something lash into his chest and the side of his neck. The plane howled over him, so close that it nearly took off his head. The wheels rushed past. Somehow, his scrabbling hands caught hold of the rope, tearing the skin off his palms. The end twisted around him. And then he was jerked into the air, so hard that he felt like he was being split in half. Pain jolted through his arms and down his spine. His shoulders felt completely dislocated. He was blacking out.

But his feet were in the air. He was being dragged up and now there was nothing beneath him except white foam, the bellowing water, crashing cement. Higher and higher. He wasn't even sure how he was holding on.

Somehow the rope had tied itself around him. The ground was rushing past.

Behind him, the Simba Dam disintegrated and the lake surged forward, free at last, hundreds of thousands of gallons pouring down into the valley. All the remaining Kikuyus were swept with it, mercilessly battered to death before they could even drown.

Dangling from the plane, Alex was carried away.

The water, blood red in the setting sun, continued pouring into an ever-widening sea.

In London, the prime minister was on the telephone.

"Yes." He listened for a moment, a tic of anger beating in his forehead. "Yes, I quite understand. Thank you for keeping me informed."

He put the phone down.

"Who was that?" Charles Blackmore, the director of communications, was in the office with him. It was 5:15 in the evening, but the day's work at Downing Street wouldn't end for a while yet. There were papers to be signed off, a planned phone call with the president of the United States, and at six o'clock, a cocktail party being held for all the people who had been working on the London Olympics. The prime minister was looking forward to that. He still enjoyed seeing himself in the newspapers, particularly when he was supporting a popular cause.

"It was the RAF in Cyprus," the prime minister said.

"Is there a problem?"

"Not exactly." The prime minister frowned. "It seems that this whole business in Kenya was a complete waste of time."

"Oh yes?"

"We actually deployed three Phantom jets down to this place . . . the Simba Valley. The pilots had the exact coordinates. Fortunately, they decided to take a visual sighting before they fired off their missiles. And just as well . . ."

Blackmore waited, a look of polite inquiry on his face.

"There were no wheat fields . . . no sign of any crop at all. There's just a giant lake there. They circled over the entire area, to be sure that there wasn't any mistake. So either the information given us by MI6 was inaccurate, or this boy, Alex Rider, made the whole thing up."

"Why would he do that?"

"Well, he's only a child. I suppose he was seeking attention. But it just shows that I was absolutely right. Remind me to call the Joint Chiefs of Staff. I think I should have a word with them about Alan Blunt. I'm afraid this puts a serious question mark over his judgment."

"I agree, Prime Minister." Blackmore coughed. "So what did the Phantoms do?"

"What else could they do? They turned around and went home. The whole thing was a complete waste of time and money. Perhaps we should start looking for someone else to head up Special Operations." The prime minister stood up. "How long until the party, Charles?"

"We have forty-five minutes."

"I think I might change. Put on a new tie. What do you think?"

"Maybe the blue one?"

"Good idea."

The file that Blunt had brought to the office was still on the desk. There was a photograph of Alex Rider clipped to the first page. The prime minister closed it and slid it into a drawer. Then he went out to get changed.

24

UNHAPPY LANDING

THE AIRPORT WAS ON THE OUTSKIRTS of a small town made up of brightly colored houses and shops and seemed to be a stopping point for tourists on their way to or from safari. There were half a dozen private planes lined up beside the single runway and a fancy clubhouse with wooden tables and sunshades where passengers could wait. Everything was very neat. The lawns and the hedges could have belonged to an English country house. There was a small playground with swings and a seesaw, and the children who were playing there were well-dressed and quiet. The evening was completely calm, with the sun setting behind the great mass of Mount Kenya, and the occasional clatter of a propeller starting up or the buzz of a plane landing seemed strangely inappropriate. Surely they could find somewhere else to go about the business of air travel!

Alex Rider took this all in as the Piper J-3 Cub came in to land. They flew low over a row of chalets with the word LAIKIPIA painted in large letters across the roofs, and he guessed that this must be the name of the town. They had been flying for about an hour, heading southeast. He knew they couldn't have gone much farther. Looking over Rahim's shoulder, he had watched the needle on the fuel indicator begin its downward journey. It had arrived at zero a while ago.

After everything he had been through, climbing into the rear seat of the Piper had almost been too much. Pulling himself up the rope, inch by inch, while being whipped through the air at eighty miles per hour and six thousand feet above the ground, he had forced his mind to go blank, to concentrate—totally—on what he had to do. He didn't look down. He wasn't sure he had the stomach for it. But nor did he look up. That would only taunt him with how far he still had to go. All he could do was cling to the rope with his hands and his feet, trying to pretend that this was just a PE class at Brookland, that there was no wind rush on his face, no engines buzzing in his ears, and that when he got to the top he would be given a quick round of applause and then allowed to get changed for French.

The whole thing would have been impossible if the crop duster had been equipped with a closed cockpit. But there were no windows or doors, and when Alex reached the top of the rope, he was able to grab the edge of the plane and pull himself over and into the backseat. He landed awkwardly, his face and shoulder burrowing into the soft leather—but it felt wonderful. He was safe. And he was leaving the Reverend Desmond McCain, the Kikuyus, and the Simba Dam far behind him.

"Untie the rope!"

Rahim had turned around and shouted at him, the

wind snatching the words away even as they were spoken. Alex did as he was told, untying the rope from the wing strut and letting it fall back to earth. He watched it dwindle in the distance until it was no more than a wriggling worm and reflected that it could all too easily have been him, free-falling down to the earth far below. He couldn't believe what he had just been through. He sank back into the seat, belted himself in, and let out a deep sigh of relief.

The RAW agent hadn't spoken again, and Alex was grateful. He was utterly drained and although sleep was impossible with the wind battering against him, he tried as best he could to relax, somehow to recharge his batteries, to put this whole business behind him. He wanted to go home. With his eyes half open, he watched the landscape slide away beneath him, the different patches of green and brown crisscrossed by roads and dirt tracks with tiny buildings scattered here and there and hinting at some sort of life—normal life—carrying on in the vastness of the Kenyan bush. The Piper's engine droned on. Rahim was wearing his camouflage jacket. Alex only had his shirt and pants, and as the evening drew in, he began to shiver. Very soon it would be night.

But even though the sun had gone, the sky was still glowing softly when Rahim suddenly shouted into his headset, getting permission from air traffic control at Laikipia to land. The little plane wavered in the air as if finding its balance. The ground, a long strip of tarmac, rushed toward them. Then they bumped down and taxied to a halt. A few airport workers, dressed in bright yellow overalls with TROPICAIR stenciled across their chest, glanced curiously in their direction. It wasn't often they saw such an old-fashioned aircraft here. And a crop duster! There weren't any crops for miles. A few tourists sitting outside the clubhouse stood up and watched them come in. A couple of them unfastened their cameras and took pictures.

Rahim turned off the engine and the propeller began to slow down. He took off his headset and twisted around. Alex wasn't sure what he had been expecting, but he was taken aback by the anger in the agent's face.

"What did you think you were doing?" Rahim exploded. He still had to shout to make himself heard, but from the look of him, he would have shouted anyway. "You could have gotten yourself killed. You could have gotten me killed!"

"Rahim . . . ," Alex began. He wanted to climb out of the plane. Couldn't they have this argument over a cold drink and something to eat?

But Rahim was in no mood to go anywhere. "You stole my equipment. I cannot believe what you did. You left me there—"

"I had to do it."

"No! My job was to kill McCain. That was all. We could have dealt with his plan afterward. You disobeyed my instructions, Alex. Do you have any idea of the damage you've caused? And how do you think my people are going to explain all this to the Kenyan authorities? You took out an entire hydroelectric and irrigation system!"

"Well, maybe you can tell them we saved thousands of lives. They might like that."

"McCain is still out there. He got away."

"I left you your gun. Why didn't you just go and shoot him?"

"Because I had to come after you." Rahim shook his head in exasperation. "I should have left you to the crocodiles."

There was a brief silence. The propeller was still turning, but more slowly.

"Where are we?" Alex asked. "What are we doing here?"

"This is Laikipia. We have to refuel. I'm leaving you here. I've contacted my people and they'll arrange for you to be picked up."

"What about you?"

"I'm going—"

That was as far as he got. To Alex, it appeared as if Rahim had snapped his head around the other way. At the same time, he was aware of a sudden spray of red vapor filling the air in front of him. Alex looked back to see Desmond McCain, dressed in a brown linen suit, walking toward him, the Mauser pistol in his hand. He turned back to Rahim. The agent was dead. He had collapsed forward over the controls. There was a gaping wound in the side of his head.

Alex felt a wave of anger and disgust. He was also sorry. Despite everything, Rahim had come back for him and saved him . . . for the third time. Alex hadn't even had a chance to thank him.

The propeller stopped.

McCain stood beside the plane, right next to the wing. The gun was now leveled at Alex. How had McCain gotten here? Alex was too shocked to think, but it occurred to him that if Rahim had chosen this airfield to refuel, then McCain might have landed here for exactly the same reason. All around him, he was aware of people—aircrew, tourists, children—running for cover, in panic. They had just seen a stumbling giant of a man, with a silver crucifix in his ear, appear from nowhere and commit murder for no obvious reason. They must think he was insane. If they only knew!

McCain didn't seem to know where he was—or even to care. He had seen Alex and he had come to settle the score. Nothing else mattered.

"Get out of the plane," McCain said. His voice was steady, but his eyes were bloodshot and unfocused, the skin around his face stretched tight. He was trembling slightly. He was doing his best to control it, but the muzzle of the gun gave him away.

Alex stayed where he was.

"What do you want, Mr. McCain?" he demanded. "I'm not going anywhere. Nor are you. Your wheat field is at the bottom of a lake. There isn't going to be any plague. It's all over."

"Get. Out. Of. The. Plane," McCain repeated. His finger tightened on the trigger. He was holding the gun as if he were trying to crush it.

"Why?"

"I want to see you kneeling in front of me. Just for once, I want you to behave like an ordinary child. You're going to cry and beg me not to hurt you. And then I'm going to put this gun between your eyes and shoot you dead."

"Then you might as well shoot me here. I'm not playing your games."

McCain dropped the gun a few inches so that it was aiming at Alex's legs. Alex knew that the skin of the Piper Cub would offer no protection at all. "I can make it slow . . . ," McCain said.

Alex nodded. He took one more look around him. It didn't seem as if anyone was going to come to his rescue. The whole airfield had emptied. The other planes—and now he spotted the Skyhawk that had first brought him to Simba River Lodge—were silent, unmoving. Surely someone would have called the police by now . . . assuming that there were any police operating in a remote town like Laikipia.

"All right," he said.

He unbuckled his belt, gripped the sides of the plane, and began to pull himself out. At the same time, he glanced into the front of the plane, past the slumped figure of the pilot. He knew that Rahim had a gun. But there was no sign of it and no way he could search around without receiving a bullet himself.

What else? His eyes fell on the metal lever between the two seats. He thought of the two rubber pipes running underneath his feet, connected to the plastic tanks at the back of the plane. The pipes that had sprayed a wheat field with death.

The whole system must work on pressure, with the tank pumped up by the engine. They had been flying for an hour, so there had to be enough pressure in the tubes. But was there any of the mushroom spore left in the tanks? Alex didn't dare turn around and look. McCain was still standing under the wing, waiting for him to climb down.

Alex stood up. As he swung his leg over the side, he pretended to stumble. His hand shot out, slamming the lever down. At once he heard a hiss—and a mere second later, a film of gray, slimy liquid squirted out of the pipes. McCain was taken by surprise. For a moment he was blinded, caught in the middle of the shower, the mushroom brew splashing over his head and into his eyes.

McCain fired his gun—but missed. After slamming the lever, Alex had thrown himself the other way, tumbling over the far side of the plane and down to the grass below. He heard the bullet thwack into the fuselage, inches from his head. At the same time, he hit the ground and cried out, a white flash blazing behind his eyes. He had landed badly, twisting his ankle beneath him. Worse still, the tanks had only contained a few dregs. Alex had barely got to his feet and begun to limp away before the shower stopped and McCain, cursing and wiping his eyes, was after him.

Alex could barely do more than hobble. His foot wouldn't take his full weight. Every step was an agony that shot up his leg and all the way to his neck. He knew he wouldn't be able to go much farther, and anyway, there was nowhere to go. Behind him, the grass and the landing strip stretched out, flat and empty. The perimeter was fenced off with an open gate leading to the edge of the town, but it was too far away. He would never reach it. McCain didn't seem to be moving fast, but like a figure in a nightmare he was getting closer with every step.

Alex came to a line of drums stacked up on the grass right next to the tarmac, each one marked TOTAL ESSENCE PLOMBÉE. Leaded fuel. Why was it written in French? Mc-Cain fired five times. The nearest drum shivered and fuel began to splash out, spouting in five directions. Alex dived for cover behind it. His ankle burned with pain. He wondered if he would be able to get up again.

McCain stopped about ten paces away, as if this was a game and he had all the time in the world. Casually, he took out a fresh ammunition clip and reloaded the gun. Meanwhile, the fuel continued to gush out.

"You can't hide from me, child," McCain shouted. "'Vengeance is mine. I will repay, sayeth the Lord.' That's Romans chapter twelve. A vengeful god . . . isn't that a wonderful thing? And now, finally, the time for my vengeance has come. Let me see you."

Alex tested one of the drums. It was full of fuel and too heavy to move. But the drum that McCain had punctured was emptying rapidly. Lying on his back, he pressed both feet against it and pushed with all his strength. It toppled over. Now Alex was exposed. There was nothing between him and McCain's gun. He got to his knees, leaned on the drum, then rolled it over the tarmac toward McCain.

McCain smiled. He walked forward and place a single foot on the drum, stopping its progress. He had a clear view of Alex and at this range he couldn't miss. Alex was still kneeling on the ground. It was just what he wanted.

"Is that the best you can do? Send a drum to run me over? You _are_ a child, aren't you? This isn't a game, Alex. Do you know how many years I spent planning this operation?" McCain asked. His voice carried across the short distance. He was leaning forward, one foot still perched on the drum, his elbow resting on his thigh. "Do you have any idea what it meant to me? All I wanted was my rightful place in the world. Money is power and I was going to have more than you could possibly imagine.

"And now *you* are going to pay. I'm going to shoot you now. Not once but several times. And then I'm going to walk away." He lifted the gun. "Good-bye, Alex. You're going on a slow journey to hell."

"Let me know what it's like," Alex said.

The fuel drum exploded. In the seconds before he had sent it rolling, Alex had attached the black gel-ink pen that Smithers had given him to the metal surface. He had activated it with a thirty-second fuse. And it had worked. One moment, McCain was taking aim, the next he had disappeared in a pillar of flame that roared into the sky. It really was like a judgment from heaven. He didn't even have time to scream.

Alex was already twisting away, trying to put as much space between himself and the inferno as he could. He was too close. Blazing droplets of aviation fuel rained down from the sky. He felt them hit his shoulders and back and with horror realized he was on fire. But the grass had recently been watered. It was cool and damp under his hands. Alex rolled over again and again. His skin was burning. The pain was horrific. But after spinning half a dozen times, he had put out the flames.

He looked back at the tarmac. The charred, unrecognizable figure that had once been the Reverend Desmond McCain was on its knees. One final prayer. The silver earring had gone. There wasn't very much of him left.

He heard shouting. Police and airport workers were

running toward him. Alex couldn't see them. He was stretched out on the grass, trying to bury himself in it. Was it really over at last, the journey that had begun in a Scottish castle and had led to an airport in Africa? How had he ever gotten himself into this?

He couldn't move. And he was barely aware of the men who lifted him as gently as possible, laid him on a stretcher, and carried him away.

25

SOFT CENTERS

THE SNOW THAT HAD BEEN PROMISED in London had finally arrived.

Only a few inches had fallen during the night, but as usual, it had brought chaos to the streets. Buses had stayed in their depots, the subway system had shut down, schools were closed, and half the workforce had decided to take a day off and stay at home. Snowmen had appeared suddenly in all the London parks, standing under trees, leaning against walls, even sitting on benches . . . like some invading army that had come and seen and decided to take a well-earned rest before it set out to conquer.

It was the second week in February, and the winter had taken a grip on the city and seemed determined never to let go. The streets were empty, the parked cars huddled beneath their white blankets, but Jack Starbright had managed to persuade a taxi to bring her to St. Dominic's Hospital in one of the northern suburbs of the city. She had been here before. It was a favorite place of the Special Operations Division of MI6 when its agents were injured in the field. This was where they sent them to recover. Alex had spent two weeks here after he had been shot by Scorpia.

Mrs. Jones was waiting for her in the reception area. She was wearing a black full-length coat with leather gloves and a scarf. It was hard to say if she had just arrived or if she was on her way out.

"How is he?" Jack asked.

"He's much better," Mrs. Jones said, and it occurred to Jack that she could have been talking about someone who had just recovered from a bad cold. "The burns have healed up and he won't need any skin grafts. He won't be playing any sports for a while. He fractured his ankle at Laikipia airport. But he has amazing powers of recovery. The doctors are very pleased with him." She smiled. "He's looking forward to seeing you."

"Where is he?"

"Room nine on the second floor."

"That's the same room as last time."

"Maybe we should name it after him."

Jack shook her head. "I wouldn't bother. He won't be coming back."

The two women stood facing each other, each one waiting for the other to speak.

Mrs. Jones could see the accusation in Jack's eyes. "This really wasn't our fault," she said. "Alex met McCain quite by accident. That business in Scotland had nothing to do with us."

"But that didn't stop you from sending him to Greenfields."

"We had no idea that McCain was involved."

"And if you had—would that have stopped you?"

Mrs. Jones shrugged. She had no need to answer.

There was a plastic bag resting on a chair. Mrs. Jones picked it up and handed it to Jack. "You might like to give this to Alex. It's from Smithers. Some chocolates . . ."

"Oh yes? And what do they do? Explode when he puts them into his mouth?"

"They're soft centers. Smithers thought he might enjoy them."

Jack took the bag. She glanced toward the elevator, then back at Mrs. Jones. "Promise me that this will be the end of it," she said. "From what you've told me, this time it was worse than ever. It's a miracle he's still alive. Do you have any idea what this must be doing to him . . . inside his head, I mean?"

"Actually, I have a very good idea," Mrs. Jones countered. "I asked our psychiatrists to run a few tests on him."

"That's very thoughtful of you. But I mean it, Mrs. Jones. Alex has done enough. I want you out of his life."

Mrs. Jones sighed. "I can't promise you that, I'm afraid. First of all, it's not my decision. And anyway, as I said, this didn't begin with us. Alex has a knack for finding trouble without any help."

"I'm not going to let it happen again."

"Believe me, Jack. I'll be very happy if you can prevent it." Mrs. Jones pulled up her collar and tightened her belt. "Anyway," she said, "Alex is waiting for you. You'd better go up."

"I'm going. Please thank Mr. Smithers for the chocolates."

Jack took the elevator to the second floor. She didn't
need to ask for directions. The layout of the hospital was
all too familiar. As she approached the door of Alex's
room, a woman came out carrying a breakfast tray, and
Jack recognized Diana Meacher, the attractive fair-haired
nurse from New Zealand who had looked after Alex once
before.

"Go right in," the nurse said. "He's been looking forward to seeing you. He'll be so glad you're here."

Jack hesitated, composing herself. Then she went into
the room.

Alex was sitting up in bed, reading a magazine. His
pajama top was open and she could see that, once again,
he was heavily wrapped in bandages, this time around his
neck and shoulders. His eyes were bright and he was
smiling, but he looked bad. Pain had stamped its memory
all over him. He was thin. The haircut that Beckett had
given him when he was smuggled out of the country
didn't help.

"Hello, Jack."

"Hi, Alex."

She went over to him and kissed him very gently,
afraid that she would hurt him. Then she sat down beside
the bed.

"How are you feeling?" she asked.

"Terrible."

"As terrible as you look?"

"Probably." Alex put down the magazine, and Jack saw that even this movement made him wince. "They've taken me off painkillers," he explained. "They say they don't want me to get addicted to them."

"Oh, Alex . . ." Jack's voice caught in her throat. She had been determined not to cry in front of him, but she couldn't keep the tears from her eyes.

"I'm fine," Alex said. "I'm already much better than I was a week ago." In fact, Alex had spent ten days in the hospital in Nairobi before MI6 had flown him home.

"I wanted to come out and see you."

"I'm glad you didn't."

Jack understood. If he looked this bad now, she could hardly imagine what he must have looked like then. He wouldn't have wanted her to see him like that.

"Are you angry with me?" Alex asked.

"Of course not. I'm just relieved to see you. After you went missing, I was . . ." Jack stopped herself. "When can you come home?" she asked.

"I was talking to the nurse just now. She says that if all goes well, it should only be a couple of days. Tuesday. Wednesday at the latest."

"Well, thank goodness for that," Jack said. "You know what Thursday is."

"No." Alex had no idea.

"Alex!" Jack stared at him.

"Tell me . . ."

"Thursday, February thirteenth. It's your birthday, Alex. You're going to be fifteen."

"Am I?" Alex laughed. "So, what are you going to buy me?"

"What do you want?"

"I want to go home. I want peace and quiet. And I want that new version of Assassin's Creed . . . it's just come out on PlayStation."

"I'm not sure those violent computer games are good for you, Alex."

Jack didn't tell him that she had already bought it and that a few of his closest friends were waiting for her call, hoping to come around.

Surely MI6 would leave him alone now. They had stolen almost a whole year of his life. But never again. Jack made herself that promise.

In front of her, Alex settled back into the pillows. His eyes were closed and even as she watched, he smiled and fell asleep.

ACKNOWLEDGMENTS

IT'S ALWAYS AMAZING how many people are willing to help me, giving up their time and opening doors that might otherwise stay closed—and it seems only right to name them here. I try to make the Alex Rider books as realistic as I can, and it simply wouldn't be possible without them.

So to start at the beginning, Martin Pearce and Colin Tucker from British Energy showed me around the Sizewell B nuclear power station in Suffolk. I'm assured that security there is rather tighter than it was at Jowada. I then visited the John Innes Center, which is part of the Norwich BioScience Institutes (and bears no resemblance at all to the Greenfields Center in this story). I was given an extensive tour by Dr. Wendy Harwood and Dr. Penny Sparrow, and they very kindly explained the principles of GM technology and demonstrated the gene gun that I describe in Chapter 13. I owe a special debt of thanks to Dr. Hugh Martin, a principal lecturer at the Royal Agricultural College, who first suggested to me the method by which Desmond McCain poisons the crops in Kenya.

Jonathan Hinks, who is the chairman of the British Dam Society, introduced me to the concept of the double curvature arch dam and arranged for me to see one. I spent a very pleasant day in Scotland with Kenny Dempster, from Scottish and Southern Energy, who gave me an extensive tour of the Monar Dam (the only double arch dam in the UK), located in the very beautiful Glen Strathfarrar.

Lea Sherwood, the brilliant stunt arranger who appeared in the film of *Stormbreaker*, assured me that Alex's escape in Chapter 23 would have been possible, but perhaps you shouldn't try it at home. The Gaelic translation in Chapter 2 was provided by Dr. Robert Dunbar at the University of Aberdeen. And I owe an apology to Professor Robin Smith from London Imperial College, who gave me a lengthy lesson in physics that sadly didn't make it to the final draft.

As always, I have relied on the guidance and advice of my three editors: Jane Winterbotham and Chris Kloet at Walker Books and Michael Green in New York. Also in New York, Don Weisberg and the rest of the Philomel team moved mountains to make publication possible. My agent, Robert Kirby, gave me some great support when I needed it. My assistant, Olivia Zampi, organized everything with incredible patience and precision. And my son, Cass, was once again the first to read the manuscript, even though he's now much too old for it.

Finally, thanks to my wife, Jill Green, who had to live through the writing of this. It wasn't always fun.

Alex Rider was only *part* of the story. . . . Turn the page for an excerpt from the prequel to the pulse-pounding Alex Rider series.

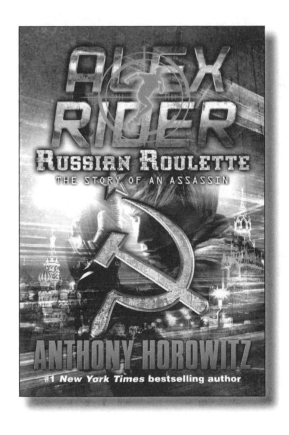

PROLOGUE

BEFORE THE KILL

HE HAD CHOSEN THE hotel room very carefully.

As he crossed the reception area toward the elevators, he was aware of everyone in the area around him. Two receptionists, one on the phone. A Japanese guest checking in—from his accent, obviously from Miyazaka in the south. A concierge printing a map for a couple of tourists. A security man, Eastern European, bored, standing by the door. He saw everything. If the lights had suddenly gone out, or if he had closed his eyes, he would have been able to continue forward at exactly the same pace.

Nobody noticed him. It was actually a skill, something he had learned, the art of not being seen. Even the outfit he wore—expensive jeans, a gray cashmere jersey, and a loose coat—had been chosen because it made no statement at all. The clothes were well-known brands but he had cut out the labels. In the unlikely event that he was stopped by the police, it would be very difficult for them to know where they had been bought.

He was twenty-eight years old. He had fair hair, cut short, and ice-cold eyes with just the faintest trace of blue. He was not large or well built, but there was a sort of sleekness about him. He moved like an athlete—perhaps a sprinter approaching the starting blocks—but there was a sense of danger about him, a feeling that you should leave well alone. He carried three credit cards and a driver's license, issued in Swansea, all with the name Matthew Reddy. A police check would have established that he was a personal trainer, that he worked in a London gym and lived in Brixton. None of this was true. His real name was Yassen Gregorovich. He had been a professional assassin for almost half his life.

The hotel was in King's Cross, an area of London with no attractive shops and few decent restaurants, a place where nobody really stays any longer than they have to. It was called The Traveller and it was part of a chain; comfortable but not too expensive. It was the sort of place that had no regular clients. Most of the guests were passing through on business and it would be their companies who paid the bill. They drank in the bar. They ate the "full English breakfast" in the brightly lit Beefeater restaurant. But they were too busy to socialize and it was unlikely they would return. Yassen preferred it that way. He could have stayed in central London, in the Ritz or the Dorchester, but he knew that the receptionists there were trained to remember the faces of the people who passed through the revolving doors. Such personal attention was the last thing he wanted.

A security camera watched him as he approached the elevators. He was aware of it blinking over his left shoulder. The camera was annoying but inevitable. London has more of these devices than any city in Europe, and the police and secret service have access to all of them. Yassen made sure he didn't look up. If you look at a camera, that is when it sees you. He reached the elevators but ignored them, slipping through a fire door that led to the stairs. He would never think of confining himself in a small space, a metal box with doors that he couldn't open, surrounded by strangers. That would be madness. He would have walked fifteen stories if it had been necessary—and when he reached the top, he wouldn't even have been out of breath. Yassen kept himself in superb condition, spending two hours in the gym every day when that luxury was available to him, working out on his own when it wasn't.

In fact, he was on the second floor. He had thoroughly checked the hotel on the Internet before he made his reservation, and number 217 was one of just four rooms that exactly met his demands. It was on the second floor, too high up to be reached from the street but low enough for him to jump out the window if he had to—after shooting out the glass. It was not overlooked. There were other buildings around, but any form of surveillance would be difficult. When Yassen went to bed, he never closed the curtains. He liked to see out, to watch for any movement in the street. Every city has a natural rhythm, and anything that breaks it—a man lingering on a corner or a car passing the same way twice—might warn him that it was time to leave at once. And he never slept for more than four hours, not even in the most comfortable bed.

A DO NOT DISTURB sign hung in front of him as he

turned the corner and approached the door. Had it been obeyed? Yassen reached into his pants pocket and took out a small silver device, about the same size and shape as a pen. He pressed one end, covering the handle with a thin spray of diazafluoren—a simple chemical re-agent. Quickly, he spun the pen around and pressed the other end, activating a fluorescent light. There were no fingerprints. If anyone had gone into the room since he had left, they had wiped the handle clean. He put the pen away, then knelt down and checked the bottom of the door. Earlier in the day, he had placed a single hair across the crack. It was one of the oldest warning signals in the book, but that didn't stop it from being effective. The hair was still in place. Yassen straightened up and went in using his electronic pass key.

It took him less than a minute to ascertain that everything was exactly as he had left it. His briefcase was 4.6 centimeters from the edge of the desk. His suitcase was positioned at a 95-degree angle from the wall. There were no fingerprints on either of the locks. He removed the digital tape recorder that had been clipped magnetically to the side of his service fridge and glanced at the dial. Nothing had been recorded. Nobody had been in. Many people would have found all these precautions annoying and time consuming, but for Yassen they were as much a part of his daily routine as tying his shoelaces or brushing his teeth.

It was twelve minutes past six when he sat down at the desk and opened his computer, an ordinary laptop.

His password had seventeen digits and he changed it every month. He took off his watch and laid it on the surface beside him. Then he went into eBay, left-clicked on Collectibles, and scrolled through Coins. He soon found what he was looking for: a gold coin showing the head of the emperor Caligula with the date 11 AD. There had been no bids for this particular coin because, as any collector would know, it did not in fact exist. In 11 AD, the mad Roman emperor Caligula had not even been born. The entire website was a fake and looked it. The name of the coin dealer—Mintomatic—had been specially chosen to put off any casual purchaser. Mintomatic was supposedly based in Shanghai and did not have Top-Rated Seller status. All the coins it advertised were either fake or valueless.

Yassen sat quietly until a quarter past six. At exactly the moment that the second hand passed over the twelve on his watch, he pressed the button to place a bid, then entered his User ID—false, of course—and password. Finally, he entered a bid of $2,418.12. The figures were based on the day's date and the exact time. He pressed Enter and a window opened that had nothing to do with eBay or with Roman coins. Nobody else could have seen it. It would have been impossible to discover where it had originated. The message had been bounced around a dozen countries, traveling through an anonymity network, before it had reached him. This is known as "onion routing" because of its many layers. It had also passed through an encrypted tunnel, a secure shell that ensured that only Yassen could read what had been written. If someone had managed to arrive at the same screen by accident, they would have seen only nonsense, and within three seconds a virus would have entered their computer and obliterated the motherboard. The computer, however, had been authorized to receive the message, and Yassen saw three words.

KILL ALEX RIDER

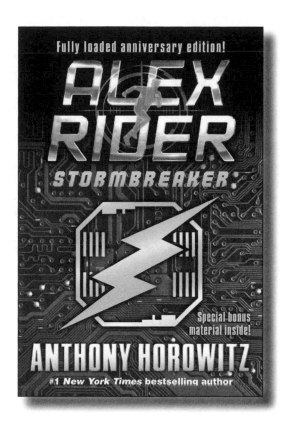

Fully loaded anniversary edition!

ALEX RIDER

STORMBREAKER

Special bonus material inside!

ANTHONY HOROWITZ

#1 *New York Times* bestselling author

They said his uncle Ian died in a car accident. But Alex Rider knows that's a lie, and the bullet holes in the windshield prove it. Yet he never suspected the truth: his uncle was really a spy for Britain's top secret intelligence agency. And now Alex has been recruited to find his uncle's killer. . . .

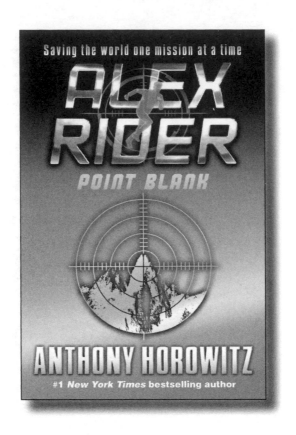

Saving the world one mission at a time

ALEX RIDER

POINT BLANK

ANTHONY HOROWITZ

#1 *New York Times* bestselling author

Kids are dying mysteriously at a Swiss boarding school, and Alex Rider, reluctant teen superspy, is going undercover to find out why. But the mystery he uncovers is more nefarious than he'd ever expected, and now the clock is ticking on Alex's mission. Is his luck about to run out?

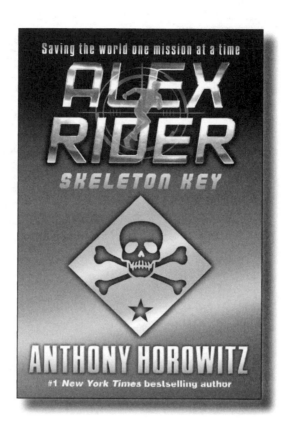

Working as a secret agent, teen superspy Alex Rider has seen it all. But Alex is about to face something more dangerous than he can imagine: a man who has lost everything he cared for, a man with a nuclear weapon who will stop at nothing to get his world back. Unless Alex can stop him first.

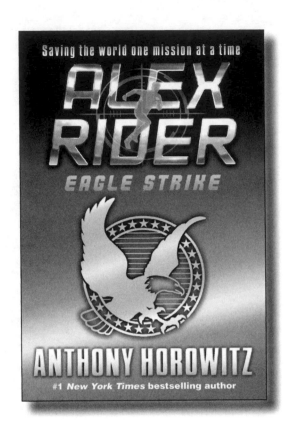

Teen superspy Alex Rider has seen his share of criminal masterminds. But none like Sir Damian Cray, the most popular man on earth, who also happens to be a madman bent on destruction. Only Alex can stop his evil plan . . . but this time, Alex Rider is on his own.

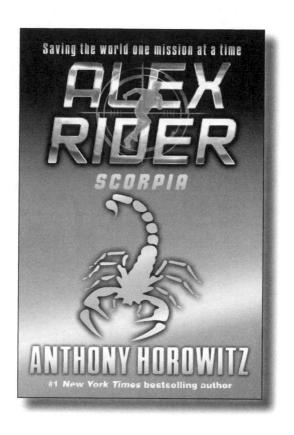

Teen superspy Alex Rider's world shatters when he discovers that the father he never knew may have been an assassin for Scorpia, the deadliest terrorist organization in the world. And now Scorpia wants Alex on their side, and will stop at nothing to get him.

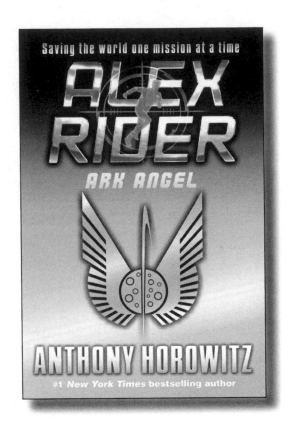

Saving the world one mission at a time

ALEX RIDER

ARK ANGEL

ANTHONY HOROWITZ

#1 *New York Times* bestselling author

The sniper's bullet nearly killed him. But Alex Rider, teen
superspy, survived—just in time to intercept a kidnapping
of billionaire Nikolai Drevin's son. Drevin's been targeted
by a group of deadly eco-terrorists who think nothing of
killing millions to achieve their goals. Unless Alex can stop
them in time . . .

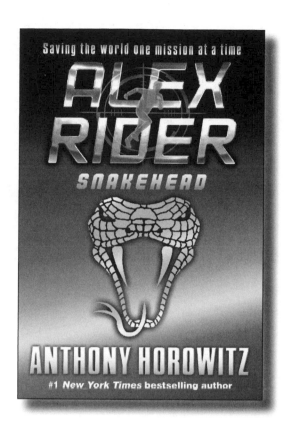

They murdered his parents. They shot him and left him for dead. And yet Alex Rider, teen superspy, thought he was finished with nefarious terrorist organization Scorpia. He was wrong. But even Alex can't turn down the prospect of learning more about his parents—even if it means venturing on his most dangerous mission to date.

Saving the world one mission at a time

ALEX RIDER

CROCODILE TEARS

ANTHONY HOROWITZ

#1 *New York Times* bestselling author

Realizing that there's big money in charity—the bigger the disaster, the bigger the money—a con artist is poised to create the biggest catastrophe known to man and release an airborne strain of virus so powerful it can destroy an entire country on a single gust of wind. The antidote? Teen superspy, Alex Rider.

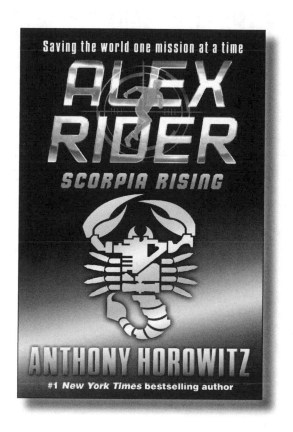

Saving the world one mission at a time

ALEX RIDER

SCORPIA RISING

ANTHONY HOROWITZ

#1 *New York Times* bestselling author

Scorpia has dogged Alex Rider for most of his life. They killed his parents, they did their best to con Alex into turning traitor, and they just keep coming back with more power. Now the world's most dangerous terrorist organization is playing with fire in the world's most combustible land: the Middle East. No one knows Scorpia like Alex. And no one knows how best to get to Alex like Scorpia. Until now.